THE HYPEBEAST

Adnan Khan

The Hypebeast

A NOVEL

Publisher: Meghan Macdonald | Acquiring editor: Russell Smith
Cover designer: Laura Boyle
Cover image: istock/draco77

Library and Archives Canada Cataloguing in Publication

Title: The hypebeast : a novel / Adnan Khan.
Names: Khan, Adnan (Novelist), author
Identifiers: Canadiana (print) 20240459903 | Canadiana (ebook) 20240459911 | ISBN 9781459754478 (softcover) | ISBN 9781459754485 (PDF) | ISBN 9781459754492 (EPUB)
Subjects: LCGFT: Novels.
Classification: LCC PS8621.H34 H97 2025 | DDC C813/.6—dc23

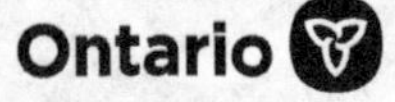

We acknowledge the support of the Canada Council for the Arts and the Ontario Arts Council for our publishing program. We also acknowledge the financial support of the Government of Ontario, through the Ontario Book Publishing Tax Credit and Ontario Creates, and the Government of Canada.

Printed and bound in Canada.

Rare Machines, an imprint of Dundurn Press
1382 Queen Street East
Toronto, Ontario, Canada M4L 1C9
dundurn.com, @dundurnpress

One

1.

This is my favourite spot. The Oberoi hotel in Bombay and its precisely landscaped interior lawns and light fixtures that glow like veneers. It's true that Muslims are fanatic about gardens. All our kings obsessively tended to their greenery — from Delhi to Baghdad to Cordoba, the trail of conquerors is pruned. Now it's shawarma shops: tahini sauce and tender meat, hungry students, cab drivers, late-nite drunks. What happened to our greatness? How did we go from conquerors to Uber delivery, from emperors to 7/11?

One year ago, I was still in Toronto when I had my last stab at greatness. Starved after an Al-Anon meeting, I was in a slit of a shawarma shop. Meat and vegetables on the left side steaming in metal pans, and on the right, a short bar and mirror reflected the servers back to themselves.

There was always a new kind manning the counter. Usually Pakistani, often Somalian, the occasional Arab. That day it was a disdainful Persian too elegant for fast food. I'd run inside after rain began, heavy with heat at the start of the summer, which, before I'd realized its strength, was up to my ankles. My loafers — caramel butter suede with a hand-stitched apron and pegged soles; let's not talk about the price — were soaked. My feet squeaked.

I'd rushed to the Al-Anon meeting after my shift at the store I owned and needed my blood sugar calmed before seeing Natalie so I didn't make things worse. I'd dressed in white chinos she liked and a navy polo she didn't, both on sale from a small boutique, still over a hundred dollars each, and a gold bracelet Grand Seiko watch I'd taken from the lost and found box at my last summer job ten years ago. The polo was a little tight but broadened my shoulders. Its tight cuffs maximized my biceps. I flexed my foot and enjoyed cool air where the sole bent away from my instep.

We were to celebrate our second anniversary. I prepared to fight. On the phone her voice was tight and curt. I predicted what she was going to say later by the way she spoke now. A bad sign: exhausted at upcoming exhaustion.

I needed to go straight into the fight with Natalie. That was the way I was then. I hadn't learned how to be honest with myself, not like now, and I wouldn't admit that action — headfirst into battle with Natalie — was my way of dealing with anxiety. Anxiety about Natalie, sure, but about everything; death too, as ambitious as that sounds. Back then I believed if I wasn't always applying force onto the world I was dead. The puttering engine of mine powered me by telling me no matter what, I needed to act. That to *do* was the way to live.

A small Mexican man, five-foot-two and drunk, swaying, a glob of garlic sauce on his pimpled chin, broke off from his pack and stared at me staring out the window at the big raindrops. He touched my arm to confirm I was real and moved back to his group. The group shuffled to seats near the door and I took their place at front so the Persian could hand me my shawarma. I gobbled the tube down, careful to have my arms extended so no sauce would drip on me. Raindrops burst against the ground, scattering water like seeds. Weather was my proof of God. That's what we were taught: if the weather change was abrupt, it was him. A girl in grade 5, chubby with pink cheeks, once told me when it rained Jesus was spitting on us.

"You're that guy," the Mexican said. He spoke confident. Garlic sauce breath and sharp cologne. He was up to my rib cage and his drooping eyes, eyelashes almost covering his dilated pupils, the whites streaked red, locked onto me.

I was halfway through my meal. His gelled black hair caught the overhead lights in their short-spiked stalks. The Persian behind the counter continued his assembly line. The Mexican's friends turned to watch. All three wore tapered light wash jeans, clean fades, T-shirts with surf or skateboard brands. All new but their shoes were scuffed and torn. Cheap. "Salam alaykum," the Mexican said to me.

I had no idea who he thought I looked like. And it was difficult to get mad at this casual confusion since likely he'd been at the end of it millions of times. His menace broke into a goofy smile. He put his hand on my shoulder and squeezed, his breath beaming across at light speed. Garlic with cologne and the meat stench; my wet foot sliding around my leather loafers, the woozy yellow walls.

He showed me his cellphone, which was on the Instagram page of a very familiar face: Abdul Mohammed.

Oh, Abdul.

Abdul had been in the news most of my life. Even before we met it felt like I knew him. When we were both fourteen he was arrested for shooting an American soldier in Afghanistan and sent to Guantanamo Bay. For the next decade he fought to get out of Guantanamo. After much legal squabbling between countries he was released a few years ago.

Since gaining freedom he appeared on the news and in public regularly, building a social media following by always willing to be a smiling spokesman for the Muslim experience in the West. He'd moved from a shady character accused of striking the heart of America to creating a profile as a respected figure of civic society, buoyed by a multi-million-dollar settlement from the Canadian government for their handling of his ordeal.

He wasn't wholly embraced. He angered many by not disappearing. But his insistence on remaining public kept me in awe.

Even now, after all that happened, after what I know, after what Abdul did to me, his fury fills me with admiration.

I'd always been envious of him. I'd actually met him very briefly two years prior, but could barely speak when I did. I was overwhelmed by the feeling of knowing him. He'd grown up a few streets over. He could have been a neighbour, a boy I played soccer with. He could have been me. But he'd held so much power. He'd cradled a noble force by shooting that soldier and becoming part of history. He'd wrangled death.

Almost as long as I could remember Abdul in my life I'd been anxious with death, worried about the shape it would take, its hue, colour, shading; the way it could manifest out of nothing to change all. It was truth, ice-cold water on a hot day.

It was the leash pulling me through life. No matter what was happening, death's light would always be there.

The Mexican played a video from Abdul's page, which was like the dozens I'd watched before. Abdul sat in a car, thick hair swept back, speaking directly into the camera. No sound but white text on the screen said: *Should your Wife NEED to work?* (17.3K views). I hadn't seen this one. Me and the Mexican watched the muted clip together. I didn't mind being confused for Abdul; he was handsome.

The Mexican's friends laughed and turned away, leaving him with me. Hanging on the wall behind us was a photograph of the Mogadishu skyline, with a dull, blue sky reaching over short white buildings. A white with ponytail and flip-flops entered and ordered a chicken shawarma. Another photograph behind the cashier declared the skyline Damascus in small letters. The white was the tallest in here, his ponytail half the height of the little Mexican and he wasn't wet anywhere except his fat pink feet.

"May God be with you," the Mexican said, now in English.

The rain stopped: like that, as if the channel changed. The white's red goatee sparkled, the Mexican left me.

I checked my watch on the inside of my wrist: 7:00 p.m. There was early summer light. A blue wash before a brief gasp of pink at sunset. I was going to be late to see Natalie.

The Mexican knew who I was more than I did. Now, a year since that meeting, I know that confusion was the last warning — if I'd seen its light it would have led me to safety.

Or, that's false — what happened was always going to happen and the Mexican was no prophet, no more no less than Abdul; Abdul whom I'd always known.

So, really, whatever light I missed that day with the Mexican, the phantom life I didn't lead meant nothing, because the ending — me, here, in a hotel bar — was guaranteed. Abdul was always with me.

Now, at the Oberoi, a year after all that happened with Abdul, after we got to know each other in that small dark room, I'm still in Bombay, in this golden Bombay sun and its light that quenches desire. Even in this hotel building and through the pollution the light is magnificent against the azure crash of the Arabian Sea, like we're nestled in the centre of a radiant jewel. One that is pockmarked with overweight Indians looking to show off, next to the worst kind of man — the European on holiday, full of resentment because to feel rich they've had to leave their continent and put up with Indians — but still, a jewel. Light reaches all in this city, from the buttoned-up waiters mimicking colonial protocol to the clerical class hoping surface trimmings will keep clients happy. And in the haze outside, the cluttered city, the cutthroat city, what beaten-down locals will say is the real city, with a sneer and a spit, the famous Indian throat-clearing and hawk, light reaches there too.

Light: last week the car I rented broke down in the lot itself and the owner refused to give me back my money. He shrugged. There'll be a different car tomorrow. Come back then. He went back to his desk and to his mobile. I laughed. I let it go. I've changed.

Light reached this hotel and brought my journey with Abdul to its end.

Light: this custard is sent straight from the manager. I know him, he trained at a Michelin-starred restaurant in California. The day we met he apologized to me personally for Modi's treatment of Muslims and said with a sympathetic head bob, at least everyone has a toilet now. Thank God no one is shitting in the streets. It's the lower castes, he assured me, that were responsible for Modi's party winning the Indian elections on a platform of nationalism and anti-Muslim ideas, not him, not his middle class, not his fat, Pepsi-addled, internationally aspiring middle class. The dessert is on the house. There will be no gelatin in it. Everyone is very mindful in places like this.

•

That day in Toronto, I exited from the sliding doors, nodding to the Mexican's friends, making sure to make deliberate but limited eye contact, making sure each one knew I saw him.

I walked toward the sun. Wet on wet on wet there was damp heat trapped in my pants.

I was nervous about Natalie, if she would be drunk when I arrived. She was twenty-eight, had been living in Toronto for five years when I met her and never once flew back to visit her parents in their tiny Vancouver basement apartment. Her goal was to save as much money as possible so she didn't visit but would say she planned on retiring them in the Philippines. They both did a sort of factory work. When I asked to meet them over FaceTime, she brushed me off with "They don't speak English."

For a week afterward I studied every Filipino I spoke to, finding them mostly at Tim Hortons, and while they were accented, they spoke perfect English.

Her secrets about her parents were out of character. Over our first dates she eagerly shared stories of her youth, telling me over glasses of wine — before I kept track of how many — what her foundational experiences with friends and boyfriends were. That she kept her parents shrouded attracted me immensely and made me think we could have a future where our pasts would not reach.

Even when she was smeared silly by booze she didn't chat about them the way I expected habitual drunks to, the way most people at the Al-Anon meetings suggested they did when complaining about the burden of information they held on to from their loved ones. All it took was a few thimbles of alcohol and these lunatics were revealing tales of complex PTSD, abuse, and trauma — but Natalie would never talk about her parents and the first and only hint I got about their treatment of her was in her refusal to watch TV or movies featuring children and families.

That late afternoon, before what was supposed to be the evening's two-year celebration, I'd attended my fifth Al-Anon meeting — at her suggestion. She didn't attend AA but thought I could benefit from its partner program Al-Anon, for people who are "worried about someone with a drinking problem." The someone was not Natalie. According to her, the problems I had with her drinking were really problems I had with my father's drinking.

That old joke.

The meeting was held in the basement of a church. Its policies were affirming and positive. Anti-racist, pro–gay rights, a "community of faith, justice, and the arts." The Al-Anon meetings were open grieving sessions, everyone taking turns trying to close festering wounds. The church was named after Paul, which is the least Biblical name I've ever heard; it sounds like the name of an electric-car salesman: *If I speak in the tongues of men or of angels, but do not have love, I am only a resounding gong or a clanging cymbal. If I have the gift of prophecy and can fathom all mysteries and all knowledge, and if I have a faith that can move mountains, but do not have love, I am nothing. If I give all I possess to the poor and give over my body to hardship that I may boast, but do not have love, I gain nothing.*

Its outside was as most churches are, with great brown blocks making up its pillars, and it squatted on a square of valuable downtown land. Sunlight dazzled off the stone but otherwise there was nothing holy about the building. It was too noisy. Seagulls circled and swooped for discarded bagel ends and stuck their faces into empty chip bags. Filthy men sat on the exterior stairs and one mumbled to himself in a low pitch. A woman panhandled out front. On a patch of grass near stairs were two silent crows. Pigeons cluttered the entryway, flapping up when I came to enter. Natalie's father used to hunt pigeons when they were first in Vancouver. They seemed easy to catch.

The sternness of mosques, the white purity of their facades, their austere coolness, promotes the holy. It needs quiet to come out. The church was too much. Too much between me and Allah.

Inside, the building was cordoned off into corridors and sections for various activities. I was an infiltrator, of course, too scared to check out the pews or see if there were any. There was all sorts of positive-language signage and already I'd been asked too many times how I felt. It was an intrusive environment.

That was my last meeting. I never went back but I'm still not supposed to talk about Al-Anon. That is made apparent at the beginning when they told us if we see a member on the street to not acknowledge them. That was fine with me because obviously the place reeked of vulnerability. Al-Anon encouraged sharing as a way to process, to roll grief through our fingers and unpack it, but they also wanted to keep the stories within the space to administer a level of control. The first of their controls was to take our control: to accept the basic premise that alcoholism was an infliction or a disease. The bottle a manifestation of an invisible wound. A cry for help. I hated it.

I hated it — but from the meetings I attended, listening became a kindness I learned to value, because it requires so little, and does so much. It turned me into a blabbermouth. The release upon revealing … the first time I felt it … developed the ability in me to talk to strangers at length about private details and take a detached perspective, as if I was recalling the plot of a movie. I was new and told my story over and over again to fresh empathy, brand-new head nods of recognition.

I was terrified because everyone's story was … the same. The small details differed but the damage, the denial, the mechanics of the histories were the same. We lived similar lives and all of us in the basement shook for someone to hold.

At that fifth meeting I recognized the same pudgy white faces — I'd never seen a "person of colour" there — and this bothered me. Everyone there to complain about a partner and almost everyone traced the complaint back to a parent. I was trying to avoid that trap. It was easy psychology. That's what stopped me from going back. I couldn't understand, if we all knew what the source of the problem was, why could we not chase the agony away? The gap between knowing and feeling Al-Anon could not close. We were all diagnostic experts but it left us holding our shit in our hands; the smell strong.

Kids activities took place in the same basement space and their litter was left behind. A few superhero toys, dump trucks, a small portable green chalkboard, tiny plastic chairs, and a waft of baby powder and piss. There were small rectangle windows that light creeped through. We sat in a loose circle within handholding distance. I sat a little bit back, in the circle, but a little bit back. The only way I could make myself come to these meetings was to maintain that dynamic. It was women, all white, two men, eight of us total. Different ages.

All the women wore jeans. One lady had fake dyed-blond hair with a dark patch cresting the top of her skull. She leaned back in her seat. She spoke. She reminded me of a cigarette. Then someone else. Give and take. Endless repetition, trusted when they shouldn't have, betrayal a snake in the grass, botched responsibilities, again and again. Father/son, wife/husband, the shadow that loomed over their lives — some for decades! — was drink. It's too easy to say that in the basement we were addicted to the push-pull of those relationships and that need was the knot we spent our lives unravelling.

That small underground room of prayer shivered with meaning. It allowed us a simple hope.

That things could change …

2.

I met Natalie three years ago in an Airbnb I'd rented for the weekend in a neighbourhood associated with start-ups. The life I'd wanted coming out of school. Renting a condo there for weekend blitzes was the closest I got.

Marwan could not believe the unit. At its entry was a ten-foot mirror, its gold frame carved with spears, winged demons, and cherubs playing the harp or shooting arrows. A rug, embroidered with roses, led to a sunk living room with a brown leather L-sectional and glass table that had several remotes, one for the massive TV, another for the Bose sound system wired throughout the unit, and two we never touched. Marwan ran his fingers over the fake marble countertop.

"We are going to mess this place up," he said.

A cowhide led to the balcony and he slid the doors open to a view of the CN Tower. I walked the hallway lined with prints of

Japanese woodcarvings to the two bedrooms. The linens in each room were patterned with intricate flower designs, from the curtains to the covers, all coloured with red, orange, or brown, taking inspiration from a potpourri bowl. The bedside tables were real wood and a sleek white plastic diffuser puffed in the corner. I held the curtain fabric between my fingers. It was a thick weighted material that returned to its wavy shape when I let go.

In the kitchen Marwan lined up four empty bottles of Grey Goose on the counter. He examined the lips for grime and wiped them clean with a damp paper towel. One of the bottles was losing its label to peel but would hold out for one more evening. We refilled the bottles of Grey Goose with cheap Iceberg vodka and I told Marwan to throw the empties out. I took our one genuine bottle of Goose and made a small tear in the label for recognition.

I took photographs of the walls and surfaces and fiddled with the drawers and handles to see what would break easily under drunk weight. It was a two-bedroom spot with two kings and two bathrooms. At least one more person could sleep on the couch. We were splitting the weekend rent with a Punjabi meathead friend of Marwan's, but he would only pay if he pulled that evening. It was my weekend to organize, so I got the master, but realistically, I would have to sacrifice it — at least for the duration of a nut — if I met no one.

Our weekend ritual: downtown treks to obliterate ourselves at clubs. We pooled with different groups to rent the weekend's condo so no one had to Uber back faded to their parents.

I tossed my duffle onto the bed and took out my dopp kit. The Punjabi was coming with a crew in V-necks and collared shirts embroidered with dragons and lions. Most of them would be vomiting in the bushes by 9:00 p.m. The women would be dripped into tight, intense-coloured dresses that stopped mid-thigh, bodies smooth with coconut moisturizer, on their cellphones by 11:00 p.m. trying to arrange an alternative to the buffoon they came downtown with puking in the shrubs.

I loved the accessories: women with layered extensions, sharp clattering nails, thick contoured makeup; men in pointed shoes, creatine muscles, spiked gelled hair, and too many bracelets.

We knew why we went out and what we wanted.

Tonight we'd move from club to club drinking our guts out, losing members if they paired off. I dressed badly then, but at least I wasn't dragon-shirted; I was proud of my attire. Hair swooped back into a fresh fade every weekend, clubbing in a business casual getup of chinos and tight, collared shirt with fake leather shoes. After six gin and tonics I would undo my top buttons to show off the divot between my pecs that I had spent at least four hundred hours on. A gold-plated chain with the word Allah in Arabic drew the eye there. I had a little taste — I was careful to cologne just my wrists and neck, two spritzes, not the Arab style of half the bottle.

Marwan stood on the balcony with a cherry cigarillo between his lips. Seven or eight clubs were within walking distance. He wore a cap backward and cupped his small belly under his white T-shirt, patting his track pants for a lighter. All Nike, a brand he'd been loyal to since high school. He'd come from the gym and was excited for the shower. I let him use the one in the master bedroom, which had multiple nozzles, including one that was removable and attached to a hose. He was eager to tell me about the water pressure on his asshole, the cigarillo bouncing between his lips, laughing at his story as he told it. He sparked and said, "Tonight's going to be good. Start of the summer. It's hot. Hot hot. I got paid. I'm going to be good."

"Did I tell you I quit?" I asked.

"What? Why?"

"'Cause we got the tax thing going."

"Bruh," he said, "that's not going to take off for a while."

"That's if we half-ass it. We got a little money out of it already. If I focus —"

"You're putting too much pressure on it," he said. "It can't be your only source of income."

I'd quit my job doing brute-force telephone sales work. Strict instructions and a script. Internet and cellphone upgrades over the phone, minimum wage with commission. I'd done it for two years, hated it, but learned how to sell. It wasn't being suave or smooth or even charming, but the repetitive drone of the script and a sales pitch that made it out like there was no option but to upgrade, plus the right customer flummoxed by moderate confrontation.

"And if we don't focus on it — then what?" I asked. "We'll be half in–half out for too many more months. We'll never get anywhere."

"Don't get crazy thinking this is the only way to make money. It's one way."

"Why you always arguing with me? Commit. Be a friend."

"Don't even say that. How many hours did I spend on the phone this week? I'm committed," Marwan said, and pulled the cigarillo out of his mouth.

The telephone skills honed selling upgrades were perfect for our new tax gig. It had started two months before when I got a robocall: *This is the Government of Canada calling to tell you your tax assessment has been re-assessed and you owe an outstanding balance. Your visa may be in jeopardy. Hit one now to talk to a representative.* I'd gotten these calls for years, assuming correctly it was an Indian going down a list of names and calling over and over again until someone hit one.

Everything mysterious is simple. There's always an Indian behind it.

"Mentally," I said. "I want you to commit mentally. We turned twenty-eight this year."

"That's young," Marwan said.

"Come on, man. I want money. Proper money."

"Don't force it, that's all I'm saying. That's how we'll get in trouble."

The tax scam was the same as my legit job. I had to be persistent, consistent, and steady, waiting until I lucked out with a doofus on the other end. It was easy to find them, it just took time. I tried on my own using numbers from work with minimum success. Then I reconnected with an old high school friend, Hussain, finding his number in my company's system, and through his connect, got us a vetted contact list of phone numbers from people who had fallen for similar scams previously. Our hit rate had gone up, but we had to throw him a chunk of change for the list.

"I couldn't do it anymore. I can't be on that phone selling upgrades," I said.

"Calling up dudes and scaring them into paying 'taxes' doesn't involve you being on the phone?" Marwan asked.

"It's our phone at least."

Selling cellphone upgrades to old whites had been perfect practice for scaring immigrants. It was a risk but we needed it; I needed to *do*. I changed the subject.

"Your homie coming tonight chill?" I asked.

"He's chill," Marwan said. "Nothing to worry about."

"He can handle his drink?"

"Nothing to worry about."

"Because last time …"

"He was coming off a break-up."

"That was messy."

"He's bringing his cousin tonight," Marwan said. "She's from Jersey. Some other girls."

"I'm going to say it just to say it so it's clear: Don't start anything."

"Don't with me. I can handle myself. I won't start nothing. I won't start a fight. Or an argument. I won't even talk," Marwan said and his right arm yawned open. He ran his fingers through soft black pit hair. "Should I shave my armpits?" he asked.

"If you start now you'll have to do it forever."

"You right. The stubble will be mad itchy. But it would be so smooth."

We moved to the living room and cranked the A/C and had a small fight about smoking indoors until he stubbed the cigarillo out. The deposit was on my card. Marwan leaned back with his feet on the table, wandered TV channels, and sighed. We were tired; we'd been doing this for years. Without a word he got up and went into the bathroom, stripping his shirt before he entered, raised the volume on the speakers, and when I turned to shout, he'd taken off his pants and watched himself in the mirror, examining the hair on his ass, his thighs, and finally, his drooping cock, hanging over his balls, completely shaved. He hacked at his armpits then applied shaving cream over his chest and pits and slid a razor blade neatly over his fair skin. The crashing water mixed with the Future playing and for a moment I was sealed forever in the condo, never escaping. White light, steam, heat, the soft chemical smell of shaving cream, and the jingle of hi-hats roiled together and my stomach clenched: what if this was my life forever? What if I never made it out, never made money or did more than my father and his pathetic middle-management job? I got dizzy. The bathroom fog rode into the living room and sunbeams lit the furniture up.

I took big breaths and counted in eight and out four. Again. Again. Dizzy went away. That out-of-body didn't happen often around Marwan. I coiled my fear and used it to spring into preparation for tonight's nonsense. The fuzz of a vodka-Coke relaxed me quick.

•

A durag-wearing Punjabi came in shouting, dapped up Marwan and took over the aux. Behind him, grouped at the entry, a crowd posed for selfies in the hall mirror until she broke away for the kitchen — my heart jumped at this first sighting of Natalie. She didn't look at me for a long while, chatting with friends, refilling her plastic cup, and I snuck strange glances at her, getting caught twice.

She wore a white top that showed off golden skin, all shoulders, collarbone. When she laughed she threw her head back and the shirt pulled up, revealing her stomach. She sat on the arm of the sofa, swung one leg over the other and let a scuffed heel dangle from her foot, flicking it so it slapped against her. Her dark skirt worked with the blond streaks, fake burgundy nails. She cupped her hand around her large mouth, ran into the corner and sneezed so loud we all turned to look. She laughed: her head cracked back exposing her neck; a slight moon-face and light-brown eyes that darted. Her clothes were new but not special. Not like the dragon shirts kept in the closet until special nights out. The skirt was lightly frayed, and a small, very small stain, chocolate or wine, almost like a mole, was on her white top where it met her naked lower back. She mixed her own drinks.

I circled. The Punjabi boys were fine to talk to and I got that over with. I worried about their tight T-shirts with images of lions over the heart. The casualness might limit the clubs we could go to, but maybe not, since we had an important two-to-one ratio of women to men. Marwan made sure the guests were relaxed by filling drinks, rolling a spliff, ordering a pizza that few people ate, fiddling with the lighting. An hour into it a random boy puked in our bathroom. Marwan brought him a bottle of water and found the girl he had come with. She left her friends reluctantly. He would spend the next two hours face-first in our toilet, then fall asleep, and no one would answer her pleading texts about our location.

Marwan really went out of his way to make the men relaxed. He was six-foot-two and his muscular frame caused many problems without him realizing, men and women both mesmerized by his easy physical presence, a kind of repulsion they couldn't move past. He had a dedicated workout regime, wrapped measuring tape around his biceps daily, and entered his diet into a spreadsheet. It was the casual joy he carried his frame with that caused problems. People liked to fight him.

One of the Punjabis tried to lean against the counter and missed.

The women were in an in-joke bubble. A man I hadn't introduced myself to leered at them, misunderstood a reference, blurted out what he thought was a funny response, and thoroughly ignored, went back to his cellphone.

The Punjabi got off the floor and did a shot.

I circled, not seeing Natalie. Two women were having a conversation apart from the others. I refilled my drink and one of them asked me my opinion on a club; easy. I settled into a boring monologue and saw Natalie dash onto the balcony for a smoke. I kept talking, looking at the ember tip of her cigarette swing from her lips to her friends and back. My conversation was so boring it wouldn't be rude if I left. How to?

On the balcony Natalie's friend pivoted, opened the door, and clanked across the living room to the bathroom.

I could go now. I could join. What do I say. I don't smoke. I can smoke. Oh: fresh air. I love fresh air. I came out for some fresh air.

To the two women, I said, "Yeah, but you don't actually know, really, what he's about, right, so, does it even matter, if you don't know, I mean, how could you know, really?" and they turned away from my blathering in disgust.

I wiped my palms on my pants.

She was lit by the sole balcony bulb. It cast her in an eerie yellow gloom, making the white tendrils of smoke solid before they dissipated. I slid the door shut, noticing her body twitch, becoming aware of me, the last time before the first time we spoke. Street-noise audible.

She turned to speak to me, her cigarette coming to an end.

"This Grey Goose tastes funny." Natalie rattled her cup and pulled into an exaggerated face of repulsion. Two ice cubes on top of each other in four thumbs of vodka.

"You need a mixer," I said.

"Not if it didn't taste cheap."

"Goose ain't cheap."

"You sure this is Goose?" she said and cocked her head into

an open, confused face; by the end of the night I knew what it meant to be mocked by her. It was one of her favourite tools.

"Nah it's Goose," I said.

"I used to bartend," she said. "This just … I don't know. It tastes funny."

"Bad batch."

"*Bad batch*," she said back to me.

"It happens."

"It almost tastes like … like … Iceberg?"

"No …"

"I did see an empty Iceberg bottle under the sink," she said and laughed. "You forgot to throw it out."

"I mean, I dunno, I'm not in charge of the drinks —"

"Really? Who do you know here?" she asked.

"Everyone. I rented the place for the weekend."

"You live with your mom and dad then?"

"Hell no. I ain't one of those boys. I live far. It's easier to chill here at the end of the night. What about you?" I asked and leaned against the balcony, trying not to get too close.

"I know Gurneet. I used to be her manager at the salon. What you do?"

"I work in sales," I said.

"You're one of those Toronto knuckleheads, eh?"

"You here to have fun or be mean?"

"Who says they're different?" She took a sip of her drink and I froze, not knowing what to say, feeling pressure in my chest. "I'm just playing," Natalie said and touched my forearm. "Don't sulk."

"You can't be from here," I said.

"I'm from Vancouver."

"What was that like?"

"I'm here, aren't I?"

She laughed at my stammering and moved on to making fun of how pointy my shoes were.

We got drunk. The memory is a pure vision of what we could be. Loose with booze I learned what details she made herself up with. Parents in Vancouver, the debt she had to them, a feeling so intense she left the city, work first as a bartender here, now managing a nail salon. She had a sharp way of speaking, interjecting jokes when she could, a degree in psychology no one knew what to do with. The mundane details of her life, rather than flattening her into an image I could see clearly, deepened my curiosity.

We got drunk. For me to see the seams of a woman's attraction to me so early was exhilarating. Her nails chittered on the metal railing. Her hands were prematurely aged, wrinkled like faded flowers.

Later, it always brought me comfort to hold them, as if they were a glimpse of our future together.

•

The line was loose at the end and tightened up near the bouncers. One Black, one white, both wearing black outfits with shorn heads and Sunni beards. They took breaks from chatting to match IDs under penlights with the faces in front of them. Three skinny Indians they could probably smell were turned away. They protested but the white bouncer literally moved the littlest one out of the line and they left glum, their dreams unsatisfied. There should be a handbook given out on the plane for these guys. How to assimilate: Step one, deodorize. Step two, three white women for every Indian man.

Groups of women got in quick and any group of men without women was eyed with penetrating suspicion, like they were perverts on prowl, which, in fairness, they were. I watched a single man with a big camera and flash beg for entry, promising he ran a successful Instagram account. The classic urban pair of white man–East Asian woman got inside with no hassle. A few Korean women in the line huddled close and side-eyed Marwan. Their legs flashed with glitter. Korean women were always scared of us and he couldn't resist the negative energy.

"You aren't on the guest list?" Natalie asked me.

"They don't have lines in Vancouver?"

"Where are you from?"

"What it sound like? I'm from Toronto," I said.

Natalie rolled her eyes.

"Don't be an ass. I'm not white," she said.

"I'm from Bombay. Came here when I was six. What about you?"

"Manila. Came here when I was ten."

"I could speak English, though."

"I didn't say you couldn't!"

"Could you?" I asked.

"From birth. My parents always wanted to come here," she said.

"You speak Filipino?"

"It's called Tagalog, dummy. What about you?"

"I speak a little Hindi. You ever go back?"

"When I was a teen. Every few years with my parents. I want to go without them," Natalie said.

"For what?"

"It's my country too. Maybe I'll live there for a few years."

"Damn, you a FOB for real."

Three more white people were let in while we spoke. My most reliable tactic for getting into clubs was slipping by without fanfare. We were a big, brown group, but the women were well groomed, quiet, and polite; this, plus their numbers, should override any other principle. Except the Punjabi boys were ruining it, getting louder and louder in their complaints, pulling from a Coke bottle infused with vodka.

"Yo bro I swear this line needs to move," one of the Punjabis said.

I didn't understand yet how Natalie's being Filipino ranked her. She was too dark to always pass for East Asian, so not super high, but higher than me, and way, way higher than me and Marwan together.

"What's going on with these bouncers, guy," a Punjabi continued.

My best chance was to break off with Natalie and present as a pair. An East Asian woman in a miniskirt? Bin Laden could be her date and they'd get in. The two Punjabi boys swerved in and out of line, barking at passersby, playing music on their phones, being fools. My blood rose but I didn't want to ruin the evening. Marwan nestled into the group of women and urged them forward. He was light-skinned, tall, and groomed enough to make it work. We had to be quick before the Punjabis detonated. I looked at Marwan to communicate that we were about to dip and I'd meet him inside. He understood.

"I swear to God yo. IsweartoGod," a Punjabi said. "If this line doesn't move. I swear to God."

All they needed was an errant bump. A short white chud in front of the line stumbled off and puked a green arc onto the sidewalk. He apologized to the crowd. Another, smelling and seeing the vomit, stepped forward and blasted the sidewalk with his hamburger dinner. The violence of the throw-up shuddered through the crowd.

"That's nasty," a Punjabi said. "That's nasty. You two are nasty."

The puke had agitated the Punjabis. The pukers left. One of them apologized again. A small rumbling erupted into a shove and one of the players bumped into one of our Punjabis, who were waiting for it, and responded with wild swinging arms.

The bouncers descended to control the fight, leaving their posts empty for a split second before they were replaced. The Punjabis squared up with a bouncer each. I tugged Marwan and told him to come with us. The line shifted away from the fight and we now had groups of innocuous whites in front and behind us, our Punjabis much farther back in battle; Marwan made a joke at their expense, binding us to the whites, weaving us into a friendly group of good vibes, inoculating us in their aura. Seamlessly, our IDs checked, we slid inside.

•

I didn't care about money that night. I pushed through to the bar and let Marwan on my card to show off. I told Natalie to order what she wanted. We commenced with shots of rum, paired with rum-and-Coke doubles, ended the night with tequila. I don't know how much of each but I still thank God every morning we didn't order Red Bull.

I wasn't counting — four hundred and fifty dollars over the evening — because nothing mattered when Natalie grabbed my hand and pulled me to dance. Roaming overhead lights slugged over us, in rhythm with hot, dripping bass; wet, moving bodies. Natalie moved close, moved away, moved close, moved away, men flew around like bats, their eyes going from woman to woman. I touched her skin between shirt and skirt and she pushed against me, her hair in my face, her throat visible for a second, a burst of citrus perfume. Her body so warm, hotter than the club, hotter than anything.

We pushed to the back and out a side door where they had cordoned off a smoking area. Outside, the summer air hit sharp and almost cold against us. She bummed a cigarette off a giant tech-bro before returning to me. He glared, deceived.

"You came here to be a nail salon manager?" I asked.

"At least I don't work in *sales*!"

"Nah — no, sorry, I didn't mean it like that."

"You're so sensitive," she said. "My parents chose to move to Vancouver from Manila. I didn't, you know? I felt nothing for it. I wished they'd moved to America, so I'd have more cities to choose from. Where else was I going to go? Calgary? Yeah, right. Montreal is too much, they're too crazy there."

"You tight with your folks?"

She took two puffs while she thought of her answer.

"They're my parents. It doesn't really matter. That doesn't change. No, we aren't close. But they're my parents."

We went back inside. An hour before last call. The rhythm was as always: Shots drink dance, shots drink dance, shots, piss, drink dance. Piss.

The night blinked to a close. People coupled off, some blacking out, a last-call hunt and dodge for others, a few sullen on the sidelines giving up. I pushed, she pushed back; she put my hands on her hips and kissed me. Hot tongue. I pulled her toward me, hard. I wanted everything. The songs ended. She stopped. Lights up.

"Let me go get water," she said and left.

Marwan slunk out from a corner.

"You have to help me," he said.

He put his hand on my shoulder and rested his weight on me. His forearms totally dry. No pit stains either. He'd gone to the bathroom regularly to pat the sweat off his body with cheap brown paper towels. We were in an overripe fruit. We were overripe fruit. I needed that water. To get to cold air outside. Marwan pointed to a blond white woman sipping from a straw dipped in a short glass. She wore gladiator sandals with straps that crossed up her calves to her knees. Thighs that were slabs. Light khaki shorts and a teal top that revealed she was shredded. From a distance she seemed sober and out of place.

"She thinks I'm rich," Marwan said. He panted. "Like. A rich person in Mumbai. A tech guy. Like the Google guy."

"Why does she think that?"

She had the same muscle-packed body as Marwan. Swayed her hips waiting. Men would fly by on the way to exit and she batted them away. The club floor covered in plastic cups, liquid; I stopped myself from looking. Glitter scattered over Marwan's shirt. His mouth hung open.

"I told her that."

"Why you tell her that?"

"It came out of my mouth," he said. "She asked what I did for a living."

"She said that? In the club? What do you do for a living?"

"She's very formal."

"You think she believed you?"

"She laughed a little when I said it. She's so hot. I don't know. She's going with it. I sold it. I said tech shit."

Natalie came back with two bottles of water and her hair in a bun. She wanted to eat. I wanted to go home away from the noise and into my bed. Warm bodies. Cool sheets. No light. No noise. Marwan sauntered away drunk, like a giant growing into his limbs, and brought the woman to us.

"This be Brittany."

She waved. Natalie spoke to her but I didn't hear because Marwan leaned in to whisper.

"I need the master bedroom," he said.

"No," I said. "You know the rules."

"Your girl wants to eat first."

"No."

"Imma be there first."

"No."

"Let me show off," he said. "I can't use the second room."

"Don't do this."

"Imma go."

"This isn't what friends do."

"We going."

"No," I said.

"Bye."

•

One of the Punjabis was naked and passed out face down on the couch. Another neck deep in the toilet bowl. A woman in pink patted him on the back begging him to drink water. He scolded gibberish, she stomped into the kitchen, saw us, retreated to the bathroom. Marwan scrambled to the kitchen in his boxers, grabbed the legit Grey Goose, two glasses, ice, and a squished joint rolled earlier. Morning light would break soon.

I closed the door on the Punjabi and slid the balcony shut, picked up a few empties, and threw out a McDonald's bag. Natalie wandered into the second bedroom and opened the window. She turned on the bedside lamp, took her hair out of the bun, and undressed, showing off a matching set of black sheer underwear. Her nipples obvious behind the bra. Two copper coins. She pulled the sheets out from their corners and placed her packet of Belmonts and a white lighter on the bedside table. The diffuser puffed and weak blue light along with cold air entered from the window. She stood in the doorway looking at me in the living room.

"Come in, dummy," she said.

Her crucifix and two other chains left on. One by one she pulled the rings off her fingers and stacked them next to the cigarette pack. I unbuttoned my shirt, pants, was in the room. She opened the white sheets and slid inside but stopped me from following with her foot.

"Take it all off," she said.

I removed my watch and chain, put them on the bedside table, socks, stared at her. I snapped the elastic on my boxers. She stopped me once more.

"We're not going to fuck," she said and I couldn't help but laugh.

There was the room, her. No street noise, no one outside our door, anywhere in the world. Only the room. She took her panties off and tossed them at me. There had never been anything before this. Our limbs stark brown against the white sheet, our bodies folded into the light that flowed in through the window. She waited, laughed again, turned the lamp off, grabbed my hands, and pulled my face into hers.

I woke to her smoking. Gold sunlight spilled on her body and the window frame made spokes of shadow on her face. She heard me stretch and groan and stubbed the cigarette out and apologized. She came back to me, shivering.

"I'm a little drunk," Natalie said.

"Me too."

"Have you ever been in love?" she asked.

"Maybe," I said.

"That's a bad sign. It means you haven't loved."

"I said maybe! Have you?"

"Yes," she said.

"How did you know?"

"Five years ago I was on the West Coast. What were you doing five years ago?"

"Probably this," I said.

"Shut up. Don't joke. Can you have a serious conversation?"

"You have to be taught to love," I said.

"Someone has to show you?" she said and turned to face me.

My fingers between her ribs.

"How did you know you were in love?" I asked again.

"I've been in love twice," she said. "It doesn't matter if no one shows you. You can want it. Learn it. I still miss them."

"I don't miss anyone."

"How old was your father when he had you?" she asked.

"Twenty-eight."

"How old are you now?"

"Twenty-eight," I said.

"Uh-oh."

"Have you ever had your heart broken?" I asked.

"Never," she said.

"Lucky girl. How'd you avoid that?"

"Have you?" She asked.

"Yes."

"Then you've been in love."

"What about friends?" I asked. "That's love. Do you have a best friend?"

"Are we in high school? A best friend? Who has that?"

"That's my best friend we can hear pumping away in the next room," I said.

"I've had best friends, always. Like in middle school, then high school, then university. But it always goes away," she said. "It's super intense for a year or two or three, and then … the class finishes, or the grade, or whatever."

"What about right now?" I asked.

"No. Not really. There's people I like. People I talk to. Like I'll have someone to complain to about work. Or someone to talk to about, whatever. To go drinking with. But not one person."

"Should we be best friends?"

"Isn't that what everyone says now? That you should date your best friend?"

"That's crazy," I said.

"Right! I don't want to date my best friend. I want to date my boyfriend. I don't want to kiss my best friend. I want to kiss my boyfriend. I don't know if I can be friends with someone in *sales* anyway."

"Come on, now."

"What do you do, for real?" she asked.

"I sell shit. Over the phone. It doesn't matter."

"Is that all you want to do?"

"I want to make money," I said.

"Doing …?"

"It doesn't even matter," I said. "What about you? You using that psychology degree at the salon?"

"I want to make money too! But I don't know why. For my parents, I guess."

"Money's money. It doesn't matter. I just want … you know. A good life. Whatever."

"I want to buy my parents a house," she said.

"Where?" I asked. "In Vancouver?"

"No. We never talk about it. They hustle hard. They came here for me, right? I didn't ask them to but they came here for me. How can I forget that?"

"You didn't ask for it," I said.

"No — of course not," Natalie said. "I believe that. But they still made the choice. They didn't have to. They didn't have to leave. I wouldn't do it. Would you leave Canada to go back to India for someone else?"

"That's a little bit different," I said. "Have you been to India?"

"It's not different," she said. "It's the same. You get used to it. Whatever it is, you get used to."

"I'll buy you a house."

"Oh, is that right? Minimum wage plus commission for selling shit over the phone is gonna buy me a house?"

"You the meanest girl I've ever met."

"You like me, though," she said.

"I like you, though."

"You've really never missed anyone?" Natalie asked.

"I'll miss you."

"Shut up," she said. "I like you. But no talking. No talking. You a bad talker."

Natalie kissed down my chest, flicking my nipples, to my stomach, then turned her body so I could taste her. She directed my arms around her torso and we moved in a slow groove like this, twinned together, my hands all over, her legs squeezing my head when I finished into her mouth; she pushed up to sit on my mouth, the wave of her long black hair falling against her back. After she came she curled into me. We fell asleep.

3.

The living room had been tidied. The Punjabis gone. I sprayed cleaner into the toilet bowl to cover up the vomit smell. The TV, coffee table, and fixtures had no damage. No tears or stains on the couch. Empties under the sink. A small stack of tens and fives on the counter next to Marwan's charging phone — $375, exactly what they owed us. I put in Marwan's code and read the text from the Punjabi:

wicked night

My phone was dead. I took Marwan's out and plugged mine in. We were supposed to meet Hussain's connect — the man who'd provided the vetted phone numbers — to take over directly. We were waiting for confirmation.

Marwan was right. The tax thing was fine but it was sporadic and relied too much on luck. I wanted more in my life. The only legal work I was hired for were anonymous phone-sales gigs alongside college graduates in their first "real" jobs and new immigrants happy for scraps. Enough money for fake leather shoes and trendy polyester pants but not more than maintaining my credit card debt.

It's not polite. It's gross, it's common, not pleasant to say out loud — it's leaving a New Era sticker on a baseball cap, the leather tag on Timbs. But I wanted money. Not stocks, investments, real estate, but cash, bills, paper. Rubber-band stacks. Forget wealth. That required the future. I could not think five years into the future. I did not plan. When I looked that far ahead it was black.

I could not have my father's life. After slinging us here from India he had burrowed into a job at a credit card company, worked a nothing job for a nothing wage, content to leave no mark on the world except for his nights of six or seven red wine glasses; a snide remark or wild slap common. His ambition extinguished itself getting us to the country. Its bitter pit remained.

This was our history. Like bureaucrats for the Mughals or the clerks in East Africa, administrative paperwork is what Indians excelled in.

When I left university at twenty-three a corporate job was my bull's eye. For three years I worked the jobs I could manage, always a temp, never brought on as full-time staff. There was a corruption to my personality that kept me from advancing in any way. It might have been the disdain for my father manifesting. It might have been that growing up under his anger made me incapable of existing in a professional world. It didn't change fact: I wanted money.

Our first success in the tax scam was a soft-spoken Indian, intelligent and articulate over the phone. I was exhausted when she answered, assuming she'd hang up, but she asked question after question, believing my bullshit. In the end, we met at a Tim Hortons, her in a mustard-yellow sari, me in a cheap grey suit. She gave me four thousand dollars.

We got a Pakistani on the hook last week. We were meeting him later. It was simple. If the voice who answered had an accent we followed an easy script: their taxes had been filed incorrectly, they owed thousands of dollars to the government, and if they didn't pay, they would go to jail or be sent back to wherever.

We didn't try to convince. There were lots of people who would walk into a trap propelled by fear. Bengalis, Indians, Egyptians: if their home country had a corrupt government, our threat was within the realm of possibility — maybe, they thought, the West was not so different.

We didn't play with Somalis or anyone from the Balkans.

I dreamed of the potential in Hussain's connect. Me and Marwan had run small things over the years. Selling TVs of unknown origin, moving tax-free cigarette cartons, a failed weed delivery enterprise, lots of tiny moves that topped off our wages without culminating in anything substantial.

We'd heard the connect was new in town and trying to make a push through backroom gambling — that's what I wanted in on. He came from a prominent family based in Bombay and Dubai. Proximity to him meant money. He was the person who could take us from small scams into actual money. Not criminal. Not seriously criminal. If people want to part with their money they should be allowed to.

Apparently, his roving gambling operation went from mansion to mansion and needed reliable management. Baccarat, poker, roulette, someone said they even had big-money dominoes. My imagination was limited but precise: a simple job that would put me in regular contact with the monied connect and his clients. Despite myself, like everyone, I aspired to be a middle man.

Hussain had not planned to introduce us to the connect. We usually paid him five hundred dollars for each list of numbers to call, which he received direct from the connect. Hussain was saving for his way out, apparently going to get into the textile business with his brother. Then he got in trouble. Inhaling a joint in one go, he told us the government was after him for his Twitter presence — he couldn't shut up about ISIS and loved yapping about guys like Abdul — and his lawyer said he was about to get hit with a peace bond. He studied the park we met at with wide eyes. Violence oozed off him. He spoke rat-a-tat-tat fast and made little sense when talking about his problems. If the government was after someone, it was probably him.

He had needed a favour, he said, tossing his roach into a bush. He asked us to hold onto a shoebox filled to the brim with bills and jewellery. Later, me and Marwan sat down and counted twenties and fifties until we hit ten thousand dollars. And the jewellery was gold: five sets of earrings, two onyx signet rings, and a thick necklace that reached Marwan's belly. Hussain gave us the box and a stack of papers with names and numbers. He'd be back for it in a few weeks.

And so a few days ago when he came to collect his box we made it simple: we wouldn't give it back until he connected us to his man.

He was so frazzled by then he didn't care. We agreed on a final payment of seven hundred for the intro, plus returning the shoebox. Now we waited.

We were doing nothing in our lives. What went in came right out. I'd lived the same life for the past decade. My mother had fled to Bombay three years before and my father had moved to his tiny apartment a few kilometres from me. Did I miss them? It was more like a phantom limb; I knew what was supposed to be there.

The Airbnb that weekend reminded me how much I hated what my sales job would get me. I lived in a one-bedroom basement apartment at the end of the subway line under a Korean family who occasionally sent meals to make up for the mould crawling up the walls. Small windows hinted at light outside. Often I would see the feet of raccoons or skunks before they got into their regular evening scraps. Their battle cries over food lulled me to sleep, the hot air a glove over my body, the dank seeping into my clothes, mice loud above and under me.

I'd learned from the phone job it was cheaper to simply refund some claims rather than investigate. I furnished my apartment from an online store, Wayfair, by claiming the items were delivered broken. They refunded a coffee table and two stools without asking for proof. I stopped after they refused to refund a hundred-dollar lamp.

The rest I decorated with a mattress on milk crates, a vintage Toshiba TV from Value Village, a fake-wood breakfast table, two folding chairs, and a rack for my clothes I found on the street. I paid cash for an ugly KAWS toy marketed to morons like me. A seventy-dollar ashtray I did not use. A hundred-and-twenty-dollar bong.

This shopping was revenge. Growing up my father told me our furniture was from The Brick or Leon's or any other regular, middle-class store. I learned at twelve, riding along to help him load a new couch, that we'd been buying from the

Goodwill down the street and that I'd been coached to tell people a lie to hide where we made our purchases.

If I closed my eyes during the day it was easy to pretend I was elsewhere. The slithering moss smell arrived only at night. I rented the apartment because its ceilings were higher than normal.

Two raps on the door of the Airbnb pulled me from sleep. It was a delivery of brown bags stuffed with burritos. Marwan came out of his room in a robe, turned on the coffee. He allowed himself one fast-food indulgence every month and I was never allowed to say anything about it. He'd ordered for both of us.

"Natalie still here?" Marwan asked.

"She went to work."

"You gonna see each other again?"

"For sure," I said.

"I didn't hear you two last night."

"Don't say that. That's weird. Britta?"

"I love her."

"No, man."

Marwan prowled back and forth in the living room with his hands squeezed around the burrito. Britta had left at dawn. She gave him her number.

"I love her," Marwan said. "I know what you're going to say. It doesn't matter. It doesn't matter. But I say time doesn't matter. No you're right I don't love her. You're right you're right. I could, though. I could. That matters. That's basically the same thing. It's almost the same thing."

"You had sex, you're excited. Simmer down."

I poked the rolls and picked one.

"No way man. Don't say I can't be in love. Everyone believes in love at first sight."

I wasn't sure he was speaking to me. He mumbled while tidying up, straightening the rugs, adjusting mirrors, and then spraying and wiping down the counter. He tried to keep his voice down but excitement took him over as ideas rushed. He moved around the apartment like a sniffing hound.

"Soulmates what about soulmates?" Marwan asked.

"Are you still drunk?"

"No."

"What about soulmates?" I asked. "People say that to fill the air."

"People believe that. People always believe that. I had a real life-changing moment. What you think about Natalie?"

"I like her a lot."

"How's that different?"

"We're saying two different things entirely," I said.

"You have to believe in soulmates to have a soulmate. Twin flame. You heard about that? It's all over my Instagram."

"You being serious?"

"I feel for her."

"I feel for her too bro. You nuts."

"That's how you dismiss people," Marwan said.

"Don't be weird with her," I said. "She was nice."

"She was lovely."

My phone pinged. It was Hussain.

•

We cleaned up and zoomed over in Marwan's champagne Corolla. Hussain never drove anywhere, was always there already, an endless cigarette hanging under a curved bird nose that seemed desperate to fly off his face. His fade tight and high but slightly crooked and he was the kind that wore a windbreaker all the time, even throughout the summer.

Marwan parked near Hussain standing under the shade of a maple. He dapped us up with clammy hands.

"This him," Hussain said and texted me a link to an Instagram account. ArabTarzan, 50K followers. Marwan read over my shoulder and I scrolled down the page tallying up different birds, turtles, and assorted small reptiles.

"This who?" I asked.

"This him. The guy. He's got a job for you," Hussain said.

"This your connect?"

"Yeah, dog. Don't say anything when you see him."

"Don't say anything about what?" I asked.

A black Chevy Tahoe jerked into the lot, ran over a curb, and parked. Music poured out from the SUV. Darkened windows. We waited. After a minute, the driver opened the back door and a skinny man with a massive red keffiyeh held in place with an agal came out. The sun reflected against his aviators. Thick leather sandals snapped against his skin and his white thobe was fresh out of the box; it had creases from being folded so long. A gold watch, the face too big for his skinny wrist, hung loose. Hussain paced and smoked six million cigarettes in the time it took for the Arab to walk to him, and then lit the Arab's cigarette.

I leaned against our car while they murmured to each other. ArabTarzan. The son of a gangster. Aspiring crime lord. Summer rain tapped on leaves above us.

"A desert oasis, eh?" the Arab said to us before turning back to Hussain. He was wearing a classic Middle Eastern outfit, missing the hawk and glove, but his features gave him away. He wasn't Arab. His complexion was dark brown and his nose flattened in the centre of a chubby face. He looked like my cousin. When he spoke to Hussain he bobbed his head in the Indian way. I couldn't stop staring. The Arab beckoned us over.

"Salaam," he said. "Hussain says you're good people looking for work."

His accent was Indian strangled with TV English and twisted with Arabic. His family's business sprawled from Bombay to Dubai, which is where they fled and opened their base of operations after the '93 Bombay blasts. He'd been sent here as a scout, Hussain claimed, to see if there was room for another ethnicity in the crime businesses. ArabTarzan was his own thing. His passion. I hated Hussain. He was an idiot. I was an idiot. He was an idiot. The Arab had not been sent here to "scout," but to be hidden, a failed rich kid, last in line to inherit the empire, kept out of sight from a disappointed father.

Money to be made, however. A mansion in the suburbs that hosted dozens of small birds, reptiles, some dogs. What the Arab wanted was a cat. A big cat.

He ordered Hussain, "Send them the link."

My phone buzzed. BOWMANVILLE ZOO OWNER TO FACE ANIMAL CRUELTY CHARGES AFTER PETA EXPOSÉ.

"I tried to buy it but he won't sell," the Arab said. "No one I know will do this for me."

"What you need?"

"The cat."

He pulled gently from his Benson & Hedges. Hussain stared at me with pleading eyes and Marwan squeezed his little belly, which he did when he was nervous or confused. The Arab went over the details: we had to steal the cat. He'd pay us three thousand. We'd then have direct access to a vetted list of names and phone numbers we could use to cold call. It needed to be done soon. His usual crew too scared or confused or not ambitious. He dismissed their complaints with a wave. Hussain scratched his hand while trying not to look at me, looked at me. The Arab agitated as he explained the details of the zoo to us and the troubles of the owner — the poor cat was being fed frozen Costco chickens.

The Arab and Hussain gave us space to talk and I sat in the Corolla with Marwan.

"What you think?" I asked.

"Maybe I could bring Britta up there to the mansion. She'd be into that. Look at his Stories he's always got parties with the animals."

"Bro."

"Sorry, sorry. It sounds easy. He's going to provide the van. You think Hussain's getting paid to introduce us?"

"Probably. Let's knock that off our fee."

"And what about the three thousand?"

"What is it — it's a heist. Let's do four."

"Let's do five," Marwan said.

The Arab got back into his SUV. I turned to Marwan, wanting to make sure he was good with the work.

"It's an insane job," I said.

"It's good money," Marwan said.

"It's stealing a jaguar."

"He said he's got a dart gun," Marwan said.

"A dart gun. Say it again."

"Dart gun."

"Did you ever think you would say dart gun out loud?"

"You said you wanted to work," Marwan said. "Wanted real money."

"I'm good with it. Are you?"

"You heard how he talked about his boys. We show up, be good, we get more work."

"You think it's too big a risk?" I asked.

Marwan googled the zoo and we skimmed news articles and pictures.

"It's a bum-ass zoo. PETA is after the owner, so are lawyers, the police. Nobody cares about this guy," Marwan said. "He's let the zoo get totally run down. We're helping the animals."

"Why he call himself ArabTarzan?"

"What's wrong with it?" Marwan asked.

"He's not Arab."

"He's not Tarzan either."

Hussain's grinning face at our window. He knocked twice. He had a yellowing tooth and white lined gums.

"What's going on, man?" Hussain asked. "You gonna do it? I set this up for you and everything."

"We going to do it. You negotiating or him?" I asked.

"Negotiating what? Three thousand is a good fee. Don't be a custie," Hussain said.

That made me mad.

"A'ight, tell him five, plus he covers your seven hundred," I said.

"Yo what —"

"Nobody else will do it."

"He came 'cause I said you'd do it for three," Hussain said.

"Why you say that?" I asked.

"That's a good price. He doesn't even come normally. This is special to him."

"Good price says who? You ever steal a jaguar?"

Hussain left furious and the Arab wouldn't let him in the SUV. He spoke to him from the window. Hussain came back.

"He says four. He's upset though," Hussain said.

"He's not upset. Five plus your seven hundred."

"I can't ask him to do the seven hundred."

"How much he paying you?"

"Nada."

"How much he paying you?" I asked.

"If you guys do it then I get eight hundred."

"Sheesh. What you need our seven hundred for, then?"

"Yo."

"I got your shoebox. Tell him five."

They spoke for five minutes. The SUV screeched out of the parking lot. Hussain came back to us.

"Five's good. You'll get a text in three days. He's gonna set up a place with the van and the gun but his cousin is gonna come too," Hussain said.

"Who's his cousin?"

"I dunno man, his cousin. I dunno. Can I have my shoebox?"

•

We went back to my place to hop into my 2001 Acura Integra. I'd gotten it back from a Chinese guy who promised to add a JDM front end and Halos for a few thousand and I wanted to show off. Marwan didn't notice.

Today was big: we had a "tax gig" for a possible seven thousand dollars. From my place we drove to a Coffee Time in North York, at the tail-end of a plaza with a Jamaican grocery store and two Hakka restaurants. I found us a spot in the lot across from the shop's front window and waited. It was half full. I'd found our Mr. Ahmadi's photograph on his LinkedIn profile but recognized no faces. Marwan complained my A/C was busted.

"But you got the cool headlights."

I was itchy and hot in my Value Village suit. I didn't want to be seen in it but Marwan insisted it was perfect for the role. It had its original shoulder pads and wide silhouette pants and way-too-large lapels and the cheap polyester inhaled my sweat and held it. It was twenty dollars so fine, whatever. My pit stains grew. I opened the window. Marwan dug into my glove compartment for the bag of pistachios he'd stuffed there.

"You saving for retirement?" Marwan asked.

"Are you serious?"

"My dad asked me if I had a Tax-Free Savings plan."

"I don't," I said.

"Check this: oh you who believe! Be careful of your duty to Allah and relinquish what remains due to usury if you are believers."

"That your dad?"

"It's from Abdul's latest post. We're not supposed to gain interest. Haram."

"I knew that," I said.

"Money has to be tied down."

"How much did Abdul get from the government? Ten million?"

"He's buying a building downtown. Land," Marwan said.

Abdul was in the news a lot then. When he'd been released from Guantanamo Bay he sued the Canadian and U.S. governments; Canada had recently settled. I tapped my steering wheel, amazed at the figure.

"Ten million dollars. Wow," I said.

"Would you go to jail for ten million?" Marwan asked.

"How long was he in? Ten years? And that place — Guantanamo. That ain't jail-jail."

"And he said he's innocent. That he didn't shoot anyone. That's why he got the money," Marwan said.

"Forget that. He shot that guy. But what was it? A soldier shooting a soldier in war."

"He wasn't a soldier," Marwan said. "He was a kid. He's our age. You see those posts I send you?"

"Yeah yeah, he's great," I said.

"Ten years."

"Ten million though," I said.

"Fourteen years old when he went in. Twenty-five when he came out. You think he's a virgin?"

Most of Abdul's money went to lawyer's fees and the ongoing U.S. case; he funded the defence for a few other detainees. The remaining chunk went to a new home he bought and to a four-story building on prime real estate downtown. It unnerved the country that he'd received millions. The city was upset that he bought land downtown. His lawyer had released a statement saying he had public plans for the building.

"I think you're a virgin the way you talk about Britta."

"Why you always so rude?"

"You're telling me he's got ten million dollars and it isn't making interest for him? This country would lose it if people couldn't make interest," I said.

"He's saying money has to be connected to us. Money can't make money. Money as a tool, not life. You read the posts?" Marwan asked.

"I read the posts," I said, "yeah."

"Then you know he's talking about fairness," Marwan said.

"That the guy?"

A short man in a green spring coat and grey slacks, balding, opened the door, checked the customers out and sat at an empty corner table facing the window. He took out a manila envelope from his coat and placed it in front of him. He laid his hands over it. I couldn't read his face from so far. His hands clasped one over the other and then shoved into his pockets. Then back out. He was nervous. Good.

Marwan double-checked the official-looking documents he'd Photoshopped. He shoved his hand into the pistachio bag.

"Probably. You got a name?"

"Hamid?"

"A fake name?" Marwan asked.

"I'll use yours," I said.

"Shut up. Do Shah Rukh."

I rolled my eyes and practised a fake signature. I'd wanted to call the lady from that first successful job again but Marwan ruled we couldn't hit up the same person more than once. It was tempting when someone gave in easily to tap them forever but that moved from teach-them-a-lesson to cruel too intensely. Anyways, the more we saw the person, the likelier it was they'd put it together. Marwan closed his eyes, murmuring names to himself to see what fit.

"Do Dale," he said.

"I'm not gonna say, 'Hi, I'm Dale.'"

"I got it. You want it? I got a good one."

"Give it up," I said.

"Mohammad Mohammad."

"You're an idiot."

"Mo-Mo. It's so good. Easy to remember."

The man examined the faces in the coffee shop. He hadn't ordered. It was for sure Mr. Ahmadi.

"You nervous?" Marwan asked.

"Yeah," I said.

"Really?"

"A little," I said.

We sat in the car, quiet.

"You want me to do it?" Marwan asked.

"Nah. Nah I got it."

"You're not Hamid being Mo'. You're Mo'. You're Mo-Mo. You're Mohammad Mohammad the tax collector. There's no Hamid. Only Mo-Mo the best tax collector the government has."

"Actually, it's Mohammad, not Mo'."

I said Bismillah and swung out of the car, Mohammad now.

The suit crackled at the frigid indoor air. I really hated that suit. It made noise when I walked. There was no line so I bought a coffee and took in the customers. Five or six seniors read newspapers and a group of kids, all friends, laughed with each other, some who had hit puberty and were clumsy-limbed with sparse chin hairs, and some who were waiting for it, small, a doll-like glaze on their faces.

I read the text again: Farhad Ahmadi. We made eye contact and he rose in his seat. It was him. His trousers baggy and a faded yellow polo underneath the coat. He was stressed and eager, with bags under his eyes, wrinkles lining his face, and a moustache bunched over his lip.

"Mr. Ahmadi?"

"Yes yes, thank you. Would you like a coffee?" he asked.

"Um, no, I'm okay, I have one. Uh, this doesn't have to be long. You spoke to my colleague on the phone. I'm Mo'. Mr. Mohammad."

"You're so young," he said. "Your parents must be proud."

"They're okay, sure. Uh."

I sat across from him. His mouth was dry and he smacked his lips, licked his lips. Sour breath. His clothes were cheap. His open eyes relaxed, relief pouring out of his body. I tensed. My mood spiked. He was my father's age. How could he be so dumb? Doesn't he have family to look after?

"I'm so thankful for this," he said. "I'm sorry. My son usually helps me with my taxes but this year he wasn't able he's so busy at work. Last year also. He has a son now."

"Did you tell him about this?"

"I couldn't tell him — that I filed this incorrectly. It's my fault. My problem."

"I get it. I understand," I said.

I removed the paperwork from my thrift-store briefcase. Mr. Ahmadi shuffled and skimmed through the sheets.

"Once again I want to apologize for this inconvenience," he said. "I didn't mean to do it wrong."

"Use a tax guy next time."

"The amount here, it says seven thousand dollars in back taxes. From the last two years? Can you explain to me again what these fees are? You said over the phone it was an income thing, that the wrong boxes were ticked, but I didn't totally understand."

"They're back taxes. You said you had two jobs? It's from that."

"But the error in my paperwork?" he asked. "I don't want it to happen again."

"You didn't declare enough income. And … you didn't declare what kind of income it was. We should have taken more at the source. If you sign the documents you won't have to worry about it."

"I understand … but I mean for next year. I'll have to file my taxes for this year. So I can learn."

"Hire an accountant," I said.

"I can't afford an accountant," he said. "Especially after this."

In this dumb suit, in this dumb coffee shop, with this dumb idiot in front of me.

"I have a full day," I said. "I'm here to help you. This process needs to move along. There is another fee for delayed filing after an error is discovered. And you know, if we begin to involve the courts, there's more money involved, there's repercussions down the line. Right now your good faith is helping."

"Oh, no, no, of course — I understand."

Mr. Ahmadi shrank back into his seat. It was easy to see why he was a target. My tone crunched him down easy. He skimmed the papers again and moved his lips to read. I took breaths to not lose composure. Others were scared of anger's corrosive nature but I could guide it and shape it for my benefit. It was the seed in me that grew every day, grew where I didn't look, grew to take me over. Mr. Ahmadi took the pen I'd lain on the table and signed the documents. I took the paperwork back and put it in my briefcase.

"Do you not sign the paperwork?" he asked.

"What? Oh — of course."

I took the paperwork back out and made a show of signing both our copies. We stood up together and he thanked me once again for my help and handed me the envelope.

"Do I need to count this?" I asked.

"No, no sir, of course not."

We shook, both of us clammy. He sat back down empty-handed.

4.

My phone buzzed and buzzed. Buzz for voice mail, buzz for a text, buzz for voice mail, again. I shook from Mr. Ahmadi, ready to confront anyone over anything; it was better not to answer that phone call. I wouldn't be able to control myself. I couldn't be like this in front of anyone but Marwan.

I drove Marwan to his Corolla. He knew who was calling me. He didn't say anything at first but couldn't keep his mouth shut. He reminded me we could chill at his place and blaze. We'd made money. We could have fun. Half the fun of getting drunk was the groggy hangover. Since we were teens Marwan had pulled me into his life with ease, showing me in his patient, kind way, what family and grace were.

I ignored him. He told me to breathe. Four in, eight out. We sat in the car and did a grounding exercise he found online. Start by clenching feet, then calves, thighs, working up to the top of the head to get out of the head. The phone buzz tightened my spine and cemented my head into place with stress. With this anxiety, anger would arrive to control the situation; I would get angry at getting angry. My phone buzzed for a text again. The only person this annoying in my life was my father.

I read: Pick up.

I had an appointment with him.

I drove off the main street and slowed into the curved road that led to a three-building complex, my father's building the first on the right. He had downsized automatic when my mother moved out three years ago, as if he'd been waiting to compress his fifty some years into a one-bedroom. As I parked I saw the buildings crumble and collapse, the ground open and take them in. Or a tornado manifest. Or a fire, a gunfight in the lobby, a bomb explosion, my father's bloodied arm sticking out of the rubble. Heaven's dark light could take him up and away from me.

Up the elevator with the ding of opening doors I drowned in the wet leather smell of cabbage. Somehow, in a neighbourhood full of Afghans, a building full of browns, he managed to rent on the floor full of whites. Maybe Russians, I never spoke to them, but the eyes-to-the-ground of the wives, and the bare, shit-eating grins of the kids was Slavic. The browns of Europe, at least. The carpet hummed with decades of weird cooking.

He lived at the end of the hallway. Always a different light bulb was out. I stopped in front of his door to examine new splotches darker than the carpet. A short fat lady with a scarf around her head sized me up.

I unlocked the door. All as it always was. The kitchen on my left with its sink full of cleaned and stacked frozen empty dinner trays waiting to be recycled. Four cleaned empty jars of premade grocery-store curry next to that. Each surface scrubbed. Seven empty wine bottles. No beer, no liquor; except whiskey at weddings, he drank red wine exclusive. The living room spotless and bare. Two leather recliners were positioned toward a sixty-five-inch TV I had bought him. One recliner had a divot from his body, the leather pale, almost yellow; the other pristine in plastic wrap. A few patches of mismatched drywall. There was nothing else I could see in the apartment. No table. I never figured out where he ate.

He was on the balcony holding a cigarette between his index and thumb. The sun turned the air purple, softened my vision, and dropped. 6:00 p.m. and it was possible he wasn't tipsy. His lungi caught in the door as he came in, he didn't notice, kept walking, and it tore. He ignored it. His eyes were glassy. He washed his hands for thirty seconds, spat in the sink, and sank into his recliner.

When we lived together he started drinking at 6:00 p.m. because that was when he walked in the door. He would nurse five or six glasses of wine and by 9:00 p.m. no one could talk to him.

He started his hand stretches. He'd risen to some steady cog at Visa's call centre where he could lord over a team. Whatever happened to his attitude after my mother left infected his work and he was knocked down to a data-entry position alongside recent Indian immigrants who couldn't understand his backward trajectory. He couldn't even sustain a life dedicated to mediocrity. The energy and ambition it took to uproot him, my mother, and me to this country fizzled upon landing and that space filled with mysterious grievance that drink cajoled out. I used to feel guilty, like his choices were my responsibility, but now I didn't care; I hadn't asked to be brought here.

"Did you get it?" he asked.

I handed over five small blue packets of plant food. He took them to the wall underneath the window with the five plants my mother left behind. There'd been fourteen when she left. His walk had changed. Was it a limp? He held himself differently, slightly tilted. He shook his hand, flexed his fingers.

"She brought it up again," he said. "Divorce."

"You knew it was coming," I said.

"I've heard all the bullshit before. I'm sixty years old. I've heard all that bullshit before. Why should I do what an email says?"

He sprayed the plants with water and emptied the sachets.

Three years before, my mother had knocked on my apartment door, a black eye spreading, a scatter of scratches on her face. Swelling taking over her left cheek. She'd always been fair and freckled and new colours — red, black, blue — distorted her. It was January 1, New Year's. It had happened before but I'd never seen marks. I'd been a kid. The girl I was dating stood behind me, naked but wrapped in a sheet, then dashing around the apartment for water and ice. I asked my mother to sit and stood stunned. I boiled water. I dressed completely. I didn't know what to do but find him and kill him.

"What's going on with your hand?" I asked.

"Don't worry about me."

"Do you need anything?"

"I work. I have money. I'm your father. Don't ask me stupid questions."

The girl — I can't even say her name — fluttered and fixed that night, dabbing my mother's wounds. I'd told her about my father but she'd never seen it. My mother and me the room clouded with grief. A small sliver of me was happy: see, proof, I had an origin to my temper, I wasn't telling tales.

The girlfriend had never met them. She thought it was because she was blond, blue-eyed, her skin ice-white; I let her. I couldn't bring her over to them. I tried to pretend they were fake the moment I moved out. They lived ten minutes away and I saw them once or twice a year.

I was stuck in the moment I opened the door to my mother's changed face. The bloom of my father's anger, violence, drink. After two months it was clear I would never thaw. We broke up. I hated her for a long time but eventually I let myself realize she'd done the right thing. When I remember her I filled with gratitude, happy she exited our bad situation so neatly.

My father fiddled with the plants. I'd never been inside his new bedroom. The door ajar. I couldn't see in.

"I'm going," I said. "Text me if you need anything."

I could stand the unit for ten minutes max before the thrum of memories overtook me. I'd known my whole life he hit her but I never looked at it directly. Until she knocked on my door that night I had deniability. Fragments. Notoriously unreliable childhood memories.

I reminded her that day he'd hit me too, trying to draw a bridge to her, but she only saw another person damaged by him. She spent the morning on my couch drinking tea, smoking cigarettes — a habit she'd kept hidden from me growing up, even after I found out.

The first time I saw her smoke was when she ran away after an all-night fight with my father. She burst out the door screaming she'd never come back. My father watched her cross the street and told me to chase her, and no matter what, to not lose her. I followed the trail of vapour, stunned she'd kept a secret from me; I was ten and learning the surface didn't always match the interior.

He told me to chase her but not what to do. She stopped on a park bench. I don't remember what I said. She said she was not coming back. She had no bags or belongings, just a packet of smokes; not even a lighter; she used one to light the other.

She came back home.

5.

Three days later, Samir, the Arab's cousin, backed up the vehicle the Arab provided. It was big, white, and conspicuous: a cargo van. Perfect. It was so common no one would bat an eye. The Arab already used it to transfer his animals so it was prepared with a cage that could be taken out, blue tarp, a lock box that held a dart gun and five darts of different dosage marked in a way I didn't understand. The cat's dosage was supposed to take five minutes. She would be agitated from the prick, hissing and bearing fangs, prowling and panting until a slow-down turned into sleep.

Samir exited the van to greet us. He wore a black T-shirt and pants and shaking his hand I got a whiff of cumin and B.O. He reached my chin but his arms and legs were much longer than mine, as if they had stretched late in life to accommodate his energy. The skin on his arm had white scratches from dryness. He was formal and tried too hard to make a serious impression. His hair was pulled tight into a bun, with a band slid over his forehead to further hold it in place. His features were classic working-class Indian male: youthful around the eyes, but otherwise cragged, with the wrinkles of a fifty-year-old Westerner.

The Arab texted me a link to a new PETA video on their website: insider footage of the owner whipping the lions relentless, turning the violent act into a mechanical movement of boredom. We'd be saving Bagheera, he texted.

The van clunked out the garage. We left our phones in our cars so they wouldn't ping a trail with the corresponding towers. I'd printed out the route instructions from MapQuest and read them to Marwan. We had a two-hour ride and would reach at 11:00 p.m. Marwan re-accustomed himself to stick shift, Samir let his arm swing from the shotgun seat window. Me in the back on a folded chair bolted to the side. I sneezed; sawdust lined the floor.

The Arab had visited the zoo several times in his failed negotiations and his appraisal of the place was that it was a shabby den deserving our poaching. We'd hovered over a laptop on Google Maps and plotted our route in and out. Security? We assumed none. The zoo had no money. The owner had been selling the animals to pay for legal fees. An exotic bird equalled two hours in a room with a lawyer.

She was named Bagheera, not after *The Jungle Book*, but a TV show called *Amazon*, about a group of travellers lost in the rainforest and having to make do. The show ended in 1999. The cat was ancient. We weren't stealing a sleek, skulking, death machine, but a retiree happy with frozen rotisserie. We wore pitch-black outfits with latex gloves and thick ski masks.

Samir spoke. His voice loosened and dropped the formality. He'd been in Canada for a few months. Officially an international student studying animal biology, in actuality a vagabond criminal hoping to make good for his family back home. He opened the dart gun case and slid his finger across the metal barrel and plastic parts. Whether it was a gesture of familiarity and comfort, or newness and apprehension, I couldn't tell. Chamber empty, he pulled the trigger so the hammer clicked. Again and again he did this aiming the gun at his feet. He hadn't wanted to let Marwan drive until we patiently explained the route. For every action we suggested, he offered another; no matter how small, he wanted to express his opinion. His energy was pulled tight and the constant trigger-pulling irritated me. The white and yellow sodium lights of the highway illuminated his face as he spoke.

"She'll be my first pet," he said. "I think she'll be better off with us. I've never had a pet. She'll be happier. I hope her health is good. A sick cat is a sad cat. There's very little you can do for them. The big diseases — cancer, I mean — I don't think they can get. My very first pet."

I called out the sign marked Clarington and Marwan took the exit. I'd gone through several spikes of anxiety by now and steadied myself. What if the cat didn't fall asleep? What if she roared? I couldn't know all the ways it might go wrong. I told Samir to stop pulling the trigger and after doing it twice more, he listened.

Marwan stopped the car. I got out, put duct tape over the front and back license plates, and jumped back in. We weren't far now. We crackled the walkie-talkies to make sure they worked. Five minutes from the zoo we slowed for the dirt transport road where we would park.

Marwan pulled the parking brake and we stepped out. Looking at a zoo map we walked single file far off the road to avoid oncoming car lights. A full moon above and wind shifting trees. Closer to the entrance the branches came lower touching us on the shoulders.

We could see inside. There was no activity. The zoo was small and surrounded by fence. A single light in the distance, inside a portable, was on. I saw Bagheera slashing at Samir's face, his howl of pain, the panic of the swipe. This was a bad idea, I knew. That didn't mean anything, I knew. It had to be done. Bagheera patiently pulling Samir's organs out of his stomach, the look of surprise on his face, her mumble of delight. Even caged, bloodthirst wouldn't leave her.

We walked alongside the fence, then followed it as it broke right and walked two more minutes, our eyes scanning for movement or cameras. Every article online talked about the financial hit taken by the PETA claims and the general rundown nature of the place.

Piss and hay stench. I heard a machine noise: was there a camera? Behind the fence was a squat building made of brick and I could see a metal door. Probably a generator acting up.

I climbed the fence, dropped, and ducked behind the building. What did I just see? Movement in the corner of my eyes. I waved at Marwan and Samir to hurry and they crab-walked to my hiding spot. I peeked and saw nothing. I whispered to them. Samir didn't believe there was anything. We stayed quiet. I looked. Two crows on a low branch cawed. I scanned. A low whistle, a tune. Was that real? I put my finger to my lip and made them quiet. A melody.

We waited.

No — nothing.

"Don't be a pussy," Samir said and we walked twenty metres west through a maze of trees, a block of bathrooms, a lizard and bird section. Not a single animal interested in us. The full moon spilled white light onto plastic and metal surfaces. Bats flew. The heat was flat and the sound of trickling water came from the cages. It was an old-school zoo, one that you would expect to see in the '50s, or in Asia today. There was usually a pile of hay, a shallow pool of water and a sad, obese animal resigned to its easy life. What were we doing? I was being foolish. Marwan's warnings about patience and diligence flashed in my mind. Slow and steady was Marwan's method. He's often right. Bagheera's claws, extended same as a tabby's, gripping my forearm, tearing my flesh, playing with it like a toy.

The lion exhibit was empty. A camera hung, hopefully turned off. We took the fork to the left for another ten metres, crouched low and slow, knowing she would appear at any time. The air thick with animal. A sweet smell, sweat, meat, foliage. Flutter of wings. Soft scratch against a cage. We were in the peak of night. Us, the animals, the moon.

We would deliver Bagheera and head to a party at the Arab's. I was excited to see Natalie and to take her there, to my rich friend's house, to impress her. This kept me moving. The cool of night, the mammal glamour of the zoo, I was here to get to the end, alone with her in a room, a bed, an idle light, a maple glimpsed through the window, the rest of it pushed away.

Samir slung the gun over his shoulder and Marwan had the tarp.

I read the place card that said we were at the jaguar exhibit. The green plastic board nailed onto a pike read in faded letters:

BAGHEERA, AGED 10, was found in the jungles of India and trained to be the star of the hit TV show, AMAZON. Retired,

Bagheera lives a life of relaxation and ease and loves showing off for children.

She was way older than ten. There was no information about the type of jaguar she was or her evolutionary history. None of the usual facts on these things. We rose from our crouch and peeked inside the cage. There were some rocks, a flock of chicken feathers, a few fake trees, and a weak stream that curved through the encampment.

All three of us examined the space. It was quiet but not. Our bodies loud. Our insides telling us to run away. An ancient anxiety told me to get out of there. My breathing shallow. We looked.

"There," Samir said and pointed with the gun. "There she is." Bagheera lay like a log flat against the ground, ears down and back, eyes on us. Marwan watched while Samir loaded the weapon.

Click-clack.

Hearing the the gun load, she got up and walked back and forth, her focus never turning, her eyes always on him, her body across the cage quick. She was a black jaguar, at home at midnight. Yellow eyes never settled.

Her breathing heavy.

Samir gave me the gun. "I can't do all the work," he said. He wouldn't go closer. I hopped the small fence between place card and cage, got on one knee, and inserted the barrel through a gap in the mesh fence. We were two metres apart.

Bagheera watched me.

I controlled my breath. Long and deep inhale-exhale.

I shot: the gun made a noise like a slammed phone book and the dart hit her in the chest. She jumped in surprise, eyes wide, her front paws lifting off the ground with a small noise from her mouth. When she landed her lips peeled back over her teeth and a growl rumbled from her.

The zoo stayed quiet. She paced. Samir timed on his watch. The dart fell out of her chest and she watched it drop, slow, stopping, finally lying fully on the ground.

She closed her eyes.

She slept.

We waited ten minutes. Samir urged me to hop the fence. I refused. Was she asleep? I strained to watch her. Maybe she was just pretending. Her belly rose up and down. The dart dosed to knock her out for two hours.

No one spoke. Samir pushed me again, telling me to go over the last fence and closer to her.

"You go," I said.

"Should we shoot her again?" Marwan asked.

"No," I said. "It could kill her?"

"She's huge. I don't think so. Shoot her again," Samir said.

"Shut up."

Her lips trembled. Her fur almost blue. Samir looked on the ground and found a small gathering of pebbles and began throwing them at her. A few hit. She didn't move. Confident she was asleep, he went up the fence and landed with a loud thump.

I waited until he was within striking distance. He watched her body. He knelt. I could smell her, I thought. He ran his hand across her fur. I waited. She didn't move. I climbed the fence. I was jealous he was so close.

The crackle of the walkie-talkie burst the silence. Marwan had scrambled past an adjacent fence and through the access gate and I could hear the cough of the van engine as he came close.

Samir picked up the dart from the ground and pointed to where we should roll the tarp. I forced a deep breath. Every way we moved our eyes remained fixed on her. We went to either side of Bagheera. I grabbed a massive paw and squeezed the rough pad, hard and soft at the same time. It was wrong, holding her knocked-out like this, and thrilling; I'd never be this close to a wild animal. Pure nature, no reason. I wanted to touch her claw but was too scared.

We pulled her onto the tarp. She was huge. I was sweating. My body in full panic, ready to run, run, run, so I focused on breathing. The dart was working. It was fine.

She made a small noise, a chirp, and we jumped away from her to the far sides of the enclosure and I grabbed the fence and climbed halfway up before stopping. We stared. We looked at each other, at her. Just dream noise.

We had to hurry. I wouldn't last much longer. I went in the black hole of her cave to find an exit. The Arab was confident there would be an access door at the back where her caretakers could enter so she could be fed or treated. He was correct. A small tunnel led to a door for humans. I opened the door to a room with peeling green walls, a table, and a clock. Another door in there led to a hallway with signs to the service road. All the lights were on. No security cameras.

When I came back Bagheera was rolled up. Samir had found his bravery. The Arab was right to send him. I don't know if I would have been able to do it alone. The radio crackled to let us know Marwan was close and ready. Bagheera's body warm and I lost myself staring at her paws, wanting to touch again but frightened.

We slid a chain through the holes around the fringe of the tarp. She must have weighed two hundred pounds. Samir and Marwan each grabbed an end and I directed them out the door.

The red parking lights of the van spilled over the dirt road. The back doors open. Samir halfway through a cigarette. The sky a purple wash, an alien dome. The trees lining the road swayed with wind. Birds in the branches flew away from us. Cold sharp air. Our hair matted to our skull with sweat and we ripped off our ski masks. I was terrified but baited myself with the promise of Natalie at the end of this. Marwan moved without fuss.

"One, two, three."

We heaved her body onto the van and into the cage.

"Should we take her out of the tarp?"

"Should we shoot her again?"

"What if she roars?"

"I cannot believe we did that."

"Is she okay?"

"Who's sitting in the back with her?"

Staring at her, Bagheera's lips trembling in dream, we unwrapped the tarp. Marwan and Samir rushed to the front and got the van into gear. I was lost in her needles of black fur. She had faint spots. She murmured as I locked the cage.

6.

Samir chain-smoked the whole way back. Marwan's left arm hung out his window, the highway empty, while Samir stared ahead with the gun loaded between his legs. Bagheera, still and sleeping, jerked when the van bumped over the on-ramp, terrifying us with a soft kitten mewl. She blinked, folded one paw over the other, yawned, and made no more effort. She had the sweet smell of rich earth, like well-tended soil. Job done, the obnoxious buzz that surrounded Samir ceased. His commotion was limited to swinging his arm up and back down for his cigarette. We'd forgotten to pack water and were parched, our mouths thick and dry.

The Arab's men met us at the parking lot and took snoozy Bagheera.

I picked up Natalie and rolled into the Arab's at 2:00 a.m. The Arab led us to the backyard with drink, music, and hookah, bloodshot weed eyes and jittery coke limbs. At least twenty people. The exterior was visible from a mile away, probably from space, covered in a garish beige stucco, small bulbs illuminating the surfaces, the front ornamented with Greek-style columns and two lion statues. The house glowed with Indian wealth, a kind that made sure everyone knew.

We were given a room upstairs in a corner that overlooked the backyard. Noise came from the group outside taking turns jumping from the rectangle pool to the hot tub at its end. Next to that was a barbecue system with built-in gas crowned by a gazebo and dining space. Gentle lights pulled across the lawn, which led to separate, defined areas: a natural, but maintained garden, with purple and red flowers; bursts of bush; a selection of hanging hammocks; and sporadic crowds of chairs, as if no one knew how to fill the large space. Music from speakers bolted into the ground on poles.

The room was one of ten and I wasn't sure it had ever been used. A short grey vase of dried flowers sat on a white dresser with mirror. A plush California king bed, covered in slate linen, and bathroom with sunken tub and shower. White curtains ceiling to floor. I googled the tag on the mattress: three thousand dollars! My feet sank in the white carpet. A bougie room in an insane asylum.

Behind the yard was a forest with trees I could barely make out at this distance and dark. The drive had been long, up and off the main highway, down a side road to this house far away from everyone. It belonged to the Arab's parents.

Back downstairs, we dropped tired into chairs. The pool surface wobbled. Brown and green bottles scattered lawn lamps light. There were so many people and so much music. A couple in the pool slashed through water until they went silent kissing. Another two cuddled on a lawn chair. Natalie puffed a thick blunt. Mango smoke. A bonfire surrounded by sleepy ones. Closer to the speakers was shouting with dancing, bare limbs swinging, men and women wet and shining from water.

"How do you know this guy?" Natalie asked. "Does he work in *sales* with you?"

"I work for him," I said. "A little. I started. Tonight."

"You know him through the official network of Toronto knuckleheads?"

"Yeah, the Muslim chapter."

"Are you Muslim?" she asked.

"What else would I be? You Christian?"

"Catholic. I go to church."

"No, you don't," I said.

"I do!"

"There's no way."

"I love church," Natalie said.

"Do you believe in God?" I asked.

"Of course I do. You do too," she said. "When you do something, is it for him?"

"I don't know," I said.

"Will your parents get mad if we date?"

"We're allowed to date 'women of the book.'"

"That's convenient."

"We got good rules," I said. "No popes, nothing like that."

"I believe everything I do is for God."

"There's no way," I said.

"I do. I have to. It's the only way. But I don't feel anything. I just do it."

"Your parents taught you."

"We always went to church. And I told my mom I didn't feel anything and she said it didn't matter. It doesn't matter what you don't feel. You just do. You feel a connection?"

"Sure," I said.

"I guess it doesn't matter. How I behave is more important."

"You don't feel any kind of connection?"

"Maybe I don't know what it is. Maybe I feel it. Maybe when I feel happy, that's it, that random happy feeling, waking up with happy instead of anxiety. Maybe that's it and no one told me."

Then we were drunk. After an hour Natalie was too drunk. Marwan hazy in my vision talking to a woman. Hookah passed to me I filled my mouth with peach. I took Natalie upstairs and she retched into the toilet. What came out was clear and sticky.

"I'm sorry," she said. "I'm not usually like this."

"You like to drink."

"You like to drink," she said. "Don't be an asshole."

"I'm not trying to be."

"But somehow ..."

I filled a glass with water.

"I'm sorry," she said.

"It's all good. It happens."

"Sometimes when I start. It's hard. Of course you know. To stop."

"For sure. Don't worry about it. Maybe you didn't eat enough."

"That's it. I did not eat enough," she said.

"Want me to get you some food?"

"No, baby."

I turned the bathroom light off. She pressed her face against the floor tiles. We could hear outside all night. She lay next to the toilet refusing water, tried to light a cigarette. She took off her shirt, bra, pants, panties. She was naked save her jewellery: long chains, rings, painted nails, hair clips, a storm of pubic hair. Red lines from underwear elastic etched into her skin. Slid into the bed. I took two steps and she was snoring. Spit around her mouth dry.

•

I woke up with pressure in my chest, like I'd slept in mud. Natalie gone. The sheets were tussled where I expected her body to be. The pepper-and-smoke smell of her perfume remained; her rings on the bedside table. No noise in the bathroom. Several black strands of hair stood out against the milk white of the sheets. There was crud on her pillow with specks of food. Orange and red. Vomit crust. A membrane of spit had dried. It stank of cheese.

I patted around for my phone. I'd smoked a joint before bed but I remembered putting it on the bedside table. I stretched and saw it was on the dresser now. I was locked out of it for fifteen minutes from too many attempts at the password. I pushed the obvious thought down. Couldn't be. It couldn't be that she had tried to unlock it. I was already committing myself to her and ignoring what didn't suit that.

I left my phone and opened the curtains and squinted while putting on my clothes. A bird circled the backyard above five white women in bathing suits near the pool. Five brown men hovered around the hookah and the Arab at the end of the pool wore a thick glove. The bird stopped mid-air then made a great, fast dive, before floating onto his hand with grace. The Arab bowed and his audience hooted.

Marwan cooked meat on the barbecue under sheets of blazing midday sun. I didn't recognize the women or men. They may not have been the same people as last night. In the bathroom I squeezed toothpaste onto my finger and wiped my teeth. I turned to leave and felt a rancid spread in my lungs, as if I'd done something very wrong. I was angry in front of the mirror. I did my grounding exercises, hoping the muscle clenches would dissolve the anxiety. I visualized air flooding my limbs.

I came downstairs greasy from last night's adrenaline and Natalie's whippet body. Empty beer bottles framed the pool, like a connect-the-dot drawing revealing last night's frenzy. The unattended hookah's coals burned, the tentacles of pipe flailed for a mouth. A blond in a bikini was closest to me and I asked her if she knew where Natalie was. She replied with an extended exhale from a blunt, the cherry burning like an angry eye, her eyelids closing and trembling with the hit of the smoke. She nodded her head toward the grass and the women lying on lawn chairs, each beside a small table with an ashtray, a bottle of Voss water and a bubbled glass full of drink. Near the foot of their congregation was a boombox playing Top 40. Half the women recorded themselves on their cellphones. One was on her knees at the edge of the pool getting a friend to record her. Natalie not there. Four men on paved ground filmed themselves dunking on a lower-than-regulation basketball net.

Marwan now sat with his feet in the pool. He raised a glass to me and belched as I came close. The sun hurt my skin.

"Where's Natalie?" I asked.

"There's too many rooms."

"Where's Natalie?"

Marwan verged on passing out from the sun, drink, and exhaustion. He swished his feet in the water, telling me the food was almost done. I caught a waft of the meat. Behind him on a table was a stack of animal biology textbooks. He squeezed a bottle of water onto his face.

"Check downstairs," he said.

"Where's the Arab?"

"Who?"

"You all right?"

"This sun, dog. Check downstairs."

I invited myself into the lagoon cool of the main floor. There was a staging area that broke into a larger room with a bar that hugged the entire side wall. Its surface covered with bottles at different stages of empty, multiple everything I'd ever seen — Fireball, Bacardi, Smirnoff, Crown Royal, Azure, Malibu; bulging packets of herb sitting in black baggies marked with silver ink — Fire OG, Rockstar, Milk Chocolate; a half-eaten burrito; a textbook about animals with crumbs of cocaine on it; clear bottles of Sol beer. The room was dank, a large large-screen TV on the wall in front of a leather couch, a pool table, darts, a *Donkey Kong* arcade machine.

I heard a sucking sound, then a loud, theatrical spit, and saw a brown bald head, the skin stubbled, the body sunk into the couch so the head barely appeared over the ridge. My chest ripped with anxiety and I creeped over so I could see. Kneeling over him, working her mouth furiously over his lap was a broad-shouldered brunette. Both wore flip-flops. The football game on TV lit up their bodies in red and blue.

I stared to confirm it wasn't Natalie and watched a little bit more, entranced by her rhythm and his soft, babyish moans, but left before they could feel my eyes on them, walked toward the basement entrance, a door-wide darkness where Natalie might be.

The staircase was pitch black and I made my way deeper into an antiseptic smell, straining to hear any voices. As I went down, I heard the soft shuffling of bodies moving and what sounded like the clink of a cage closing. The basement stairs turned with a landing to a second door and pulling it open I exchanged the vacuum of darkness for white fluorescent light. A row of cages, each with its own animal. Snake, bird, turtle, a small old monkey with no legs.

Natalie shoulder-to-shoulder with the Arab. Tending to the dive-bombing falcon was Samir, his forearms brittle-thin, a stiff straight posture, and curly hair falling to his shoulders. He wore gold-framed glasses, a blue face mask and latex gloves and was surprised when he saw me. Green coral eyes examined me up and down. I stared back until he shifted his eyes. Natalie turned and smiled, her skin grey from hangover, drained like a boil. The Arab stroked the bird and shut her cage before speaking.

"Hamid my man. Samir is the in-house vet. Not really. He's not really a vet. Just for visa purposes. But he does like animals. Loves animals."

Natalie came by my side and cozied her hip against mine.

"They're so calm here," she said. "It's great they can be calm."

What I felt for her was like a tender bruise. I needed the blush of pain that came when she pressed on it.

The Arab cooed at his falcon. Bagheera in a corner cage on her hind legs. There was a de-feathered and raw chicken in a metal bowl. She watched.

"What are you doing?" I asked Natalie.

"I told you: for a coffee. I woke you up."

"I don't remember that."

"It's a big house brother, she got lost," the Arab said. "Listen, come up and find me in the garden after. There's swimsuits upstairs. Brand-new for guests, I promise."

The Arab flashed a grin and bobbled his head. Natalie squeezed my hand and went up to shower.

Once they left, Samir turned to a sink filled a quarter-inch with blood.

"I help with the animals," he said. "I'll feed them in an hour if you want to see. Truly, I don't like working with these animals. Except her, Bagheera, my girl, my pet. You work for us, right? For the family I mean. All of us. Me."

A brown lizard in its aquarium flicked its tongue. A lamp blasted hot orange light. Samir reached into the sink and pulled the stop for the blood to drain. He took off his gloves with a snap, removed his face mask, and revealed a calm expression, two dimples on round cheeks, and pulled his hair back.

"I need help with the food. For our lunch," Samir said.

From an industrial-sized fridge he pulled out a small cage with a shroud on it. I heard panicked birdsong.

"Do you want to help?" he asked.

He lifted the cover off the cage and revealed it was packed with tiny screaming birds.

"This dish is called assafir."

His hand went into the opening and pulled out a single bird.

"You eat the body," he said.

In one smooth motion, like flicking a coin, he popped off the little bird's head into the garbage. He threw the body into a metal bowl.

"You want to pluck?"

He moved to a second bird and repeated the motion. It clonked into the bowl. He took them one by one. The other animals agitated now that death appeared in the room. Bagheera watched. The old monkey backed himself up in the cage away from the noise. The little bodies bled out fast. His hands moved from bird to bird with little snaps. Being so casual around killing shocked me. I didn't let it show, met his eyes, and shrugged it off.

"I have shit to do," I said, my voice almost cracking.

•

Outside, the women dragged their lounge chairs under the shaded awning. There were pairings with men. I couldn't tell who chased who. Marwan sitting at the edge of the pool watched a race between Natalie and another girl. Natalie reached the wall first, disappeared under, and appeared a few metres away, barely disturbing the surface, stroking with precision.

"Britta won't come," Marwan said. "Too far. Uber too expensive. I offered to pay and she said no, not today. I should send one of these guys. It'll be like a fancy personal driver."

"Did you show her Bagheera?" I asked.

"I took a photo of her in that dungeon cage. It's depressing. He's going to move her outside into fresh air. I'll try again then."

Marwan pointed to the side of the house where I could see the fence disappeared into shadow.

"I can't stop thinking of her," Marwan said. "Like. It was just like. Like, I was just there. The vibe was right away. It was crazy. Like right away, boom, we went in the bedroom and it was just like, boom. No, before that."

Marwan drew a shape of her in the air. He was far off. Lost but happy, travelling a great distance in his head. The Arab came out in a fresh white thobe and red keffiyeh around his skull. Behind him followed three short and dark Indian men, frail bodies like boys, wearing black pants and brown sleeveless shirts. Their collars starched. They hustled to the barbecue and took over.

The Arab came to us.

"Follow me, follow me."

We trailed him to the side of the house to open-air cages. Water dripped from Marwan's shorts. Two grey pit bulls barked and jumped in their enclosure. A tiny Indian went into their cage and they nuzzled his leg and followed him to their food bowl.

"Kublai and Genghis," he said and the dogs dug their snouts into food. The worker left, his eyes to the ground, leaving behind loud gnashing. "She's going to get one of these cages. The big one. See, it has shade. You did a good job. A really good job. Very cool. Bringing her to me was great. There's nothing in the news this morning. I wonder if he'll even report it. Whatever, I can pay lawyers. That was fun. You know what's next? You wanted to bring your bitch, right?" Marwan winced when the Arab said this: a tendon in his neck popped; body flexed for battle. He took a breath. The Arab continued, not noticing. "She's not coming? Doesn't matter. I have something better. Way better. Samir says in a week we can give her a pop again. He doesn't want to agitate her by moving her around too much. But he's got a low dosage he can give her so she's high but not knocked out. Lazy high, hazy high, in-da-couch high."

The Arab showed us his Instagram post that advertised a DJ night in one week featuring a special guest. It was a rooftop club downtown in a generic hotel. An elevator ride released onto a pool with bar and lounge-chair service. It mimicked the Miami model, half-indoors, half-outdoors.

"This is my event. Animal beats. I'm gonna bring Bagheera. Special guest. We dope her up. You invite your chick. I bring the cat. Come, work the night for me," the Arab said.

"Bruh, is that … what … ?" I said.

"Don't worry. Permits? I got permits. Special permission. It's all good. I've done it before. Not with a cat, with birds. Same difference. You know those pics of people in Thailand with tigers? Same thing. How impressed is she gonna be when you bring her? You can say it's yours. Just to her. Not to anyone else."

"Does Bagheera like crowds?" I asked.

"She's a TV star. She knows people."

They brought a picnic table to the middle of the backyard. It was expensive cedar, specially made. Three Indians draped a white tablecloth overtop, erected three umbrellas to cast it in shade. Buckets of beer with ice melting, warm pita bread, cloth napkins, and silver cutlery. I smelled fennel seed and za'atar.

From the barbecue area three workers carried trays of chicken, beef, lamb, smaller plates of tomatoes, onions, lettuce, and placed them in the centre of the table next to the stack of birds Samir killed, black char marks across them. Two roasted tomatoes leaked on the plate. The liquid had a blood sheen.

The women were Samir's classmates. Third year studying animal biology. They sat at the table and the workers placed plates in front of them. Marwan shooed one of them away and tossed a giant salad. Three bowls of tabouli were placed at even distance. Lemon water. The men came and sat each with an open beer. Marwan was a natural entertainer and gave a sense of equal attention to whomever he spoke. He was smooth. Water flowing downstream.

The women continued:

"I think to diagnose you have to think about the contralateral side."

"No. The book. Page one-forty-two. The test. Think about the test. What's going to be on the test. Agalactia."

"There's no mammary disease!"

"That's why it's agalactia. I think that's what it's referring to. 'Partial or absolute milk flow with the absence of mammary disease.' Literally in the book! We have to follow the book."

"Sorry! Jeez."

"I don't want to do this test."

"I hate memorization tests."

"Ask Sam. Sammy did you memorize the terms already?"

Samir smiled and waved a pair of tongs at them.

"You have to really know the terms," Samir said. "This is beyond memorization. You can't innovate without the base."

The smell of meat filled my mouth. We ate using our hands. Greasy fingers and debris stuck in teeth. The Arab popped a bird in his mouth and licked his fingers. I rolled a cold beer bottle across my forehead.

Natalie came out in last night's clothes, hair wet and smelling like soap. She loaded her plate and ate without a word. A hamburger — tomato, mustard, onions; hot dog — ketchup, relish; Greek salad; the tiny bird, plain, not asking what it was. For five minutes talk stopped. Jaws chewing flesh the sole sound. Filling up, talk began again, dishes passed, a woman picked up the small bird asking what it was.

"Poultry," Samir said and laughed. He picked meat out from between his teeth. Examined the fleck and ate it.

Grease covered Natalie's lips and coated around her mouth. When she was done with meat she had a bowl of vanilla ice cream floating in amaretto; when she hit her foot hard against the table without an exclamation I realized she was drunk. She finished the bowl, grabbed a beer, and tugged on my index finger, asking me to come upstairs. I had no choice. I wanted her attention. Behind me a cannonball into the pool. Lunch over. We slipped upstairs.

"There's a lot of money here," she said.

"There is."

"Family money? He didn't earn it."

"Maybe in a past life," I said.

"Muslims don't believe that."

"I can't hate on him for his family."

"But you do," she said.

"I don't hate him."

"You're envious, I can tell."

"I do like money," I said.

"I like that you're ambitious."

"Good."

"I've dated a lot of … you know. Whatever guys."

"We dating?"

Natalie ignored me and herded me to the sheets. The bed had been made and a stick of incense lit. Sunlight from the gap between curtain and ceiling. The room hot like candle flicker.

"Could you imagine being this rich?" she asked. "I could disappear. In this house. I could stay in this house forever and disappear into it and every day would be so carefree."

"He has problems," I said. "He's all worked up about his Instagram page."

"That's because he's always been rich. He has no perspective. I would enjoy it." She grabbed my hips and pulled me and kissed me. She tasted like meat and vodka. It made me want to stop but I couldn't. She pulled me back. I didn't want to kiss her but couldn't stop myself. She was drunk. I asked her how she was feeling, she said yes; misheard me. Grabbing hands. I squeezed her hips hard trying to bring myself back to reality. Her tongue dashed into my mouth.

"I'm having fun," she said.

"That's good."

"I don't have a … thing."

"A thing?"

"A problem," she said.

"With what?"

"Don't. Like. I don't want to talk about it. I always have to talk about it."

"Let's not talk about it," I said.

"You like me?"

"You're cute."

"You like me?"

"I like you," I said.

She stopped and held her hand on her stomach. We were naked facing each other on our knees on the bed. She was sick; she couldn't anymore. She apologized and lay down facing away from me. Her eyes fluttered toward sleep. I left to piss, straining my erection toward the toilet bowl, watching myself in the mirror. On the counter a bottle of vodka and an empty glass. She was partying, it was fine. She didn't have a problem. We were partying, it was fine. Late afternoon, it was fine.

7.

Even now, so many years later, I can feel her flesh in my grip. The memory threatens real life. It wants to come forward and take over. That memory is where I hide. It doesn't matter what happened after. Only a few memories ever become lifelike, so vivid that when I recall them it's like they're happening again. That small remembrance of her flesh in my hand opens up a whole world and its possibilities.

This city, Bombay, has always been the city of possibilities for me.

A few weeks before we left for Canada, I wanted to go to the Arabian sea. My parents were planning the move and eager to see the major sights one final time. We went to Marine Drive, but I was upset there was no sand, so we went farther to Chowpatty beach, which my father loved. The sand was junk but the water and its possibilities were there. That's what mattered. The lives in the ocean were infinite. Maybe that was the first time I felt the possibilities of death: that it was a door opened, not closed.

I wasn't used to so many people doing so many things around me. I was disoriented on the beach. Groups of friends dotted the sand, men walking and selling, shouting, clashing languages, the big punch of sun. I stood staring while my parents went for bhel puri and when they returned I was a lump on the ground. I'd fainted. Water on my face brought me back to my parents laughing because I couldn't handle the heat. It wasn't the heat; it was the possibilities in the swirl of sea …

After, we drove to my auntie's house. We encountered an open-roof Jeep, clearing the streets with its blaring siren.

We drove quickly. We hid in my auntie's apartment while the violence went on outside. I'd learn a decade later that this was the Bombay riots of '92 that extinguished Muslim lives. I asked to go play cricket and my father slapped me across the face and when I bent over in fear, he hit me on the back of the head.

"You don't know what will happen if you go outside," he said. "If you go outside, you'll die."

We moved to Canada a few weeks later.

8.

I had a single cheap burner phone. Marwan had bought a dozen and we were supposed to throw them out and use a new one after a successful transaction but I sold them instead.

It meant Mr. Ahmadi could reach me. He was never supposed to call and I ignored it the first evening but then it happened three times the next morning. I didn't like that at all. He wasn't supposed to call. He was supposed to hide. Beyond losing the money was the humiliation. He'd been had. Spelled out by someone else, the con was evident; him, stupid and gullible. What did it amount to? I asked for money and he gave it. How could you be so dumb? The charm of the con was that most people were too ashamed to tell anyone.

I'd have to pick up the call. I'd seen how the Arab lived and wanted that life. It was self-sustaining: the drive for money driven by the drive for money. Marwan talked about buying new gym equipment or a car but all I could see was money. Its power came from itself. Power brought to the ground. Earthbound Godliness. I couldn't ignore the phone calls and let Mr. Ahmadi become a bigger problem. I had to tie up this business so I could be free to take on more work from the Arab. Mr. Ahmadi could be a stepping stone or a roadblock. It was my choice.

He continued calling throughout the day. That night I answered. I stepped outside my basement and walked down the silent street. I didn't want my landlord to eavesdrop.

Mr. Ahmadi told me he'd spoken to his son. His son asked him why we didn't show ID and why there was no online record. His son took over the call. He asked for the infraction to be explained. I circled:

"We showed ID," I said. "The online record takes time. The particulars of the tax problem are complicated. Why don't we meet tomorrow? No, the office is being renovated. Let's meet at the same place. Your dad knows."

I called Marwan. Mr. Ahmadi was from the last list of the Arabs that Hussain had provided, but we couldn't bring this to him. Our future was dependent on our dependency. The Arab loved us after the Bagheera run and we had the club night tomorrow. We'd learned more about the Arab's business — money coming in from coercive loans, sports betting, card gambling a big money maker, stolen goods. We'd sold ourselves as men he'd never have to think about, there to eradicate headaches, not bring them.

I explained Mr. Ahmadi's phone call. Marwan sighed into the phone. "What's the point in waiting?"

I slid into my Integra and motored over.

Marwan was arguing with his parents when I arrived so I parked near the curb. Hussain walked up and down the side-walks waiting in a way that could get a nosy Neighbourhood Watch to call the police. We liked him for that effect. A hol-stered gun I hoped never to take out.

I didn't want to be stuck in the car with Hussain so I let him be and turned to my phone. Abdul was in the news: he'd applied to the government for more money to help him turn the downtown building he'd bought into a type of public re-habilitation centre for former Guantanamo Bay detainees. The details bare, but his new, million-dollar request had an-gered many, even those who believed he'd been wronged as a fourteen-year-old. His audaciousness forever impressive.

The livid blogs were accompanied with a new photograph of his sly look. Hair coiffed perfect, the four-in-hand knot of his tie just askew. His determination to not disappear and live on a tropical island with his millions fascinated me. What had he *done*? What had been *done* to him? His ability to surmount what they had done to him. To move beyond and make himself whole again. Or my fascination with Abdul was simpler, like the Mexican would notice, drunk and swaying: we were alike and so I was curious. A tribal lure controlled me.

Years ago, when news of Abdul's capture first became public, they showed two images most often. The first was probably taken on school photo day. He stared ahead, a line for mouth, basic haircut, his demeanour shapeless and mild. Ordinary. The second, him surrounded by U.S. Army medics, his clothes torn, bloodied gouges on his shoulder and chest, the dust of the Afghan wilderness dirtying him. They were bitter: he'd killed a soldier, they'd shot him, and now were obligated to keep him alive.

I obsessed over the images. Photographs of his family in their blue Afghan burqas and Taliban beards hit newspapers. Completely different from my family, until I found out my paternal grandparents were from Kandahar, near the same place as his family in Afghanistan. We would have allegiance. Could it last through generations, distances?

At first, I didn't care about the politics. Over the years, as Abdul's social media influence spread, Marwan dug deeper into his teachings, but I had no feeling for worldwide Muslim grievance. I couldn't imagine myself as one of the hooded detainees at Abu Ghraib or as a kid with a shrapnel-speckled skull. Those boys and bodies were in the wrong place at the wrong time; not me. But Abdul was a neighbourhood boy, like me in so many ways, but grand, with the ability to control an impossible force I was mesmerized by: death.

Following Abdul's photos led me toward what I'd lacked: a sense of history. We lived in Canada without any extended family and I had no cousins that I spoke with and remembered little of family life in India. I heard my mother's hushed phone calls back home, but my father's disdain for his family meant that we worked as an isolated unit cut off from any idea of our history.

Keeping up with Abdul, I began to understand how I fit into the world. When Abdul made the news, I learned about us: I learned from the images of him, but also Iraq, Afghanistan, Saddam, Binny. When the photograph of Khalid Sheikh Mohammed, 9/11 big boss, was released upon his arrest, sleepy-eyed, disgruntled, scratches of hair around his shoulders, sideburns tipped grey, I laughed: he looked exactly like my father. The war images showed me where I placed in the world.

I thumbed through old articles and images of Abdul on the battlefield. Many more had been released since he'd got out of

Guantanamo. I had access to photos of his hideout, his fellow fighters, the American soldiers. Enough to construct a full life for him.

Marwan honking pulled me out of my reading. Hussain leaned against the Corolla. I got out, Marwan opened the trunk and we grabbed ski masks and metal baseball bats.

Hussain wanted his pay upfront so Marwan gave him his two bills and we drove to Mr. Ahmadi's bungalow at the far end of the city. He lived in a neighbourhood of legacy whites in Scarborough who'd bought property in the '60s and hung on as the suburb darkened. We stopped across the street. Two cars in the driveway and we could see the living room light through a sheer curtain.

We'd done this before. The first time when a storeowner didn't pay for a stack of PlayStations. People push back a little, they want to protect their money, they test limits. They take what's given.

I knew two ways to do it. First, fast talk. If that fails, a little ruckus. Most people are not used to facing violence. The elevated heart rate scrambles the mind. In the moment they'll agree to anything. The aftermath is worse. Chills as the body calms. That night's sleep gone. Random sounds scary for a while. The long wake of the threat solidifies our position. They won't call again.

We crossed the street and pulled on the masks. We slid between houses, moonlight caught on the pricks of grass, and found the back door wide open. The noise of the TV carried outside. I opened the screen door and we walked through a messy kitchen to the living room. It was him, the wife, the son, watching *Law & Order*. There was no thinking after this. I let my body do its thing.

I pulled up my mask.

"Hello."

The wife cross-stitching, the needle in the air ready to come down. The son dropped his phone onto the mustard carpet. Mr. Ahmadi's jaw slowly opened and his eyes widened. Marwan and Hussain stood behind me.

"You're not going to call me ever again."

Mr. Ahmadi stared at me as I spoke. The TV switched to commercials. Their son glanced at them for reassurance, a child again. I kept my eyes fixed.

"Say okay."

"Okay," Mr. Ahmadi said.

"It's seven thousand dollars. It's gone. What's seven thousand worth to you?" Hussain swung and smashed a lamp. The pieces flew frantic, landing on the wife's lap, and she screamed loud and quick, stopping abrupt when she saw our glares. Mr. Ahmadi saw the pieces, Hussain, and made the connection.

"What's seven thousand worth to you?" I asked again. "I don't want you to call me ever again. I don't want to hear from you ever again. Do you understand? Never."

"Yes," Mr. Ahmadi said.

"Say you understand."

"I understand."

I pointed my bat at the son.

"I understand."

I pointed at the wife.

"I understand."

The cross-stitch rolled to Hussain's feet and he tucked it under his arm and we left.

9.

The Arab hinted at his special guest all week on Instagram. He posted a close-up of Bagheera's fur captioned with a sentence from *The Jungle Book*. A Photoshop of Mowgli with the Arab's own face superimposed. A bizarre mock-up in the forest behind his house, dressed in khaki like a Raj, with cardboard cut-out elephants, Indians dressed like servants, and two white women posed to suggest concubines, captioned, *From the earth We Created you, and into it We shall return you, and from it we will call you forth for another time.*

The day before the event, a photograph of Bagheera's front paws one on top of the other, *And there is no creature on the Earth or bird that flies with its wings except that they are communities like you. We have not neglected in the Register a thing. Then unto their Lord they will be gathered. Bottle service available. Contact Club Mirage.*

He'd tagged Abdul. The Arab wanted the legitimacy of an association with Abdul and found a potential entry in animals.

Abdul's latest video was him once again face-first into the camera with a serene expression, this time in a high-end kitchen, stainless steel sparkling, speaking softly.

"The two things you must ask your future husband: One. Does he have a porn addiction? Two. Does he know your rights as a wife? Be careful: does he ask you to take off your burqa, or hijab, or covering, in public? To do so is within your rights but the flowering of such a thought should come from within. The seed should be planted and tended by you — not from him. The modern Muslim man might be transfixed with your veil and its connotation against evil. But remember, the veil is a signal of resistance. The word of man is not the word of Allah. Your husband cannot force the covering on you. There is a gap between the words of man, and in that space the Qur'an is available to you. The Qur'an is forever alive. The Qur'an is always speaking to you, as Allah is. Bring yourself to it."

Abdul continued. His gaze was mild. He'd made a post about the orange crabs that exploded from the sand after heavy rain in Guantanamo Bay, another about its iguanas. Most recently about the Prophet's love for cats and how the feral population on the Cuban island was taken care of by *Operation Git-Meow*.

The tag worked: Abdul was going to come to the club.

•

I'd arrived at Mirage in the late afternoon as it switched from its lunch setting to a nocturnal vibe. The Arab's phone had gone dead. A new number, saying it was Samir, took over our communications. Unnerved, I hoped to catch them to figure this out. I parked in the underground garage in the section marked for Mirage club management. A crowd surrounded a Sprinter van in the corner.

I couldn't tell who was in the group. I watched from the hood of my car until Samir poked me in the ribs with the dart gun case. He'd let his hair out and was wearing an all-blue camo outfit. Sharp cologne with several pieces of gold. A diamond stud pulled his earlobe down. His eyes never locked in on the person he spoke to. He'd look up, look at you, look at a flash of movement, look at you, let his eyes investigate elsewhere, look back at you.

"Silver," Samir said. "Nice. This is a sexy car. It's clean. It's fine. You don't let people eat inside. You're one of those. Listen. You're surprised. I should have explained. My bad. It's too much to talk to him directly. You know this. He needs distance. Talking to you about Bagheera? He loved it but no. Too risky. Anyway, she's mine, I'm the one cleaning the cage. ArabTarzan let him be. Long-term thinking. We're good though. We good? Work is coming. We like you. I like you, yaar. He's still the top, okay? But me and you, we do work."

I agreed to keep telephone distance and thanked him even though every alarm bell in my body rang.

"Let's meet the man," he said.

The group fluttered open. Bagheera in the cage in the van panting. Abdul arguing with the Arab. Abdul in light-wash Levis and a short-sleeved green button-up with a camp collar. Scars up and down his hairy forearms. His crew was two white hijabis and two white men, the men hollow-cheeked and tall like ghouls, the women starch-white, all their clothing brown. The boys from the backyard party surrounded all of us. Exhaust sputtered from the van, kept on so Bagheera could have some A/C. Abdul's movements were slow, as if he was all glued together.

"I appreciate what you're doing," Abdul said to the Arab. "You've been especially thoughtful to invite me. But this is not the way to do things. This all is a little bit rough, don't you think? This is not something I really want to be part of. Her in a cage."

The Arab tried to work him.

"No, no, this is temporary, see the photos, she has a big enclosure at home. This is a little party for her. She's socialized. She misses people. This is good for her."

Bagheera made a sound no one had heard before. A low grumble rolled into a grunt, laced with threat. She put her paw on the mesh cage and pulled. The Arab offered a weak smile. Abdul offered his hand to the Arab. They shook, Abdul's hands closing over the Arab's and pumping while looking into his eyes.

I was dumbstruck trying to reconcile a decade's worth of images, news reports, and video clips with Abdul's physical self in front of me. While my mind flipped through media memories my body stuck. He nodded at the rest of us and we automatically parted for him. He brushed against me and I tried not to look at him. He smelled like citrus and rice, flashed his teeth, the back two molars gold. His gang of new Muslim converts following, he got into the back seat of a black BMW, the windows tinted totally, the car gliding away and out.

The group dismantled and preparations for the evening began. Embarrassed by my speechlessness, the memory of that brief meeting is smudged; I remember his smell, the element of his character I couldn't have known, and the expectant way he moved through the crowd.

•

I waited fifteen minutes in the lobby for Natalie. She was nervous the ride up the elevator to the rooftop. She pushed her body against me, arms around my torso.

"My mom called me two days ago," Natalie said. "She asked for money."

"Like grocery money? Or rent money?"

"Four thousand. The car. Their brakes need fixing."

"That's a lot for brakes," I said.

"It's probably other stuff too. Who knows. She asks for it in a lump."

"You need cash?"

"You gonna pay my bills?"

"Why not?"

I was terrified of this idea but couldn't stop myself from offering it.

"I got money, don't worry," she said. "It's stressful. To have your parents ask. Like, why do I have more money than them? That isn't right. Your parents like that?"

"No, never," I said. "My dad would flip if I bought him a coffee. I probably have more money than him now. He been acting dumb as hell."

"My dad is the same," she said. "I told him I would send them money every month. Or let me pay the phone bill, cable bill, some small thing. He didn't talk to me for three months. Then, my mom calls, asking for money."

"They don't work no more?"

"He works," Natalie said. "He works all the time. She works all the time. They can't hold on to it."

We got out the elevator and were in the club, on the roof. Tepid daylight and clouds, like a moist tea bag, covered two pools, a cabana setting, a few tiki bars, and an elevated DJ booth. The interior was sleek and modern, two bars, a group of white bottle girls in black T-shirts and skirts chatting, dark brown bus boys wiping down tables, laughing with each other, their eyes trying to look everywhere but the women.

Marwan squirted oil on his skin. He'd come earlier and secured a spot — near the bar, the pool, overlooking the city — for himself and Britta. House song after house song played, a blood leak in my brain from it, and inside, the Arab and his crew fussed with organization.

A club in daylight is different. People mingled with kindness, the doorman and bartenders polite, the vibe effusive and relaxed without snobbery. There was a secret acknowledgement that real life existed outside and that the door fee sealed us from it. The tiki bars reminded us we were not in Hawaii, but that pretending was good as. It worked.

News of Bagheera's kidnapping had emerged but blame was automatically on PETA. Who else would it be? The mystery wasn't who took her but what they were doing with her. The Arab's rich-kid confidence meant he was sure no one would figure it out. Guests at the club asked about tonight, injecting the atmosphere with their anticipation and the expectation that they were going to see an event majestic and stupid.

Samir switched to ill-fitting Billabong shorts almost dragging on the ground, Natalie in a hot pink dress, and we moved into a group of the Arab's friends, drinking and eating. Despite what was happening that evening, I was relaxed. The Arab had been welcoming, paying us five hundred for the night "in case I need you," and Natalie's new energy thrilled. I was happy for Marwan, who was smitten by Britta and eager to show off.

I guzzled two beers and one shot of whiskey to calm my nerves; Natalie matched with doubles, tired after a long week.

It cooled with sundown. Marwan waved me over to one of the bars where he was now with Britta. Four tequila shots and limes ready. He spoke to the Arab in whispers. Britta asked me if there really was a jaguar and I winked and told her to wait and see. We took the shots, Natalie without lime, and she pulled me from the bar to the centre of the club, close to the elevated stage where Bagheera would be displayed. Wobbly from drink, we danced, making out in spurts as songs faded into each other. Together, we could lose track of time; the greatest benefit of our relationship. Even two years later we never lost the ability to carve out our own space, on a couch, burrowed into each other, or in a bar, talking shit about work. We ordered small plates of hummus, pita, and chicken shawarma and stood in the corner as the club filled.

"My mom ends every call with prayer," Natalie said.

"That's kind of sweet."

"She doesn't ask me if I go to church anymore. She used to and I always said yes but now she doesn't ask."

"When was the last time you saw her?" I asked.

"Like in person? Five years."

"You never want to visit?"

"For what?"

"Do you miss them?"

"It's like they're just me. Like so totally me. So what's to miss? I don't miss myself. How often do you go to a mosque?"

"Are you freaking out I'm Muslim? I'm not, like, a weird Muslim."

"I think it's cute."

"I go when I go," I said.

"Do you pray five times a day?"

"Wow. You read the Islam Wikipedia page?"

"I started to pray," Natalie said. "Like, four, five times a day. Is that crazy?"

"What — you face Mecca and everything?"

"No, dummy, I pray, like my prayer. I read about Muslims praying five times a day and I was like, why not. I try to do it. For like one minute."

"What you pray for?" I asked.

"Nothing. I just think. I think about God. I try to just think about it. I close my eyes."

"And you go: 'God!'"

"Honestly? Yeah. It's so silly."

"It's not," I said. "I do pray, yeah. Not five times a day. I pray when I can. Like everyone else. When I'm sad. When I need it. The standard."

"I think that's why I started," Natalie said. "I need it so much. I felt guilty. So I said, maybe if I make it regular, I won't need it so much."

We finished our plates and Natalie asked me to flag the waitress making her final rounds before the bar shifted fully into its night mode. The waitresses had been avoiding me because I paid in drink tickets the Arab gave me and also because I wasn't tipping. Tipping is fine. I tip on cocktails. For a mixed drink on a drink ticket?

The waitress had her revenge. I stepped in her path to scream two double vodka sodas into her ear and made a show of handing over four drink tickets bundled with a twenty-dollar bill. By the time she returned years later I was in the corner hunched over a bottle of water, gulping for my life. Natalie at the bar. Her skin melted into the harsh colouring of her pink dress. White sandals with thick soles I couldn't believe she was dancing in. I was dressed stupidly, in navy shorts that ended right above my knee, a collared white shirt, two braided bracelets for some reason, and cheap black fake leather loafers. It cost less than two hundred all-in but still makes me cringe. Samir joined me, sober. He'd re-applied cologne. He didn't speak, pulled his hair back, tipped his Corona into his mouth for a few glugs, then left, cutting through the floor and toward the washroom. Pink lights over the floor. There were women dancing in pairs or threes, laughing loud and playful.

Natalie came to me with two blue cocktail pitchers and refused to tell me the contents. They were sweet and dug cavities into my skull. The two DJs switching spots messed up the transition. The house beat changed mid-song to trap. The lights shifted to blues and reds and dimmed. It was 9:00 p.m., early, sunlight hanging on, but the club full. The Arab's social power had pull.

The Arab whispered to the DJ, who lowered the volume on the music and kept asking for quiet over the mic. It took five minutes, then he asked:

"Are you here to see what you're here to see?"

The mundane question muted the crowd. He switched to a blunt statement:

"Do you want to see a cat?"

We screamed. The Arab's men created a path from the elevated stage at the centre of the crowd to two swinging service doors.

The lights swivelled to the entrance.

Two men opened the doors and two men pulled on thick, oversized chains, wearing all-black outfits. The cage rolled out. It was a classic he'd rented from a movie prop store with ten-foot iron bars and a giant silver padlock. Bagheera crouched low to the ground, her stomach against the floor, her ears flattened, and her eyes scanning the audience, lips twitching.

Behind her was a triumphant Arab expecting a warrior's greeting, holding a bullwhip, happily recorded by phones. Behind him was Marwan with his hand around Britta's waist. She had a face of skepticism.

Bagheera recoiled from the lights but had nowhere to hide. The crowd noise, stopped by shock, started again, and she scurried to the centre of the cage, as far away from the bars as possible. A drunk stuck his hand in the cage and one of the Arab's men slapped him away. She paced. The crowd's noise turned into shouting and screaming. It was clear the Arab had no real plan.

Samir had given her a mild shot before she was brought out, hoping the crowd would appreciate a little wildness before the dope kicked in. The majesty we'd seen in quieter moments replaced by flattened savagery. Her lips curled back. He placed a silver bowl in the cage and squirted a murky dosage that would put her to sleep.

The crowd pressed against the bars shouting at her. The Arab's men were swarmed and hands flashed inside as people tried to get her attention for a selfie. She sat in the centre on her hind legs watching. Maybe the drugs kicked in, because she watched everything coolly, with a distant appreciation, like going through a menu.

Me and Natalie were at the outer rim of the crowd about twenty feet away but Bagheera's agitation was palpable. The thick, coarse black fur that enamoured me at the zoo was gaudy under the club lights. Samir spoke sadly, saying they'd left her thirsty for a few hours to make sure she would finish the job by drinking the knock-out juice he'd added to her water bowl.

"I think she's shy," Samir said. "She was shy earlier. She doesn't meet my eye."

Bagheera settled in. The men slid her cage onto the platform. Her stillness was designed to hide her plans. Cellphone cameras clicked and Bagheera turned to a woman with her back to the cage. The woman leaned against the bars and her flesh rippled in between the iron. Bagheera licked her lips. She yawned and the woman moved away, happy with the photos her friend had taken.

Bagheera moved to the bowl and her big pink tongue lapped up the water, betraying her vulnerability, and when the bowl was empty, she continued licking, pushing the bowl until it dropped out the cage.

I watched her circle until the mixture hit her. Her walk slowed until she lay down and put her head on her paws to sleep. The attention of the crowd waned, the thudding volume of the beat rose, and people moved away from the cage and to their original business of getting drunk. A few animal lovers, here for the cat, not the club, obvious because of their bad clothing, stayed and took photos. Marwan talking to Britta, their backs to the cage, and after an hour, I told Samir that maybe it was time to put Bagheera in the back. Watching her nap, the novelty already worn off, her mission accomplished, he agreed.

She was a house cat snoozing. A model of the Sphinx. The crowd hanging around was wondering what was going to be next. Was that it? The animal lovers hassled the Arab, asking to get closer to her. The men grabbed the chains and pulled her back inside the cool, dark interior. One of the animal lovers asked if maybe there was a sort of a leash she could be put on.

The Arab batted down this idea as a slow, looping laugh cut through. A white, short, really short, muscle-packed man in wife beater and checkered blue shorts past his knees, with two skinny white men hanging behind him in similar outfits, came to the cage and banged on the bars. Bagheera opened a lazy eye.

The short man circled the cage, grunting. His eyes never left Bagheera and her ears noticed him, perking in time with his grunts, and then she raised her head and her eyes followed him around the cage. Completing a circle, he stopped in front of the Arab. He laughed and showed off his twinkling blue grill. He had a tattoo of a koi fish on his neck.

"Are you going to let her out?" he asked.

Bagheera was groggy, not asleep anymore. She huffed. She didn't want to be with people. She didn't move but watched. The little man persisted and the Arab didn't know what to do, until a chorus of East Asian women in short dresses that he'd been trying to seduce broke out in a single chant:

"Let her out! Let her out! Let her out!"

Infatuated, the Arab considered their suggestion. I jabbed Samir and he left to talk to the Arab. He leaned into his ear and whispered, the Arab nodded, and ignored him. The animal lovers stood back tense. They knew it was wrong, but what an opportunity.

The flashing lights, women in dresses, their skin, the incessant barking of the little white man flooded the Arab's senses. He wanted the women and hated the man. Of course he would do it. I didn't move. We watched. Samir backed away toward us.

"He's going to do it," Samir said. "I can't say no. I said no but he won't listen. He's going to open the cage. And go in? She's okay. She's sleepy. She's okay. She'll sleep. Good girl. Good girl."

The Arab pulled out a single oversized key from his pocket, showing it off like he'd performed a magic trick. Bagheera faced the little man, who kept up his agitating. She was mildly interested. Her eyes clouded. She seemed stoned, locked in the well of her solitude.

The Arab slid the key into the chamber. He turned it to the left and we felt the weight of the lock shift then clink open. Bagheera didn't move. Marwan, still playing the role of the cat's owner, formed a line at the front with Britta to his side. Bagheera curled her head toward the door, which was closed.

"Get your phones ready!" the Arab shouted and pulled the door open and sucked his teeth.

Bagheera waited.

Bagheera pounced.

The Arab landed on his ass. The crowd scrambled away from the cage and made a small path: Bagheera jumped at the swinging service doors to push them open.

She was gone.

There was silence.

Then, screaming. Everyone rushed out to tell the others what happened. The DJ shouted over the beat. They were telling people that Bagheera escaped but it wouldn't process.

The Arab still on his ass. His men stood still. Samir shouted for no one to call the cops. He told us he was on the phone with them taking care of it. He pulled me and Marwan aside and asked what he should do. Calling the police was not our first option, since this was all our doing, and he wasn't actually on the phone with anyone. Natalie walked to the swinging doors and peeked through the little window and into the service corridor.

"She's going to fall asleep? You shot her," Natalie said. "She couldn't contain herself. Let's go get her. I bet she'll find a corner for a nap." Natalie shrugged and held the door open, her dress blazing against the hard grey concrete of the corridor.

The fire alarm went off. The crowd scrambled. The DJ bleated safety instructions.

We got behind the cage for safety. Natalie propped its door open so we could push it at Bagheera and she'd jump in. That was our solution.

Natalie led, checking behind kegs, boxes, bar debris. There were two more doors far off leading into a kitchen. The light off. We looked through those door windows for Bagheera. Natalie pushed the door and turned on the light, quickly pulled her arm back in. The windows were plastic and made everything blurry but it didn't seem like she was in there. The fluorescents collected as pools of white light on the steel surfaces. We pushed the cage, following Natalie, who was already peeking and probing in the corners.

The service elevator led to the loading dock. I pushed the button and got back behind the cage and convinced Natalie to do the same. The booze was there, at the back of our brains, charging our decisions.

The digital counter showed the numbers as the elevator made its way up.

Ding.

The doors opened.

Bagheera on her hind legs.

She sniffed the air.

We watched.

The elevator was recalled, it chimed, the doors closed, and it dropped back downstairs.

It stopped at the garage. We pressed the button again and waited. Samir aimed the dart gun.

Ding.

The doors slid open.

Empty.

We pushed in, Natalie, Samir, Marwan, and I, quiet.

Two gold chains on Natalie, a saint, a crucifix, overlapped. Marwan and Samir scared, light trembling on their bodies, but Natalie determined, her face fixed.

Ding.

Downstairs. Parking level.

Cars and trucks silent.

It was bright like daylight.

A car far away, a honk.

The Sprinter was there, the driver's feet stuck out the window, a river of cigarette smoke floating out. We walked closer, hearing the DJ talking about the last track.

Natalie got on her fours and looked under the cars. Samir pointed the dart gun and peeked in between. Marwan looked behind the cars parked against the walls.

We moved slow.

Slow, slow.

Don't surprise her.

Samir called out to the driver who snapped to attention. He jerked his body, trying to stuff his feet into the van, got stuck, swore, said sorry, and laughed. Natalie at the end of a row of five cars. Marwan slid against the wall, looking behind a Toyota pickup.

A movement — flash of black.

"Argh!" Marwan screamed. "Help!"

I turned to him. He was flat against the hood of the Toyota, Bagheera pinning him down, her entire body rigid. He held his arms up to protect his face.

A strike, a bite.

She jumped to the next car. The next.

She gnawed her new toy.

Marwan staggered.

His left forearm ended without the hand.

I saw the shape of his hand where it used to be. My eyes lagged behind reality. Tendons torn, gristle, vibrant bone, red against his face, blood drooling down his arm like a melting ice cream cone. He was quiet. Samir fired a dart at Bagheera. Marwan fell and I held him, his weight pulling us both down. He lay against me. Blood on my clothes. Metal taste on my tongue. His blood on my skin. A sharp, bitter taste in my mouth. I didn't know what to do. I cradled his face. He was cold. Pale. I loved him, I loved him so much and he was vanishing. I didn't know what to do. I held him. Samir on the phone. Natalie in her underwear next to me wrapping her dress around his arm, tightening, stopping the blood. The pink dress all red now.

Marwan closed his eyes.

10.

Years passed quick from that night, moving us far away from Natalie's heroism. The trauma that bound us turned mundane, taken over by a domestic cold that entered our lives, settling on our lamps, tables, expanding to fill empty space.

The wrinkled fingers that once brought me so much joy repulsed me. Now the flash they gave of our future made me aware of weakness: she'd left her parents behind in Vancouver, alone and estranged after bringing her to the country, and that act, which I first understood as strength, her getting away, making her own, filled me with dread; I came to consider it a failure.

For the two years we'd been together since Club Mirage, we obsessed with finding each other's wounds. I focused on her relationship with her parents. It took a year for me to convince her to speak with them regularly and not only when there was trouble. When they called, she would exit the room, shut the bedroom door, leave me with our new furniture and my quiet glee: I was responsible for fixing that rupture. I often overhead conversations in Tagalog. If I asked for details she waved me off. If I pried it led to a fight. And I didn't pry often; I didn't actually want to add the burden of her parents to my life, I wanted it solved, for the drink to go away. It had no effect on her drinking; I tracked it. She drank no more no less after a phone call, even if I overheard a fight or minor squabble.

I began counting drinks when we went out. I even stopped drinking. It didn't slow her down and it became contentious that I stopped so easily.

We'd gotten a place together after two months, sliding slick into domesticity. A two-bedroom rental on the third floor of a mid-town condo. Gym, pool, concierge, not as fancy as it sounds. Property management hired a lanky Indian from a security firm for a few dollars over minimum wage, paid him to sit behind a desk and watch videos on WhatsApp. The pool had a green scrim of grime covering it.

I took pride she didn't have to pay for groceries, bills, then rent, when we needed a couch, a TV, a bed — I bought it. We never spoke about it. I ignored my credit card bill. She worked full time managing a nail salon. Because of the money she saved, she began sending her parents a monthly allowance. I got us matching gold signet rings with onyx stones to remind us of the cat.

Her retort to me urging her to reconnect with her parents was to demand to meet my father. So, just after we moved in together, I took her. She was right. I wanted to be adult. To move on. I couldn't be a cliché. Childhood pain a snarling bear trap. I couldn't blame my father for everything.

He was drunk, it was late, a bad idea. He knew we were coming but hadn't prepared. Not true — he drank from a stemmed wine glass rather than his regular water glass. He was happy. He'd had his first phone conversation with my mother after a year of silence. She said she missed him. His spirits up. In the kitchen, Natalie between him and the fridge, he stopped, a wide grin on his face, turned his cheek to her.

"Kiss me," he said.

I heard him from the living room.

"Just on the cheek."

Anger filled me. Rage like before, that New Year's. I pulled her from the kitchen and got between them. He stood dumb with vacant eyes. His head tilted. He'd already forgotten. I couldn't move. My mind raced but my body was locked. I couldn't talk. We stared at each other until Natalie took me by the shoulder and we left without speaking. I was dead. That had been a genuine provocation. I'd done nothing.

We went home without speaking. I couldn't look at her.

Natalie took off her dress, bra, panties, and jewellery piece by piece. We did not speak. I took off my clothes and in my underwear drank a cold glass of water at the sink. She lay in bed looking at the ceiling, her body covered by the sheet. My body was hot. I slid in the bed, in the dark, naked, numb, not touching her but side by side. No talk, not for a long while.

"Has he done that before?" she asked.

"No. No, of course not," I said.

"You didn't say anything."

"It — it caught me by surprise."

"It was gross."

"I'm sorry," I said. "I didn't know what to do. I'm so sorry. It was gross, I know. I just. I just …"

"I don't want to see him ever again," she said.

"Never. I promise. I'll talk to him tomorrow."

"You don't have to."

"I will."

"It's fine," she said. "It's whatever."

Again, I didn't know how to respond. Then she spoke so small and simple, what I'd been waiting my whole life to hear, so obvious and pathetic that it pulled me back to life.

"You're not him," she said. "I'm glad, I guess, that I got to meet him. I know that you worry. You don't have to. You're not him."

You're not him. Man's great fear — to become his father. Small and simple, those three words spilled into our entire relationship. I would forgive all because of that moment. The balance forever in her favour. I would follow her anywhere for the gift of those three words again.

•

I was nervous to meet on the patio for our second anniversary. I got off the streetcar, my clothes dry from the earlier rain, my brain soft from the Al-Anon meeting, and my loafers soaked and damp, already exhausted at our upcoming fight at what was supposed to be a celebratory dinner. I chewed four mints to get rid of the shawarma breath.

We hadn't spoken in a few nights since she'd been brought home blackout drunk by a co-worker, Claire. They'd gone out for drinks and Natalie said she was going home, left. Claire left the bar fifteen minutes later and found Natalie on the sidewalk passed out. Claire brought her to me at 3:00 a.m. Natalie could not stand. I carried her to the bathroom. She forgot to put down the toilet seat. Fell into it. Then fell asleep on the floor. She tried to hold my hand. I left.

As I came closer I saw her at the far end of the patio. She was wearing my favourite cotton white dress. A good sign. The brown of her nipples was visible behind the fabric and I wanted men to gawk, clock them glancing, see them snatching a second look, then look at me to make sure I hadn't seen. I would catch this second stare and they would scurry their eyes back to their plates or girlfriends. We did it together — she wore it whenever I asked — and all day the tease sent bolts through my body. She was coming home with me. We would talk about it after, pushing hard into each other, her body held down.

Two laughing white men flanked her, an easy joke told. She was in the shade of an umbrella, a short sweating glass in her hand, a lime rising to the top. Her gold crucifix hung flat on her chest and caught a stray ray from the sun. I entered the patio and pulled a chair out and sat.

We hadn't slept together in a month. Every weekend she blacked out, stumbled home, which I saw if I was there.

In response, I stuffed myself into the shop, staying away, dreaming about her. I wish I could decide which scatter of memories were the ones I came back to. A blue night, a hotel bed, she bites her own bicep while I move into her. A white light, grocery store, her fingers testing broccoli. In my car, shouting, Coca-Cola spilled over the seats. A smell, butter, sugar, her warm against me at the movies.

Those are the ones now, years later in Bombay, that come when I'm alone. They are well-worn gouges. Occasionally, when I'm lucky, I remember a moment I've never recalled before, a moment lush with fresh meaning, our history present in front of me like new.

Natalie took a sip and put her glass down. The men, not knowing what to do, continued to talk and she replied in one-word answers. One of them spoke to me. I didn't want to talk. Confused, they gathered their drinks and wandered off to a nearby table. The waitress took my drink order — club soda, ice, two limes — left, came back, and we still hadn't spoken. Her hair fell behind her shoulders just as it fanned against our white pillows. Those moments in privacy, as one, stretches of morning light, why did they make the rest worth it? Deep in me was the old feeling for her. Her perfume the same pepper and smoke. I'd asked her to keep it like that. She finished her drink, ready to talk.

"I feel like going to the middle of the sea so far that I can't see any land," she said. "That's what being around you makes me feel. How much money did you make this week? Does it matter? Where do you think it takes you? When you look at me, what do you see? When I see you looking, I know what you see. What's it like to live with someone who disgusts you? Are you looking at my eyes? Are they glassy? Are they wet? Am I drunk? Thank you for using your money on me. I keep mine. Do you know why? I used your money to keep my money. Do you know what I'm going to do with it? Have you thought about it? Has it crossed your mind, ever? I disgust you. Can you believe that?" She tapped her ring against the table. The waiter came by with a double vodka, one ice cube, a psycho's drink. The way Natalie looked at me shifted, a glimpse into a depth of her personality I'd never seen. Even then, so late into the relationship, I discovered a new self, another mystery for me. She was far away. She tapped her ring against the table and spoke again.

"Who cares," she said. "I want to vanish."

"That's natural."

"Shut up."

"What do you want me to say? I'm trying to help you."

"Help me with what?" she asked.

"To stop drinking!"

"Did I ask for your help?"

"You passed out on the toilet three nights ago," I said.

"So what? So what? So what? Close your eyes! How much money do you have? In cash. Right now," she said.

"Eight hundred dollars."

"Give it to me."

"Relax," I said. "Natalie, I love you."

"You do. You love me. I want to go. I want to go away."

"Do you want to visit your parents?"

"Are you going to pay for my ticket?" she asked.

"If you want me to?"

"Ugh."

"You know what they tell me at these meetings. This is a sickness. It's not you. It's … you know. Like if you had a cold. I don't hate you because you have a cold. You can be annoying and whining if you have a cold, and maybe I hate that, but I don't hate you. I want you to … I want you to not drink."

"I love drinking," she said.

"Don't say that."

"I love drinking," she said.

"What am I supposed to say to that?"

"I want to vanish. And I don't know why," she said.

"I can go away," I said. "For a week, a month, whatever. You're addicted, right? This isn't you. Please listen to me."

"Who's addicted?"

"You."

"Then why isn't this me?"

"That's what they say!"

"That's what they say!"

"Please."

"You think two drinks makes me drunk? I'm not drunk."

"They're doubles," I said.

Natalie bottomed the drink at my reply and left. I thought she was going to the bathroom, so I stayed for five minutes before realizing she was not coming back. Forty-five bucks for two vodkas and a club soda? She wouldn't go out with me anymore if I didn't tip, so I put a fifty down and chased her.

I knew where she was going. Each week she somehow made new friends, forming temporary lifelong bonds at bars and cafés, her genial nature sucking them in. New friends but the bars stayed the same. She liked one close by that was narrow and dark with cheap pints and a long happy hour.

I caught up with her at a stoplight. I walked after her, slid inside the bar behind her. My shoes stuck to the ground. It smelled like beer. Most of the light came from a TV hooked above the bar rail.

"I don't need you to be happy," Natalie said.

"What do you mean?"

"I think I felt it, finally," she said. "I was praying. I was at work. I was praying. I started praying with intensity. Before I was only praying, almost fake, you know —"

"What are you talking about?"

"I think I felt something?"

"I don't think it's like that, you don't just feel —"

"I never see you pray."

"I go to the mosque," I said.

"When?"

"Are you drunk?"

"I've had two drinks, Hamid. What did you say: I am an addict. An alcoholic. Do you think two drinks are going to get me drunk?"

"You're freaking me out."

"I was saying. I felt … whatever. I felt. I was praying, I have been praying. And I felt … I don't know."

"That's good," I said. "That's good. I'm glad … I guess. I guess I'm glad."

"It doesn't mean anything," she said. "That's what I finally understood. My mother prays at the end of every phone call with me. Just a little line. I haven't asked her if she feels anything, or if it's just habit for her. But I realized. It doesn't mean anything. If you feel …"

"… God, you can say it."

"If you feel Allah," she said, "it doesn't mean anything. It all stays the same."

"I'm sorry," I said.

"But it's not supposed to. That feeling has to be a guide … to something. I want to find … something."

"I love you," I said, panicked.

"I don't need you to be happy," she repeated.

I'd run out of games and tricks. The energy to convince myself I was fighting for a worthwhile relationship. That two years could be everything and nothing was a surprise. What was left to do? I saw a lanky rice king in the corner — *Akira* T-shirt, dunks, skin flash white, pimples rotten on his face, an overbite, red hair freckling his arms — looking at her, wondering if I was going to leave. She drank beer at the bar and I left a twenty, telling her I'd be at Marwan's again.

Yes — Marwan was fine, if annoying. It was his left hand he lost, the evil hand for unclean tasks, that he used for masturbating, wiping his ass, and so it had to be a sign from Allah. A message. The paramedics told us Natalie's dress saved his life. He passed out as they closed the doors of the ambulance that scooted him to the ER.

The Arab had come down directing his men. Lawyers were on their way. Lawyers were on their way to the Bowmanville Zoo, too, with a wad of the Arab's cash. By the time the police arrived he and Samir had invincible grins on their faces. He told me to shut up, and I did, watching him bob and weave to minimize disaster. The Arab got hit with a ticket: no permit. The police loved Bagheera. Marwan wouldn't speak to the cops.

The Arab fell in love with us. Our silence proved loyalty and reliability, exactly what we were trying to express. He insisted on diya. Blood money. What's a hand worth? We were gifted a shop in the corner of a plaza in Scarborough, our names on the paperwork, no connection to Samir or the Arab, and we moved small, stolen electronics — vacuums, humidifiers, fans — whatever fell off that week's truck. They kept us in steady supply.

From the bar I paid fifty dollars to Uber to Marwan's place after grabbing hamburgers for us. Marwan continued living under his parents. He had his floor redone and bought a washer/dryer set. Otherwise it was the same set-up.

His red prayer mat was out, and to its right, hanging on the wall, was a calendar of Britta in a body-building pose and green bikini. He'd found it online. He never saw Britta after that night but followed her online presence silently.

We couldn't share a bed so I slept crooked on the pull-out. He'd been having nightmares and shouted nonsense in his sleep. He twitched and jerked while dreaming and wet the bed with sweat. He liked me to rank the bio-sheets of prospective wives his parents got for him, so I laid them on the table in my order of preference, fell asleep quick, woke up at dawn for namaz with him, eggs, toast, and the subway back to the condo Natalie had insisted on us renting. I didn't move here to live in the suburbs, she had said. It was a tremendous money suck.

At 8:00 a.m. I was in our building. A new Indian security guard. I wanted my bed. We wouldn't fight this early. I'd be able to slide into bed, murmur an apology into her nape.

I knew before I unlocked the door.

The closet doors were closed, so were the dresser drawers, but I knew. On the shelves in the kitchen, her favourite snack, pretzels, the family-size bag I'd bought, gone.

An envelope on the coffee table. A letter inside.

She was gone.

Two

11.

Forget the envelope.

First, I checked the top of the bedroom closet, in the corner, in my duffle, under a performative layer of clothes; I had fifteen thousand dollars there. I pulled the bag out and sat on the couch with it on my lap.

I counted it. Fifteen thousand. Fine. My savings plan.

Relief, then. Like a dam broken, cool water rushed into me. It's finally over. No more nights worried what drunken smear will come home past midnight. No more counting drinks over dinner. No more checking the bottle at the back of the cupboard. Fine.

The envelope. White and thin.

I fell asleep on the couch with my arms wrapped around my money.

The envelope wasn't sealed.

> Hamid,
> Thank you for everything. Thank you for your generosity, your kindness, and your love. Thank you for holding me close as long as you could and for those bright days that took me out of my darkness. I'm sorry I couldn't always be what you needed, but I'm happy we had those years together. I will always love you.
> Thank you, thank you, thank you.

Thank you! Thank you? Thank you is what I say to a cashier after a tidy transaction. To my bank clerk. Thank you! Fine. Thank you, to be said without thinking, a punctuation mark to seal a conversation shut.

I paced around the apartment not surprised she left. She wants to break up. Fine. I want to break up. Agreed. Does that mean that we break up?

She hadn't taken any of the furnishings. I went to the bedroom and pulled open the dresser drawers. My underwear and socks as before. Empty and serene wire hangers in the closet. She'd taken a few wooden ones. On the top shelf, left behind, a cheap Michael Kors clutch I'd gifted her. Fine. Our linens left behind. Fine.

I was terrified to go into the bathroom. I was already nostalgic for a toilet crusted with booze vomit. Her special shampoo and conditioner gone. Fine. Nail polish, creams, deodorant, bobby pins, all gone. Fine. A wet bar of white soap lay in its holder. Fine. She'd used it that morning. Fine. A single strand of her hair looped around it. Fine.

A memory sideswiped me to my knees. Her almond eyes. Her fingers tapping the side of my ribs. Pepper and smoke.

I curled into myself on the floor. All at once the relationship was present in me. Things I'd never thought about. She liked to mix Sriracha with ketchup. Our first New Years, drunk, dazed, laughing, my shirt unbuttoned, the taste of champagne, gold chain around her neck.

Thank you. Thank you. Thank you.

I called her phone:

The person you are dialing is no longer available.

The pain physical. I made a pathetic noise. Air leaving a balloon.

I searched the rest of the condo for her trace. No notes or indication of where she'd gone. Her social media accounts dormant for days. Did she go to her parents? No. She wouldn't do that.

I regretted our last conversation. Not at the bar, but before, before she came home drunk a final time. We'd been up all night playing psychotherapist. Talk talk talk. We went backward, from traumatic incident to traumatic incident, creating the image of ourselves. She said once again, serious-faced, her mouth a hard line, my problem with her drinking was not her, it was my father's drinking, I was taking that out on her. The next night, dribble of vomit on her chin.

How long had this plan been in motion? Why didn't she tell me? I would have stopped her. What did she say — she had plans for that money.

I went back to the couch and my reflection in the TV. I went to the bed. It would smell like her. I slid into the cold sheets. They smelled like our detergent. She'd changed the sheets before leaving. A final cruelty. I sniffed the corners of the duvet, her side up and down, all laundry fresh. I stuffed my face into her pillow and caught a whiff of her.

I slept until evening. I rolled over and checked my phone: no messages. I stepped onto our balcony hoping fresh air would give me clarity. There are practical things to do after a break-up. We were not conjoined. No bank account linked us, the lease was in my name, no car payment together. She could leave without trouble.

Our balcony gave me a view east and west of a banal midtown street. The fake Irish pub patios fat with customers. Stray scurries of conversation floated up. A light mist above the sidewalk settled onto the road, a cloud come low, impossible at this time of year.

Across the street under a light pole was a man dressed in black with a covering around his face that left his mouth exposed. Pink lips. He faced me. The lamplight swirled around him in the mist. He watched me. I felt crowded, like he was on the balcony with me. He was thirty, forty feet away, across two lanes of fast traffic.

It rained. The bubble of humidity should have popped, but it stayed, and cold, fat drops sliced down. He stood under the rain without moving. A knock on my door jarred me out of my teeth — the burrito I'd ordered. I went in and ate while listening to the patter outside, like loud footsteps in an empty hall.

I wasn't going to be able to sleep. After eating, I took time to shower, shave, and change. I went back to the balcony to see if the rain had stopped. The brash fluorescent light from the convenience store signs lit up the puddles along the sidewalk. Music from the bars dribbled onto the street alongside the groups of men and women wobbling. Under the light pole was the same man in the same position.

His left arm rose very slowly. His palm facing the sky, he beckoned me toward him. I didn't respond. He did it again. Was he really looking at me?

He repeated the gesture.

He was looking at me.

I slipped on my Air Maxes and my North Face raincoat and ran out the apartment, double-timing it down the stairs, almost crashing. It was the invisible rope, pulling me toward the horizon. I didn't want to think about Natalie. I didn't want to think. This stranger was a godsend — to *do* was to live and this chase could take me away from thoughts of Natalie. I looked east and prayed: Thank you. Thank you. Thank you.

The rain fizzled. I exited from the back and squeezed between two black Beemers, dashboards lit up like jellyfish.

The concrete walls of my building were lit by small lamps every few steps. I walked through, my shadow zooming every which way as the light hit me at new angles. A drunk in a suit pissed into bushes. I kept my eyes fixed ahead. The man who beckoned me stared. We were across the street from each other now, cars and taxis passing, a streetcar in between, so I couldn't cross. He wore a balaclava and black track suit.

He turned on his heels and took strong strides as if he had a location in mind. I crossed and followed. Stumblers fortifying with pizza slices for more drink. The rain turned into a fine spray. He turned right, off the main street, and I followed, but the game made no sense. He knew I was there. I kept back. His gait was stiff, on the verge of a limp. He took a turn left, not looking back to see if I was following and we continued along a street paced with massive trees.

Squat apartment buildings on our right, an empty park on our left. He turned once more, close to the main street again, and this time looked back. We'd walked a circle. A taxi passed, the headlights taking turns cracking over us. This was getting stupid.

"Yo!" I shouted. He stopped. Turned to face me. Raindrops loud against metal contours like gigantic teeth clattering. I approached. The air cooler, the humidity popped, but I was hot. I wiped away sweat on my brow.

We stood ten feet apart. I couldn't place him but I recognized him in a way I didn't understand. He was my height and build. A spook went through me at this smudged double, like I was seeing my own self in a broken mirror. A passing car backlit him then hit me in the eyes. When I squinted he burst into a run.

I chased. He turned right onto another side street, then right again, now away from the main street once more. We ran at the same pace: I wasn't getting any closer, he wasn't getting any farther. On our left was a school, two stories with a field out front, and a basketball court. He veered off the street onto the school grounds and I chased him across the field, the only sounds our thumping feet against soggy grass.

The back of the school was lined by another side street and small houses. He headed there. He turned a corner of the building and I lost sight of him. The rain stopped. I turned the same corner. He was gone. Two black cars were parked on the street, one in front of the other, engines on. A lowered Honda drove past, its tinted windows showing a bare sketch of passengers.

I had to catch my breath. I crossed the street toward a porch with its light on. There was a foursome lit by a weak bulb. Moths gathered. Old men and women, cigarettes dangling, sitting around a table with drinks, playing mah-jong and ignoring me.

An animal blasted out from the bushes and into my side. I stumbled and twisted, my feet tripping me up. I fell into the wet mud. There was nothing in the bush. The animal was on my right, it was him, he was standing with his hands clenched into fists. He let me get up and I sprang forward with my knee, but he sidestepped to let my momentum carry me into a weak wooden fence that crushed under my weight. I twisted my torso and threw a plank at him. He swatted it away with his forearm.

He took two steps toward me and went to work, a right into my ribs, then a left into my kidneys, his breathing steady and hard. He wore thick gloves. He repeated the punches. I threw an elbow into his gut, which allowed me to get up fully. He drove a knee into my stomach. He stood above me as I took breaths and coughed. I managed to get to my fours. He let me get to my knees and I grabbed a handful of his track suit but he knocked my hand away.

"It's finished. Do you understand? It's finished," he said. His accent was faraway and familiar: Arab, Saudi, like that, with some Canadian twisting through it. I tried to look at him and he shoved my face away. A pain in my neck stopped my thoughts. "No more."

One of the black cars pulled out of its parking spot and did a U. Using his foot he pushed me into the ground. I scrambled toward the mah-jong table.

He was gone.

One of the women brought me a Styrofoam cup of water. The men lit new cigarettes.

12.

I went home, iced my emerging bruises, inhaled an enormous joint, and fell asleep on the couch. I woke a few hours later, the thread of dawn blistering on the horizon, drank a glass of water, fell asleep again.

I refused to think about what had happened.

I did not know who that man in the track suit was or what he meant. What was finished? Nothing. Who could that man have been? I thought through names: Hussain, Mr. Ahmadi, the half-dozen men and women we'd run through the tax scam. Maybe it was our first victim, the gentle Indian woman — perhaps she had access to goons we never knew about. The list of potential perpetrators overwhelmed. What about Saif, the new kid from Pakistan who I'd pushed down a hill in grade 6?

I refused to think about what happened.

I could not think about what happened. Really, I did not want to know: it did not matter to me who that man was. The gift was the invitation to *do.*

I was practised at not thinking about violence. Silence was my tool. When there had been violence at home it was never useful to think through. The moment I was struck by my father would replay in my head as I tried to find meaning for it. But there was never meaning to violence. It was just my turn.

I did not think about that night ever again. I tried not to think about that night ever again. I turned the confusion into anger and let it flow. It was the easier thing to do. Reaching into my nightstand for an Advil, I found Natalie's gold chain with its emblem of Saint Lorenzo Ruiz. She'd forgotten it? It was in my side drawer. She never used that drawer. I layered it with my usual chain, got into my grey Nike hoodie and sweats and into the Integra. I was due at the store in an hour for a shipment. I had work to think about.

•

I parked between the owners of the Chinese grocer, the Tamil grocer that ran small table games in the back, and the Bosnian owner of a hollowed-out furniture store, who sat behind a wide plastic table and talked on a landline all day.

Our store was at the corner of the plaza. When it was given to us it already had a white sign above the door with blue bulbs that spelled out CANADA ELECTRONICS. The past owners had sold A/C units, fridges, big items with terrible margins. Usually, by the time I rolled in at 10:00 a.m., Marwan was behind the counter haggling with some brown. Today it was a Sri Lankan upset his calling card wasn't working and believed we ripped him off. Marwan patiently walked him through the steps of how to connect. When Marwan had to burn a few cents off the card to show him the procedure, he demanded a new one.

A driver unloaded kettles for us. We were, again, trying a new tactic. The gift of the store and its responsibilities as a hub for the Arab's various businesses — gambling, an assortment of real-estate scams, loans; basically the crumbs of illegality — had boomed our monthly income to ten thousand. So five thousand each, plus money from the occasional small-scale theft or vague violence that we did for him. But it wasn't enough. I scrambled to cover expenses. I'd pissed off Samir by charging his cousins five thousand per to pretend to be their employer for their Permanent Residency applications, while in the last two years — when I hadn't seen the Arab once — Samir had become much richer. He managed all the Arab's business with us and much more I wasn't allowed access to, much more that I did not know about.

The signs were there: smoother skin, his gold jewellery lost its green tint, his Honda always detailed, no more smooth polyester Walmart shirts. His hair cut short regular and he'd dropped the Bollywood affectations. No more dollar-store aviators. Now he wore a pair of Tom Ford sunglasses. He kept us at a distance. I took joy knowing if I wore a new piece of clothing, he'd soon be wearing a similar, crass version. The Tom Fords mimicked a pair of chunky Italian glasses I'd worn once, after a night of stoned Grailed.com purchases. They were dumb: I tried to dress in a subtle way these days, but it meant it was rarely clear how expensive my clothes were.

I made obvious I wanted more but I could never hop over Samir to the Arab. The backroom casinos were expanding to rich slices of cottage country and talk was about heading westward, but he never invited me to be involved. Me and Marwan needed to be clean, Samir insisted. We needed to have roots and an above-board paper trail. We were taught to maintain books so we had a legitimate income stream. Even the stolen goods had a fake, real wholesaler.

Samir undervalued us. I wanted brain work, to have to figure out a scheme, to see the different angles of a problem, but instead we were busy with small tasks that swerved in and out of legality. I spent the days side by side with Marwan doing paperwork and watching TV. We paid Samir's cousins five dollars an hour to help around.

Reluctantly, I was trying to accept we'd reached our peak with Samir, and so these kettles were my latest attempt to separate. We'd purchased a small shipment with lightly damaged electric cords and hoped to sell them wholesale. No one was buying. They'd spent a week in the van going store to store. The driver and salesman, another cousin of Samir's, had dark sweat stains, coffee-browned teeth, and a bad haircut. He spoke excellent book British English, but was meek around men, and likely why we couldn't offload them. Samir insisted we use him at the store. I'd have to get in the van and try myself now. It wasn't the kind of idea I liked. Labour-intensive with minimum gain. But it could help me and Marwan expand our web.

The Sri Lankan left after Marwan sold him two more calling cards. Marwan finished his daily currency organizing while watching YouTube on our TV above the money exchange. Our shop was small. We sat behind an L-shaped glass counter with cellphone accessories, cases, headsets, the wall behind us with the same junk; three rows in front had stacked boxes of toasters, toaster ovens, microwaves, blenders, various household appliances with dented boxes, ragged electronics, all of disreputable origin. A single set of shelves housed smaller, random pieces. A lava lamp. Mismatched computer speakers. Half-broken, cheap, Google Chromebooks the banks liked to give out if you opened an account with them. All under hot white lights on a decades-old blue carpet. We spent our days alone inside, counting inventory, making small sales, relying on the Arab and Samir to provide us product.

The corner of the L had a currency counter Samir set us up with for money exchanges and wires. This was one of our steadiest moneymakers and he was our biggest customer. I sent sums of his cash back home almost weekly to a few different accounts in India. In two years he'd sent at least a hundred thousand dollars.

The TV was on a recent video of Abdul in conversation with a pallid white news anchor.

"I think it's an honourable and respectable step. Of course, I value and appreciate what the government has done in regard to me. I will always appreciate that. They made right by me. But I want this money to go towards something positive and I had many brothers in Guantanamo Bay that haven't been as lucky as I have. And yes, after two years of preparation and planning we are proud to announce that we are venturing forward — with government help, along with private funding — with a therapeutic and resettlement program for former, wrongly accused, Guantanamo Bay detainees. At the moment I've used my own settlement money for the centre. The program will eventually branch out. But right now we want to focus on new therapy techniques and educational programming and specifically this cohort of young men. There are two men, one who they attempted to settle in Serbia, the other in Yemen, who are on their way. The first patients. I will be promoting therapeutic techniques that were so successful on me. Our downtown building will be the heart of this project, a project that, in its very essence, is Canadian. There will be therapy sessions of course, but also English classes and general programming. With the help of private investors, we are offering a scholarship to help them begin school or vocational training. They will be integrated. Productive. Canadian."

Abdul had 225K followers now and was always on TV, the face of local Muslims. When someone attacked us he was the one they spoke to. His hair was lustrous, wavy, beard lines sharp. His new mosque was in his downtown building and offered social programming even to non-Muslims, and he had a flock of forty white converts, plus twenty normal Muslims who attended events regularly. He was big time. That group now included Marwan, who after Friday prayers with his father at his mosque, zoomed downtown for Abdul's weekly dinner and chats.

Marwan fussed with the register. He asked me for his prosthetic only when he was stressed. He didn't believe he should hide his stump. The prosthetic's colouring was pink and it was missing its pinky nib. The dinners and conversation with Abdul had strengthened his belief that the accident was a message from Allah and the pain that came when he was agitated he considered reminders he was straying. I opened the drawer near me and handed it over.

"I masturbated last night," Marwan said. "That's why this hurts. It's hard."

"Jerking off with your right hand?"

"Abstaining."

"It's the Britta calendar staring at you," I said. "You miss Britta."

"Don't worry about the calendar. The calendar is normal. I don't know how she got so far in me. How she infected me. I don't want to say infection but I don't know what else the word is. Two, three months ago, Abdul did a relationship talk, the one Natalie went to, you remember, he said this, he said that it was the most important choice, your partner, but that it shouldn't be stressed, because humans can change. We're malleable. We think new thoughts every day. Like one day, you can randomly have a thought you've never thought and boom! Everything goes in a new direction. So love is an action, he said, and you can love anyone because you can act toward everyone."

Did I remember a dinner Natalie went to? Marwan spoke about Abdul so much, and Natalie had been around for those conversations, but I didn't remember her going to a dinner. Marwan babbled. I thought about telling him about Natalie's letter but I didn't know how to order the story. I'd have to tell Marwan about Natalie soon. He'd brush it off and say she'll come back. Who would be taking care of her if I wouldn't? She needed someone to guide her home to a calm landing spot. It wasn't done between us. She'd have to have planned this breakup for a while. A friend must have helped with the move-out — but her belongings would have fit into a single suitcase. Had she made me angry on purpose that night so I'd leave? I hated talking to her about money. She knew that.

A customer came in for handheld vacuums and Marwan shouted for a Samir cousin to help. We saw on the security TV under the counter Samir himself pulling into the parking lot. "Did Samir talk to you yet?" Marwan asked. "He's got an idea. I don't know what I think about it. I like some of it. But it's Samir, you know?"

Outside, I watched Samir direct a cargo van into our smallest spot. After kissing the wall, the van lurched forward a foot and the driver and associate came out with a gust of tobacco smoke to begin unloading blenders, smoothie makers, knock-off Vitamix, larger electronics; mini-fridges, humidifiers. Multiples of everything. Samir ordered his squad of cousins to take the boxes and stock the items for us. While I waited, I grabbed a broom to disturb the crow's nest being built high up in a corner. The birds squawked but wouldn't move. I wouldn't hit them and so gave up.

Samir's thick black hair was gelled into a hard shell, his pale scalp skin visible in segments. Yelling at a cousin, he lit his cigarette with a shopping mall Zippo that had a glittering skull engraved onto it and retucked his faded red polo into his pressed jeans. Before I could say hello, he stopped me and reached down to flick dirt off the horse-bit loafers he said were Gucci.

He was always making effort to remind us that he was, in many ways, our boss. Instead of authority, he fixated on his clothes, shouted orders louder when me or Marwan were close by, occasionally forcing cousins into needless tasks to prove that he could. For our part — for me, anyway — there was jealousy. I considered him to be an idiot, but cunning; stupid, but ambitious — dangerous. He'd earned his spot next to the Arab through proficiency and that deserved respect. We needed him and he was annoying about it.

"Let's go brother, I got a job. A personal job," he said to me and whistled at a skinny cousin, whose family hadn't had a nutritious meal in several generations, about four-foot-eleven and dark-skinned, looking like he'd been dropped from a sweatshop and into our plaza the night before. The cousin jumped into the driver's seat of a grey Toyota Camry without speaking or shoes. Samir motioned for me to join him in the back.

He tried to manifest power in overt silence but was always awkward when he held back from speaking, his mouth agape or he'd make a small noise and stop himself, as if remembering what he'd read in a book about power. We drove for a ways, out the lot, to the highway. He fidgeted with prayer beads, then his cellphone clip, then yelled at his cousin for not choosing the right radio station; he wanted me to ask where we were going. We drove farther into an area of the city I didn't recognize and the English signage on restaurants, grocery stores, and general real-estate riff-raff transformed into Chinese lettering. Finally, the cousin slowed into a neighbourhood of tangled streets and stopped.

"A favour: the man inside owes me money," Samir said. He pointed to a house that had started off as a bungalow. The back now had a two-story attachment to it painted pastel blue. The original bungalow was a rust-brown. In the driveway was an orange Beck taxicab and a car whose make I didn't recognize that was missing two front wheels. The taxi was finely cleaned and shone under the afternoon sun. The property was wrapped in a broken-down green fence and children's toys crowded the lawn.

"Why?" I asked.

"I floated him."

"You're not supposed to do that."

Samir loaning money meant the gambler had been denied by the Arab. The Arab rarely denied anyone, which meant it was a big deal.

"Can you go talk to him?" Samir asked me.

"How much he owe?"

"Fifteen thousand."

"Yo," I said.

"You'll get yours. But it has to be, very, you know —" He raised his index finger to his lip. "And then afterward, let's talk. I have a good thing for us."

He knew his leverage with me and Marwan. He knew why we couldn't get rid of the kettles. It wasn't because of the cousins's sideways teeth or constant farting, but because no one knew us. Even to get rid of ten, twenty surplus items in one go we'd need his name. Everything needed a name or an intro. We only knew him, and so diversifying our web to exclude Samir would only happen if Samir made phone calls on our behalf first.

"No more broken blenders," I said.

"I'll help you get rid of them. But I got something else too, bhai."

"Is the guy inside Chinese?" I asked.

"No no no, man, not like that, nothing crazy," Samir said. "It's simple. I don't need all the money back now. Just go talk. Get the ball rolling."

"For real: is he Chinese?"

"No!"

"I don't want to knock on that door and some next Chinese man to open," I said.

"He's not."

"I don't want that Chinese shit."

"Nobody wants any Chinese shit."

"Is he Viet?"

"No no no, wow yaar, no way, come on, I'm not crazy, he's from UP, he's from Benares he's good he's chill he's a good guy."

"If he's Chinese I'm coming back," I said.

I stepped past an overturned tricycle and knocked on the door, which opened as soon as I finished my last rap. A stubbled brown face peeked out. I shoved the door open and the smell of a thousand sweating men hit me, then a mix of cooking spices, then noise: a radio playing an ancient ghazal in a far kitchen; NDTV news on the living room TV; and from the depth of the house, the new addition, a baby wailing in rhythm with thumping. The living room a disaster. A three-seater couch with rough green-and-brown fabric was covered in a plastic tarp, which was covered in areas by loose blankets with different Taj Mahal designs on it. Above this the single piece of elegance in the house — a black board with gold Arabic lettering for the Shahada. The shabbiness leaked into a dining area with a table covered in more cloth and an assortment of bowls each with their own type of nut.

The man who'd opened the door didn't say a word and went back to his La-Z-Boy chair and sank in, his faded yellow sweatpants matching the walls.

The smell overwhelmed. I opened a window without asking and saw Samir's cousin's feet sticking out the driver side and Samir pacing the sidewalk talking into his phone. I looked back to the man — Will, he said his name was — and decided what to do. Will moved through the channels and flicked his cigarette into an ashtray he'd cut into the La-Z-Boy's armrest. He scratched his feet and popped a nut into his mouth. He was sick, as if grey colouring had been injected into an otherwise brown shell.

"Back home," Will said, "there was a boy named Lakath who would do whatever I asked. A beautiful small boy. His family lived in the tenant behind our house and he was our domestic from day one, not servant, a domestic, and he would fetch me what I needed. Water, khana, cigarettes, and he ironed all my clothes, and growing up next to him my son would have learned so much. Who knows what happened to him? Who knows what happened to all these boys?" Will knew what I was there for but didn't expect me to be able to take much money away from him, so he remained calm. Maybe he could pay Samir back over a year, two years, the money in small sums. But the Arab would let him continue to visit the tables. Samir had to wait in line. Will had other debts to pay off first. He gestured to the hallway that led to who knows how many doors. He'd turned his house into a rental property. Three families lived in the scowling addition, and seven single men, Indian international students, in the basement apartment. They lived in bunk beds, helped each other with cooking, everything good, everything perfect, Will said with a head bob.

The wailing child was his son's, who, he explained to me, without any emotion in his voice, was a stupid moron. Will had his own gambling debt; on top of that, the Arab had lent the son twenty-five thousand to start a business: Café Paan. The son's genius idea after reawakening to his Indian roots on a summer trip abroad was to open a betel-nut business like he'd seen in Delhi.

Paan — the betel-nut glob that Indian taxi drivers and construction workers chewed, often mixed with tobacco, resting in the mouth for the day and spat at intervals onto the floor, walls, any available surface, staining it forever red. It was a revelatory snack that identified your upbringing. No self-respecting Indian abroad would be caught chewing the cud and spitting out the extract onto a white Canadian surface. In India, spitting in public was a national pasttime; in Canada an egregious trespass. Will understood this — he drove a taxi, spoke to many influential men — but his son did not.

The son rented a small shop downtown for the imported ingredients and hired a graphic designer. Explaining the concept was hard enough, but once the bitter, foul-tasting mixture entered a mouth, any formerly prospective client was horrified. And while many drivers learn to line their betel-nut package with cocaine and related miscellany, his son wasn't offering these services. What was he offering then, exactly? The business failed within four months. Will corrected himself, the business failed at the word go, but it took four months for stupid-moron to notice. Even the Arab didn't purchase from them and forbade any of his workers to. It was too conspicuous. Paan without the Indian apathy to spit was a no-go.

"'Why not simple money,' I asked my son. 'Why not be a landlord?' You're how old?" Will asked me. "You're his age, no? You have a good job. Let me tell you. It's good, it's honest, it's steady. Six, seven men downstairs, each paying me eight hundred dollars a month. And now see, I can house my son's family, my daughter, both are in the back, along with my wife. No, he wants to do all this, to be proud of his identity and to make his mark. Identity. He doesn't even go for Friday namaz." Another TV clicked on in the house. I wanted to get out of there as soon as possible. The noise and smell was a physical presence that provoked an old, erratic fear I couldn't place. I could feel the basement dwellers in there with me, smell the curry from a fortnight ago like I was about to eat it; I saw his mail on the coffee table, which reminded me of Natalie's letter, and I dropped into a worse mood.

Will said he could pay back maybe fifty dollars a month to the debt he owed Samir. Whatever his connection to the Arab was, he made it sound substantial. He knew he couldn't be pressed, but I had to leave here with Samir satisfied. I couldn't get his money back for Samir but I could put Will to work. Will spat shells and said, "Surrounded by the Chinese here.

Next door, China, across the street, China, the shop signs are now in Chinese, did you see? China China China. They come here and do what? They don't drive taxis. You ever see a Chinese drive a taxi? They do Uber okay, but no taxi. You know, they can't work with other people. They don't work with anyone else. My son, he won't do any work either. Not like those Filipinos and whatever they work for whoever, wherever. No, I must own a business, my son says. The Indians today are like this. They won't do any shit-kicking work. They come into the country and want to be an engineer or accountant or doctor. Look at my son and tell me he's an engineer. He's good for the factory. I tried to explain a union to him. But no, he wants to be on TV with his big businesses. *Dragon's Den.* Every night he watches *Dragon's Den.* He takes notes. To a reality show. He takes notes and says that it's business school."

I felt for the moron son. Who could blame him for wanting his own way of life? His father had grown into the shape of so many old Indian men full of resentment and bile, unable to see their good fortune and unable to view their sons with curiosity. Was it migration? Had the journey sapped these men of their ambition for life? Did they convince themselves that the move was the start of momentum, and not, what it might be, the end? It was the anger in-built in men like Will — I moved here for *you* — and it was plain his son would never pay it back. "Back home," Will said, "we had three, four, servants. Night and day. For nothing, you know. You understand. For no money. They were like family. But they worked. No complaining. No crying. They wiped his ass when he shat. He doesn't know. He doesn't understand. You bring those servants here and they will clean this country right up." There was a thud and smash of dishes in the kitchen. Will rolled his eyes. "The genius has arrived," he said, above the baby's crying. I wanted Will to fail, alongside his whole family.

"Forget the fifteen thousand for now," I said. "You want to do work instead?"

"I'll always work, okay? I work every day. Twelve, thirteen hours a day, and I come home just for TV and no bullshit —"

"Okay, okay, relax." The work was simple, I promised. We'd recently come across a Point of Sales clone. Essentially, he had to get a customer to swipe their card and input their PIN number while taking a debit or credit card payment. Our little machine took all the info down and we'd be able to drain the account until they noticed. Will shifted in his seat, apprehensive. He tried to wave it away. I reminded him of the debt and the potential consequences. He waved me off unbothered, totally sure nothing could happen. I struggled to keep control. His dismissive attitude, the total surety that I couldn't affect him was giving me few options. I pulled a chair out from the dining table and winced, the bruise from last night fully formed on my ribs now. His son came into the living room holding the sleeping baby.

"I'll do it," the son said.

Will tried to interrupt, getting up from his seat.

"No, no, no —"

"I can do it," the son said. "Let me take the taxi for a few hours."

"No, no!"

"It'll be easy, Abba. I owe for the store. Let me do this for you."

"I don't want you to get involved."

Fear on Will's face. His sins could be managed as long as his family wasn't dragged in. The son stood upright, the opposite of what I'd expected from his father's whining. He had smooth skin, freshly shaved, and wore neat, clean clothes, Gap-stylish and not over the top. I expected the kind of entrepreneurial goof you met downtown, but he had the fresh face of a striver, and more surprisingly, given his failures, a face of innocence and vulnerability. I agreed to take him on and got up from my seat.

Will turned to me. "Don't you get involved. Don't get him involved," and stepped close. He stopped then, unsure what to do. The son began again, trying to convince his father it was okay. No one mentioned the culprit, the gambling debt. Pleading passed over the father's face. This was the first time, I guessed, that the son had become entangled in his father's activities. It was defeat.

•

Samir was confused when I explained what happened. I told the son he'd be able to keep 25 percent until the debt was paid off, and then him and Samir could renegotiate. As we drove back Samir liked the plan more and more.

We parked behind the store.

"Brother, can we talk? Where's Marwan?" Samir asked.

"He's inside," I said. "He's obsessed with Abdul. He's probably watching his videos."

"Really? Good. There's a reason. Let's talk about 'ArabTarzan.'" He fiddled with a sunglasses case. "My man wants to be community-minded," Samir said. "The ArabTarzan social media thing is great — fun. But we need more. His parents expect more. We need you and Marwan for a favour. It's a big-time move for you and he'll be in major debt." A cousin brought him half a bagel with butter. He chewed while he spoke. "I asked Marwan to show you the clip: the Resettlement Centre for those Guantanamo Bay guys that Abdul is setting up. A great thing. Great thing. Abdul is a great, great guy. We want to help. We want to be part of the Resettlement Centre. How else? Money. Abdul is talking about funding from government and using his own money, of course he made those millions, and we want to add to the pool. To be partners. Brothers." Samir turned his phone to show me the centre's website. He flicked his thumb down the page, muttering approval to himself. "Don't forget: we can also get lots of other people to donate money. GoFundMe and all that. We know lots of people. Lots of local-wocal businesses will donate. Abdul will see how much charity we can do for him. All we ask is that we be part of it. Simple. That next to Abdul, our names are used also."

"I don't really have that much money," I said.

"Bhai, you don't really have any money. We're talking money-money. Not your loose change."

"Why you need us then?" I asked.

"Easy, simple. Nothing complicated," Samir said. "You remember Abdul bhai came to the party for Bagheera at that club, Mirage? Maybe Abdul is upset now because he's not taking any of my calls. And then … on paper yaar, our money is not great. Not exactly so legitimate. It's complicated. Not totally our fault. You know, like sending that money you do for me, to India, we have to move money around to make magic from it, otherwise the government gets very curious. You know what these people are like with us, right, with Muslims, we give money, especially international money, what do they to think? Big Taliban natak. Let's not joke. Our money is not exactly legal in all places. If we put bhai saab's name on a big-money donation directly to Abdul's centre then we run the risk of an audit. An audit is very bad. So we want you to put the money forward for us. Our money, using your store. The store, remember, we gave you. Donate the money to Abdul with the store's name. Under your name. You can become the big-shot too. Then it becomes all of us helping the community."

A cousin brought him rose lemonade in a plastic cup. He stuck his hand in, gathered the ice, and flung it to the ground. Chugged the sour drink. "Local business owner Hamid bada saab," Samir said. "That's you. Small businesses. Small business owners are everything. These people are obsessed with small business owners. If an accountant pokes around they're only going to find my two boys, Hamid and Marwan, small business owners, donating, perfectly legit. I have a friend, don't worry, he will make everything good, make sure you have an increase in sales to match the donation amount. No problem." He'd smoked three cigarettes talking.

"And what we get?" I asked. "You gonna pay us?"

"No, no, bhai, no. Listen, you have to help us a little. Do one thing, organize a meeting for us and Abdul. Marwan goes to those Friday dinners. He knows Abdul, no? Marwan is refusing to set it up. So far we haven't actually been able to sit down with Abdul and explain our plan to him. We want to be part of his public team. When Abdul goes to an event to speak about his charity, we want to be there alongside him. This is what we need. This is our ambition. Our next step. He's going to be meeting a lot of people — CEOs, politicians, bureaucrats, that kind, and he needs us to introduce him and help him navigate that new world. He's a big-shot online. But in our world? Who knows him? Who trusts him? He needs us to help with all these little people. But not just him. You'll be there also. We give a little money and he brings us along. Very simple, no?" Samir waved a cousin over and ordered a new packet of cigarettes and fresh coffee, double-double. "You want more, I know," Samir said. "This is good for you. I told you before, we notice everything. This is what you want. You want to sell kettles your whole life? Okay, fine. You want this? This is here too. At every meeting, I promise you bhai, you will be there with us, side by side, and everyone in this city will know your name. Talk to Marwan. He's being a little … I don't know. I don't want to say. He watches too many of Abdul's videos. Thinks he's a good guy now. All I want is to meet with Abdul, give him the idea. Look at your face. Marwan's face didn't look like yours. You earned this. Don't think you didn't. Don't think we haven't noticed. This is because of strength." He threw his cigarette into a drain and shouted a new task to a cousin. I walked him back to his Honda. "You want a water? It's a Fiji Water," he said. "You know Fiji? Four bucks a bottle. You want one?"

13.

I wanted what Samir was offering. I knew the kind of man he was inviting me to be. The figure in local newspapers, bus stop ads, sponsoring community softball teams and children's soccer, poorly made plaques with their names hanging in pizza shops. The local bigwig. The man whose power existed in a small area, known to the local politicians, whose office the mayor would stop by during elections and forget about upon victory.

It was a first step for the Arab, who surely had grander, million-dollar ambitions, but for me, it could be perfect. I was humble. I wanted a little visibility that could push me toward a gig with long-term stability that didn't involve peering into every corner for spare coins. I would be involved with more than myself, but not everything. A something that wasn't at the fringe of the world but directly in it.

Inside, Marwan watched another video of Abdul on mute while he fiddled with the microwaves. I waited until he noticed me and then spoke.

"You don't want to introduce Samir to Abdul?"

"It's Samir," Marwan said.

"He's a crook."

"But it could be a good thing for us. I agree."

"Then?"

"I don't want to be the one to introduce Abdul to Samir," Marwan said. "Samir trying to buy access to Abdul. It feels like I'm sullying Abdul."

"But it will go to charity," I said. "For Abdul's little Guantanamo Resettlement Centre? We're helping. The ummah. Any money Samir gives will go right to Abdul and his projects."

"Have you ever known Samir and him to give away money for nothing?" Marwan asked. "What else does he want from Abdul?"

"All they want is to go legit. To appear to go legit. So let him. Let's gain from it."

"I don't want to do that to Abdul," Marwan said.

"He's not your pet."

"Why do you want to do this?"

"What we doing here? Selling microwaves? Bro, why not?"

"You were happy with this two years ago," Marwan said. "Too much money has grown your vanity."

"Don't say that. Whenever you watch his videos you talk like that."

"You want to be good," Marwan said.

"I am good."

"Are we? Who are we good to?"

"Exactly," I said. "This is an opportunity to be good to our community. Samir is not perfect — so what? Do we know what happened with Abdul in Afghanistan? He confessed to shooting the soldier."

"He was a child being tortured."

"He was fourteen. You knew not to shoot someone at that age."

"What kind of guidance did he have?" Marwan said. "It was a war. I know you think you need this to go forward."

"When I look in the future I don't see anything," I said.

"That's because you're depressed," Marwan said.

"Bro."

"Is this the thing to fix it?"

"I feel like if I was depressed this would help."

"We make good money here. I don't want to be the person that brings those two together."

"What do you think is going to happen if we say no to Samir? All our product is from him."

"They won't do nothing," Marwan said. "They need us."

"We could do so much more."

"I don't want to give Abdul dirty money."

"And what's the government money he gets? They bomb our brothers —"

"Don't pretend to be political —"

"I'm not pretending."

"Our government isn't as involved as other —"

"Don't draw lines between good and bad money," I said.

"Come with me to the mosque."

"I'm not going to no Abdul mosque."

"This is appealing to your vanity," Marwan said. "To be a big man."

"Bro, shut up."

"I want to say no. The root of the money counts."

"This is for Abdul's charity. You should be jumping on this."

"I don't think Samir is a trustworthy person."

"We work with him," I said.

"For Abdul. He's not trustworthy for Abdul."

"Abdul isn't better than us," I said. "Samir just wants to do lunch. There's going to be other people. You aren't the only person who knows Abdul. We could miss out."

"What do you actually want?" Marwan asked.

"It's an opportunity. A door. Remember when you had ambition."

"And then I lost my hand —"

"You wanted that cat in that club. You couldn't close the deal with Britta and that ain't on me. Man, if I'd lost my hand in a club like that —"

"What? What would you do?"

"That's a great injury," I said. "Great story. You act like you lost it in some ghetto redneck tractor. You're so moody about it."

"Samir will use Abdul's reputation to launder his. We won't be better, we'll take on all their dirt."

"My man. Every single item in this shop fell off a truck."

"These are electronics," Marwan said. "Goods. Prices are unfair, people can't afford necessities. I want to say no. But. But I want goodness for you."

"Don't talk like that to me," I said. "You're not allowed to watch more than two of Abdul's videos per day."

"Don't be shitty."

"I'm sorry," I said.

•

Natalie's leaving caught up to me. I stayed in bed for two days. I iced my bruises. I texted Marwan I wasn't coming in and didn't answer Samir's phone calls.

I did not think about the man in the track suit.

My father texted and I told him I was sick.

I did not think about the man in the track suit.

No one could take care of Natalie like me. I'd have to go to her work at some point to ask about her. There was no activity on her social media. I had no phone numbers.

I daydreamed I'd run into her disoriented and confused and I could take her back in. I was ambivalent about finding her even if I was compelled to. That we'd avoided a growling break-up fight brought me anxiety. We needed a full stop.

I couldn't remember her parents' names. They all moved here in the '90s. Her father's first job was at a Vietnamese restaurant, in a basement kitchen, lime-stained fingers, bean sprouts crowding a dish of hot soup; an inept cook, maybe happy to have a job.

My father's first job here was as a waiter in a restaurant. It was run by an Indian who locked up the cooks in the basement on cots every night. The best deal they would have, he promised them. My father was fired quick. He spilled chicken vindaloo on someone and wasn't very sorry. Six months after he left there was a fire. Four or five cooks slept in that basement sending money home.

I had to bring Natalie back into my life. What was it that Track Suit had said to me: "It's finished. It's finished."

For three days I walked the city forgetting where I was going. Marwan kept texting so I finally told him about Natalie. Then he called over and over.

Was the absence in me always there or was it her? Why did I miss her if I hated her? Why did I feel compelled if I wanted it all to be over? That first moment of relief already receded, pushed back by my body's need for her presence. I couldn't make simple decisions without her to bounce off. I looked in the mirror expecting her to look back.

Marwan kept calling. So did Samir. The shop wore me down. For the last two years we worked twelve hours daily. I saw Marwan and whatever crook of the Arab's came in for the day. No one else. At home, Natalie flew in and out seeing friends, co-workers; dinners, movies.

Marwan found a positive way to be in the world. Abdul provided him with rules of engagement for life and he thrived, always a sympathetic ear, keeping me alive with patient listening after I worked myself up over a trivial issue. Marwan would brew coffee, count the till, nod, make small agreeing noises.

He was reluctant about Samir because he saw his vanity on full display. He saw it in me and he knew he himself was under its thrall. Vanity a cheap thrill. An easy way to clear inner rubble.

Marwan had struggled but was better; Abdul helped. Marwan kept his workout regime going but stopped posting lifts on Instagram. I'd seen glimpses of his mental strength over the years but since losing his hand it became hard and sharp. To be admired, like a diamond. But for every instance I admired him, a pain burst in me, illuminating my lack.

While he rooted himself in Abdul's neat mingling of Western and Islamic ideas, I struggled, even with Natalie. What were dreams of the future made of? Who gave them to you? In university, my peers were either gently guided by parents, or listened attentively to counselling. I could do neither.

And I couldn't move myself forward. Instead, I grabbed at the shreds of dreams others had, hoping one would push me into my own specific future.

What I wouldn't accept: I was closer to Samir than I was to Marwan. So what was Abdul, then? A figure in the distance I could rise to.

•

I'd been waiting ten minutes at the restaurant Samir had suggested. It was a bare white-walled space, with a grey plastic table covered in see-through tarp, two patio tables with Styrofoam plates and cups resting on top. No art on the walls. A drinks fridge in the corner and a hastily written out-of-service sign stuck to the bathroom door. The lone worker visible leaned over the counter watching a video on his cellphone. Fluorescent tubes ran the length of the ceiling uncovered and I requested one be turned off.

Samir came in talking on his Bluetooth accessory and jangling a new gold bracelet on his wrist. He plopped a box of frozen rotis onto the counter, re-adjusted his phone clip, and, noticing the bulbs turned off, snapped Hindi at the cashier who pointed at me. Samir let a smirk crawl across his face.

"I own the place," he told me, gesturing to the white walls. "Isn't it nice?"

He wore faded blue jeans and a black Ralph Lauren shirt with a gigantic red polo player sewn above the heart. I filled with envy.

I was always taken aback by his wiry frame, with long arms spindled with black hairs, oiled scalp and fanny-pack-looking paunch that was highlighted by his tucked-in shirts. I saw him often through the shop window at the spot in our parking lot that he liked to hold meetings at. A small pile of his Benson & Hedges gathered when he'd been there. If they weren't swept up he'd complain about the state of things.

I was repulsed by him but I couldn't stop myself. He understood what money meant. He spread his arms wide, happy to be in his restaurant.

Like many North Indian Muslims he obsessed with his Pathan heritage and owning an Afghan restaurant fed into this source of pride. An active link to the past. The server dropped off Styrofoam plates loaded with wilting lettuce, brown carrots, and two oily samosas. Only two years ago Samir was pretending to be a shy veterinary student conducting experiments in the Arab's basement.

He was nervous. He sat, stood, yelled, showed off. Food came in rounds. He mumbled business was good. He expected me to turn Marwan in his favour. At the time, of course, my thoughts went to the Abdul project he'd talked about. Like always, I failed to see the different mechanics in others; I could only see what was directly in front of me. I bit into a samosa and oil oozed at the corner of my mouth. A plate of brown circular kebabs arrived. He broke off a piece and gestured for me to eat.

"Do you know where Natalie is?" he asked.

Why did he care? He tossed off the question casually. How did he even know? Marwan probably told him. They talked, I guess. Why had she thanked me as if I'd filled her grocery bag? He picked at the leaves from a fake plant crawling across the wall behind him.

"Yes ..."

"That's all right. This happens. Tonight we'll meet someone who can help. Do we have trust between us, brother?"

A hot plate of channa arrived. He stuck his dirty fingers into the grease. I took a piece of naan and a bite. It was fine. I asked about his life but he avoided answering. He had nothing to talk about, he promised. He was all business. I'd cobbled together facts over the years: His family lived in India, he'd grown up poor as an ignored arm of the Arab's extended family. They'd married in. He sent regular money back. People relied on him. He delivered a banal speech on responsibility whenever he asked me to wire cash home.

"You're going to come with me tonight," he said. "I'm going to show you. I wanted to show you this restaurant first — because even if I work with you, I work with my family, I have this, I have my own thing. This is not my only place. I have a shop, like you. I know Marwan is a funny guy. I know. But you can make a decision for the two of you. For the store. For your independence. That's what money buys. To be your own man. I don't want to get between the two of you but you're your own man, of course."

"Why not just go to Abdul's centre? Approach him directly?"

"Brother. You'll see tonight. Family is connection. Money is connection. The most beautiful thing is introducing someone to an opportunity. A gift. Let me give this gift to you." Half a chicken, then a plate of lentils came and went and small glasses of Coca-Cola were the last things brought out. His heavy-lidded eyes never left me. The earlier nerves gone. "I want to show you my life. Wash your hands, let's go. Don't worry about Natalie. I'm sure it will be okay. These things happen."

His black hatchback was parked in front of the restaurant. The windows tinted, the wrap polished to a vulgar sheen, blue lights tracked under the doors, and gold rims pulled it together.

The inside upholstered with leather and a Bose sound system. The steering wheel had fur covering. All black.

"Why would you do this to a Honda?" I asked.

"It's a good car. Lasts a long time."

"It's a Honda."

He took no offence and jerked the car into traffic. The engine had a UFO purr. He wiggled his eyebrows at me, his eyes away from the road.

"You know what I call her? The name of my first pet."

I didn't want to say it.

"Bagheera!" he said and laughed, slapping the wheel. "I modified her with the pussycat in mind." He slid through two lanes without signalling, heading westward toward the sun. We drove five minutes and then stopped in front of a take-away shop called HOLY CHICKEN. Across the street was a mosque.

We slipped off our shoes, rushed our cleaning, and joined the evening prayer.

After prostrations was a line of handshakes. Samir spoke Hindi and I caught slips of words and responses. I was being introduced. Old brown men grabbed my outstretched hand with both of theirs and shook vigorously, as if I'd promised them my prize goat. Samir pointed at a short man wearing loose grey clothing and broken slippers. He'd missed two patches shaving.

"He owns six Wendy's."

A man with chubby child's cheeks came to me. His hands were wet. I was forced to meet each and every old man. Samir said a magic phrase in their ears and they greeted me with hungry eyes. Each toothless senior sang his praises. He donated money. He spoke to a wayward grandson. He helped with a marriage. The walls of the city collapsed and I was transported to a small village in India, clustered and claustrophobic. My hand wet from all the sweat and after each shake I had to wipe it on my pants. I caught that my name and Abdul's were being linked. We went through about ten men in twenty minutes before I finally asked, "What are you doing?"

"Smile at everyone please. We have to build you in the community."

He gave everyone an equal thirty seconds during which he remembered a fact about them, memories produced like gold nuggets. They loved to be remembered. There was a group of young men in the corner waving off any effort to speak to Samir. Sullen and alone. No families. They watched while whispering to each other.

I followed him like a tail and met a different kind of man wearing a sleeker suit, a flash of an expensive watch, and as the audience got younger, richer, I got introduced more and more as Abdul's bhai, or friend, the link between us becoming substantial. These men got serious, to-the-point conversations.

After an hour Samir announced it was time to go. The sun dropped and gone. He lit a cigarette as we stepped outside and stood as if he was waiting for someone to drive his car up to him.

"You ready baby, you ready baby?" he said to me in a sing-song voice, his eyes wide and mad. He laughed at himself and I followed him across the street to the car.

We roved west, in and out of lanes toward the horizon. Samir concentrated on everything but his driving, the radio stations on perpetual flick and at every pause on the road he went through his phone. We were going to Brass Rail, a strip club in the centre of the city.

"The guy we're meeting is going to set up our website, GoFundMe, all that stuff. Once private funding comes in the government gets a little less shy. They have lots of money. What do you do with money?"

"What you mean?" I asked.

"You spend it? This is money you can't even spend it's so big. Do you understand that we are at a high risk in this country? The banks, the government, they're all watching how we move."

"That's a little paranoid."

"No, no, no, no, no no, no no no no. Money is every, single, thing. Whatever you want to know about a person is in their money. How they spend their money. What. Who. Where it's kept. Money is simple, easy. There's nothing out of reach of money. It's the most obvious thing on the planet. That's why Abdul is so important to us. You can understand a man like that, right? He wants to make something — ten years in prison, that's a long time, a long absence. That need to make money in him. Holy. Simple. Clean. You know some people, they're okay in prison. They don't mind. Their life outside barely exists anyway, work, shit, shampoo, home. But someone like him in that prison for ten years. If you have even a single spark of ambition what happens in those years? For most, it goes, poof. Who cares? But when you look at Abdul — do you think that? He gets ten million dollars and the first thing he does is sink it into real estate." Samir slid the Honda into a parking spot. He spun his keychain around his finger. "We're drivers. They don't want us to be but that's what we are. Pushers. Me and you. We have to make our own room in this country."

We went around the lot to the front entrance. The facade giant lit-up plastic tubes with pictures of women. They were stuck, like a fly in a fossil, in their '90s hairdos. Samir opened a door and walked down a blue hallway. I glanced up and down the street to make sure no one I knew was watching and rushed in behind him.

The dark corridor empty except two bouncers in black-and-white vests and bow ties manning the front. The end of "Black Beatles" spilled from the speakers, and then a polite, steady voice took over: "Give it up for Starlight! Starlight will be on the floor in a minute and make sure to tell her how much you enjoyed the show. Up next is Bi-an-ca! Bianca, ladies and gentlemen." Samir walked in with a nod to the bouncers but a beefy hand on my chest stopped me. The shorter bald one, his head covered in an unreal blue light, asked for ID. The taller one reached down to my pants pocket, caught the fabric between his index and thumb, and rubbed it together.

"Are these sweatpants?" he asked.

"Hell no. These are pants."

"Really? They're thin. They feel too thin."

"It's Egyptian cotton."

They'd cost $250 and in the month I'd owned them this was the first comment I got. The bouncer returned my ID.

"Sweatpants aren't allowed."

"They're soft, summer pants."

"You can't wear sweatpants in here."

"These are regular pants!"

Samir slung his arm around my shoulders to vouch for me. The bouncer, content, warned me not to wear sweatpants next time. Samir pulled me away before I replied.

Spread across the floor were women in various fabrics: lace, leather, polyester, all cut in different shapes and patterns to highlight a muscle or curve.

Past the bar was a seating area, and this early, filled with solitary men with eyes locked forward onto the stage. No one made eye contact as we moved to our table. Classic desire on display: average men for beautiful women.

The women bent over tables to speak so others would be free to look over their bodies and decide. Invited to sit down, they put a bandana on the surface of the chair. Most often, the man shook his head, offered a meek smile, and said he wasn't ready. They didn't linger. Smiled and a coy voice let them know they would be back, later, maybe. The exchange transparent. In the corner, shaded by the overhang of the bar, was a fat white man in a blue polo, telling a dancer about his day, a brown bottle of beer in his hand, a clear glass in hers.

No man looked at me. As we reached our seat, my eyes landed on a bespectacled East Asian wearing a windbreaker spotted with dandruff that glowed under the UV light. He snapped his eyes away when I caught his and then the white dancer on stage, an intricate pattern of tattoos around her breasts, was existence for him. She held herself sideways on the pole.

Samir sat at his favourite four-person table with clear sightlines. A wall of asses for us to stare at. Across from him was Samir's friend Bilal, who spoke to almost every dancer that walked by, holding their hands for too long. It was clear he wasn't going to pay for a drink or dance. Samir introduced us: we would be going over bank transfer details, organizing paperwork, and rummaging over the last year of our accounting to increase our sales, in order for the bigger donations to Abdul from the Arab to make sense. Bilal would set up the GoFundMe and a website where people could donate directly to Abdul so we could pretend this was a legitimate exercise and lessen Samir's fear of an audit. Any meddling from the country's tax agencies could threaten their entire empire.

Bilal was scrawny and bald and a thick Cuban link chain dipped into his chest hair. He looked older than me and Samir, but spoke to us like a younger brother. A loud laugh that purposefully attracted attention. The women left after he held their hands and his eyes would go limp.

Bilal was four or five drinks in. I ordered a club soda.

"You don't drink?" Bilal said, gawking.

"I'm Muslim."

Samir's head on swivel.

"What's your cut?" I asked Samir.

"This is charity. I can't take a cut. Abdul won't go for it. Even Bilal is free."

A new girl appeared on stage every three songs. Bilal spoke nonsense to me like we were lifelong friends. He leaned into my shoulder. His jaw dropped at every new woman. Sad, but at least he was enthusiastic. A short Black dancer walked by and my heart stammered. A glance at her was enough to open up a path of happiness in me. I wanted her at the table, in my hands, around my body, just like everyone else.

"I don't know how I can convince Marwan to set up a dinner for you and Abdul." I said.

"What's his problem? Me?" Samir asked.

"No. No," I said.

"Imagine your name and face on those little pamphlets they give out during Eid. Imagine buying all that biryani. For the community."

Closer to midnight groups of drunk men arrived. Five or six in a group absent of self-consciousness. The evening shifted. The music louder, more dancers on the floor, the solitary men leaving and those who stayed ignored. The women approached groups in pairs.

A Pakistani-looking blond stood beside me, her arms folded over each other. She was barely five feet, but her platforms and hair that reached her ass made her seem taller. Her face was small and her smile reached either end of it. Samir held her hand and introduced her: "This is Bianca. This is my girlfriend, my baby," his voice gentle like I'd never heard before. Bilal gathered himself to resemble sobriety and said hi. Samir and her left together to the back.

A blue light pulled over Bilal. He ordered another Red Bull vodka. A muscular brunette in a leather harness shouted in his face, "Do you want a dance?" He bobbed his head and said no. She didn't bother with me and went to a group of Chinese boys all wearing different-coloured Anti Social Social Club hoodies. Bilal sipped his drink.

"You fuck?" Bilal asked.

"Hunh?"

"What's your body count?"

"What?"

"Your number?"

"Bro, what?"

"How many women you screwed?"

"I don't know," I said.

"Not paid."

"What?"

"Oh, it's like that," Bilal said. "It's like that. Don't tell me. It's private. You're shy."

"How long you known Samir?" I asked.

"Enough time. Our parents know each other from India. Damn, check that chick. You don't know my parents, do you?"

"No, dog."

"This place," Bilal said. "A test. It's better for you to practise self-restraint."

"Where did Samir go?"

"Those who follow their lusts go astray."

"Do you need another drink?"

"Man was created weak," Bilal said.

"You good?"

"I'm at five. Pathetic, no? Paid though — oh wow. I can't get a girl here."

"That's a surprise," I said.

"Right? I got money. It's a cultural barrier."

"Don't go after white chicks."

"I don't 'go after' white chicks," Bilal said. "It's the Indians my dude. I meet an Indian and I go: okay. What are you? It's cumin, when they say we stink, it's the cumin that comes through the pores. I never stand next to an Indian at the gym. But it hurts the heart to have a woman watch the clock always. How many hours working in front of the computer equals one hour with a woman? How much is touch worth? You can't invoice touch. It would be easier on my spirit if I could write it off on my taxes. I don't want to be rule-breaker, but in a country like this, in the winter, what can you do? And we always meet at boring business hotels downtown. For once, I'd like a personalized room, picture frames, a laundry hamper overfilling. For one hour it's no problem to enjoy a fantasy of love and all that. And then I send the same sum back, to my parents. What kind of car you drive?"

"An Integra."

"A little rice rocket? You study here or back home?"

"Bro, I'm from here."

"IT?"

"Business administration degree."

"That's good, bhai, that's good. I had to study in one of those little colleges that disappear after one year. I got mine though. You don't drink — you're Muslim. Good boy. Like me."

I couldn't tell if he was being sarcastic. The question always came up: am I Muslim and, if so, what kind? I always disappointed with the kind of Muslim I was, that, back then, I often forgot my prayers, I chose Halal if it was there, but at least adhered to the absolute red line for all Western Muslims: I did not eat pork. Pork was the barricade in the battle for the Muslim soul and if it was not breached, all was okay.

Bilal's round head shone. His eyes followed a woman across the floor. Then he asked, "You cut?"

"Bro."

"You said you're from here. Do they do that here? I met this convert, this white guy, red beard, he got cut at fourteen. Would you do that? I wouldn't do that. Do you date a lot of women?"

"Not — no … not really."

"But you like to …"

"I'm … young," I said.

"Do your parents pressure you for marriage?" Bilal asked.

"My parents don't pressure me."

"Mashallah. What wonderful parents. I was dating this Sikh girl. You ever date a Sikh? Those people … they're very … it's a big deal …"

I warmed to him with this confession. I'd seen a Punjabi girl once for two months. We saw each other once a week and she enjoyed reminding me how upset her parents were that she was dating a Muslim. Bilal paused after sharing, the singe of the relationship still real for him.

"I did once," I said.

"Really? Here? Did her parents ask if you're cut?"

"Bruh, no one in my life has ever asked me if I'm circumcised."

"It was my fault," Bilal said. "I lied to them. I said I was Hindu. I thought they would like that better. They surrounded me, pulled my pants … they inspected my cock, can you imagine? They beat me!"

He was probably going to show me his penis but Samir slid back into his seat with Bianca once again by his side.

"Go with her," Samir said.

"I don't think so."

"Go with her go with her. I have to talk to Bilal."

Samir gave me small pushes to get me out of my chair.

"I'll pay for it," Samir said. "Don't worry you cheap-ass. I want you to see."

Samir put her hand into mine and she tugged me to the back of the club where there was a small section with low chairs divided into semi-booths. Bianca gestured to a sunken seat and stood above facing me. She put a bandana on my lap. In the back each booth was lit by its own bulb. I was a little terrified. This was Samir's girlfriend?

"I'll wait till the next song," she said.

"Or Nah" finished and "Closer" came on; a dancer switch. Bianca moved over my body, pressing close but maintaining distance. She straddled me and moved my hands on her hips. I squeezed.

"How long have you known Samir?" she asked.

"A few years."

"So you know what he's like," she said.

"I don't know him well."

She took her top off, turned, slapped her ass, and turned back to face me. She smelled good, like cheap moisturizer, and I focused on her two small pink nipples. Across from us a white stripper wagged her ass in front of a faded white dude in a suit, his eyes boring into her asshole as if he was going to find the secret to life there.

"If you give me two hundred dollars I'll tell you what Samir told me," she said.

"What does that mean?"

"If you give me two hundred dollars I'll tell you what he told me."

I was turned on by the way she stated her request. She moved my hands up to cup her breasts. A new song came on and she asked me if I wanted to continue. I gave her the two hundred. She counted, grinding against me.

"What he say?" I asked.

"He said: make sure he has a good time because without him I can't get what I need."

"That cost two hundred?"

"How he said it, that's important."

"What that cost — one hundred?"

She turned and stomped her heel just before my crotch.

"How he said it. How he said it costs fifty."

I was hard; uncomfortable, turned on. I gave. She tucked the bills into a small purse I hadn't noticed.

"He didn't say it in a —"

A roar erupted from where Samir and Bilal were sitting. Samir appeared next to Bianca. Two bouncers shoved a sloppy Bilal out of the side door.

"We gotta go," Samir said.

"What did he do?" Bianca asked.

"I didn't see," Samir said. "I was in the bathroom. We gotta bounce."

He kissed Bianca while she was on top of me and their tongues flashed together. I throbbed. My hands smelled of her.

Outside, Bilal stood in front of Bagheera like a child waiting to be scolded. Samir hit his Honda's auto-lock and the two beeps frightened Bilal.

"What you do?" Samir asked Bilal.

"I was itchy. My underwear bunched up. I was adjusting myself. It was not what they said."

"You stupid," Samir said.

I was a few steps behind. I needed distance. Did I lose that money to Bianca for nothing? Obviously he needed me. He told me. I was an idiot. A quick con. Good for her.

Still: I'd been warned. My father taught: every single person will want to take from you. Every interaction they will try to take, take, and again take. Samir lit a smoke and asked again about the dinner.

"Can you convince Marwan?"

"I don't know if I want to."

"He'll do it if you ask."

"It's a big ask."

"This is a big opportunity. Do the right thing." Bilal got into the back seat. Samir sucked the cigarette to its nub. "One more stop," he said and started the car.

•

We drove north of the city. Samir was trying to learn more about Abdul. An interview with him played in the background.

"The Western idea of Muslims is that we don't drink — wrong. We loved wine. Ask the Persians, even those who might be reluctant to claim Islam. You love the Sufis and they loved their drinking cup. The whirling dervishes are an easy way to the heart of Islam ..."

Samir parked in a plaza lot with a few cars, a pickup truck that looked like it lived there. A pizza parlour had a yellow-orange sign on. It was warm without being muggy. Many of the stores had their neon lights going and they reflected a wine-stained hue against the pavement.

Bilal and Samir cackled to themselves walking through the lot. I walked behind them.

"Hey," Samir said, looking at me, "the Uber driver's following us."

They laughed at their joke. I tailed, insulted but curious. The plaza was squat and seemingly extended over and over again at right angles. They stopped in front of a unit with tinted windows, white bars, and in neon letters a sign that read, ENTRANCE.

Bilal buzzed and looked at the security camera above.

"Three of us. It's Bill and Sam."

The door opened to a small room. A buzz again. The second door opened.

It was all red mist inside, the colouring part of the air. Jasmine incense and on the front counter a gold Buddha statue. Three women approached from darkness. Coming to me was a woman in a short blue kimono and red bodysuit underneath. Her skin marble and bangs ending abrupt above her eyebrows. A glittering jewel on a tooth. Her hands over my chest. Two women led Samir and Bilal off. There was cold air being pumped in.

We went farther into the unit. A small TV near a drinking lounge played Japanese porn with the noise off and another TV showed a Japanese woman dancing in a bathing suit with soap bubbles covering her. Samir watched the porn: the set was a bus and a struggling woman in full clothing passed around by men in eyeglasses. All the men wore black pants and white shirts along with trench coats. Their cocks, peeking out from their unzipped flies, were pixelated.

We sat on two couches, each with a woman. Samir in another world. A short, stout, Sri Lankan–looking woman in a robe sat on his lap. Her breasts flowed from the opening. Bilal spoke to a small woman in a burgundy cheongsam. They were familiar. Their fingers lingered on each other. I made small talk with my girl, Rose, and she ran her hands up my forearms, brushing my arm hair.

We were in a private room. A waitress in all black stood in the corner organizing our drinks. Music played in our room at a low volume. I could hear noise outside our door; when a song finished or there was a lull, the low moan of a woman or a series of stuttered grunts from a man in another room creeped in.

Rose asked questions about my life in front of a red wall covered in gold Chinese lettering. The waitress leaned to me and handed me a small pipe. Samir and Bilal had their own. They exhaled chains of smoke and the sweet scent of hash hit me.

Rose leaned into my body and I absorbed her warmth and sandalwood smell. There was a sharp current of body odour. She ran her hands over the crotch of my pants as we spoke and curled her palm over my erection through the fabric.

Samir's partner stood and dropped her robe. She wore a vivid blue two-piece, cut in the style of Jasmine from *Aladdin*. She danced in full view, swivelling her hips while holding her arms up, and he leaned forward to touch her when he wanted. His shirt was off. The woman straddled him and when she stood back up, his pants were undone and his cock had slipped out from the gap in his boxers. Bilal laughed and reminded him we had all night. She tried to kiss Samir but he clutched her face and pushed back.

Rose whispered Chinese into my ear. Her skinny body and sharp angles would stay permanent in my memory. Her breath was coffee and peppermint gum. Her face eager and practised. It didn't dilute my feeling for her. She was an expert and her confidence turned me on. Hipbones that wanted to rip through skin. She sat in the blue pool of her satin kimono and moved very slowly with me, aware I was new.

The Sri Lankan said, "Yes baba, please baba," and took Samir's hand and pulled him up so they were dancing together, Samir swigging from his drink. He was at half-mast now and the woman pulled at him softly. He watched Bilal take his shirt off. Samir swirled across the room. Bilal sucked noisily at his partner's nipples, his slobber shining on her skin like fresh paint. Rose ran her hands over the pants of my crotch, my erection full now. Samir and Bilal's bare shoulders bumped. Samir held Bilal's arm and gently moved him away. They looked at each other while touching their women.

Samir stopped in the middle of the floor and pulled his girl close to his body, watching Bilal, grabbed her forearms and spun, falling back onto the couch, so she was against him, moving in waves while he held tight. His right hand went up her torso, brushing over her breasts, squeezing one, then slapped it. He moved his hand around her throat. He squeezed. She squirmed. He looked at Bilal. He tightened. She coughed, bucking forward, but he pulled her back by the throat. She continued moving over him. He tightened. Spit at the corner of her lips. The Cantopop beat turned. The waitress lit a stick of incense and the sound of the girl's choking was hidden under song. Samir's left arm held her in his grip. She struggled. Her heels fell off. He tightened. Rose rubbed me. Bilal next to Samir their eyes locked. Samir relaxed his grip on her throat and she took in a breath of air. They kissed, their tongues churning, and moved apart, a white line of spit connecting them, then Samir pulled her back to him, his hand around her throat once more, choking, slapping her cheek, and he put his mouth into her ear and whispered while staring at Bilal. A vein in her temple throbbed, her eyes watered, she put her hands around his, tried to pull him off. He tightened. Bilal watched.

I stood.

I stepped toward Samir and swung. My fist hit his chin. The girl jumped off his body. Rose screamed. Bilal stared. Samir put his hands up. He didn't fight. He took deep breaths. I didn't want a fight. We stared at each other.

14.

"Pick up" texts from my father all night while I slept. Three missed calls. He needed to keep better hours.

The hard immobile letters of the message moved me. Pick Up. I'd gotten my monthly email from my mother too. *Beta, I hope things are good. Auntie is sick. Dabir found another good job in a call centre. Your father is going to ask you a favour.* She always wrote me in a disaffected, detached voice, a bullet-point list of updates. She was all right. A photo from her balcony of the bridge and the racket below. Most of our family of inbred hillbillies in Uttar Pradesh wouldn't easily acknowledge divorce, if my parents ever did finally take that step. We hadn't spoken on the phone in a year. Now, she repeated I could visit anytime. She and her widowed sister lived in an apartment near JJ Road that their family had owned since the 1960s.

•

Entering his apartment, the old anxiety twisted in my chest. He was waiting, flitting around the unit when I came in.

"She has a storage unit," he said. "She wants you to assess its worth."

I hadn't seen him in two months. His skin hung from bone. His hair gone from silver with black streaks to stark white. He pulled at a black hair curling out of his earlobe.

"You can't go yourself?"

He tended to the plants. When he fiddled aimlessly waiting for his son's answer he was pathetic. That's when I felt our connection. It was surprising he would ask a favour so loaded with emotion.

"You won't go," I said.

I'd bought him a plant a year ago, I don't know what kind, it was seventy-five bucks and big, and it was already dead. Down to three of my mother's plants. He turned from me and dropped into his chair. He'd developed an addiction to documentaries on the royals; Will and Kate on TV. I flashed forward to old age: his anger would be impossible if he lost his mind.

"Address is on the fridge," he said. "Key there too."

He knew I would do it. I made myself believe there was vulnerability in his request.

The kitchen never out of place. I opened the fridge: pickles, condiments, jars of curry, processed meat, an entire shelf devoted to eggs. The freezer had a seriously varied selection of frozen pizzas. The cupboard meant for pots and pans had two boxes of red wine. One full, the other, a dribble left. In the sink a glass, its bottom forever stained red.

Last week I dropped by Marwan's when he and his father were chatting. Small talk, back and forth, light but laced with love. I couldn't stand it. I couldn't stand him. I hated myself for it, and it twisted and turned into anger, like everything I felt. It was my father. I blamed growing up under his anger, that it snarled me into a person always on the outside. Marwan grew to embody his father, glad to take on the same shape in the world; I withered, unable to grow in the dark of my past.

In small moments on the subway, or at lunch, dreams, unasked-for, would appear: hanging from a ceiling, a gun and its warm metal in my hand, an easy overdose.

My need to come back here over and over and fulfill these kinds of small requests was a punishment I did not understand … each time hoping he would be a little different, that each time I would gain …

•

I ran home to mope. I'd forgotten to close the curtains and the sun had cooked the living room.

The night in the room with Samir and Rose had fogged my brain. My hand hurt. Marwan was right about Samir. Samir texted me with apologies about that night. I opened and closed my fist. Marwan was right. We shouldn't get involved. Samir's particular violence was foul: I could not ignore it.

I pulled up a clip of Abdul on YouTube. It showed the famous photograph of him at thirteen with chin pubes. The common sullen, muted expression of a teenager. Next, a drawing in a courtroom, Abdul in an orange jumpsuit, the beard filled out, his expression dead. I clicked and clicked.

He'd never given many details to the media. There were document leaks about torture and one news report focused on the way he walked and how enhanced interrogation had shaped his growing body. The montage continued with shots of the blazing sun on Guantanamo and a voiceover: more soldiers had been fined for harming iguanas — a protected species on the Cuban island — than for violence against detainees.

In the video, Abdul's face is flat, steady; impossible to tell if he's holding back. Is he controlling his emotions or have they been taken from him? The entire swing of his youth behind bars.

Even now, in Bombay, I return to these videos. He's taken down his social media, but history remains on YouTube, or on old, long-forgotten web pages. I can't help myself. No matter what backroom I'm in, what chai stall, at any moment, a spill of memory can arrive. I take my Hero Honda to Nariman Point and watch the sea flush in and out, hidden among couples sneaking kisses, and watch videos for an hour or two, dumbly staring into my phone. Inevitably it leads to Natalie, but I don't realize that will come in the moment — I'm fixed on him, replaying our last night together: the dark room, his track suit, the whimpering smell of copper.

It's his coherence that attracts me, how he moved through the world unfettered by his own past, or so I thought. I recognized serenity and contentment. He'd made peace with his own complicated history. I envied him. What he surmounted powered his magnetic pull.

That day in Toronto, I watched his early interviews, when he struggled to talk normally, eyes flickering as he spoke about Guantanamo with no emotion. He said the same things over and over. He didn't try to make his case. He stated facts. His skin pale and his hair grew in patches. He didn't like looking at the camera or into eyes: he didn't like looking.

For the first year after his release, under severe parole restrictions, he stayed in his room, quiet. There were no media appearances. He replaced the jail cell for a room in the apartment in the suburbs living with his lawyer's cousins. They said he was happy but did not speak. He read. He studied. He wanted to become a social worker. After a year of silence there was a burst. He conducted YouTube lectures. The first dozen did not make mention of who he was.

He talked into the camera.

Why a man must SERVE his Wife
2.1K views.

The WOMAN is the link to ALLAH
1.1K views.

Motivation for the REVERT
4.2K views.

While he gave his opinion on Islamic issues directly, his follower count remained small. He took questions and answers in a soft voice. He stuttered awkward, unsure; uncomfortable with his message and delivery.

Then, there's a change. The background fills with green books with Arabic on the spine. His beard, a wild mess previous, becomes refined, shaped. His moustache clipped neatly. He wears a shirt, tie, and a jacket he takes off during the lectures. He speaks at length with a patient demeanour, his eyes full of light. He moves his hands when he speaks. He reminds me of a young boy with his first crush.

Yes, Islam can THRIVE in the West
15K views.

Save your seat in PARADISE
12K views.

Unity creates STRENGTH
19.4K views.

Finally, there is one more shift. He's been out four years. He is confident, grinning, perfectly choosing angles, making small jokes. Charm ooze. His beard cropped closer, turned friendlier, he angles his phone so his brown eyes shine. He's gotten a stylish low-fade haircut. He wears hoodies, T-shirts.

Some videos are lighthearted jokes about Islam but the philosophy is serious. One post is text: *When your parents are ill and Allah is ready to take them, will you have memories full of joy? Wealth isn't about living large. It's about what you hold inside and how you're there for those close to you.*

Another text post: *If you're looking for a wife, ask yourself—are you truly ready to give yourself over? Being the man of the house isn't about glory. It's about dedication, hard work, and sacrifice. She deserves the best of you.*

All beings are EQUAL
80.1K views.

Kindness is reserved for ALL
110.8K views.

LOVE is the path
120K views.

The seriousness remains even if he smiles more.

My ringing phone interrupted my scrolling.

"This is Claire from The Beauty Bar?" Natalie's work. Natalie and two others were assistant managers, and Natalie only liked the daytime one, who did hair on the side. This was her. "You're listed as her emergency contact?" Claire continued. "She hasn't been in, in like two weeks. She booked off a week but hasn't been back. Where is she? It says you're her boyfriend?"

"We live together."

"Whatever, I think she's fired. She has a paycheque here," Claire said.

•

The Beauty Bar was a short drive away. When Natalie told anyone about her job there she followed up by saying it was temporary and she was going back to school for sure.

It was my first time inside. Claire pulled an espresso shot. The energy warped when I stepped in. All the women eyed me while trying to appear nonchalant. I wore light grey Nike sweatpants and a matching hoodie with Roshes, trying to be as basic as possible, knowing I'd be viewed as a vague threat the moment I stepped inside. I wanted to look boring but I probably looked like every bozo who'd hollered at them from a street corner: I was every bozo that hollered at them from a street corner.

Claire, her T-shirt flecked with coffee grounds, blond hair with turquoise streaks that matched her nails, asked in a loud voice if she could help me. I'd only met her recently, when she'd gone out with Natalie and brought her home drop-down drunk at 3:00 a.m. I re-introduced myself and could see her trying to work out the situation in her head. If bad happened to Natalie, I was most likely the reason.

Claire led me outside.

"You really don't know where she is?" she asked. We were in the alleyway behind the salon. The compost bin lid off and on the ground, the sour vegetable smell mixed with hot garbage air. She expertly lit a Parliament with a barbecue lighter and exhaled. My eyes followed the freckles up her white arm; she looked me up and down, not hiding it. "Are you a Muslim?"

This again. Now?

"I don't mean in a judging way," she said.

Claire swung her arm down and kept her eyes on me while she waited for an answer.

"Why?" I asked.

"I don't want to be rude but I think it's easier if you answer the question."

"Yeah, okay," I said.

"Yeah, okay, what?"

"Yeah, okay, fine."

"Don't be like this. Natalie told me you were like this. Are you guys still together?"

"I don't know."

"That's a no usually. Are you Muslim or what?"

"I'm a Muslim, fine. There is no God but Allah and Muhammad is his messenger. Ameen."

"Natalie started wearing a hijab at work," Claire said. A croak escaped my mouth. Disbelief and laughter. The alley shrank. Claire watched me trying to understand. "Like an hour before the shift was over," she continued. "She would go to the bathroom and then come out with it on. I didn't ask her questions, I'm not like that, I'm not rude. Once, it was a customer's birthday and I gave her a glass of champagne and she took it. She took it but she didn't drink it. She left it on the counter. Isn't that weird? I mean — for her. Don't get mad at me for what I say next. There was this dude, this guy. And he came in one day and they talked and I don't know, I don't remember exactly, this was like six months ago. And I think the hijabs started coming on. And he got his nails done every week after that, a clear coating, and his tip was like, the price of the service. Like a sixty-dollar tip for sixty-dollar nails. And he had …"

"What …?"

"He had pamphlets," Claire said.

"What did they say?" I asked.

"I don't know, she put them in her purse right away. But it's not good, babe. Anyone gives you a pamphlet, they're messed in the head." Claire told me to wait, stubbed the smoke, went inside, came back. "Here: he entered a business raffle." She gave me a white business card with a symbol of two birds intertwined. No name, but a number and address. "They would leave together sometimes. It was weird. Not like bad but weird. He was hot, like muscular."

I thanked her and waited for her to leave. She came back with a bottle of water and the paycheque. I could not walk or I would fall.

The simplest answer, that she'd left me for someone else, hadn't even occurred to me. Her in a hijab gave me a headache.

I stumbled to my car.

I reminded myself: drinking was her shadow-self, the darkness she didn't want. The thing that distorted her true personality. The true self of Natalie was the one I loved and the one I wanted to chase. It had to be. I had to split them.

Old ideas powerful in me. What damage drink failed to obliterate, we could conquer together. I could create a world with her that took me out of the smoke of my inner life, the beam of Natalie clearing the path.

I squeezed my eyes shut again and again and tried all the breath exercises I'd learned over my life as a way to calm down. I dialed the number but did not call.

The address. There was an address on the card.

15.

I went to the address. The home was behind a massive sloped lawn, in between similar houses hidden on a downtown street, shaded by centurial trees. Many of the houses were shabby from age, giving off a casual, unkempt air, but the cars in driveways — BMW, Mercedes, Audi — gave hint of the money inside. I was close to the lake.

The grass recently trimmed and bush covered half the front window. Three black BMW 5 Series parked back to back to back. Two houses in the neighbourhood had Sotheby's real estate signs and I googled: three point two million each. How was I going to compete with this dude? I probably couldn't afford a bathroom.

I walked close to the front door not sure what to do. The first Beemer had a flat tire and broken tail light. Two windows on the second floor, surrounded by red brick, were covered by black shade. A brass circle on the front door had the same intertwined bird logo as the business card. The fixtures on the house shone new.

A crow shouted from the tree behind me. There were two on opposite branches. They squawked and broke away. One carried a shiny object in its mouth.

In the backyard was a built-in gas grill, dining furniture, and lawn lights leading to a small pool for fish. Frivolous water near the lake. Always a sign of wealth. I opened the grill. It had never been used.

Pollution made sky light purple and strange and there was low wind.

I tried the back door. Locked. I went to the front, checked under the mat to be sure, then scurried to the backyard again. Behind the grill on the other side of the house was a small garage extension. Neatly arranged tools and lawnmower with an exercise bike and squat rack.

And an unlocked door that led inside.

First, quiet.

Then, maybe, music, a barely heard riff down the stairs.

A heavy wood coffee table in the living room surrounded by two Herman Miller couches I recognized from online window shopping. I googled them: ten thousand each. On the walls were black-and-white photographs of bodies twisted, stretched, curled. Models posing in impossible painful shapes. A stack of magazines on the table with the address and ADMINISTRATIVE OFFICES printed on the label.

I smelled charred meat. The lights off in the kitchen. I went to check. No one. I opened a bottle of Voss water and drank half.

Thuck, thuck, thuck, from upstairs, like fists on punching bag.

I waited.

A rough guitar riff.

The same song repeating.

I took the stairs slow.

Thuck, thuck, thuck.

There were four doors at the top.

Two closed. One room painted entirely white with a white chair, white table, and a circular piece of stainless steel hanging, polished into a mirror. A drain in the corner gurgled.

The room smelled of bleach.

The other open room had a metal grill drilled into the ceiling with a thick chain dangling down and a wet tarp on the ground. A metal chair folded in the corner. There were soaked towels with an empty canister for water on a table with open straps.

Thuck, thuck, thuck: coming from the room with music.

The track repeated.

A moan from the room.

Was that Natalie?

Guitar, moaning, pause, thuck.

The noise of bodies hitting.

Grunt. Exhale. Thuck.

I didn't know what I was doing.

I should have walked out. Thuck.

I opened the door slowly. Thuck.

I didn't want to see.

A man in a black mask and track suit stopped, his arm pulled back, a nightstick in his grip. Another man naked to the waist: a pole slid behind his back to hold his arms up and a chain hanging from the ceiling looped around his body bore all his weight. His torso a splatter of old scabs and fresh wounds. He tried to control his hanging body. It smelled rotten, like roadkill under the sun; warm, fermented meat. He moaned.

Track Suit wore protective glasses. Blood marked the wall. He pulled a curtain that revealed a half-door to a tiny cubby room. Track Suit opened the half-door. Another brown man, crouched in his underwear. Shit and piss sharp and warm on my tongue. The man jumped to the door knocking over two buckets, one water, one his toilet, the brown mud mixed with clear liquid. The chain around his torso snapped him back. He fell into the mess. Track Suit closed the door to a scream.

"What did we tell you before, Hamid?"

I was blocking the entrance.

"It's finished."

He swung the baton again and again against my forearms. I lunged while he wound for another hit and drove my knee into his gut. I fell. We scrambled, scratching each other, and I put my fists up. He had the baton. The hallway tight so I closed space between us and he couldn't swing. I pushed shoulder-first into him but he dodged and I crashed into the wall. I fell onto one knee and covered my head with my arms bracing for the crack of the baton.

He was gone.

Through my blood rush I hadn't heard him run down the stairs. The two men in the room shouted. About to enter the room, I stopped and followed my instinct: ignore.

I ran away through the front door Track Suit had left open.

Night had broken. Cool air. I doubled over gasping and saw the baton on the grass. I scanned the street and Track Suit was in the distance walking south and then turning west.

I took off. My arms screamed. My head. I thought my nose bled but it was snot. I trailed him at a distance. He wasn't running, just walking fast. He didn't look back. He knew I was there. He knew me.

He took a right into a labyrinth of side streets and old buildings.

It was cold, cool.

He turned into narrow streets. The strange purple of night disappeared, replaced by sporadic artificial light. We passed group after group of drunk whites who parted wide swaths for both of us. My breath back to normal. Where was he taking me? We headed closer to the lake and the temperature dropped.

It was quiet. Groups of smokers all we saw. My skin wet I patted myself down in panic. There was no blood. A light fog fallen. I shivered. Where was he taking me?

We were close to each other now. A burst of speed would catch me up.

I could go away, call a taxi, ignore all I'd seen.

No: I wanted to finish it.

Track Suit's strides purposeful.

We went onto a side street and at the very end was a four-story building, faded yellow brick and a blue neon light above the door, spelling in simple font: WELCOME.

The building half-fenced. Track Suit popped in, spoke on the intercom, glanced at me for the first time since he'd left the house, and walked into the building.

Twenty metres away.

I was being pulled into this.

It was loft-style units. Some lights on. Most off. At the back was a larger unit, maybe the largest, but the fence prevented me from going farther.

I waited, then I opened the main door he'd gone through. Through the glass to the foyer it was total dark. In the lobby was a metal number pad and speaker but no directory.

The door buzzed and broke my concentration. The lock clicked open. Stunned, I stared at it, waited too long before I pulled. It locked again.

I waited, not moving, and it buzzed, I pulled, it opened.

The air dry.

Track lights turned on one by one leading me down a hallway. On both walls were photographs.

The collection began simple.

THE LONG HISTORY OF ISLAM IN THE NEW WORLD

THE FIRST MUSLIMS IN CANADA WERE REVERTS: JAMES AND AGNES LOVE, WHO REVERTED IN SCOTLAND AND ARRIVED IN 1851

Barns, winter landscapes, pencil drawings of James and Agnes.

AFGHANS USED CAMELS TO EXPLORE THE AUSTRALIAN INTERIOR AS FAR BACK AS THE 1860s

The photograph was a grainy black-and-white, poorly scanned, a group of men on camels. Faces blurry.

ISLAM WAS INTRODUCED TO AMERICA WITH THE FIRST WAVE OF SLAVES

Ships, Black men, chains, routes across the Atlantic.

ISLAM IS A MULTICULTURAL RELIGION

Drawings of people coloured in different shades. A breakdown of Islam by ethnicity into percentages and country distribution.

I put my ear to double doors. I turned the knob cautious, very slow, praying for no creaks, and glimpsed in.

An auditorium painted white and cream. There were around fifty people in the room, crouched, sitting or kneeling on green carpet, facing Mecca. Total silence. At the front and centre was a single man, seated at the same level as them, cross-legged, with a giant book open on his lap. Four men flanked him at a distance and in the corner I could see the same symbol I'd seen on the card: two birds intertwined with each other, but now there was a sprawl of Arabic underneath.

Abdul sat in the centre. He breathed heavy. He seemed to stop, seemed to look at me, a warm smile slashed across his face.

I shut the door and ran.

16.

I scanned the news the next morning, the morning after, the morning after that. My swollen forearms iced until it was safe for me to go outside. Marwan and Samir texted me non-stop. I called in sick. Drove by the house during the peak of day when there was sun everywhere.

What had I seen, I asked myself, knowing exactly what I'd seen. Those two men hanging like meat.

Under afternoon sun, driving by, not daring to stop, the house was a quiet, almost invisible building, no reason to notice it without knowing what was happening inside.

I was thirty years old and said I'd hated him for most of my life but when my gut shrivelled tight I needed to speak with my father.

The phone rang. He'd be at work. It went to voice mail.

I put my phone down. Those two men in that room hanging like meat. The bucket of shit and piss.

The man in the track suit leading me to Abdul.

Five minutes after I called, my father called back.

"I'm at work," he said. "What is it?"

"Nothing."

"You called me."

"Nothing," I said. "Listen … Nothing. Don't worry about it."

"I get two fifteen-minute breaks a day," he said. "This is one of them."

"Sorry."

"What's wrong? You need money?"

"No. What if … I don't know. I'm in this …"

"You need money?" he asked again.

"No! What if something happened?" I asked. "And I don't know what to do."

"Are you in trouble?"

"I feel like. I don't know. I feel like. I don't know. I should. There might be. Something. For me to do. I saw something. And I don't know that I should have seen something. But I saw something."

"Did you get hit in the head?"

"Just listen. When you see something … you're supposed to say something."

"Do you need to get involved?" my father asked.

"I mean. I don't know. I mean. I saw something —"

"Is it actually your problem?"

"Not right now."

"What does that mean?"

"No. No, it's not."

"Then?"

"Yeah. Okay. Thanks."

"Did you go to your mother's storage yet?"

"No."

"Go today. And don't call me at work unless it's an emergency," my father said and hung up.

And so the evening's memory retreated into colour and shape, jumbled impressions that turned into desire and force of action: not introspection. My father was right. There was nothing for me to do about those men and what I saw being done to them.

I had to always remember: to *do* was to live.

I knew this. It was my life's lesson.

But I could not stop my mind from wandering.

What did Track Suit say? It's finished. The same as the man outside my apartment.

Never mind.

Were they the same man?

Never mind.

It doesn't matter.

I had to earn this wad of money. I had to *do*.

What was important was that Track Suit led me to Abdul, which led me to Natalie. The way to Abdul was through Samir. It was another gift from above.

It was easy to put the thought off and say I didn't know. That I didn't think. Thinking is for the mind. The body cannot hear thought.

I would push directly into action, getting closer to Abdul, which would take me toward Natalie.

I stayed indoors, closed the curtains, and turned my phone off. A/C on high. I'd gone there for Natalie. Let the memory rearrange itself. What did I need from that night? To know where Natalie was, anything else a frill to be discarded. Not useful, not for me.

What did Samir say? We're drivers: we create the world for ourselves.

17.

A plump Tamil, arms like chicken drumsticks, grunted in the direction of a mysterious hallway off his front desk, then flicked a switch that turned on the lights with a loud electric shudder. I followed their path but returned confused. In a gibber of grunts, milk tea dripping from his moustache, he gave me a paper map, circled my mother's storage unit in red ink, drew an X through the circle, pointed his thick finger to where we currently stood, and then dragged the appendage in the exact route I should take. Landing on the storage unit he tapped four times, then looked at me, frustrated I'd distracted him from his day's true task of watching videos on WhatsApp.

"Got it?"

A gigantic prison for discarded memories. I was obligation's cur; I didn't want to be there any longer than I had to. I was thankful Natalie left no clutter in my unit.

Every step echoed. I slid the key into the brass lock and the shutters sucked up to reveal a ten-by-ten storage room of old, old shit. A couch, checkered red fabric, shoved into the corner with plates and cutlery, folded linens, and assorted junk resting on top. A dresser and mirror adjacent, reflected me: I wore an indigo-dye T-shirt from a small shop in Vancouver I'd found online that sourced its material from Japan, notable for its heavy weave and tender drape across my shoulders, and cheap forty-dollar light-wash jeans — I could never get into raw denim, the kind that took half a life to become comfortable, whose fans, typing on Styleforum with one hand, insisted should be put in the freezer to kill germs in lieu of washing with detergent and water — that rhymed with my pair of caramel loafers from Allen Edmonds, which cost — I can reveal the price now — six hundred dollars. Obviously I wore no socks.

Morning was the breeding ground for my vanity and I took my time that day, slowly selecting the day's plain outfit to provide me the insulation I needed before re-entering the world. I'd shaved patiently, lathering cream onto my face with a brush, letting it settle for a few minutes, then carefully stroked the blade against my skin, not going over the same area more than twice. I finished with a fifty-dollar Kiehl's cream swirled into my face after a warm water wash with Cetaphil — not soap — and a spritz of a Bleu de Chanel, which the salesperson promised me smelled like woodsmoke in the middle of a forest in the darkest moment of night, when even the animals were quiet. I was shopping-mall fancy. My hair, thick and mostly straight, medium-length, and easy to maintain, I worked with a Kent comb and then applied a Baxter cream pomade. I did little to it except cut it every three weeks, wash it once a week, and let it relax into its natural shape, a perfectly cresting wave about to break on shore. Then, my jewels: I clasped my Grand Seiko, layered my two chains, and slid my onyx signet ring on; I was ready.

A couch, plates, cutlery, dresser, linens, a whole life. I'd grown up with these objects. Their memories tried to rise, chained to an anchor lost in me.

I picked up a phone that had been stuck to the wall in the kitchen. The first time I tried to *do* for my mother, I was too young and couldn't reach the phone high up on the wall. Frustration: why had it been placed so high? I got on a chair to reach. My mother asking my father over and over if he was going to hit her. Almost a taunt. I didn't exactly know what events calling 911 would unfurl but I knew to call it. My father, the adult sense of danger, grabbing me before I could dial. The memory resurfaced in my neck. The next morning I heard them in their bedroom laughing and I asked how they were. Joking, lovers again, the sun through the window on their puffy faces of no sleep. They were laughing at me for wanting to call 911.

Household nonsense. I came for this? This is what they would leave behind for me when they died.

My assessment of the storage room: worth zero point zero zero dollars in a divorce. Two bucks' worth of gas in expenses for me. The most useful thing in there was a spider on its web. Two caught and wiggling flies awaited him. This is what her life in Canada accumulated to.

No wonder she left.

18.

I hadn't spoken to Marwan since the house. I scanned the news for those two men. My bruises faded.

The memory of that night shaped the way I wanted. Into nothing. I learned this online alongside my breathing practice for anxiety: allow a thought to enter the mind without judgment.

Let it pass.

A thought is imagined — not action. Not real.

The two men hanging like meat.

Let it pass.

Track Suit outside my apartment; Track Suit in the house; Track Suit to Abdul; Abdul to Natalie.

I knew what to say to Marwan. I drove to the store.

He stocked shelves in a white shalwar kameez and Jordans, not saying a word as I tidied around the counter.

A man digging into his teeth with a pick asked about his washing machine repair. A fleck of food flew onto a vacuum cleaner. Marwan was mad at me so he shouted at the man and chased him out, telling him to wait for a phone call. Outside, he swore at us, but a Marwan glare sent him to his car. I cleaned off the food.

"I haven't been in," I said.

"No."

"I'm sorry."

"Sure," Marwan said.

"Have you thought more about setting Abdul up with Samir?" I asked.

"Samir has been coming by every day asking me the same thing. Asking where you are."

"I'll text Samir. Get him off your back."

"What if I say no?"

"You're thinking of it as a favour to me," I said. "It's not. It's for us. Trust me."

"How Samir makes his money is important to me," Marwan said.

"What about what the money is used for? The good it would do at the Resettlement Centre."

"It can't wash who Samir is. What he does."

"What we do," I said.

"We've been over this."

"Natalie is with Abdul," I said. "Natalie. With Abdul. She's joined his little group."

"How did you find out?"

"Her co-worker gave me an address. I guess it was his home address. From there, I went to the centre. The mosque. Whatever he calls it."

"Did you see her there?" Marwan asked.

"No."

"She didn't tell you she was going?"

"You knew?" I asked.

"She'd come to dinner with me — I told you."

"You knew she'd gone there?"

"Only that she was interested," Marwan said.

"She's wearing a hijab!"

"So?"

"Bro: Natalie, my girlfriend, my Catholic, Filipino, drunk-ass girlfriend —"

"That must be a shock," Marwan said. "But it could be good. People in trouble. Abdul is good with that."

"Natalie going to Abdul is good. Abdul is good. But Samir —"

"Please," Marwan said. "Why does it have to be me? If Natalie has gone and is healing —"

"What does Abdul do down there?"

"We read the Qur'an. Talk. He has rooms for boarders seeking intensive treatment."

"What is the treatment?"

"It's spiritual conversation. Natalie was hurting, you know that."

"It's just talking?" I asked.

"Of course. We discuss. We read. The reverts have their curriculum. The born Muslims have a different conversation. And then the resettlement for the Guantanamo detainees is their own program."

"What does he do to them?"

"I don't know. It happens at his home."

"Does Natalie ever go to his home?" I wondered if Natalie was in danger: would she be in one of those rooms?

"No: she's a revert. She stays at the centre with the rest of them."

"You have to help me," I said. I held onto the idea of Natalie in danger. "This is so simple. This is so small. Organize a meeting. Just vouch for me — for us."

"Come to a dinner," Marwan said. "You can meet him there."

"No, bro. I'm not coming to dinner like a fool looking for Natalie."

"You want Natalie back — is that it?"

"I want you to vouch for Samir to Abdul."

"I can't ignore where Samir's money comes from," Marwan said.

"What did you say to me? That we're helping people here with low prices. What's that? That's you ignoring the money, ignoring where this comes from."

"You think General Electric is hurt because we sell stolen kettles?"

"You're making that decision," I said. "You're choosing what to say yes to."

"You trust Samir too much."

"I know we can use him."

"Abdul asked about you," Marwan said.

"Of course he did."

"He remembers you. You met."

"At Club Mirage, yeah. The hand, yeah."

"Don't start with that."

"I don't have what you have," I said.

"Don't start with that."

"What's the biggest difference between us?" I asked. "Even when you lost your hand you didn't flinch. The ground beneath you is stable. Every night you go home to your parents, man, you're thirty and you go home to that love. And what are they doing? They're trying to find you a wife right now so you never have to be out of love. That's why you don't need this."

"I'm lucky," Marwan said. "I know that. It doesn't mean you don't have family. Have you spoken to your mother lately?"

"What?"

"You have to try. You have to talk with them. I know your father is difficult, but you have to try."

"Half the time you don't want me to —"

"I want you to be safe but it's important you keep trying," Marwan said.

"It's like talking into a black hole. That's what's beneath me. A gaping hole. That's why I want more; it's not more, I don't want more, I want something, something at all. You don't get it. Everywhere you feel your parents' presence. That stability. If you fall, you don't fall far. It's not like that for me."

"So what do you think? That by doing this you get fixed?"

"Nothing is going to get fixed," I said. "There's nothing fixable."

"Just come to a dinner," Marwan said. "Abdul will make you feel part of something. That's what he brings. It's not easy. People search their whole lives. If Natalie is there … We can just be still, Hamid. It's not bad to be still. Your whole life isn't your father."

Marwan shifted in his seat. Another man came in through the doors and asked about the vacuums, speakers, the microwaves, currency rates, calling cards, about everything we sold, and left without buying anything.

"Forget all that," I said. "He needs money to get the Rehabilitation Centre going."

"You know what it means when someone breaks up with you?"

"What?" I said.

"It means don't follow them."

"You know what Natalie means to me."

"You want Natalie? Or Abdul?"

"Right now they're both the same thing."

"What if I say no?"

"You been saying no."

We sat for ten minutes, an hour, four hours, customers in and out, complaining, buying, I organized our inventory and prepared to go over our books with Bilal. I filled Marwan in on the steps and he was quiet. He maintained eye contact whenever I spoke but wouldn't reply.

Our shop faced west and we watched the sun slink down. A bump of customers at 7:00 p.m. and by 9:00 p.m. the sun gone and black fallen outside. We sent the cousins home. We counted the till and shut off the lights, left, locked the door. Marwan turned to me, on the verge of speaking, his face shrouded with sadness and resignation, but also always hope.

"Don't come crying to me if this gets messy," Marwan said.

"Who else am I going to cry to?"

We hugged, my face above his shoulder, his musk transferring some of his hope, and walked separately to our cars.

19.

The Arab booked a meeting in the Shangri-La right downtown. I drove too fast and was early. In the lot I eyeballed the Beemers; they way exceeded my bank account, sure. But I'd never gone for a purchase that outlandish. And I was curious. With a small item, like a two-hundred-dollar incense holder from SSENSE, the mild happiness it produced lasted a week or two before dissolving, but could reappear when light hit the brass object in a new way. I drooled at the eighty-thousand-dollar car — how long could that happiness last?

Things moved fast. A few nights ago, Marwan broached the subject with Abdul. We thought it might take convincing but we received an answer in a day. The next day Abdul met the Arab for dinner. They agreed to work together. It was simple. There was money to be made. The day after that, the ArabTarzan Instagram page directed its following to a

GoFundMe (specifically for the former Guantanamo detainees' living expenses) and to a separate web page Bilal had organized with FAQs, pictures, and where organizations could privately donate and inquire. That day, the Arab made good on his first promise and arranged for us to all meet with government bureaucrats at the Shangri-La to convince them to reach deeper into their wallets. Next week we'd begin introducing Abdul to the Arab's extended circle.

I tried to make Marwan come to the meeting with the bureaucrats but he refused. But it was Friday so he'd be at dinner afterward. I was hot, sweating, the sun woke up this morning expressly to roast me. Nervous, like I was about to deliver a book report in school.

I looked good: a navy Zegna suit with tasteful chalk stripes and brown Allen Edmonds wingtips. Both on a credit card I was no longer keeping track of. I winced at the continental clash, but the Italian suit and English shoes worked together, so I decided it was not a faux pas.

I wore an excellent Rolex Oysterdate replica. It was an older style, so the watch face was smaller and Natalie liked to wear it. I didn't let her often because she didn't know it was fake. I told her my father gave it to me. She definitely did not believe that. One of the things I loved about her: she allowed me delusions.

Samir called last night with final details for our approach to the meeting. As important members of the Muslim community we were taking an interest in supporting Abdul through his charity. We were donating our own money but also encouraging others and massaging our connections.

Abdul existed in an odd virtual space with thousands of followers online but few on-the-ground connections with people that you needed to make projects go: administrators and bureaucrats at corporations and government agencies. This was what the Arab dangled in front of him. At the Shangri-La, we were to show the government workers that we moved in lockstep and that Abdul was vetted.

That day's ask: we needed more money from the federal government to continue the program for certain approved former detainees — who, we stressed, had 100 percent been wrongfully scooped up — to enter our resettlement program that eventually allowed them to live normal lives. Therapy, education, that kind of thing. Abdul had already paid the government for secondary background checks and administrative fees. Then there was all the staff. Money was urgent: the first two detainees were already in Canada. After a few months, we'd establish a scholarship for the former detainees in the Arab's name; next year, in mine.

The resettlement program easily created publicity. I watched news clips of guests trying to talk around a basic elemental fear: brown men. It wasn't whether they were innocent when picked up in Pakistan, or Yemen, if they even could be innocent in those countries. It was, what did ten years in Guantanamo do to you?

At the meeting I was to sit, talk about the Canada Electronics business empire if needed, and nod my head about how much the community supported Abdul.

The government was apprehensive, but greedy: Abdul's program had the potential to be a massive success, and for us, even a "small" government investment would number in the millions. The Arab just had to massage these low-level government bureaucrats enough to convince them Abdul was a reasonable person to work with and pave the way for contact with their superiors.

Then, the Arab could use Abdul in the Muslim community for a more meaningful credibility, away from internet frivolity, the charity work a springboard to deeper government contacts. That, I believe, was his end goal. His money from his parents in India had done a lot for him in the country, and he had built an admirable network of low-level goons, but he was an immigrant lacking the natural connections of the West-born. Money was one hurdle, reputation the next.

The resettlement plan was a great idea even if impossible. How do you undo disaster? The two fools already in the country were lined up for us to throw education, therapy, and money at. Both had spent a decade alongside Abdul in Guantanamo Bay. I watched documentaries about their treatment, read news reports; neither brought me closer to understanding what had been done to them and what they'd be like.

In the lobby I watched a digital wall clock change to 1:00 p.m. My leg rattled off nerves up and down bouncing.

Doors opened and Samir led the way in an ugly brown suit, dressed like a 1980s couch. Behind him was the Arab in a dark green thobe, his powerful cologne stanking up the lobby. He readjusted his carefully placed red keffiyeh and his leather slippers clapped his soles like a private audience following him. Two brown guys in black suits, Abdul's accountants, came in after, with two solemn white men I never heard speak, who waited outside the meeting space.

Finally, Abdul. He glid through the lobby, his head on a pivot, absorbing detail. He stopped at a plant and lifted the palm-sized green leaf, crooking his head to the side while taking it in. He wore black trousers faded from being washed in hot water and a black Nehru jacket. Ready for a newspaper photoshoot. A woman in a cream hijab, white or Lebanese (don't call them brown), continuously took photos of him on an iPhone. The worn pants and cliché of the Nehru jacket worked to create softness. A real gold Rolex on his wrist.

I shot up. My body hurt as he approached. He was familiar — I'd met him, of course, but now it was intense, primitive. We shook. His hands hot and callused.

"I feel like we know each other," he said.

Warm-milk voice. He followed Samir into the meeting room. His accent had a foreign lilt I hadn't noticed in the videos. They said he picked up bits of Saudi, Pakistani, a mix of others from the multicultural detainees.

In the room we took five minutes to make sure everyone shook hands. Abdul across the table: brown eyes, a boyish smile, and hair pushed back in all its thickness. Lowering himself into a seat, his movements were stiff and his body stuttered, but when he checked his watch he was graceful, smooth; elegance where I didn't expect. He was handsome and I'm happy to say that yes, the Mexican was correct, we did look alike. He let people talk, watched, spoke after thought. A man used to being alone.

The bureaucrats treated him with awkward reverence. They were not exactly sure how to engage. The question of his innocence filled the space. Had he shot a soldier? And if he had, was that okay? Had he been, at fourteen, a child soldier or a man? What was a coerced confession worth?

Abdul knew how to play the tension. He spoke quiet but was not soft-spoken, forcing them to lean in. Our eyes connected in allegiance.

Samir began a PowerPoint Bilal had created to convince the bureaucrats we were worthy of long-term financing. It started with depictions of the Arab's legal businesses and then an assessment of the centre's potential value. My thoughts toggled between choking Abdul to death and him entering Natalie.

I disassociated, unable to get the thought of Natalie in a hijab out of my head. Had she been forced into it? Was he doing it to her? I knew no coerced hijabis, but the thoughts were difficult to vanish. At some point I spoke about our business and got affirmative nods in response. I loved bullshit. Abdul turned his eyes to me as I finished. I saw him and Natalie intertwined, their hands on each other's throats. An odd, distant intimacy. I'd seen him so many times on the news over the last decade.

My temper. I couldn't hold it. I was going to speak. My forearms in pain. Body remembrance. I needed to force a confrontation. The fighting, Natalie, Track Suit, the chase, all struggling to come to the front, demanding I act. I focused on my reorganization of events and forced my body in line with my mind.

I excused myself. I went to the bathroom to hide. It was massive, with eight sinks, and shining with silver- and gold-coloured fixtures. Mirrors in every direction and eight bone-white urinals lined up against the back wall, side by side, and I was in front of one when one of Abdul's men came in. His skin was a thick white, like it had been painted on. He stood at the stall right next to me.

"As-salaam alaykum, brother," I said. "It was good for you to come."

"Anything for Abdul."

"Yes … anything for Abdul."

Was this Track Suit? Of course not. Abdul and Natalie, gold skin, spinning together, spit and tongues, choking each other. Samir and Bilal; Rose and her hip bones, peppermint breath. My throat constricted. Forget it; the money. My body and mind would not sync. The goon zipped up and left without washing his hands.

Samir on his last slide. What a stupid suit. It was the worst brown, almost yellow. A government bureaucrat cleared his throat to speak.

"There's questions about how exactly, under what umbrella, this would be run, and how would the donations be ordered and organized."

This was the same question left out in my discussions with Samir. The Arab and Abdul were coming together in a charitable venture, and eventually it would not simply be the Arab facilitating donations. Would there be a more forceful joining of organizations, funds, legal paperwork? Was it on purpose? Did the Arab and Samir have an ulterior goal and had they hoped to squeeze the question by?

Samir leaned forward in his seat ready to answer. I played dumb and had a sliver of a second to show off. "We plan on organizing as a non-profit." I said. "With all of us under the same umbrella. Incorporate it that way. Great for taxes."

I wasn't supposed to offer ideas today. I smiled stupid. The bureaucrats mumbled in agreement. Samir scowled at my interference.

I never learned what Samir would have answered — maybe it wouldn't have been important, maybe it wouldn't have had an effect on what happened next. A non-profit would be the best way for the Arab to entrench himself to Abdul, along with a veneer of legality. A non-profit in the Arab's name, alongside mine, would give us an alternative enterprise through which he could launder his money without involving our store. In my arrogance, I tried to shield Canada Electronics and Marwan.

As the glad-handing began my importance puffed up. This power transfer was genuine. The bureaucrats shook my hand and thanked me for coming. I thanked Abdul for listening, my chin tilted. Promises whispered and money heavy in the room.

I was here. Integral to an event that would affect the world.

•

The upper floors of Abdul's building had been used in the '90s by a porn consortium before being bought by a cluster of Chinese families when the British handed over Hong Kong. It was a bizarre spot for a family but they'd purchased them sight unseen, fearful of what the mainland would do and how soon. They needed an escape. Two families remained on the topmost floor, refusing to leave, and halting the renovation process. Abdul wouldn't strong-arm them out. They had their gardens and routines and one of them ran a small restaurant nearby.

Samir halted outside. He turned to me.

"I don't like what you did there."

"You hadn't thought of a non-profit?"

"That's not what I said. We'd agreed on what your role would be."

"It was a good idea," I said. "No one had to take it."

"Don't get smart."

I let him have his space. Just a little outburst.

We went through a side entrance that opened directly into the hall. Three plastic tables had been pulled end to end in the middle of the cavernous room I had stumbled on the week before. It was lit carefully with lamps, creating valleys and peaks of shadow. The tables were on four rugs, each with a different bird design sewn into it.

In one corner a man on a ladder fixed a series of clocks that told different times: LONDON, BARCELONA, ISTANBUL, KANDAHAR, MUMBAI, BEIJING, SEOUL. The kitchen doors swung open with new sounds and smells whenever a person came out. Abdul at the head of the table and Marwan next to him. Marwan spoke and gestured with his hand, Abdul giving him attention fully as if all he'd ever done was listen.

That was his magnetism. There was a discreet confidence that made people want to talk and talk and talk. Receiving his attention was a gift.

The rest of us took our seats. Two women came out with a tray of yellow saffron rice with raisins speckled through and shredded carrots, two gigantic mutton bones in the middle, the remaining dish peppered with chunks of meat. Brown kebabs with char marks loaded onto a tray in a pyramid, the spiced beef next to orange pieces of tandoori chicken, black in spots from the oven, and served with chopped lettuce, fragrant purple onions with a fresh hot bite to them, and fat wedges of salted tomatoes overflowing in their juice. Two of Abdul's men joined and the rest went to a corner where a smaller table was set up. Samir had volunteered his cousins for the cooking, and one brought out a basket of naan, its crust a toasted brown hue, too hot to touch. I tore into one anyway, its inside downy, right from the oven, the bread crisp and crumbly. I took a heaping of the intense gold-coloured channa, my spoonful loaded with onion, garlic, and coriander garnish, and as the thick curry settled on to my plate, the oil moved away, leaving a window-pane surface on my dish.

Samir saw something he didn't like. His face contorted and shifted with nerves. He wouldn't look at me. Marwan trailed off while he spoke, blinked a few times, and then continued, sorry when he met my eyes.

The women sat down after serving us. A plate of chicken slid to my left; a dark green sleeve that led to a familiar wrist, then thin wrinkled fingers; familiar rings, black onyx, the sleeve pulled up, a wrist adorned with a gold bracelet, a gift, a memory come loose.

Her back to me. I could never see her face and I'd know. I lived our relationship dozens of times right then. I couldn't take more than a shallow-short breath. I looked to Marwan because I couldn't look at her. I tried to take more breaths, my body loosened, I was made of balloons and every limb floated away, then it tightened, a python around my neck. Or is it the opposite, that I'm anchored down, my body suddenly full of gravity, not able to move in any direction I beg it to …

I reached for a glass of water but my fingers wouldn't open and I had to focus all my attention until they responded … the cool water touched my lips and that was enough relief, enough relief …

"Hamid, you should spend the night," Abdul said.

The naan burned my fingertips. Some woman spooned a chunk of paneer in a goopy spinach curry onto my plate. I hated the flat, mild smell of cooked spinach.

"Excuse me?"

"We have facilities for boarders. Those taking study sessions."

The room: the men hung under hot white light. Blood, bile, shit and piss and sweat. Was Natalie in danger? I shook the memory away.

"That would be a good idea for me," I said.

"It's good to see what you're investing in."

"How many people stay here?"

"Ten at the moment."

The cloth curled around Natalie's head cut off any sharp angles. Her moon face. I saw her from the side, a cheek glimpsed before she turned her head and directed the other staff. Her covering was floral, made of silk, and caught light. Almost like an Hermès scarf. When she went to the kitchen I regained my breath. Marwan quiet. Samir wouldn't dig into his food. The Arab had no idea who she was and I was thankful. She came out with a plate and sat at the table for the staff with four other women.

"I will one day," I said.

"Stay tonight. Why not?"

"Why not."

I shoved lettuce into my mouth, then onion. The tomato mealy. Abdul turned to Marwan. Samir picked his nose, pulled out more than expected, stuck it under the table. He'd taken off his suit jacket and rolled up his sleeves. The women at the table gathered their plates and left for the kitchen. With the double doors open I smelled my favourite scent: rice, cream, and sugar with toasted pistachios. Kheer. They brought out a selection of bowls, hot and chilled, and the sweet smell wiped out the pungent odour of curry and its spices.

"Hamid, can I be blunt?" Abdul asked.

"Yes."

"Did you pray today?"

"Yes."

"Do you pray five times a day?"

Samir and the Arab ogled me. Abdul looked at me with spotlight intensity.

"In my head."

A momentary silence. Samir peeked at Abdul. Marwan slurped the kheer. Abdul laughed, "Good. Good."

Natalie brought a tray for empty bowls and the other women carried four pots of tea. Next to me, one of the clumsy workers tried to pass a half-empty bowl of kheer to Natalie, and crossing over my legs, spilled the white liquid over my lap. I braced, expecting pain, but he had a chilled portion. The liquid gathered in the divot between my thighs.

Abdul said, "Oh," then, "Natalie, help the brother out."

I gathered napkins from the table and brushed off the concern. "It's okay," I said, "not a big deal," I said, ready to murder the man. The night at the house came forward. I had to get away. Calm myself.

I asked Natalie, "Can you show me where the bathroom is?" She nodded. I followed her down a hallway. She turned to me. I reached for her.

"Take that off," I said and grabbed her covering.

"Don't touch me like that." She slapped my hand away.

"Baby."

"Why are you here?" she asked. "Don't get involved."

"Why are you here? Are you safe?"

"This is something for me," she said. "Where I can get better. Why are you here? Don't get involved."

"Come home."

"I am home. This is good for me."

"Are you safe?"

"Of course I'm safe," she said. "Are you listening?"

"Come home," I said.

"I can get better here. Please. I've found something here. It isn't right for you to get involved."

"You can get better with me."

"This isn't about you," she said. "Don't try to understand what this is about."

"What are you talking about?"

"And now —"

"Nat—"

"I'm working toward something ... I heard something. I told you. I told you that I couldn't hear. Now, I've heard something."

"I love you," I said.

"I love you too."

"Will you come back home?"

"No. Not now. Don't get involved."

"Who brought you here?"

"I did," she said. "I brought myself here. Please understand that."

She led me to the bathroom entrance and left. I saw in the bathroom's stainless-steel mirror the white mess had ruined the suit. I stared at the stain and didn't know how to proceed without anger. By the time I returned, the table was clear. Natalie gone. Samir, the Arab, and others talking over tea. Abdul, for a second, alone. I saw someone approach. I rushed toward him and before I spoke, he took me by the elbow and walked me to the kitchen. I was one of the goats for Abraham's slaughter.

"I'm sorry about your suit," Abdul said. "Here, drink." He passed a Styrofoam cup with tea. "You're such a valuable partner for us. And a bachelor! I thought you would have been married. It's easy for Marwan and I, so blessed by God. It's so easy for him and I to remember gratefulness in our lives." He laughed. We went outside through back doors. The sullen moon. "Sit, sit." He pointed to upturned milk crates.

"Do you smoke?" Abdul asked. "I can't stop. What do you think a cigarette is? Does it have any meaning? Every time I have one, I hate myself. I'm weak. No willpower. Or it's good that I have one; it allows me to do everything else. Like a pressure-release system. Are you okay? Was the food good? Can I tell you something? Marwan told me all about you — unfair, I know. He told me everything. Like a best friend would. He told me about your parents. I'm sorry. Can I tell you my story? It's silly, I know, but it helps organize it. The doctors say it helps. Gives order, meaning comes from the narrative. It's one thing to tell it to myself, but to a new face … it's irresistible. Will you listen? It may help you."

He blew smoke into the air. Then he said:

20.

The memories of the first time I went home from Canada to Afghanistan are spare. I remember the great squabble of my family — two older brothers, two younger, three older sisters, and one brand-new baby. It was my seventh winter, and I'd been surprised by the great gusts of wind. Like everyone in the West, I expected Afghanistan to be a landscape of desert heat. It was cold, colder than I'd ever been, and the wind fierce, always threatening to lift you up and away into the mountainside. And the noise! A pressure from all sides as if it was constantly squeezing. Perhaps that's a memory trick; I had grown up in a quiet suburban cul-de-sac, a tree-lined street with mid-century bungalows on either side. There was no noise there. Almost no one raised their voice, even. Kandahar was the opposite, my Western life inside out.

While I remember, few precise details, the feeling of those moments holds strong in me; embers that provide the foundation of my life. It was mostly commotion, family running in and out of a great big house, with white walls and a courtyard in the middle where we gathered, a small fire surrounded by lush grass and dogs scattered around.

There was a great stream of people that visited my father, who brought with them long ramshackle conversations. Countless men, each of whom my father described as his best friend. He received visitors like a king — I didn't know, then, the shackles that he felt bound him to our homeland. I learned later that the explicit purpose of that trip (this was before the Taliban) was to set up a free workshop that taught college-aged men (and women!) basic computer skills.

These were skills that allowed them to open up small shops for small repairs: everything those days was minute, conceived in the quietest possible terms. Nothing grand, but as the proliferation of computers became obvious, it was an easy avenue for a merchant to establish a stable business.

Each evening, my father took five men and three women to a corner of the backyard and taught them the building blocks of computers. Not only how the hardware was made, but rudimentary IT training. The students had been recommended in the neighbourhood for having a natural aptitude for mechanics, and my father was proud to contribute to their education.

A few of the students had larger ambition to move to the West. Afghanistan was in a perpetual rumble and the younger ones wanted to settle somewhere stable. An education in computers was a wise way to bolster a visa application and before long they were using a corner-shop photocopier to create certificates of completion that my father would sign for their application packages. Beyond this, my father was helpful in the community, either lecturing on the need for a robust Muslim presence in the West to continue, helping with others' book-keeping, or continuing to simply fill out forms. There was no agitation in those days.

Our family had been in Canada since 1979, a big year for Muslims worldwide: the Grand Masjid siege in Mecca, the beginning of the Soviet invasion into Afghanistan, Bhutto's overthrow in Pakistan, and, of course, the revolution in Iran. We had been firmly established, but the first sign the root was not taking in our family would appear the year I turned seven. My sister, against my mother's wishes, and at my father's demand, had been born in Afghanistan, in Kandahar, on that trip. It reversed the westward migration they had started decades ago but it brought a permanent smile on my father's face. She still lives there. It gave permission for my father's and my older brothers' trips to become longer and longer; that was my first, and it was only a month long. After that, it was two months minimum, the whole summer, and then at fourteen, my famous year, I had been there a year.

Those first years there is nothing to remember really, but sights and sounds impressed themselves on me unbidden. It's common for others to ask me for insights from that period, but truthfully, beyond vague shapes and colours, I have no idea of what it might have been like. There is no singular overwhelming emotion.

Now, I know there are family photo books that I can look through and create stories from, and I remember my father's stories of our family's great history. After a late dinner, he liked to sit outside and as the children ambled towards him — it was the only time he was free, calm, about half an hour every day — he would begin great tales of heroes from his family line.

The memory is a flat, hard surface, purely decorative — beautiful. All my life I have felt that discovering a hidden code in those early years would answer everything ...

My father was relentless. Now I can see he was dangerous — he had a ravenous ambition that could not be extinguished. Actually, it was when he came to Canada that he seriously studied history. The folk stories of his childhood transformed into an education in post-colonialism. In the West, with institutional clarity, he learned about The Great Game and that borders of countries were drawn with an arbitrary hand, an aimless scrawl intended to protect Western interests, not Afghan. He became newly motivated by the hidden Islam in the Americas: Ayba Suleiman Diallo, Omar ibn Said, the plentiful white reverts, Malcolm X. He spoke to prisoners to understand their jailhouse-justice notion of Islam, and if you were a Mexican, Chinese, or any kind of unexpected Muslim he would listen to you for hours. This flowering of knowledge turned into anguish. He felt helpless. He needed to devote himself to a larger philosophical idea, but knew he had to choose, West or East.

His personal studies did not, at first, affect the reason he'd come to the West: to make money. Many people repeat the myth that we were poor, but it's not true. During my first years I grew up guided by a gilded hand.

My father ran one of the first mobile IT businesses in the city. It was aimed specifically at small offices, private accounting firms and the like. Throughout the 1980s he drove the maroon family minivan across the city a thousand times. By the time I was born, he had a fleet of three cars, and drove none of them; by the time I was seven, we had been walking backward into low income, as he had been sending most of his money back to Afghanistan to support the Mujahideen in their fight against Soviet forces. As it was against the Russians, there was no restriction on money flow.

The persistent American rumour was that somewhere between 1988 and 1990, when I was around two years old, he had been in Afghanistan, actively fighting. I have no memory of the time, of course, and I only heard this during my own incarceration, when my interrogators were trying to concoct a long family history of rebellion. No one in the family ever spoke of it. They showed me the stamps in his passport. What skills could he offer? My father as a fighter was unfathomable; my earliest memory of him is braiding my sisters' hair. It's easy to realize now that there was a messy rage in him waiting to be unleashed.

The interrogators never believed me. There had been business dealings with the Deobandis, Muslims who led insurgencies against the Soviets. Mawlawi Mohammad Yunus Khalis, Mohammad Nabi Mohammadi, Jalaluddin Haqqani were names found in my father's possessions, on account balance sheets. Had he worked with them? Had he sold them IT help?

The first time I professed ignorance, I was being held in solitary confinement in Afghanistan. They ordered me to stand and wrapped a towel around my neck, my hands still shackled to my legs. My head was slammed against a wall. I fell; I was slapped. It was nothing spectacular. The second time was cramped confinement; the dog box. I was put in a wooden box too small to even sit up in and left alone, curled in the fetal position. That's responsible for my shoulder.

When I came back to Canada, I had to learn the history of my invisible decade in prison. I was astonished to learn that Guantanamo had been well reported on, that it stayed in the news cycle, that the newscasters reported the small details like which musicians were used in the non-stop listening sessions.

It was confusing for me that so many people could be against the prison and yet nothing be done.

Really, what the interrogators never believed, was that my father was entirely focused on making money in the late '80s. By the time he opened the school in my seventh year, he was impatient to contribute to Afghan life. Quickly, with enormous community support, my father transformed the workshop into a school with sixty students. Fifteen he had managed to directly help obtain Canadian and Australian visas. Their paltry remittances were a fortune.

He'd moved into a one-story building, the exterior and interior painted in a variety of cream colours, abruptly changing when one can ran out. The wind whistled through the corridors and there were three classrooms with thirty students that operated simultaneously. My father thought that this was the only way Islam would survive into the future. Just as the printing press allowed the Qur'an to spread, so too could computer code. He was right, in a way. ISIS and the rest would be impossible without computers. That he foresaw this still fills me with childhood awe.

My strongest memory comes from my childhood in Kandahar: my father holding my hand as we walked through the airy compound, the earthy smell of his body odour mixed with the perfume of the afternoon air, the combustion of cars outside the gates, and the pride erupting from him as he spoke about the many rooms in the compound. I was getting large then, but he picked me up when we reached the end of the path and kissed me on the cheek, the feeling warm and moist, telling me that I have the temperament of a teacher, that I would be a great one.

Most of the work was done out of photocopied American textbooks, and the students took turns hovering around the four working computers. As a bonus, two broken computers existed for them to fiddle with. This must be my father's happiest time. The only time I can remember a certain quality of effortlessness in a life of undefined struggle.

In one year, it was finished. In 1994, a country defined by war was struggling to adapt to peacetime. Crime rates in south Kandahar were rising and we welcomed the Taliban's stability. By 1996, when I was nine, the school was operating as a madrassa. Each summer I studied in those quiet rooms, trying to mix the jumble of Arabic, English, and Pashto in my head into something I understood. My father attempted to migrate the computer school into smaller workshops in our backyard, but one night, after a night of screams, my mother wailing on the phone, and a permanent limp now induced in my father, that stopped.

In Cuba, it was the nights the heat broke when I was finally able to consider my situation. Otherwise I was mired in the day-to-day of survival, trying to make it from one moment to the next. That decade I saw my face only three or four times, always in a warped stainless-steel reflection. I could have been anyone. Yet, I never complained. I was quiet.

I was always a quiet boy. Eight siblings! I was almost an afterthought, like an errant object you place in the cupboard and are pleasantly surprised to find months later. That was fine. Growing up in Canada, my two eldest brothers were under considerable pressure, as the whole house was always filled with unarticulated expectation for them.

When I was ten, my brothers disappeared from Canada. This is a contentious issue, I know, but truly: they vanished from my life. I heard stories of their whereabouts, but nothing that would hold up in court. They didn't say goodbye — I woke up one morning and the room we shared was empty. It was January, a new year, during the cold Canadian winter. My memory of them quickly became a hard surface that even now I cannot break through. We played soccer in the field behind our house, I know that; I remember their grim faces, quiet at the dinner table, mouths like cuts on skin. When I was captured, the interrogators told me my brothers had died but I couldn't verify that until I was out.

In the cell next to mine was a boy my age. I'll spare you his name — I try to forget the names, I don't want to bring that with me. He's the only one I've met who loved soccer as much as my brothers. At night, when some of us could not sleep, he would recite his favourite soccer matches from start to finish, like a radio play. He knew everything: the advertisements on outfits, the starting lineups, when a substitute was inserted, the different names for the type of dribble moves, the precise time of scores. One of the guards said, "Impossible memory, you must be making it up." But who cared? Nothing was reality — anything outside was possible, and the way this boy smuggled in this exterior world for us was invaluable.

I loved Canada. When I turned eleven, my grandparents moved in with us, and regular international phone fights commenced. Eventually, I realized the fighting was about me. As I said, my visits had been two months in length, but my father was pressuring to extend them. He spent ten months of the year in Kandahar. Despite my father's practical computer work, his insides were rotten with idealism. He thought a future could be made in Afghanistan and wanted desperately for the family to be reunited there as proud members of the community, rather than spread around the globe. We had to set an example. It's true, there, I had my mother, sisters, but my father was always busy; my brothers were not there. In Canada, I had the two middle brothers — beyond excellent students, so they were spared — and my grandparents, who rarely spoke with me but fed me and hugged me before bed each night.

The reports came later, much later, that my eldest brothers were in those training camps, but my grandparents must have known, if it was true. The fights lasted all night as they refused to give me up to my father to bring back "home." Going backward to Afghanistan made no sense in my grandparents' eyes — my mother's parents — who had been enjoying their twilight years in docile Canada. I was young, I missed my father, but those summers in Afghanistan, at the core of it, were boring. I read the Qur'an with my tutor, practised Pashto, and was given free rein to wander the city before nightfall. Without language, without school friends, what kind of person was I? The freedom was daunting; an empty promise. I wanted to stay home, and even if I could not articulate it, as I approached my thirteenth birthday, I felt like I had to orchestrate it.

That swing year from twelve to thirteen was not remarkable; I made a friend in class, a Chinese boy named Alex. Not that I hadn't had friends previous, but this was the first time I had feelings to confess, dreams to worry about. To make me feel better he said he might be sent back to China and perhaps we could meet up.

I turned thirteen in 2000. My transition to Afghanistan would be out of my grandparents' hands. A Canadian passport was meant to ensure my safety — if Afghanistan made good on its promise to crumble, I could come back to Canada. I was full of panic: at school, I would gaze out the window, my eyes focused on the trees dotting the schoolyard. I had a small, stupid plan, full of a child's urgency and confidence.

At the far end of my schoolyard in Canada was a portable classroom. Essentially a trailer mimicking a school setting with chairs and a chalkboard. Made of plastics, it had been installed by the school board to deal with the neighbourhood's rising population; it was cheap, but the hidden assumption was that as the schoolchildren were largely from the Global South, it was still an outstanding accommodation for us. This was the moment in which I recognize myself most as my father's son.

In our basement, we had bottles of lighter fluid for the barbecue. The entry to the portable was simple as they left the door unlocked. My plan was simpler: I squirted the liquid onto the teacher's desk and on a pile of papers.

The idea arrived fully formed as I watched a crow through the classroom window hopping across the open field of the schoolyard. Children saw him and chased. For some reason, the crow could not fly, but amazingly, in its mouth, was an even smaller bird, a swallow — alive! The crow had to make a decision. It dropped the swallow and jumped into thick bushes.

Fire came as an idea, and at the time I thought it was to keep me from Afghanistan, but now I recognize its aimless, malicious impulse. In Cuba, on cold nights, I wondered if I was in debt to this sin. Once the idea came, it became impossible to ignore, unable for me to contend with unless I expressed it. All the years since, I've never once felt such decisive power. Of course, the initial inclination is that it was Shaytan's evil, but I think the opposite, that I had misheard a message from Allah.

I used a barbecue lighter and watched flames run across pieces of paper. I turned and ran too, mimicking the flame's quick strides. In my mind's eye the flames rose like a crown. My thinking was childlike in its stupidity, inelegant and clumsy. I thought the portable would burn, that it was a minor crime, that the petty trouble I got in would prevent me somehow from leaving the country. Of course, I didn't properly understand the gravity of arson, of property, of violence. I waited for the news that night and in the morning before school. My grandmother slid an omelette into my plate and I ate it greedily, fantasizing that it would be my last meal.

The portable did not burn. The papers burnt, the desk scorched, but the fire did not catch. The portable was made of non-flammable material. I heard this second-hand — we weren't allowed near the unit and no one questioned me. Only the older boys came under suspicion, but the trail of evidence was so sparse, the act so nonsensical, a total failure, that I don't know how seriously it was pursued.

I sat at my desk, watching those same trees while sadness overtook me. I thought of my father, his earthy musk, and the way he held my hand. It would be okay. I tried to reassure myself. It was meant.

A year before 9/11 and two years before my arrest, I landed in Kabul International. At the Canadian airport, my grandparents were solemn. The first flight attendant I saw had dazzling blue eyes, the second, a man, two caramel pools. He was the one that knelt next to me after takeoff, telling me it would be fine.

I have never seen Kabul except to enter and exit. My father said it was not really our country, that Kandahar, and the Pakistani province below, was the dominion of Pathans. This was the cradle he was returning me to.

I arrived in the evening to a new stiffness in the air. The only noise from merchants. There was little traffic, many shops had been shut, and the friendly chaos that reigned had retreated.

My responsibilities were minor. I spent my time at the madrassa, struggling to follow along the advanced Arabic of my peers, focused on improving my language skills while not embarrassing my family. My Pashto was coming back rapidly, like a seed finally sprouting; yet I still cannot read or write it. I never stopped dreaming in English, even all those years away.

In my dreams, my father speaks English to me. Once, he came to me as a rat, running around in circles on the patch of dirt just outside my Guantanamo cage. He had been crying.

I asked him, "What are you doing?"

He stopped his circles and said, "I hid my treasure here, and I don't know if it has been found."

I needed to know more. I asked, "Why are you a rat, now?"

He replied, "In heaven, he who thinks only of treasure will have the face of a remorseful rat. Look, and learn. Leave your treasure. Look, and learn. Leave your treasure."

The year was uneventful, truly. I was inserted into a gushing stream of activity where all roles had been preassigned. Despite the interrogator's beliefs, I never saw my brothers, even though they were there, somewhere, in the country; I saw my father in passing, my mother and sisters were often at home, but we kept a large house, full of visitors and guests related to my father's work, and they were often preparing for it. He worked long hours, gone at the morning prayer and back much after nightfall. His business was still operating but he made the canny decision to sell half of it to a Toronto-based colleague. It was busier than ever and while he had stepped back from its day-to-day management, the money it provided was ludicrous in Afghanistan. We were rich once more: we had a generator that ran at all times, a driver, meat whenever we wanted.

My father's absence was the most important thing in my life. Once, in the beginning, I believe I was still in Afghanistan, at the infamous Bagram most likely; I was hooded with my arms held up perpetually, the pain sprawling across my shoulders, the only thing they wanted to know was what my father did during those long hours away from the family. I said school, he teaches at school, but it was the wrong answer. They were relentless.

What was the correct answer? What child actually knows what their parents do when they leave the house? When you're that age, even the simple things are a mystery. I didn't know and I still don't know. They wanted to know so badly. They transgressed their own sense of self to try to know. I had nothing to say.

I played soccer in the field, read the Qur'an, had halting conversations with my mother. There was no escape. You know what happened next. Whatever my father's business was during those vacant hours, we could no longer stay in Kandahar, especially in a residence that was considered flamboyant and owned by a well-known family.

Two days after 9/11 came a four-by-four to our front door. My mother and three sisters were ordered to the back and my father stopped me and held my chin with one hand.

"They are your responsibility," he said. I never saw him again. They said he died by drone while living in a cave.

We drove for fourteen hours. Maybe more. The sky was open like I'd never seen before. We arrived in the evening after four hours switchbacking up a mountain. My sisters had been taking turns heaving over the side, and the driver refused to stop. They laughed at me when I raised my voice, trying out authority, ordering them to stop so my sisters could regain their equilibrium.

When we arrived it was dark. Generators hummed. It was a small clearing, halfway up the mountain, and there were three vaguely adjacent houses. Two pickup trucks were parked. All three houses were made from a combination of materials ranging in durability, from hay, to wood, to sheet metal, and finally, small portions of the foundation with a kind of concrete. The driver handed me a flashlight and pointed at the middle house, where we were to wait until our father came to get us. The smell of livestock. I heard goats and chickens. The air was light mountain air. I felt relief as we made our way to the house, a sense that I had been unbound from time. The flashlights cut through the black air until the driver turned our generator on and the house was illuminated.

The driver unloaded our possessions: three bags of rice, two bags of flour, three bags of dried lentils, gas. Sleeping bags, a first-aid kit, a small radio, batteries. In the closet of the house were blankets and old clothes. Water came from a well far off, but the neighbours had been paid to fetch it for us. They would also provide milk and cheese when they could. He showed us how to operate the generator and left.

Above, drones flew regularly. Gunfire crackled every so often and all day the noise of trucks came up the mountain. The days were long and no one ever visited. It was almost winter and there was nothing to do beyond chores. The occasional loud noise of a drone brought everyone outside and gave us a good look at each other. Otherwise, we mostly kept to ourselves.

That memory has hardened now. When I look back at it to try to understand, I can see it was a pivot point, where the choices I made directed my path for the rest of my life.

It was easy to see the mechanics of the world on that mountain. I did one thing, another would happen. I could perceive all the possible consequences of my actions. In our luggage, my father had placed an English translation of the Egyptian Qur'an, and I read it every day, embedding its verses into my heart, sewing them to me so that they would pierce my every thought. We had rice, a chicken for eggs, onions, garlic, the occasional delivery of potatoes and okra. When the neighbours had to kill a goat, they gave us an entire hind leg. After so long, the meat was a drug.

In the spring, I changed. I wanted my world to open back up. The sky was raw and its potential for exploration was obvious. Drones arced the night sky and all the different distant thunders got louder. Were my brothers fighting? Was my father on the front lines? I had been tasked with taking care of my family, but compared to what I'd conjured as the bravery of my brothers and father, it was a child's task. There was nothing to take care of here. There was nothing as potent as ideology informing my desire for action, just restlessness, and a yearning towards adult responsibility. The aimless ambition that informed my father grew in me.

That April, in the keep for the goats, I spotted her: Afri. First, by accident, and I was startled because I hadn't seen a woman in a long time. She was not one of the little children who came out when the drones arrived. How had she been hidden all winter? Seeing her was like having a light flashed into my eyes. And I was overwhelmed with need.

Once I learned she was there I could not stop myself. I saw her for ten seconds moving pails from outside to in. After that, I took it upon myself to clean up our backyard and organize its maintenance.

Under the guise of growing vegetables, I spent hours outside, waiting for a glimpse. I approached like a slow-moving cat, spending the first month staring, determining if any men had claimed her, concocting fantasies that I could one day take her to Toronto.

Her face was strong-boned and flashes of her wrists, ankles, were most common — one day she reached up and I saw the intricate work of her rib cage; tough curved bones pushing against light brown skin. She had thick, black eyebrows, and hair plaited tightly. She was my age. Perhaps a year or two younger.

Once, her pant leg caught on a fence, she took a step forward, and it rose, revealing the triangular musculature of her calf.

I couldn't sleep that night. We had two rooms in the house. The back room where we stored the dry goods was where I slept; it led directly to the backyard, and I went silently outside to release myself in the dirt, staring at her house, illuminated by the moonlight, thinking over and over about what I'd seen that day.

The shame after was overwhelming and I spent the next week in bed feigning illness. Eventually, shame eroded as desire returned. It had no chance. Those meandering hours solidified into resolve. I wanted her; everything about her. The impenetrable surface of the past reigns now, but I know in those moments I was only driven by pure feeling, as if I was being urged on by someone directly above. There was something ordered about the precise calculation of our vicinity to each other.

I began my approach casually. It took no longer than a month. I practised the phrase many times in the bungalow, repeating the Pashto in a low voice until it came easily for me, like birthright. I didn't know if she even spoke the language. I didn't know where we were, or where she was from — I still don't. There's no one to ask. Can you believe it? That feels like an ancient, rare experience, to not have a mapped understanding of where you were in a moment of time.

When I asked her, "Can we have some eggs?" she stopped in reaction. I spoke to her back and so could not see her face as she processed my voice. One of the goats had been attended to, and she held a pail of the fresh milk in her hand. I'd listened in the mornings for her father's pickup to drive off and I knew she was alone.

She turned to face me, unsure. I didn't know if she understood me. I almost repeated myself in English, but had the sense not to — I felt like that knowledge should be secret. She went into the small shelter for the animals and returned with three small eggs, speckled with brown spots and hay. They were warm. I took them with my left hand and grabbed her wrist with my right. She smelled like earth, like milk's sweetness. I had no plan, but I was surprised — she returned my grip with no apprehension in her eyes, no surprise, almost a dare, staring me down until I let go and looked away, ashamed once more. She pushed my hand into my chest and said, "Don't do anything if you're not ready," and left me standing there. She had spoken so fast that I struggled to translate the words in my head.

For the next month, I visited daily. The pickup would leave and under the guise of practicality we would speak: her chores, her family, the Qur'an, what was down below the mountain. As the summer heat increased, my family in the hut grew agitated. There was no word from my father. There was no longer a sense of time. Each day was judged by how well the chores went. I whittled hours away in the shade of the house, clutching dirt to cool my hands.

I was waiting for the heat to break. I knew I only needed a night. We never met indoors, only outside, alone, on that small patch. One evening, with its attendant coolness, bravery rose.

I followed her for her night chores. She had to tether the goats and ensure the chickens had been put safely away. The war had pushed dogs up the mountains and they had been snapping at the chickens' necks. The sky had gone from crimson to a washed blue.

I put my hands on her hips and turned her around. She was my height, exactly. We were wearing slippers. My excitement was obvious through the cotton of my trousers and that embarrassed me, but we began without fuss. I pushed my lips at her, too scared to loosen my tongue. We took two steps to a hidden clearing and lay down together. She pulled down her pants, and mine, and our bodies pushed until I finished and the world rushed back to me.

I was instantly overwhelmed with the anxiety and worry I had denied the last two months. It felt like I had been splintered, and sadness overtook me, as the reality of my life settled, and the possibility that this would never be repeated. In the shadow of such an act, I felt a powerful loneliness, as if bringing ourselves closer had only shown me how much was missing. Afri pulled away from me and straightened her clothing. She was too human, too divorced from what I had been imagining; a stranger. Panicking, I said "good night" in English, and she gave me two eggs before pushing me out the door.

Does one moment make another worth it? Is our life random movement, caused by the push and pull of levers unknown to us? I prayed because my shame fled quickly, replaced by a need to see her again.

Two days later, Afri's father came home without a leg. He emerged from the white pickup on crutches. He had been responsible for checking roads for IEDs, working with the Northern Alliance for our Western governments. Disarming could mean exploding them. There was increased activity for the next few days and many men stopped by our house, wishing us good fortune, dropping bags of rice and flour, heaping praise onto me about my father. As far as I could understand, he was helping in a communications role. A small man with a long beard and pristine white clothes told me about my brothers — not where they were, but that they were raising money and that their fundraising efforts, overseas and domestic, were of immense help.

My familial pride helped satiate a growing wound. Because of her father's new condition, it became impossible to see Afri privately. The growing traffic had to be constantly attended to, and once the visitors stopped, she was consigned to care duty for him. Summer turned and I had no opportunity to see her again, and as the heat turned to autumn, my time at the mountain was coming to an end.

One morning, staring at the ceiling, I heard a commotion across the way, and then a loud scream. As I rose to it, I saw Afri's father hobbling his way towards our home with a machete in his hand. It was an awful sight: he was not fully accustomed to his crutches, the weapon was throwing him off-balance, and Afri and her mother tailed him, shouting. My mother and two sisters were in shock. I hadn't seen Afri beyond a glimpse in the last month, at least. Her father banged on our door, and looking through the window, I saw Afri stand still on the small road. A gust of wind pushed against her, wrapping her dark clothing tightly against her body. She was a small woman of dense muscle, there was no fat on her, no fat on any of us anymore, and I could clearly see the beginning of life inside her belly.

Her father rattled against our locked doors but I didn't move. I ordered my mother and sisters quiet. They had started listening to me. He was too frail, too weak, and was already tired. His anger made balance impossible and he fell onto his side after pushing his wife away from him.

I was obviously the culprit of Afri's change and filled with determination to take on whatever came next. Perhaps I would marry her, it wasn't unheard of, and from then onward live my life in those fields; the bombs would leave one day. Beyond her father's anger I glimpsed a path of happiness that was made possible by mercy.

The sun went. I heard two cars pull up, stop, quiet chatter. I peeked through the window at six men.

I learned later that trust had been steadily eroding across the countryside, as the Northern Alliance and Taliban fought for the people's loyalty. The U.S. agitated matters further by instituting a bounty program that promised fortunes — at least seven of my friends in Guantanamo were from this. The program stretched across the country, and into Pakistan, and the amount — as low as twenty-five thousand — was like winning the lottery. The open secret was that the U.S. was willing to pay the sum before they determined the value of the capture. The twenty-five thousand only required pointing out a target.

The men came to gather me. There was little anger, and I was taken like a farm animal; my mother and sisters in terrified silence. Because respect for my father held them back, no one was sure how to deal with my error. Normally, it seemed, a beating would ensue, and then some sort of contract that ensured the honour of all parties was validated. Here, nothing made sense: I was barely a Pathan, from outside, but my father held enough sway that violence could not be the first answer. Afri was pregnant and would need a husband — but had she already been promised to someone? Could she not be mine? I stood next to the four by four trying to pick up pieces of the bickering.

I didn't look at my mother or sisters as I left, and when they loaded me into the back of the vehicle I stared at Afri's house, what I thought was her room, with a solitary light bulb hanging from the ceiling. The moon was full. We would have to hurry, for visibility was high, and the prowling drones were always a danger. We drove down the mountain at a high speed, taking the switchbacks quickly. After several hours we arrived at an old building, where I was to be held until my father could be contacted.

I spent three days as a sort of half-prisoner. Fed freely and allowed to roam the grounds, I saw that it was a sort of operations centre with a dozen minor buildings and huts. There was a large prison in the basement, but otherwise, it had a carefree air. There were soldiers sprawled about, radios crackling, and those captured, silent. Which side it was affiliated with, I could not say.

On the second day, a tall man with bony hands and a long beard came into my room. He had a long, prominent nose. I'd finished eating and was getting ready to sleep, trying to ignore the burgeoning anxiety about my situation. I had expected them to contact my father quickly. Was it possible that he would not come? Realizing that his protection was no longer guaranteed in my life signalled the end of my childhood. The man asked if I knew what I had done; if I knew why it was so awful. I was sheepish and contrite. We had only acted according to our nature. He repeated instructions from the Qur'an to me: "It is better for you to practise self-restraint. Those who follow their lusts go far astray. Man was created weak." The memory of the mountainside was already fading into a dream. I wanted to go back and see Afri.

"Do you know how you can help?" he asked. "To remedy the situation," he clarified. An American army unit had moved close by and was occupying two buildings in a nearby town. "You can translate," he said. He sat cross-legged, getting comfortable. "There are so many ways to help. You speak English, like your father? If the girl's father is inconsolable, then I don't know … but you can help yourself here. We can help you with him, since you can speak English. Your name with Allah can be cleansed." At this, I did not respond. Up till then, my relationship with God had been a private matter, between me and the Qur'an, between me and what I saw when I closed my eyes.

He came back on the third day, asking if I knew where my brothers were, if I knew where my father was. They could not reach him. On the fourth, they said the USA wanted to talk to my father badly, that they would pay for a short conversation. It was nothing more serious than that. The money would make Afri's father happy, and then perhaps it would open up the possibility for our future. They didn't visit for two more days. The door to my room was locked from the outside. They skipped my dinners. On the seventh day the man came back — from then on, so much of my life was determined by men whose names I did not know — and reminded me I had to contribute to balancing the scale.

I had been professing the ignorance I always had: I did not know where they were. I was nervous about helping. They brought a radio that crackled with voices; the language was fast, and men spoke over each other in shouts and whispers. War cries full of fear. It was not English. It was a European language I could not understand. I didn't even know what language.

If I could not provide information, only an action could free me and bring my mother and sisters peace. "We're worried about you," the tall man said. Again, he skipped a day, and I did not eat. On the ninth he came into the room with three others and asked me to speak English. I said, "Look at the blue sky. The smell of earth, the field in which we could roam. Do you believe in mercy? Do you believe in balance? If you believe there is no need for fear."

That evening I was fed a plate of lentils and rice. It was a large plate to make up for the sporadic dinners, but it was too much too fast and it felt like hands were tearing up my insides. I used the bucket in the corner for my diarrhea and the only respite I had from myself was sleep, so I took to the cot. The man came into my room as the sun fell and sat at the edge near my feet. He reminded me that a positive action could undo the mistake of my past and re-establish my mother and sisters' safety, especially in light of my father's absence. Would I be willing to take action? I knew what he meant. They had been sending disruptive, lone men into the vicinity of Americans. Those men never came back. What could I say? I said what I had to.

Whenever my mind cycles over the evening with Afri, never do I imagine myself taking a different action that jeopardizes the moment. Instead, I wonder about after: should I have prayed harder, prayed better, longer, was there a surah in the Qur'an that I misunderstood?

My father hated when I treated Allah like a personal secretary, taking the time to answer minor prayers and small desires.

Never pray for yourself was his first instruction. My mistake was that, I realized. I should have prayed for her. I prayed only for myself.

That same night, at its deepest point, there was a series of booms and volleys of gunfire, four or five in a row, and then there was twenty minutes' worth of silence, the kind that moves into a room and clears everything out. Then there was screaming, gunfire, and a man came by with rattling hands and unlocked the eight rooms on my floor.

Outside, tracer bullets whizzed by, and I heard the blades of a helicopter, more explosions. The structure was old and large chunks were falling out when hit with bullets. The air was hot with munitions. I had run downstairs and into the front yard, but the noise pushed me back into the building, where I retreated downstairs for safety. I assumed eventually there would be Americans, and I could plead in English, wave my arms in surrender.

My father had migrated to Canada in the winter of 1979, the same time of the Grand Mosque seizure in Mecca. My father often told me stories of listening to the news on a radio, huddled next to a radiator, he and his several housemates worried about the ongoing battle. The leader of the forces that had seized the mosque from the Saudis had declared himself Mahdi — the redeemer, he who appears at the end of times. He comes with Isa, my father used to tell Christians, he comes with your prophet also. His worries about the Muslim world were shared by no others. They'd never heard of Isa; Jesus was Jesus, nothing else, and they did not appreciate the gun battles of the Middle East. Those fleeting news reports were marked with profound, violent imagery, an ultimate transgression in the holy land. Like a good storyteller, he savoured those images of bullets whizzing by, French commandos dropping down onto our holy land, snipers perched in precarious positions. Retreating back into the building, I recalled those first flickers of empathy I must have felt for my father, trying to conjure what it would have been like for him so far away in the cold, learning that Mecca was under siege, and the only ones who could help were the French.

The stairs led down into a kind of dungeon. By the time I reached the room the gunfire was non-stop, louder, closer, like a moving wall. A generator struggled in the corner and I joined two dozen men, huddling together with long beards and sick complexions. At least half were still in cuffs, and a few were chained to the wall.

There was no way to know what was happening upstairs.

The gunfire slowed down. It became sporadic. Whenever I relaxed, it erupted again. The men spoke among themselves but I stayed quiet — were these all prisoners? What were they here for? Who was the gunfire for? Whenever I considered going outside, a fresh burst of gunfire would stop me.

We turned the generators off, hoping the darkness would keep us hidden as the bursts of gunfire decreased in duration, but increased in volume. It was coming closer. There were two vents on opposite sides near the ceiling and a prisoner shouted as thick liquid dripped from one, then another. Was it water? A man's friend gave him a boost so he could peek into the shaft. As his face rose to inspect the liquid, a hum became audible from the chamber; that hum roared into a flame and covered the man's face, the force of the fire pushing him back, where he fell onto the mass of people. He was covered in flames, screaming, the cooked scent of flesh in my nose almost as fast as I saw it, and the rest screamed along with him, filling the air as several men caught fire. Fire and smoke rushed through the vents. I was pushed to the side as men ran to the door, pulling in different directions, shrieking at each other. When the door was finally pulled open, the fresh oxygen only encouraged the flames; skin flaked off the men. Black smoke filled the room. Everything I could see was covered in a veil of black smoke. It was then, against the wall, my brain woozy from the putrid air, that I slumped, decided that I had enough, that time had come for a rest ... I could hear faraway voices of who I thought were the assailants, it was enough, I could go ...

I don't know how much time passed before I woke. I was wet — totally wet and the water level was rising. I sensed bodies near me, floating, and in the weak half-light from the doorway, these corpses seemed like crocodiles. It was quiet but the open door allowed some noise in. There was the smell of dead flesh, a scent that tells your body to get away from it. I saw some faces floating, bloated with water, death, flies already buzzing. Steady streams of water coming through the vents.

In the hallway I could see it was coming down the stairs as well. There were still some men alive, crouched against the walls, shivering, their heads above water. No one noticed me and I watched for five minutes until the pain in my leg made me groan and buckle down. The terrified men pointed guns at the door. One gave me a soaked assault rifle. No one spoke. The water continued filling in, freezing cold. At the end of the hallway was the spill of moonlight against water. A spilled glass of milk. Flashes of shadows against the surface. My skin was cold, my bones. The last time I had been this cold there was slush and sun, the cold wind getting in between the gaps of my clothing while I walked to school. I remember how startled I was when snow touched my wrist for the first time.

The mechanical noises began anew and stronger streams of water gushed in from the vents. Fire, flood. What was I being told? This was Godly. It's true, the steel in my hands gave me comfort. It was a ballast in that basement. We were engulfed in total darkness. A grenade caught us by surprise and shook my teeth when it exploded. Pieces of brick fell into the water. I pointed the gun out the door and pulled the trigger; when it barked, I lost control from the force and shot upward. I held it again, steady against my shoulder, and waited for another explosion. I pulled the trigger. This time, not surprised, I shot into the dark for a few seconds. My hands were too cold, too weak, and the gun fell into the water. I was exhausted. I was on my knees. It was over, please be over, it was over …

White light: I was dry and it was noisy. I smelled antiseptic as I opened my eyes. I was in constant pain. My shoulder was frozen. The light was too much, but I couldn't close my eyes. Panic rose and I struggled but then a warm flooding sensation calmed me down. There were masked doctors working on my body. I fell asleep.

Two men, soldiers, standing next to my bed. I was in bandages. I could not move. They said I killed a man. An American soldier. They spoke to me in English. They were white. I had taken two bullets to my chest and shoulder. Shrapnel all over. There were holes all over my body. I smelled like chemical.

I squeezed my eyes shut and there I was, suddenly, in a field, Afri in the distance.

My body got better. I could turn my head and talk. There was no one to speak with. The nurse told me she had been instructed not to. I didn't know where I was or what time it was. What month. I asked about my mother. For months I did not know what country I was in. They healed me so they could hood me, cuff me. A broomstick slid between my arms so they were always held up. The pain like knives poking down my ribs. They would come in with a powerful hose to wash everything, while I sat in a chair in the middle. I was put in a box like a coffin. They covered my face and poured water over me, so my mind thought I was drowning and my body reacted appropriately.

They asked me, "Why? Why did you kill him? Why did you kill them? Why do your brothers kill? Why did your father kill?"

There was constant disbelief. Why don't I know where my brothers are? Why don't I know where my father is? I pissed myself regularly; once, two big men, one Black, one white, grabbed me and dragged me in my piss. They were wearing blue gloves that stank like plastic. They told me they would rape me. Why don't I know where my father is? Why don't I know where my brothers are? I was strip-searched. I was made to bend over; an object tore into me, and my cry met with laughter. I was not allowed to sleep. I forgot I was alive. I lost memories, sentences, language. Even if I knew the answers, I could not speak. They healed me to apply this torture. I was in disbelief.

Moved from the building to a plane, I learned I was still in Afghanistan when I caught an errant sentence from one of the soldiers. I asked if I was going back to Canada — did they know I was Canadian? I was slapped. The plane sounded like a frenzied animal. I was surrounded by men. No one asked where we were going.

Memory dissolves into a shimmer. I only remember a few things. The size of the cage in Guantanamo Bay. My eyesight is permanently weak from being in dark confinement for so many years and so smell took over. I thought I saw the famous

Cuban iguanas regularly. The smell of piss on a leg. A bag of McDonald's hamburgers as a reward. One guard chewed gum. Everything they say happened, happened. There's documentation of everything, and even I don't believe. My body believes.

Afri in the distance; a snow-capped mountain. She was pregnant, I never forget. For ten years in Guantanamo Bay I never forget. A boy, or a girl? I never forget. If I hear a sudden, loud noise behind me, I know I will pay for it in my dreams. Life is not a continuous stream of moments: it is one, two, three moments, unpacked over time.

Look at this, look at my hand.

I still cannot make a fist.

I still cannot close my eyes.

Three

21.

After telling his story, Abdul told me to choose a room upstairs and rest. I did as ordered, eating, sleeping, and praying for weeks, peeking around corners for Natalie, maintaining a half-alive state. The room I picked was furnished with a single wooden bed, desk, and wardrobe. I kept my distance from Natalie, needing her to make her own way back to me.

I told myself it was easier for all involved if I was around for the administrative tasks. The amount of paperwork required to set up the various GoFundMe pages and new bank accounts was overwhelming. I was constantly signing papers I barely read. Samir insisted on control and accountability.

I stayed in the room for July, through to the end of August, when Abdul would be attending an Islamic conference in Delhi, visiting a few private colleges in Bombay, before continuing to Malaysia and Indonesia. Finally, he would make trips to tiny mosques in South Korea and Japan — if he could get a visa approved. The Arab was going to Bombay, too, for a wedding, and would be leaving after a big fundraising dinner to mark the end of summer. Bombay in monsoon season was ill advised but neither man would listen.

We'd arranged new bank accounts to receive the donations and began the process of establishing a non-profit. To soothe my growing anxiety with all this I'd been spending money. The bank, noticing my spending, called earlier in the week to raise my credit limit, which I accepted, and now they wouldn't stop calling. I was buying stupid things that brought me minor but necessary pleasure: a $200 leather dopp kit, an $80 twill luggage tag, $900 tasselled cordovan loafers, all delivered straight to my apartment. There was a tremendous set of Baccarat tumblers — $325, slight discount — whose weight I never held. I'd purchased them so I could see the light dash through their crystal bottoms. I never got to open the packages.

While I stayed with him, Abdul's team lent me a no-name sweatsuit and slides. By the third day, alongside a few whites who volunteered, I served toast, eggs, and coffee to a line of homeless men. Abdul thanked each man for attending before allowing them to find a place to sit and eat.

Surrounded by it all, it made sense. Direction, guidance, ritual. Narrow parameters for easy living. I got it. He wrestled yearning for spirituality down into practicality. He gave happy wanderers a tangible hold on Allah.

Surrounded by it all, I stayed back. I mumbled through group activities but kept far from the congregation. I didn't trust white people converting to Islam after 9/11. Each night I returned to my room at 8:00 p.m. with the sun out and enjoyed the emptiness. My life drained of its activity was a gift I cherished. I spent those six or so weeks in ignorance. I did not communicate with my father or mother and barely spoke with Marwan or went to the store. I did not think about those two men hanging in the room under the hot white lights. I did not. I saw no trace of them and being fed, given a room to sleep in, and the quiet comfort of being disconnected from the world was enough for me to shut down curiosity.

On one of my last nights there, reading the Qur'an in bed — really — Natalie came in. It had taken the full use of my self-restraint to stay away from her.

She knocked, turned the knob, and entered. Dark marks cupped her eyes. She'd been working as an administrative manager for Abdul. Personal and professional. I saw her at prayer times or business occasions. Eye contact when I signed and handed over a document. We'd been moving on loan applications, GoFundMe set-ups, managing online access and passwords.

I'd left the curtain drawn and window open. Humid air. My room wet and dark.

Every day she and Abdul would go out together for public events and private meetings. Being so close showed me the suave power he controlled and I was no longer surprised at the number of small donations to online campaigns, which added up quick, and major wire transfers from corporate figures.

Surprise and not; that was my feeling about the days remaining for me in the West. When he told me his story and sent me to my room he had to have known what he'd done. He reached into my murk and brought up forgotten ideas of tribal brotherhood. Hearing him tell of his ordeal, not only to me, but many times over the month to others, I pledged a quiet loyalty to him.

A rush of events was coming up before he left for Bombay. A few socials, meetings, continuing to appear in public to pull in last gasps of cash before attention moved off us. That night was a five-hundred-dollar-a-plate dinner that marked the end of summer. Two interviews for Abdul and the Arab scheduled with bigger mainstream TV channels. A scatter of small, very ethnic YouTube channels continued sending in interview requests. We'd attend to them after the big ones bored.

Natalie pulled out a chair and sat near my feet. This is what I wanted. I'd never been able to come up with the traditional "five-year plan" or see at all into my future. When I tried, my mind showed me an empty cave. That night, knowing I was leaving Abdul's soon, a small flame, kindling caught, made shadows in the emptiness. Natalie was the shape of the shadows. I was convinced my future would be all right if I could grab hold of her.

She held a plant in her lap. Its leaves had yellow marks through the middle and they drooped over the clay pot like a peeled banana. Overwatered. I mimicked her posture and sat up straight. Respecting the sanctity of the building, I'd not masturbated or smoked weed all month and so sleeping became impossible. I sat stupid-eyed in bed, determined to play it cool. She gave me her professional smile.

"Thanks for helping organize everything so fast," she said. "You've been good to us."

"Anything for Abdul," I said.

"This is for your father," she said, and gave me the pot. "He still collects plants?"

"He thinks my mom is coming back."

"Abdul said you're moving out of here."

"I have our apartment to go back to."

"We're thankful for your help," she said. Her face twitched through indecision. She squeezed my foot. "Come back, okay? But promise me you'll be careful." She stood close to me. I squeezed her hand. One more professional smile at the door.

•

The next morning a thousand shouting voices yanked me from sleep. Outside the window in front of the building were about fifty people in two groups chanting over each other. I couldn't make out what they were saying. A Chinese woman with short hair and glasses led one group and a skinny blond lady with a gaudy green backpack led the other.

I checked my phone: Marwan had texted he needed my support and asked me to meet him downtown. He'd understood my absence from the shop as an Abdul-approved spiritual retreat. I was eager to see him after so long. I was eager to leave, as well. Friday was always busy anyway, but the public announcement of our plans caused a bump of new volunteers greedy for Abdul's time; they were joined by contractors supplied by Samir acting like they'd been instructed not to work, some actual brown and Black Muslims, and various whites with unknown purpose. The building was full.

In the kitchen, Abdul, Natalie, and Samir circled a small man whose eyes screamed fear. I took quick steps toward him. He jerked back. This was Mo' from Gitmo, as Samir insisted on calling him, one of the two Guantanamo resettlement projects mismanaged by life and fearful of everything. The attention of the room turned toward me when I spoke to Abdul. His manicured finger on my chest stopped me. It was time for afternoon prayer.

A young white man led. The ten women prayed freely within the twenty men. Last week, on a tour of the facilities, Habeeb of the five Habeeb's Grocers, who was dangling regular, juicy donations, discovered the gender mingling. He stood staring as women and men mixed to pray, then took his prostrations in a far corner. After, furious, shaking, he came to me for explanation. He was old — sixty or seventy, wrinkles like scratch marks, four grey hairs flung over a bald scalp, diabetes belly, and trembling hands. He wanted to pull his money. He wanted to know what was going on. Just what was going on in here?

I guided him to the dinner table where he was presented as a guest of honour. Abdul had seen the problem and praise flew out of him in front of everyone.

"What a privilege to have a guest like you," Abdul said to Habeeb. "A member of the community who takes care of his family and the people around him. A truly humbling experience for me to show you what your generous donation will go toward."

Locking him in publicly to the money was vicious. A space where the facade of Abdul slipped and I saw what he might actually be. My night at the house, chasing him — someone? — back to this place. The men hanging. My mind tried to pull the pieces together but I forced the thoughts to float by. They would not help me. Discovering what happened there would not help me. A memory of Natalie rose like a protective spell, refocusing me onto what I needed.

Even after Abdul's speech Habeeb was not enjoying himself. Staff placed plates of thick kebabs in front of him next to biryani and paneer. Garlic and onion. Heaven smells. He poked at his food. I pried apart a chicken thigh with my hands.

"You're upset," I said.

"I don't know what to think," Habeeb said.

"Do you only sell Halal food?"

"Of course not. I don't only serve Muslims."

"Everyone should be Halal, no?"

"This is not like that. Mixing is unusual."

I tried to remind him of his own inconsistencies. I pretended to be pious and told him once again of Abdul's credentials. His struggle and fight. I was firm.

"There will be no physical barriers between the men and the women," I said.

"Not even a separation? Right and left?"

"I know Abdul is unusual," I said. "But that's also why we're here. There are certain things, considerations, that if we create more room for, will allow us to gain a stronger foothold in this city. Think big. What do people think when they hear 'Habeeb's Grocers?' If you're nervous about publicity we don't have to broadcast it. But you need Abdul to make space for us, to make it safe for us in this country. You want to be more than a Halal grocer. The money we can help you make — you can't take your treasure with you. If it's that important, fine. Remember who makes the final decisions."

Abdul swooped in after dessert. Sly, warm handshake. His accent perfect, every Arabic word popping out like from a sheikh. He crouched to Habeeb's level. He began his work. By the end of the night, there was another cheque.

The young white man in front continued in Arabic. His parents had sent him to Abdul four months ago desperate for help. He was delirious to be around real-life Muslims. His conversion had taken place online, Shahada recited over Skype. The convert's insecurity as a Muslim was jet fuel, capable of melting the thickest steel beams. This dude, at twenty-five, was trying to memorize the Qur'an.

Last week, he fluttered over to me from a corner of the room before I sat for lunch. He told me my fade was not permissible because some goofball years ago said we weren't allowed to cut the hair on the sides of our head. He also told me to roll my pants up above my ankles or that they'd be "dragged in hell-fire." No "Hi, Hello," just his demand about my pants. A rain-bow arc of multicoloured pimples lined his jaw and he spoke in a southern accent. His family were regular southern Christians terrified by their son's fundamental approach to Islam. After years of tiptoeing around him, it was a botched, moronic at-tempt at joining ISIS — stupid emails about flights to Istanbul; a credit charge on his mother's card — that finally motivated them to action. They thought if they couldn't bring him back to the bosom of Christ, Abdul was the next best bet. For eight thousand a month he got room, board, and private tutoring.

After he blurted his hadith at me, Abdul pulled him to the corner and they murmured for five minutes while I ate. Abdul sent him to me for an apology. Not for what he'd said but for his righteousness. I didn't want to have conversations but I did pity converts like him. They were angry at me for my lack of religiosity and jealous I'd been born into Islam. A heritage within it that went back centuries. My pity never transformed to empathy. I could only see that they were white people play-ing a game, a rebellion that ostracized them from their commu-nities and drew attention, and, incredibly, I worried for Abdul.

He brushed my concern off. Their zeal was powerful and their numbers gave him an authoritative momentum. I was jealous too. I envied their simplicity and true submission. They rose every morning sure of the day's tasks.

In front of the men, Natalie prayed perfectly. She moved her body with the grace of a born Muslim. Converts were extreme and the older ones usually had a history of drama, like her taste for booze. But her transformation seemed genuine. Maybe she switched channels and poured that need into religion. Is that what Abdul provided?

After prayer was a short break and the whites brought out a dining table, covered it with a dark green sheet, and served lunch. Abdul the first to sit.

In private he relaxed, cigarette after cigarette, laughter and small talk. In public, he presented himself with calmness, austerity, and tried to loop most conversations to the story he was selling: Guantanamo, Islam, foreignness, the future, the persevering hope of humanity. I didn't know which side was authentic and which a trick, or if the difference applied to him. I watched him watching the room and it was clear he didn't live in the same world as us. There was a distance between him and his surroundings that did not close.

The converts babbled swirling around us dropping off dishes, picking up plates, refilling drinks, while Natalie ordered them around. They insisted on being called "reverts" and answered every question with a hadith or verse from the Qur'an.

I sat two from Abdul next to Mo'. Mo' had arrived in Canada a month earlier after an American attempt to settle him in Serbia failed. He moved slow; barely. He brought his mouth close to the plate to eat. He did not want to be seen. He wanted to ball up like an armadillo and flinched at any noise.

I asked him how he was and he shook his head back and forth talking into his plate. I asked again and his eyes spread-eagled in suspicion. He replied mumbling, waited to see my reaction, then went on, waited to see my reaction, conversation catch-and-release for him, twisted from years of interrogation.

He'd been a math teacher in Rabat, Morocco, with a small apartment and wife. She died of cancer while he was away. His mother died, his father died, his brother cut off contact, happy to inherit a small sum from his parents and afraid Mo' would ask for a portion. His wild curly hair thinned and reached for the ceiling and his wire-frame glasses couldn't hide cracked-up eyes. As we spoke, he would twist and turn, needing comfort, his back permanently hunched, his joints crackling, and he stared into his bowl of chickpeas like he wanted to dive in and hide. He was scared and stayed in his room except for therapy sessions at Abdul's home. Until today, apparently.

Samir sat down next to me and cut in.

"I got a really good idea for my man."

Marwan had been right that Samir and Abdul would not be natural partners. Samir was frenzy, scrolling through his phone while chatting, hands reaching for anyone's pockets, three conversations at once minimum, never giving the impression of dedication. The donations rolling in, he'd reverted back to his caustic self around Abdul.

"Why don't we go out with him?" Samir said and pointed to Mo'. "A night on the town."

Mo' didn't know what to say. He begged his chickpea curry to make room in the bowl. Abdul covered Mo's hand with his, patting reassurance.

"Go out with him where?" Abdul asked.

"Let's go somewhere after the dinner," Samir said. "Let's relax. Show him freedom. He just stays in his room."

Abdul stopped eating and pressed his full attention on Samir. The room noticed.

"No. He's not ready."

"To go out? To have fun. Nothing bad. Nothing dangerous."

Samir moved his eyebrows up and down, up and down, trying to convince. Abdul shook his head once more, no, and turned away. Conversation finished. Mo', relieved, took a bite. Samir dropped his spoon against his plate, the clang his tantrum. The pitch of the protestors rose and we heard their rumbling outside the window. It was about landlords and evictions. I left the table with Samir for a peek through a window. A man held a sign with an image of Abdul blown up and a giant X marked through his face.

"Abdul hates me," Samir said.

"Don't push so much," I said.

"He doesn't text me anymore. He doesn't ask questions. Natalie contacts me instead. Can you believe that? She's his assistant. I'm dealing with the assistant."

Samir placed a cigarette between his lips and flicked his lighter. I stopped him.

"Sorry," Samir said. "Sorry. It's upstairs. The top floor. He can't get rid of them. He's given them notice but they aren't going anywhere. He won't kick them out. A state-of-the-art therapy centre and there's a bunch of rich Chinese upstairs."

"They rich?" I asked. "He offer them money?"

"We offered money, yaar. It's one couple," Samir said. "The rest listen to them. They won't leave. All this is a problem. All this noise. He doesn't get it. They want an excuse. That's all anyone is waiting for. He's not good with money. How big was his settlement? Where is it? Here, there, lawsuit this, lawsuit that, there's no cash. This building — he put a ton down for it. But what about next year? The year after? Next month? Does he have any money? He has no money! No cash! There's no cash flow!"

"Why are you always counting what's in other people's pockets?"

"Bhai, that's where the money is."

He giggled and dismissed himself. I wanted to get back into my Integra and see Marwan. I missed him. He came to Abdul's on Fridays but beyond basic greetings we hadn't spoken in a month. Then, a few days ago, without asking, he brought my car back and parked it under a tree. He was thawing.

From the kitchen the chants sounded mechanical. How could you protest Abdul? His moral armour was bulletproof. Natalie gave instructions to a volunteer at the sink. Her covering slipped, revealing a part in her hair, and she stopped to adjust it, before grabbing a garbage bag and heading outside to the bins.

The noxious air mixed with the perfume she left in her trail; pepper and smoke. A few protestors saw us but didn't know what to do and continued chanting. I didn't want to talk to her next to the garbage but I had no choice.

She heaved the bag, swivelled and stopped, surprised to see me. I stepped close.

"How long you going to stay?" I said. "I'm worried."

"There's no reason for you to be worried. I'm working. I'm listening."

"You left me with barely a note."

"I couldn't —"

"What's going on with us?"

"I have other things to take care of," Natalie said. "I don't know. We're done. Right now. I don't know the future."

"Do you still love me?"

"That's not the answer," she said.

"Are you still drinking?"

"Don't be an asshole."

"I'm sorry."

"Don't touch me," she said. "What if I am still drinking? What does that make me? No one here has ever asked me that."

"I'm asking you how you are."

"Do you want to check my room for empties?"

"No. God. What you want me to say? I'm concerned."

"You're helping Abdul, right? I appreciate that," she said. "I'm thankful for that. I warned you not to get involved but I'm thankful for that."

"Is all this real?" I asked. "Are you for real about all this?"

"I'm doing a good thing," she said. "For myself. I'm glad you're helping him. What you're doing is good. I know you said you wanted to do this, to help the community, or whatever. What you're doing is good."

"Do you miss me?"

"Yes."

"I love you," I said.

"Oh God. Stop."

"You going to the dinner tonight?"

"Yes."

"You going to be nice to me?" I asked.

Finally, a smile. A coy line hinting at our past life. We exchanged a look that held between us forever, a vision of our past, future, and current selves, the growing stack of our apologies, and moments that bound us. Abdul was the path back to Natalie and this journey would eliminate the mess inside myself. Like always, I believed eradication was the first step.

She brushed past, her fingers glanced mine, the chance to inhale her scent, and I stood still as she went inside, trying to take the smell in deep, allowing it to open the door to that past life.

22.

I scooped Marwan outside the subway station where he stood idly in his all-white shalwar kameez and Air Max outfit. He was oblivious to the arm's-length distance commuters made sure to give him on the sidewalk, innocent to the ruckus his broad-shouldered, Taliban-beard, FOB-ass, six-foot appearance caused in others. His clothes sucked up all the sunlight so he was lit up like a candy wrapper.

He slid in and dropped rolled up marriage biodata sheets on my lap.

"I'm feeling it from all sides," he said.

"Marriage is good."

"Have you met Isabella?" he asked. Isabella was an Italian-Canadian convert who had yet to choose an Arabic name. Sweat gathered above his eyebrows. "They're stressing me out. I keep having these lunches with her. Abdul keeps asking us to sit together."

"What Abdul says goes," I said.

Marwan's eyes darted to the rear-view mirror and he spotted the shoebox in the backseat.

"Whose shoes?" he asked.

"Yours."

"For real?" he said and grabbed them. "These are nice. Wow, these are nice. They replicas?"

"No man, come on. Legit."

I'd bought him Jordan mids as an apology. He stroked them, lost in their all-white sheen.

"What if what I want no one else wants?" he asked.

"You don't want to get married?"

"I want to get married, oh yeah," he said. "Or, maybe. I don't know. A relationship. Like a big serious one. We can keep it above board. Appropriate."

"That's a lot easier when you haven't gotten laid," I said. "You can't close that box."

"I haven't really masturbated in a year. I have wet dreams now."

Marwan thought losing his hand was from Allah but no one knew what the message actually was and so this turned into neurosis, making him search every new interaction for hidden clues and messages. Not jerking off was part of this. I assumed he just couldn't get used to using his right hand.

We drove to a quarter-full parking lot. No signage indicated where we should go and I let Marwan lead once we got out of my car. He was nervous. When we got to the front door he pulled me to the side.

"First. Thank you for coming. Two … two. I can marry a Christian. We're allowed."

I let the words settle and followed him in. Visual clues: stiff walks, fake tans, oversized muscles, the weak smell of baby oil. I grabbed a program. The Tenth Annual Bodybuilding Competition and Expo. Vendors on either side sold various potions and mixes. There was a freakish element to the inflated muscles and despite the controlled preening, oils, and prepared poses, a raw, wild energy. I was in shape but nowhere near this demographic. Even Marwan was infantilized by them. I was made nervous by all the flesh swinging around the place.

We walked into a full room. Two seats together at the back. Most of the audience were amateur bodybuilders except a scatter of lone men, hair frizzled or balding, who, despite the sludge of August heat, wore jackets hiding their pale skin, whether they were white, Asian, or in the rare case, Black.

I flipped through the program knowing what I would find. On page 22 a small headshot in the 135-pound weightclass: Brittany Powers. Our Britta. Marwan watched the oil-slick contestants. It was men bending into geometric shapes for judges. I couldn't tell the difference among them but admired them. The dedication to craft was clear. I knew from Marwan's workout regime the combination of nutrition, training, and discipline was difficult: I got tired reading his workout logs. Lives shaped around a single desire.

A contestant without a hand posed and Marwan hooted and hollered and I wondered if that was why we were here. A genuine reason — tribal solidarity. Immediately after, the lights went down and the 135-pound female category began. Marwan shifted in his seat once, twice, three times, then settled with his elbows on his thighs, eyes locked on stage. Models did four or five poses and walked to the corner.

The eighth was her. A light green bikini faded against her shining tanned skin. Marwan did not breathe while she posed.

She was ballooned to the brim with muscles like they might pop at any time. She was bigger than before. She did her poses. She walked off.

Three more women and finish. Lights up, the judges announced their rankings: Britta in third place. A spasm through Marwan and he gripped the chair in front. The judges filed to their right, eager for a break. Marwan struggled. An attendant handed us a flyer for the after-party at a club where a few of the star bodybuilders would be hosting.

Marwan's muscles were taut. He needed release. As the judges left the hall he got up from his seat and gestured wild with his hand.

"Third place? You blind? Is this your first competition?"

The judges ignored him and went on their way. They were used to stray comments. The crowd took secret glances at Marwan and two skinny Indian security guards drowning in their outfits approached. In the far corner of the hall, wiping herself down, was a curious Britta, staring at the mysterious behemoth fighting for her honour. The security guards offered timid head bobs and asked Marwan to leave. Three white bodybuilders approached us. Time to go.

23.

I drove us home first. Marwan refused to talk, and I did not want to know. We changed and arrived for the fundraising dinner as Abdul approached the podium. I'd picked out Abdul's black kameez and sent it to my tailor to have it brought closer to his silhouette and the length shortened. My help started when I'd caught him one morning in the communal bathroom plucking his unibrow and noted the care he took to sculpt his beard. He was thankful for my sartorial interventions and we went shopping once or twice. Then he invited me to go over speeches together with him.

The one I recorded last night to be published on his Instagram page during tonight's dinner:

"Milk in the marketplace: A young man says to the sheikh — I have a bad habit and I cannot get out of it. Whenever I go to the market, I can't keep my gaze down. I can't stop looking at women! It's even worse on Instagram. My feed is full of women. What can I do?

"The sheikh was realistic. He believed in practice. He filled a glass of milk up to the brim for the young man and told one of his students: take this man to the market with you. If he spills even a drop of milk from this glass — beat him!

"The young man trembled with nerves but took the glass through the maze of the market. He sidestepped donkeys, merchants, and orange carts, keeping his eyes locked on the glass of milk. He brought the glass back to the sheikh, not a drop missing, and it was cold to the touch. How many women did you see on the way? the sheikh asked.

"The young man was astonished. None! I didn't see any!

"And this is the fear of the true believer, of the true Muslim — the fear of Allah on the day of redemption. Allah says: Tell the believing men to lower their gaze from the forbidden. That is purity for them. Allah is aware of all we do."

•

Elevated tables flanked the podium. Abdul and the Arab were seated on either side like the angels Raqib and Atid, who are said to sit on different shoulders, each recording our rights and wrongs as we move through life. The Arab's mouth in constant motion as he introduced himself to curious faces. I reminded him to use his father's reputation as a gangster that stretched out of India and into the diaspora. The guests would be thrilled to feel that close to such violence.

The rest of us were at a table closer to the ground. Natalie in a caramel jumpsuit, white cashmere sweater, and dark brown hijab, her face resting on her ringed fingers. Samir already with his blazer off and sleeves rolled up, showing off his phone for Mo', who was staring into the screen, images flashing off his glasses.

Let's not forget my full function wear: olive Canali suit and velvety brown suede Carmina loafers. I suppose I could afford it, in the sense that I had a credit card. The bank had called three times that day. My voice mails were full.

Natalie organized catering from the Royal Bombay Turf Club: masala fried prawns with tamarind chutney; Nani's village lamb, braised, charred, and finished in a madras curry with potatoes, or a secret 1950s Calcutta recipe of chickpea masala for the vegetarians; homemade pistachio and cardamom kulfi or Silk Road gulab jamun for dessert.

This was a monied-for-generations crowd. Kids that grew into high achievers: finance or lawyers. They ate Indian food with silver cutlery, sat on boards of directors, went to the mosque only on Eid and carefully analyzed potential partners' family histories for blemishes. People that planned in decades.

These were South Asians who directed NGOs in countries worse off than theirs; a Haiti or Rwanda. They were not *those* kinds of Indians and happy to provide a list of solutions to *their* problems. Even the Muslims were a different type: Ismailis, shaded in the West by the reputation of their cosmopolitan and kinda white leader, the Aga Khan. The Aga Khan had been named an honorary citizen of Canada so the prime minister could enjoy holidaying on his private island.

Historical beef created walls of insulation. The Aga Khanis had fled persecution from a number of places and it was rare to see them mingle with common Muslims. Abdul thought their ascension as the first major wave of immigrants in the 1970s was inspirational. He confessed that his father had tried to seduce them in the '90s but that they thought his ideas were crazy. He told me if I'd heard of a Muslim politician, it was them. If I'd heard of a Muslim CEO, it was them.

The crowd's buzz quietened as Abdul cleared his throat then spoke into the microphone. He had not practised this speech with me:

"Our youth today know more about Lady Gaga and Britney Spears than about the companions of Rasool. In fact — even more than they know about the prophets. How many of our youth know the names of all the Prophets of Allah? How many know the names of the Sahaba? But ask the same person who their favourite basketball player is and they'll go down the list. Favourite point guard, favourite backup point guard, favourite centre, favourite centre from 1986. This is a serious, you could say, identity crisis, a lack of seriousness about Islam.

"We know the term jahiliyya — the ignorance of the Pre-Islamic era. We know it as a time gone, but it is also behaviour. Whatever time period is ignorant of Islam, that is jahiliyya. Is that where we find ourselves now? Do we see the connections between the past and the now? Jahiliyya comes from the root word jahal, which means exactly what? It means ignorance — this is the time of ignorance. The absence of the message. The message is there, you can say, we have mosques, and prayer, and YouTube lectures, but is it being followed? Is it being heard? We have forgotten how to listen. Forgotten how to heed. Obedience is no longer a virtue. We no longer view our fathers, our mothers, with reverence. What do we see on TV all day? Trauma this, trauma that, my parents did this, my father did that — my father didn't take me to the movies. Why? Your father was outside all day working in this country that shunned him.

"I don't mean to dismiss or negate anyone's experience here. But we know that childhood is a nebulous time, when memory and emotion are at their highest pitch. Parents are a gift from Allah, as you are a gift to them, and beyond that, there are the practical considerations — immigration, starting from scratch, the turbulence of a new country. The putrid hatred that rots man's soul in this nation. Its specific vileness. We remember that while it's in vogue today to locate all our problems in our childhood, we must not get carried away with 'abuse' or its connotations. Our parents do what they can, as they are taught, but we know Allah guides their hearts towards excellence. Consider the errant discipline, the bad memory, the angry parent, and try to determine the question behind the impulse. Try to apply empathy. To understand. We can donate to developing countries, but what does it mean to be borne from them? What does it mean for the parents who raise us here, now? We know that divine guidance, Allah's benevolent gaze, is what ultimately rules.

"Where are you now? I suspect if you're in this room, you're doing okay. Many of you know me and my story. I've been to many prisons: Bagram, Guantanamo. These were cages. Many times I was shackled. Hooded. Beaten. Tortured. But they were only cages if I let them be. They were lessons: lessons on the world, infinite messages from Allah. The hand of Allah is in everything I do, think, feel, or breathe. The invisible hand is the guiding impulse. What comes next is because of Allah. We are in danger of ignorance now. Of allowing the world to happen to us instead of seeking our true fortune. Never forget that we are here for one reason. There is nothing shameful about servitude to Allah. We are not here for earthly rulers."

Abdul returned to his seat. From the milk market video to this, I heard new aggression in his speech. He'd had an interview this afternoon in his old neighbourhood. I wondered how that went. His edge had always been there — that's why I felt safe with him — but in talks like this it sliced through to the surface. Still, he had the good will of the crowd, who were willing to consider his elliptical nature favourably and clapped once they understood it was over.

The MC took the microphone and babbled about raffle tickets. Marwan turned to Samir, remembering the conversation from lunch.

"I know where we can take him," Marwan said. Samir was surprised Marwan spoke to him. "There's an event tonight," Marwan continued. "A friend is there. DJ and stuff."

Samir looked to see if Abdul was listening.

"Like … a club?"

For the first time in a while Marwan was not in traditional clothing that broadcast his religion, but a cheap suit from Zara.

"It'll be good for him," Marwan said.

"Abdul doesn't think so," Samir said.

"Abdul is unsure about the specifics. I'll chaperone."

Samir accepted on Mo's behalf. Mo' pushed his lamb into the mound of potatoes he was not eating. He wanted the phone back.

I refilled Marwan's water. "A club, eh?" I said.

"You know. DJs. Social. It's good for him. Abdul says we have to live in the world, we can't segregate."

"Oh yeah. That's a good insight. Where you hear about this club?"

"Facebook," Marwan said.

"Facebook. You went on Facebook looking for a club to help Mo' reintegrate."

"Yes."

I knew where Marwan kept his goodies. Inside right breast pocket was where joints or mickeys of vodka would be stashed in the old days. I reached across his chest and pulled out a neatly folded flyer.

FRIDAY NIGHT RHYTHM HOUSE PRESENTS TENTH ANNUAL BODYBUILDING EXPO NIGHT OUT FEAT SPECIAL GUESTS

And it went on to list DJs, an MC, and a few of the world-famous bodybuilders, including the world's strongest man. Marwan shrugged and continued eating.

"You'll talk to him for me?" he asked.

I didn't argue. There was no reason to drag Mo' into this but I understood Marwan needed an appropriate reason to go to the club so he could lust freely after Britta. After everything, I couldn't deny him.

•

The waiters swooped our plates away. Abdul gestured to me while he ate a line of melon off a skewer. Two men with bad haircuts were speaking at him and I was rude about making them get lost. He drew confessions from every hole of a room. I understood why those two white golems always hovered protectively around him. People who hadn't spoken about an emotion in decades would blurt secrets to Abdul while he ate fruit.

"Samir is right," I said. "Mo' should go out."

"Does that truly seem appropriate to you?"

"I'll be there. Marwan will be there. It'll be good for him."

"I don't think so," Abdul said.

"It'll help. The comfort of strangers."

"I don't know about Samir."

"I can see that," I said.

"Take Marwan."

"Thank you."

"Take Natalie and Isabella too," Abdul said. "I'll let them know."

Mo' was scrolling through Samir's phone. He'd found the Instagram page for one of the clubs and leered at the women. Samir had heavy eyes, his shirt unbuttoned one too much. He'd been pulling from a flask in the bathroom, likely. I picked up a plate of fried dough seeped in syrup and told them the good news.

•

Rhythm House was the spot clubbers went to retire. Five years ago I would have hated myself for coming here. They had a 25+ policy which meant no one under thirty went. Even those over thirty only went if their life had gone wrong.

I hadn't been clubbing in years. Not since Bagheera. No line yet, not many people, and so we went directly into the space, where blue-and-purple light fell over cheap vinyl surfaces and tables. Seeing a club at half-mast was not pleasant. Because I wasn't forcing my way to the bar, hurrying at the toilet, and dodging the coked ogres down from the suburbs, I was able to take the stale environment in. Sticky floors, piss stank, men and women sloppy at 10:00 p.m. My glass of soda water had a lipstick print hanging on.

An old Black man in a blue Hawaiian shirt, with rough, wrinkled skin, white curls, and a carefree attitude that age earns, danced with two young women, both in dresses that cut away on the sides to reveal striking white skin. He turned his face to the ceiling in pure glee. The women pressed against his front and back. Ask him if money buys happiness.

Bilal took Mo' under his wing like an old friend. The bartenders were confused by plain Coca-Cola orders and hijabs. Bilal ordered enough vodka for all of us.

Abdul had pulled Samir aside before leaving and gave him a stern warning about handling Mo'. Samir sulked at his beer for a long time before finally chugging the drink and ordering shots.

Mo' was a man freed. His shrunken saunter loosened and he allowed himself the occasional gawk. Who could blame him? He never attempted to approach any women, danced in a sort of circle around the centre of the floor, making sure to keep distance from others. Bilal was buffooning with random women and pointing at Mo'. I couldn't imagine a worse wingman. Mo's dancing was rigid movements and limbs shot out off-beat. That he danced at all made me happy.

I bought Natalie a thirty-dollar bottle of Perrier. They reluctantly gave me extra limes. I watched her for signs of relapse, a small sip, a tucked-away flask, a shot of brisk, cold vodka.

I took Marwan to the bar and in a far corner, in a crowd of oversized men, we spotted Britta. She laughed with her neck cranked back. She didn't need Marwan to re-enter her life. He stared at the bartender, trying to control himself.

"I'm going to talk to her," he said.

"Please don't," I said.

"A little chit-chat," he said. "As a fan. It's not untrue."

"What if she doesn't remember you?"

Panic fanned on Marwan's face. I reassured him.

"Bro — she remembers you. I'm joking. A jaguar bit your hand off on a date. She's probably telling that story right now."

Marwan and his Sprite toward the target. The molasses feel of the night came from the hulking bodybuilders, slow-moving creatures who didn't dance. Britta a slim white knife in that gobble of orange skin moving with a pink drink in her hand. I dove to Natalie.

"Hi. I'm Hamid." She was ready to murder me. I continued, "You're Natalie, right? You don't have a Muslim name, yet?"

"You love being dumb."

"I think Nadia would count."

"It's not mandatory actually," she said.

Underneath the table, where no one could see, our knees bumped.

"Wanna dance?" I asked. She stared back at me with hate, shock, death. I splayed my hands open. Breaking the ruse, I said, "I won't touch you, I swear."

I wiggled my shoulders like a puppet until her annoyance slid into a grin. She loved to dance. I'd been a child when I'd last danced sober. "It'll be Halal," I said.

"You're not funny, I hope you know that."

We went to the middle of the floor and hid in the cove of bodies. We stood far apart. I liked to dance; I did not like dancing sober. Too aware of my body to move loose. Reasonable persons didn't dance sober. The new DJ played music we both liked, songs with booming bottom-of-the-ocean bass. I calibrated myself with Natalie by copying her movements, trying to find my own rhythm. Ordinarily a drunk would have come between us but her hijab created repulsion and confusion, resulting in open space.

We dropped into a groove and I had a release I hadn't had since my last night hammered, at the peak of drunkenness, those moments when I wasn't crushed by my own self. That was the moment we all chased. If this is what drink gave Natalie, how could I blame her? Ten, twelve songs passed, we were drenched in sweat. I moved closer to her.

"I thought you were going to be a good boy," she said.

"It's not easy with you."

"Don't say it," she said.

"Why not?" I asked.

"You think it's a magic word."

"I love you."

"I love you too," she said. Tears rushed into her eyes. I pulled a handkerchief out and she allowed me to dab. We'd stopped moving in the middle of the floor. Face to face. Her breath on my cheek. I held her by the waist and she rested her forearms on my shoulders and we swayed like middle-schoolers. "I want you to know that I think you're a good person and I do love you but you're not listening and I don't want you to think it's my fault —"

"I get it."

"Please listen," Natalie said.

"I get it —"

"You don't —" She broke away from me. I followed but she ran into the bathroom just as I heard —

"Yeeeaarrrgggggh! I don't want to do this!" Marwan shouted in front of a bodybuilder, who was on one knee, blood colouring his chin red. The rest of them had taken a step back. Marwan cranked his fist into the man's head again and he fell, his blood spraying on bare legs. By the time I came to Marwan it was over. He was panting and the bodybuilders attended to their moaning friend. The music went back up. A skyscraper-sized white bodybuilder, skin like he'd been dunked in cheese fondue, put a hand on Marwan's shoulder.

"I'm sorry he said that to you. That wasn't cool. He's drunk."

Marwan nodded and accepted the apology. The violence moved to two men arguing at the bar. Two bouncers asked us to leave and a text on my phone told me Samir was outside. We left, Marwan grinning,

"I got her number."

•

Signage outside cast an eerie, technicolour light on the drunks waiting for Ubers. Natalie stared into her phone. Bilal patted his pockets.

"What happened yaar? You're a big boy, eh? It's hot in there," Bilal said and lit a cigarette for himself and a tipsy Samir who struggled to keep upright. Samir slid his sunglasses on and flapped his arms to cool down. Sprawling pit stains grew on his torso.

"I evolved to sweat, okay? It's like a ventilation-type system, okay?"

Marwan paced from excitement; the fight or the number. He answered Bilal,

"You know what he said? Stick to your own kind."

"Maybe he meant bodybuilders," Bilal said.

Samir laughed, burped, almost swallowed his cigarette. Suddenly sober, "Yo. Yo Hamid. Where's Mo'?"

"He came out with you?" I asked.

"Hundred percent."

"Where is he then?"

"Maybe he got a girl," Bilal said.

"Do you have his number?" Samir asked.

"Does he have a phone?" I asked.

He didn't have a phone. "Burrito bro burrito bro, I want a burrito, bro," Bilal sang. I stepped onto the road so I could see farther down the street. Waddling two hundred metres away was Mo'. He stopped at an intersection and checked behind. Seeing me, he turned the corner and disappeared.

It was early in the night and he could be going anywhere. How well did he know the city? Samir insisted he'd not gone out in his Canadian month except for therapy sessions with Abdul. In Serbia he had stayed in an apartment furnished for him by the government, who also kept regular watch on him. He lived a life under constant surveillance. The occasional CCTV camera downtown Toronto freaked him into hiding here too. He could not be convinced they were not for him.

"There was too much noise," Samir said. "He can't handle sudden loud noises."

"He seemed fine in the club," I said.

"That's because I spent the entire dinner showing him all the photos of women on the club's Instagram pages," Samir said.

Bilal wandered off with the conversation, wondering what he'd be like if he hadn't seen a woman in ten years. Samir repeated the noise could have overloaded him and sent him scurrying home. We weren't too far from Abdul's building. Samir tried to convince us this was the case. But I couldn't disappoint Abdul. News media was perpetually circling our enterprise, waiting for the colossal mess-up Samir forecasted. I'd seen a future with Natalie five years down the line. I couldn't give it up.

I begged Marwan to gather Bilal and Samir and take them to their favourite after-hours. Natalie suggested splitting up; I suggested we stay together, using the unease her hijab caused — drunk men, dark night. They both argued we should call Abdul but I vetoed that. Better to tell him with Mo' safe and sound, tucked into bed, than agitate him. We'd find him soon.

Mo' had turned right on a street lined with bars, takeouts, and clubs. This was where most of the Friday crowd congregated. There were a few CCTV cameras keeping an eye on us. We slid through a basement pizza shop and checked out the blank faces. To a shawarma place. Not there.

An Irish pub's patio overflowed onto the street. We surveyed faces. At the door, up a flight of stairs, sitting on a stool, was a brown man, bearded and wearing a fleece vest despite the heat. The pub had three floors and a backyard. It was a university-age crowd and he was checking IDs with a penlight, stamping wrists for alcohol permission. I strode up and he stopped me.

"You can't come in," he said and stared at Natalie, plainly confused. "That's … a covering. No head coverings. Rules. Gangs."

"It's religious," she said.

"I know what it is. Do you?"

"We're looking for a friend," I said.

"She can't come in," he repeated. "No exceptions."

"I'm not drinking," Natalie said. "We're looking for someone and you need to mind your business."

"Listen, ma'am, I'm sorry, I don't want to get in trouble."

"Who's going to get you in trouble? It's a religious covering. It's allowed. I'm not a gangster. Are you dumb?"

"I mean religious trouble." He looked up.

"I'm not drinking. We're looking for a friend. Then we'll leave."

The bouncer's brain strained as he tried to solve the problem.

"You promise you won't drink?"

Natalie rolled her eyes.

"Yes," she said.

"I'm not going to give you a drink stamp."

"Fine."

He wet the stamp and looked at me.

"You want one?"

Natalie huffed past. We stood near the main bar watching the crowd. A drunk next to me wobbled. He stared at Natalie with yellow eyes. He fiddled with his hooked nose, pushed on his mole, and released a wet sock smell. He prepared to speak. He sipped his pint, frothed his lip.

"Lady."

Natalie turned.

"You're very nice."

He offered her a cheers and his next sip stepped him into a dream world.

We checked the other floors and three other places. The bathrooms and the back alleys had the same scramble of tipsy people shouting into each other's faces. A man pissing in an alleyway apologized and told us he couldn't stop his blast. He was streaming against a dumpster. I didn't tell him it was splashing back onto his shins.

I tried to hold her hand twice and she swatted me away. At the third bar, in a thick jam of hot bodies, me leading the way, she let me lead her by the hand. She released as soon as we broke out into the night air.

"I'm happy that this Abdul thing is working for you," I said.

"Good."

"Are you … with him?"

"Hamid."

"Wow," I said. "That's not a no."

"That's not a yes. I told you why I went to him. If I could explain it, I wouldn't be there. Does that make sense?"

"Are you still drinking?"

"Why is that the one question you ask me?"

"It's important," I said.

"It's the only thing you think about me," she said. "Do you think I think like that?"

"No, but … it's like … the root."

"Alcohol is not the root."

"Al-Anon says —"

"Please don't. There was no space with you. Every night I came home and I could feel you all over me. You wished I was drunk so you could shout at me."

"You came home drunk half the time!"

"And what was it? What was it each time? I came home, too drunk for you, we fought, then in the morning we cried, we shouted, and we rolled over and pretended it didn't happen and waited for it to happen again."

"We were getting better. We were doing things. I took that mindfulness class you told me to. I went to Al-Anon."

"Getting better for what?" she asked. "Getting better for who?"

"For each other."

"No."

"I stopped drinking," I said. "That was in support of you."

"You're such a hero," she said. "You stopped drinking and that was that. It was so easy for you and a crime it wasn't for me."

"I know it's a disease, I'm not blaming you."

"Shut up. You don't know anything," Natalie said. "Have you ever felt controlled? A thing so small, so simple, just a glass, just a glass to cool you down and make that feeling that follows you go away? Imagine that's the only thing. Imagine that's the only thing that helps. Imagine your boyfriend, your husband, your lover, you, imagine you, every time I wanted that relief, you were there, your big stupid face, telling me how easy it was to stop. Fine, it's easy to stop. It's so easy to stop. Then go fucking stop."

•

My last drink had been a year before.

I rarely drank anyway. My go-to was the foggy buzz of a joint. I never drank for relaxation but for its charged-up feeling and the permission it gave to direct my anger outward. Anger and anxiety the gift of my upbringing, two feelings that shaped me so well I didn't even know I could feel otherwise — it wasn't until I was in my late twenties I realized I was anxious all the time.

I was fifteen when I first drank. Five bottles of Labatt Blue in a row. I did that every weekend for three years, adding any spirits I could locate. Malibu rum, peach schnapps, Alizé, it didn't matter, the goal was to get so faded I became another person.

In my early twenties, I moved out with Marwan to a downtown apartment near our university, and it was then, visiting my parents once every few months, that I realized the feeling that had warped my upbringing — rage, shame — and filled every corner of that house was not in all homes.

The habit slowed. I got drunk once a month on ten or thirteen drinks at parties. I didn't know what to do around others.

I was shocked at how different everyone was at university. Fully formed, with an easy ability to laugh, or have fun, alongside plans for the future. How could I see the future when I was so clouded with my own bullshit? A girl I briefly dated texted her mother in the morning and evening. They spoke twice a week on the phone. That baffled me. Don't you want to get away from them, become your own person? I asked. I like talking to them, she replied, her face confused and newly wary of me.

I stopped drinking a year before I left the country, half-way through our relationship. Natalie had invited six or seven people to our apartment for dinner. I didn't know who they were. Her personality was restrained but she went through bouts of friendliness where she would gather new friends before dismissing them a few months later. This was a table full of new men and women. A skinny Black man wearing a ridiculous black cotton shirt without sleeves, leather pants, thick-soled raver boots, and an apricot shade of lipstick. On my right, a Filipina, Natalie's "Asian sister" who taught yoga and had an intricate tattoo of Vishnu — I think — on her six-pack. She stroked her black pit hair absentmindedly.

Natalie was in a good mood. After a month-long struggle, she'd processed an insurance claim for her parents after their basement flooded. Now they lived in a swamp in Richmond, BC, and her childhood rubbish was ruined, but the payout would allow them, for the first time, to move above ground. How would they react to the sun? They had a dream to move back home, she said, buy a house. With what money?

Three bottles of open red wine on the table, one fizzy, one that tasted like the harvester's feet, and one that most were drinking from. Natalie rushed back and forth from the kitchen to the dining table, green curry smells following her: ginger;

lime; the dense, eroded odour of fish paste. Her gold earrings and crucifix shone against her brown skin. The girls on the couch laughing, recounting their dates last weekend. Her eyes glassy. I didn't like that. It put me on alert. I was drunk. I didn't like them. I didn't know how to organize them in my head. I sat there like a gargoyle, grinding my teeth. I had four, five gins. Six, seven.

I tried not to count hers. I couldn't stop myself. She had four before dinner. Rum and Cokes. She went on our balcony to smoke and brought another with her. The kitchen a mess even with her friends helping. We sat down to eat. A clutter of plates and smells. Three long-stemmed candles lit. A lamp in the corner, a welt of shadow across the table. The rice wet. Ginger, chili flakes, and sharp lime. The curry delicious; she'd gone out and got baby corn, a low-key favourite of mine. The friends talked and I tried to follow their conversation.

Cleaning up, I was drunk. She dropped a plate and it cracked on the floor. Startled, a friend knocked over a bottle of wine, and the red oozed into a cheap rug I'd brought home from the store. They burst out laughing. They rushed to get paper towels, but not before they cackled, reminiscing of other times this had happened. I was drunk. I was mad. Natalie's satin-green dress, glimmering with light, my chest filled with a horrible tension, I couldn't stand that she could be happy when she was drunk. She knew how much damage it brought. She knew what it did to us. Her full laugh. I threw a plate against a wall. Get out. Get out of my house. A man, I can't remember more, stopped Natalie by the door, asked if she was all right, did she need anything. I shoved him against the wall, out the apartment, and we shouted: Apology, apology, apology. How could you do that to me? Shut up, shut up, you're drunk. You're always drunk. You're always an asshole. You hate me. You hate yourself. You can't look after yourself. You'd be drunk and dead on the street if it wasn't for me. You idiot. You don't even know what it's like. You don't know what it's like to be around you. You don't know what it's like to babysit you. You need help. I'm sick of this shit.

I knew if I hit her the world's order would remain in place. The urge growled in me, begged to be let loose. I'd heard that beat my whole life.

I hovered near her. I was gone, dead. She brought out feeling in me no one else could. Piece of shit, she said. You have a problem. You are a problem. You are not in control of yourself. You are not in control of yourself. What are you in control of?

I felt its tug. I was at the very end. I was close to it. I felt the thrill of hitting her in my hand.

Then I felt a tug away. Away from limbo. A tug pulled me away. What was it? And heaven He raised and imposed balance. That you shall not transgress the balance. I put my head against the wall while she shouted and cleaned. She threw the plate pieces into the garbage. A neighbour knocked on the door. She answered, blood-red under her skin, told them to stay out of it. I got on my knees and mopped up the red wine.

Exhilaration. I'd wanted to hit her. The exhilaration warned me off. I'd stopped because I wanted it.

She went to the couch, legs folded over, head in her hand, and mid telling me off, fell asleep. I lay on the floor below her and was out. In the early morning the sun washed us awake and we moved to the bed, naked, curled into each other, both of us lightly drunk, and we made promises. I was never going to drink again. I loved her. I was going to show her how. I didn't tell her the real reason. I didn't tell her where I had gone that night; how close. I thought if I didn't drink again I'd avoid falling into the shape of my father.

She was right. I was lucky. I don't feel the need to drink. It wasn't a struggle; I stopped cold. Maybe because what I'd been drinking to avoid finally showed up in my stupor. Maybe the glimpse I saw was enough. It was biological, too, my Google searches said, and maybe the alcohol gene skipped a generation. Maybe maybe maybe. I held it over her and tried to sneer her into sobriety.

•

We were quiet after that alleyway tussle but not awkward. We bickered, we knew. No need to make a fuss. We were hungry. No Mo' at two more bars loaded with the same types of faces. Now we wondered if he had actually headed home, so we went backward, knowing we would encounter more bars, faces, and possible escape routes for Mo'. We stopped at a fancy late-night grocery store, the type that carried five-dollar apples and organic turnips and had a gourmet snack bar at the back. Samir hadn't stopped calling and was on his way to meet us at the grocery store, Bilal probably in tow. Marwan texted that he'd tried his best. They hadn't gone far.

I ran my finger over spiked balls of fruit and vegetables I'd never heard of. The aisles stacked neatly and a white stockboy walked around making minor adjustments and comparing the shelves to a printout image he held in his hand. The versions of product they stocked were the most expensive and under the powerful lights I noted every item's preposterous price. I bit into an apple. True enough, it tasted different from the usual bottom-of-the-bin ones I bought.

Natalie and I walked the aisles not speaking. The first grocery trip together is always an important milestone. Our first six months we made a production of making meals for the other, from the grocery store to clean-up, one person taking complete care of the other. Those Friday nights finished the same, the TV on, a joint hanging on my lip, a cold glass of gin in her hands, her feet in my lap. A meandering, lazy fuck when the clock struck midnight. A life of small pleasures I was pathetic for.

At the back near the hot foods were four very tall white women huddled around a rotisserie chicken, ripping it apart. Sweating, they wore shiny short dresses for a club night out; the chicken dripped grease. Their lips were ringed with oil and they chewed loud while talking at each other. A squat brown worker repeated they needed to pay first. He came out from behind and put his hand on the small of one's back. She giggled and asked for potatoes. They each held a leg or wing of shredded meat. He gave them a plastic bowl full of roasted potatoes. He lingered. They ate loudly, one burped, and they broke into laughter, flecks of flesh flying. Thick thighs, long brown hair, sharp nails. He didn't know where to look. They finished the meal and needed a place to put the plastic container. He tried to give them a price sticker and asked them to take it to the cashier. They laughed, his audacity precious, a good show, and one woman stroked his cheek like she would a cat.

There was no one else but workers in the place. As we were about to leave I noticed a tucked-away aisle with the sign GLOBAL CUISINE. I turned into it. Mo' stood in front of a selection of different teas, holding a packet of paprika in his hand. He was completely still.

I approached cautious and put a hand on his shoulder. Shaken out of his daze, he snapped, pushed me, and threw the bag of spice, which hit me and burst into a red cloud. I inhaled and coughed, my nose burning. He threw a can at my shoulder and ran past a confused Natalie. I coughed, crying, and wiped my snot on my shirt and we chased him up an escalator.

He wasn't fast. His awkward stride meant he turned his body at an angle to run straight. He burst through the doors and headed south. I made it through the doors and saw he was unsure of himself. We were at a southern point of the city, near a pier that opened to the black water of the lake. As we ran farther south, the noise of cars was replaced by waves against cement. Natalie shouted after him. We all three out of breath.

Samir's car screeched behind us. It hopped the curb and the lowered Honda scraped against the ground. The waves hit the wall and broke. Mo' walked to the water. He was talking. The waves hit the wall and broke. It would be frigid black, impossible. There was no light on the water, no moonlight.

Mo' faced it. I knew the water's pull. Natalie sped up, understanding. We all did, from time to time. For Mo', probably, it was the heartbeat of life.

He jumped.

Natalie would not speak. I couldn't. We watched the water. She fumbled for her phone and her shaking hands could not dial. Shrill with terror, she asked me to call 911. Samir confirmed it, but I knew we shouldn't. I couldn't call cops. There was too much in my life for me to be calling cops. Already, life had no room to consider Mo'.

I pulled her into my chest and she cried. Samir and Bilal stared into the water, screaming his name like idiots. Bilal sobbed. The wind took their sounds away. Samir on his cellphone came to us. He would tell Abdul, he would handle it. This is where the Arab and Abdul knowing each other would help. Natalie nodded in agreement; that surprised me. Abdul had to be protected.

•

She lay in the crook of my arm for the Uber and we held hands on the elevator ride up.

"How's your father?" she asked.

"Same old."

"Did he sign for the divorce?"

"Same old."

"I'm sorry. Have you talked to your mom?"

"No," I said.

She wrapped her arms around me.

"This place is good for me," Natalie said.

"Is it helping?"

"I wake up and feel good. I work and feel good."

"I'm happy to hear you say that."

"It's ritual," she said. "Practice."

"You're one hundred percent converting?"

"Excuse me, reverting."

"Be for real," I said.

"It's practice. I'm not worried about that. I'm doing the steps. I'm trying."

She left to shower. Her room was as spartan as mine, a single bed, closet, table, sink. A room of devotion. Pipes rattled. She came back with towels around her and her hair. Hot drops of water on her body. Her makeup off, she was younger, with craters the colour of plums around her eyes. "You have to go," she said.

"I know."

"You have to listen."

"I'm trying."

Familiar, new, all at once, a person I'd never seen before. I rose to leave and she didn't move. She dumped her clothes into the hamper next to the desk but held her pair of black panties. The window was open and weak blue light pooled in. She would not move.

"Will you?"

I took a step.

She asked again, "Will you listen?" She pushed her underwear into my open mouth and I inhaled its mossy earth scent. "Will you?"

I said, "Yes," through the fabric. "Yes, yes." She let me pull the towel off and I undid my belt, my pants, let them drop. I held her waist and closed my mouth around the fabric, half of it spilling, and worked myself over, over, and over until I came, sputtering onto the floor.

24.

I drove crazy, ready for that real bottom-of-the-well sleep. True slumber. My first night back at our place. Alone, but I was happy to be in the apartment. I'd left fruit on the counter and a package of ground beef out: trash and rot. Fruit flies hovered. I was supposed to be back at the store tomorrow for inventory, stock, mindless time-fill. The Arab had flown out at midnight and Abdul would leave in the next few days, with Natalie, and I wanted to talk to him to see if I could come along. Marwan could hold it down.

I stopped at the convenience store downstairs to buy Zig-Zags and filters. My credit card wouldn't go through. The Korean working waved me off. I was a regular. I could pay tomorrow.

Even if Abdul said no to letting me accompany him to Bombay, my happiness would not be taken away. The plan was for them to be back in a month. I could imagine a future and that was enough — much more than I'd ever been able to.

Falling asleep on my couch I remembered with shock that that future was tied to Samir and how he had handled what happened earlier. I grabbed my phone to find news of Mo'. It had only been an hour but his body could have been found. I scrolled. No news. We were the only people who would report him missing and it looked like we had not. Could he be alive? I held hope; he had led a sad life, but it forced strength.

The house, the chambers upstairs. Two bodies wrapped with chains, rancid men — shit, piss, scorched faces, fear. That hadn't made news either. What could I do? My life right now was a delicate build. If I pulled the wrong nail out the whole thing would fall apart.

I rolled a joint and put it aside. It was cold on my balcony and I decided I'd allow myself to smoke indoors. My stacks of purchases sat on the dining table.

The constant voice mails from the bank. Why were they trying to raise my credit limit again so soon? My spending had been a problem lately but I hadn't always relied on my credit cards. I wasn't silly enough to ignore interest. It had been so easy in Abdul's building, lying in my wooden cot, scrolling online for purchases that gave me a blip of happiness. My bill would be due soon, near the end of the month. I went online to pay a chunk of it off and found that my account had been frozen.

The weird greyed-out app. It told me to call the bank. I finally checked my voice mails. A pleasant woman left me the first two messages: suspicious transactions. Then a reedy male's voice saying I needed to contact them. One more, this evening, from a different woman who sounded like she was reading off a script.

I pulled up my accounts on my laptop, including for the store and non-profit for the Resettlement Centre. From the joint Resettlement Centre account, there were payments flinging out to businesses that I did not recognize, for services I had not authorized. That made no sense. We hadn't paid or even hired most contractors yet.

I backtracked, clicking on statements from the opening date of the Resettlement Centre's account until the present date.

There were numerous small payments going mainly to three different businesses. I did not recognize any of them. I copied down the receiving names, which were a jumble of generic titles: Maverick324, KumarLakshay Inc., and PinkPainters222Corp. Each payment had a different memo attached, "Plumbing services," "Drywalling," "Lighting," or similar, and that week's date.

For the first three weeks, the payments to the three were small, 1K or 2K at most. Each time a donation of money came in from a legitimate source, a payment went out to Maverick324, KumarLakshay Inc., and PinkPainters222Corp.

Then, in the fourth week, there was a large transfer of 15K to a totally different account than the smaller payments: Seljuk Inc. was its corporate title. Fifteen thousand was dumb. That was too large an amount to go unnoticed by the bank. A few more small payments to Maverick324, KumarLakshay Inc., and PinkPainters222Corp.

The fifth week the account went berserk with six separate payments of 50K to Seljuk Inc. Then, a 200K chunk was wired to Seljuk Inc., but it looked like it may have been frozen for further investigation. That was very dumb. A two-hundred-thousand dollar wire transfer would have to be done in person.

Then more payments of 9K to Maverick234, KumarLakshay Inc., and PinkPainters222Corp, before a final five payments of 25K split between the three accounts.

All this last week. Yesterday, a 10K cheque made out. There was only 5K left in the account. Who was being paid? Maverick234, KumarLakshay Inc., and PinkPainters222Corp seemed to be linked. They all had activity and deposits on the same day. The other account, Seljuk Inc., which received the larger payments, operated on its own schedule.

For weeks the payments coming out of the Resettlement Centre's account were small and looked like they were designed to not be noticed. For years I'd been moving money overseas and around for the Arab, Samir, and their associates, through the currency counter set up by Samir himself at Canada Electronics. From this, I knew under 10K was the amount I could move before any bank got curious and automatic anti-money laundering procedures started.

After the attempt at the large 200K payment to Seljuk Inc. it looked like everyone went dumb trying to drain the bank account.

My personal account had been untouched, but I was linked to the accounts for the Resettlement Centre … in order to pool the funds for donations … Did Samir have access to the account? My name was on all the official documentation.

What did Samir say to me: they needed someone clean on the paperwork.

Money came into the Resettlement Centre's bank account from everywhere. The GoFundMe provided six figures. Then there was money from individual donors, rich men who bought time with Abdul and for the right to be associated with him publicly. Twenty-five thousand here, there, at least from four or five different donors. There were scattered, small donations, even outside of the GoFundMe, from random sources. Our website had a donation button, Abdul's charm a magic spell on whomever he met. There were government grants from different departments and a major construction grant recently fast-tracked. All money recorded. Everything for the cause, for the program. The perks — money, rep, vanity stroked — came after, from connections, networks. We were supposed to leave all the money alone.

Put it in one pot, Samir had said. Keep it simple. It made sense. Natalie on the horizon. I couldn't think of anything else.

Did Samir have access to the account? I tried to remember. The account was in my name, but he'd delivered the paperwork to the bank. But wasn't the Arab on the paperwork too? Would Samir steal from him? There was a bank loan in the store's name, meant to help the Resettlement Centre with cash flow. We had to move fast, Samir said, while we had the public's attention … the bank loan ended up being 250K, but maybe it was a line of credit, I couldn't remember … why didn't I know these things? Why hadn't I paid attention to numbers? They were large … daunting …

I realized with dread, Marwan would be pulled into this. Was he on the bank account paperwork?

How had I let this happen? It had been a month of meetings, dinners, executives, social bullshit, the focus on bringing the money in. That wasn't it. I had been paying attention to the wrong thing.

I remembered there was an online federal registry that gave out ownership details for registered corporations. I could look up the payees in that.

I typed in the first corporate title, Maverick324.

I read the name.

I typed KumarLakshay Inc. into the registry.

I read the name. The same owner as Maverick324.

I entered PinkPainters222Corp.

The same owner as the other two.

I missed signs. I must have. It was so clean. It was good.

The name of the owner on each account was the same.

HAMID SHAIKH.

My own name.

It seemed like I was sending money to myself. I was transferring money from my own non-profit to my own fake contractors. A non-profit exists because all proceeds are cycled back into the company; there is no profit. Angled correctly, the tax benefits are enormous. Wiring thousands to my own fake corporation from my own real non-profit … was a problem.

From my closet I ripped down the thick file of documents the bank had given me when we all went in to open the Resettlement Centre's account. In clean bold type was my name, my signature, next to the Arab's and Marwan's. Not Samir's.

It had to be Samir behind this. I hadn't given him any passwords but the Arab could have given the login details to Samir … and I also gave all details to Natalie … to help expedite, she said …

Pieces came together. The money exchange Samir had set me up with at Canada Electronics! In the last weeks Samir asked me to send a few massive amounts to a single bank account in India, claiming the Arab had a new real estate venture in Bombay that he was going to look into while he was on the wedding trip he'd just left for.

It was too much money to move from one spot without arousing suspicion so he gave me a list of friendly Western

Unions across the city and a list of his cousin's names to use in place of his. This was not unusual. It happened from time to time, especially after a major night at the casino. I got a flat payment: 5K. I counted the bills, thinking how easy this all was.

My father was right. Everyone is trying to get you.

Samir had asked me to send around 250K overseas, roughly the same total amount that went to Maverick324, KumarLakshay Inc., and PinkPainters222Corp.

It was easy to guess what happened. Samir used the non-profit to pay the fake corporations started under my name, withdrew the money, and used me — again! — to send the money overseas where it could be safely hidden. I had no access to the bank accounts for the fake contractors, but they must have been opened with my name for this trick to work.

I won't lie. There was some admiration for how he handled his business. To mark me twice was cruel, but beautiful.

But the money taken from the Resettlement Centre's account was more than 250K. I looked again at the first 15K transferred and then at the other larger payments going to the Seljuk Inc. account. Unlike the other fraudulent payments, the money to Seljuk Inc. had no memo or other information. No attempt at hiding the transfer behind a fake payment for services.

I entered Seljuk Inc. into the online corporate registry, but no information appeared, not even my name. That might not mean anything. The online forms only told me so much.

I knew it had to be Samir. I couldn't understand why after carefully moving small amounts of cash he would up the amount foolishly, but I knew it was him. The simplest reason had to be true: greed. We shared that in common. While I was greedy for Natalie, he took me.

Opening bank accounts and moving money needed one attribute: confidence. The confidence to walk into a bank with fake documents, a real smile, and introduce yourself as Hamid Shaikh, giant idiot, and repeat that over and over through the city. Once you had one account at a bank it was no trouble to open the others. The secret of crime was how easy it all was.

I knew it was Samir who had created this spiderweb where every strand led back to me. It would take two seconds for the government to discover the contractors were bogus, and four more to put me in cuffs. Worse, I realized, I'd wired money overseas to India.

Still, there was no finesse to the plan. It was brute force. The smarter thing to do would have been to fake one or two contractors and skim money over time for passive income — as had been done with Maverick234, KumarLakshay Inc., and PinkPainters222Corp. The large amounts to Seljuk Inc. were clumsy.

It was not clumsy. It couldn't be clumsy. Samir wasn't clumsy.

Why in the first weeks was the amount skimmed reasonable? Why was that hustle skilled? Then, all of a sudden ... the Seljuk Inc. account. Who did it belong to?

Despite what I would go on to do, I knew at that moment my anger was driven by willful ignorance. But that was my training: ignoring violence my special skill.

•

If Samir was a piece of shit, Bilal was his hovering fly. He'd be at his favourite after-hours. It took me five minutes to get there in the Integra.

Samir and his cronies. I didn't feel on the drive over. No urgency. Anger at its mightiest when cooled. It knew it would have its time. The flame of the future I'd seen that morning was gone. The moving money, the fake contractors, it was too large to be ignored. Someone would get caught and it would land on me. That it happened swiftly and that I wasn't able to see it because of my own greed made me upset, but I had no time to consider it. The coiled tension had to be expressed. There was no doubt.

I didn't know where Samir lived. Bilal would. Their after-hours was above a Pizza Pizza on Yonge down the block from the Brass Rail he loved. It was a few rooms, a generous array of drink and drugs, and always someone to leave with, paid or not. I stopped at the convenience store and bought a pack of Parliaments, Bilal's brand.

I double-timed the stairs, passed a fallen-down drunk, then doubled back to see if it was Bilal. It was not. Low-volume jazz filled the room. Tiny florets on red wallpaper covered the walls, peeling in spots. The loudest man was in leather pants and vest, digging his fingers, each ringed with a turquoise jewel, into the thighs of the woman sitting on his lap. She played with his leather cowboy hat. He laughed loud and looked around the room after each of his jokes hoping to pull a drunk in. There were plants in a corner, leaves ringed brown, crumpled in a heap, dying.

Bilal sat alone at a corner table lit by the orange of the pizza sign, his eyes puffed like he'd been crying. I ordered two whiskey sodas and put the drinks down in front of him.

"You straight?" I asked.

"I'm a little drunk."

"No shit."

"Yes, always," Bilal said.

"You crying about Mo'?"

"No. Samir has no news about that. It could be okay. You never know. See this?" He showed me an airbrushed photograph of a rigid Indian woman and man. A computer-generated heart surrounding them. "The Sikh girl I told you about," he said. "In Delhi. Just married."

"The one that got away."

"No, not even. Not really. I hated her by the end. She drove me crazy. But every time I see her I get sad. I don't know why. This was hard. She was the type do one thing, say another, say one thing, do another. I go crazy when I hear her name." He put back half the first whiskey.

"I need help," I said.

"From me?"

"Where does Samir live?" I asked.

"Samir? I don't know."

"You don't know?"

"I don't know," Bilal said. "I really don't."

He rushed the remaining drink.

"You want a smoke?" I asked. "I bought you a pack."

"A gift? For me?"

"I was buying gum. I thought, maybe Bilal needs a smoke. I noticed you always finish a pack when we're out. We spend ten minutes trying to buy you one."

"That's very thoughtful," he said. He examined the pack in its plastic wrapping and turned it over in his hand.

"You coming?"

He nodded and followed, telling the bartender we'd return; to mind his drink. The back exit led to a side street with trees and not much else. We walked a few steps into an alleyway full of garbage cans and back doors. Bilal lit his cigarette and offered me one. I refused. Was he lying? I smothered my apprehension. Be clear, straightforward.

"Where does Samir live?" I asked.

"I don't know."

"You guys Uber home together all the time."

"He drops me off first."

"I'm going to ask you one more time."

"Or what?"

I was at ease. Loose. Comfortable. I welcomed it.

I kneed him in the gut.

The cigarette flew and I pushed him backward into a garbage bin. He dropped.

A kick to the ribs. Two more.

I let him on his knees to breathe. Big gale-force breaths. He put his hand up to stop me, and I let him inhale twice more, then kicked him hard so he fell over and groaned. His eyes popped and he choked and I let him breathe for a little bit and then put my foot on his stomach and pushed, wheezing him like an accordion. He held onto my ankle.

"Stop stop stop I'll tell you I'll tell you."

"Tell."

"He's not at home right now. He lives in Malvern … But he's not at home, he's at his family's, the family house in the suburbs, I don't know where."

"What family?"

"Ahmed, ArabTarzan, man. He's dog-sitting," Bilal said.

"If I go there and he's not there …"

"No, no, no, not lying. Please. Chill. Chill. He's there."

"You lying?"

"No, no, bhai, swear to God."

"Thanks," I said. "Here."

I picked up the cigarette packet from the ground and tossed it on him.

•

Purity. That's what obsession admired. That's what anger sought.

The different threads dangled in front of my face but wouldn't weave together into a coherent motive. Moving large sums was stupid. Samir was patient, careful. The little blips of 1K here and there was his work. His restaurant, the vacuums, he made money in increments, thinking long-term.

I circled the amounts transferred, refusing to pounce on the thoughts that came up. We were all scrambling for money trying to make our lives worthy.

Was it fair to hold Samir fully accountable? I had played a role — I hadn't seen what had happened right in front of me. In another mood, in another way, I would admire his behaviour. If it had happened to someone else, I would say it was the appropriate price for carelessness. The vision in front of me on that drive was clear: Samir had lost Mo', he had scuttled my future, he had stolen from me. I was calm because I was not surprised. Not surprised at what Samir had done and not surprised at what I was about to do. My life culminated in front of me.

It was 4:00 a.m. by the time I rolled into the curved driveway. Emerging strings of light in the sky. His ride parked in front of the garage door, so I set mine behind his to prevent escape.

I didn't want to hide. Bilal had probably told him I was coming. Around the side of the house, past the line of open-air animal cages. The pit bulls watched over me when I went by. Her cage was at the end of the line.

Bagheera would be old and fat, slowed by age and domesticity, content to lie in the pit of her cave. Her cage had new grass, a fake tree, and a black recess. I peered in to find her. She wasn't there.

"She'll be ready soon," Samir said, holding a Heineken bottle by its lip.

"For what?"

"Feeding time. I moved her downstairs only." He motioned for me to follow. The basement was dark except for the giant TV flashing the white light of Raptors highlights. A group of crows burst from a tree. Samir finished his cigarette and flicked a perfect arc into the garbage can. He exhaled into the house and left the sliding doors open.

"Don't worry," Samir said. "They're not coming back for one month."

"You a pet-sitter?"

"Why not? She is my first pet. Don't underestimate the importance of the first. The first anything. It sets the imprint for all the rest."

"You fucked me," I said.

"First time?"

"I saw the bank accounts."

"Good for you."

"All that money you got me to send to India."

"I have my family there," Samir said.

"How much did you take?"

"A few thousand. You'll be fine. I'm going back soon."

"You didn't even try to hide it."

"It can be explained," Samir said. "There's security footage of me in the banks. I tried very hard with your signature but I'm sure the loops are off."

"Shut up."

"You're a little brain-dead when it comes to her, no?"

"Shut up," I said.

"This isn't as big a deal as you're making it. I used your name, but I'm not the one —"

"Where's the money?"

"The money's gone. You sent it to Bombay yourself. I'm gone," Samir said. "Listen, bhai, you can tell them the truth about me — I don't mind. They're not going to find me. They're not even going to try. You'll get a slap on the wrist. Unless they say some terrorism thing. You have to contain the Abdul part. That will be all over the news."

"I sent money to Bombay ..."

"That's fine. That's not terrorism. Somalia, Pakistan, that's terrorism. Why did you come here just now?"

"What kind of stupid question is that?" I asked.

"Pick up my phone. Right there. Pass is 9999. I brought it up for you already. Look at that page and then you have to go." I popped in the password to see the bank page already up. I'd scrolled through the numbers before. It was the same numbers.

"This goes back to me," I said. "You moved the money with the fake contractors. I get it."

"I can't tell. Are you being stupid or serious?"

"Where's my money?"

"It's not yours," Samir said. "That's the fraud part, bhai. Look at the funds. I wasn't planning on hurting you. I know you're angry, but it's not me, not my fault. I was going to do the reasonable thing, the gentle thing, just a few points every month from incoming donations. Under the radar. Hidden figures. Then someone moved those big numbers and I got a call from the bank."

"This is on you."

"You know those numbers are trouble. They don't like us to have big money, I told you that. Over 10K is an automatic trigger, yaar. I know that. You know that. Why? Because we do this. This is what we do. Who doesn't do this? I know you're soft in the head but you know what he's been through. You know what Abdul is. He doesn't make sense. That jail rearranges you. Everyone wants to suck his dick but they don't know what's going to come out. Except Natalie. She sucks his dick and money comes out. You watch this?" He opened the YouTube app on the TV and brought it to a clip of Abdul facing the camera in an all-black outfit with his eyes rimmed kohl and a white wrap turbaned around his head. A new video.

Abdul said, "We are in disaster. We won't admit it. We are in disaster. We thought we could come here and retain our connection to Allah, the most merciful, the benevolent. Instead, what do we do? What have we done? Why are we here? Have you asked yourself, once, why are we here? Is it for your family? Your job? Your money?"

His friendly theatrics were absent. The sly smile gone.

Abdul continued: "We look for guidance and take none. We think the search is enough. We live in spiritual squalor yet we're happy because our children pray before sleeping. I go to your mosques on Eid, for the morning prayer, do I see children? The whole new world is here for us and we do nothing. We are happy: this is a country run by people of the book, Christians, Jews —"

I tensed. Muslims should never say *Jews* in public.

"— and so we think we are not needed. We have no mission. We're happy with the schools, the government, the way our people amble in public with no direction or reason. We're not allowed to be angry. And yet, what should we be? What do they ask from us? What do they solicit on the streets, in the night, in our places of work, in our children's classrooms? And what is our reason? Do we wake up every morning for Allah? What can there be for us, except to be angry? We think a spiritual struggle is back home, wherever that is. We think the fight is for our brothers in the holy lands. We donate to Palestine, to Afghanistan, to Syria, and khalas, our job is done. We ask our money to do our spiritual work for us. We abandon them. We take the whole of our spiritual nourishment and put it in our bank account and say: go forth. What's needed is simple. A reorientation. A reorganization. The new world can be ours as it is theirs. It's a trick to think it's only for them. A reinvigoration. Our new world is the same as the old world. Our connection remains. Our duty remains to both worlds. It's all Allah's land. It's all for us to cleanse. The call for jihad to be heard."

There are lots of ways for the word jihad to be interpreted. There's generally one way it is. His speech avoided a call for action, but it was direct, and worse, angry, and way worse, recorded.

I put my hand on the couch to steady myself. The video left me with no feeling. Or was it all feeling, all at once? Samir came near me. I wouldn't let him speak. I spoke over him. If I didn't hear him, it wouldn't be true.

"Where's my money?" I said.

"I'm going back. I miss my family," Samir said. "I have a niece. I miss my life. Me and Ahmed — we aren't blood. I babysat him for three years here. Took care of Bagheera like she was mine. She was mine! This is my severance. You'll never hear from me, bhai. This wasn't supposed to happen like this. Two weeks back I get a call from the bank. Can I speak to a Mr. Hamid Shaikh please? Excuse me sir, there's been a suspicious transaction on your account: did you transfer fifteen thousand dollars? This is three weeks into it — there was a lot of money in the account then. While I move small amounts, this Abdul idiot moves fifteen thousand in one go? That was it. Made me realize. I'm done with this country. Let's see how much money I can take before they catch on. I guess Abdul had the same thought."

Samir came closer to me.

Everyone is out to get you, my father said.

The words were sinking into my head when Samir swung a bottle and cut a gash into my forehead. Green pieces flew. My blood warm down my face.

There was blank space. No future, nothing beyond the moment I was in.

We both swung, I hit his shoulder, he hit my jaw. He had me in a headlock. I shoved him into the countertop. We stood apart panting wild. His eyes searched the room. He didn't want to fight. He wanted to get away. That was our difference. I charged and he put his arms up shouting and I body-checked him square in the chest. He stumbled back and fell. He scrambled down the stairs on his fours, crawling like a dog to the medical room.

The smell of feathers, animal shit, and antiseptic as I took the stairs down, catching my breath, calming. My forehead bled, covering my eye with a red flood. My jaw. I fiddled my tongue for a loose tooth. None. Good. I opened and closed my hands.

He stood behind a stainless-steel table holding a metal pan up for protection. A knife lay on a tray in front of him. His gold bracelet shone with blood.

"Stop, stop, listen, stop," Samir said.

He was bleeding; was I bleeding? I forgot. My shoulder hurt. He talked. I didn't care. I was wrong. I had been wrong about everything in my life. Every decision I made had brought me here. I couldn't listen to myself. I wanted it to be over. I wanted resolution. He was my resolution. My body was inflating with air, floating out of control of my mind.

I knew what had happened with the money. I couldn't let him say it. He kept trying and I charged at him.

He had earned this. I slipped in blood. Then I was on him. Stop talking. Stop talking. You have the money. You have the money. His teeth cut my knuckle. I was tired. I couldn't breathe; I couldn't do it. He'd started this. His face was dark and red. He'd taken my name, my money, my life. My name. I dropped my elbow into his face. Broke his teeth. Let my body do the work. He'd pretended to be my body when he walked into those banks. Let him have it then.

He spat blood on me. I swallowed it. He had no front teeth. His nose a flat thing now. I had the knife from the table. It went above his ribs and into his body. There was no resistance. I pushed it down with my body weight to its hilt. He couldn't speak. I got off him. I pulled the knife out.

Samir's head and body shook in different directions. I exhaled. He moaned. Finished. I took a breath in and out. His nose whistled. Blood rushed from the wound in his chest. Relief. Like I'd taken a piss held in for a long, long, time.

The biggest cage was at the back. Bagheera lying in it but keeping an eye on us. She had a new scar over her eye and molted fur. She huffed. They never had found Marwan's hand. She curled her lips at me, made a noise from the centre of her torso. There was no lock on the cage. She was at the very back, as far away as possible. She got up, sitting like the sphinx. I slid the latch on the door up. Her fur almost blue. Her colour hadn't left her all these years. Poor girl. She was beautiful, made to be what she was — we were what stopped her. She made a low noise and let out two huffs of air.

Her nose twitched, eyes sharpened. I turned a tap on for her. We didn't take our eyes off each other. I lifted the latch to the side and pulled her cage door open so it was ajar, two inches. That's enough.

I moved backward slow.

I closed the exit door.

25.

In my father's defence, he had been drunk when he hit us. I had no excuse. I'd taken my own step into the world, away from his shadow and created my own violence. I'd never felt so light. I was in front of the feeling I'd had my whole life.

I grabbed Samir's cellphone, wallet, passport. Dogs barked outside. I sprayed the knife down with bleach and buried it in the woods behind the house. I changed into swim trunks and a T-shirt, walked two hundred metres away from the knife, dug a hole, squirted lighter fluid over my clothes and shoes, and spent thirty minutes burning them. The flame kept me warm in the cold dawn. No one would be by for a month. Samir was the designated keeper for the Arab's vacation. He had no one to report him missing. No one cared. I had time.

I wasn't fit for anything. Samir hadn't taken anything from me; I'd made a mistake. I never had anything. I should have recognized myself as vacant.

I was invigorated. He'd asked for it. He'd acted against me. In those woods, hidden by the trees, it made sense; I could trace my life from its beginning to this moment. Of course this had happened. I was in awe of what I'd done. I'd eradicated someone. I couldn't have been prepared for it. My memory of the events became a black zone. I did what I had to. What I always did. I went forward. Like everything, I accommodated it.

I wish I'd done it for a different reason. That he'd threatened Natalie; even Abdul or Marwan. I'd done it for myself. I'd acted out of shame. It made me vulnerable to the world in a way I had not been before. But then, beyond that vulnerability was strength. Power. The act nourished. A threshold crossed.

I'd shocked myself. I hadn't surprised myself — the difference between the two came to me slowly. All along, in some animal way, I'd known what path I was on, and where it ended.

My body had shown my mind what we truly were.

26.

There were now three protest groups outside the Resettlement Centre and their rally cries crossed over one another. Police cars arrived to monitor and paramedics were treating a weeping woman dribbling blood from her eyebrow onto her fanny pack and khaki cargo shorts. There was a TV news van alongside a ring of onlookers.

The original group of protestors remained. They did not want evictions. Abdul had tried to broker a dinner with them and his gang of pale faces but this invitation had morphed into a rumour that ignited the page of a prominent social media activist who called himself DogDad_Avenger22. In an effort to be culturally conscious toward the Chinese tenants, the post claimed, Abdul would be preparing a colossal pot of classic Chinese dog meat soup for them. Puppies were preferred and in fact Abdul had several provided by ArabTarzan. The dogs would be blanched first to remove their naturally earthy flavour and then added to a broth finished with spring onions and ginger. A humble dish.

Chasing the hundred comments down it was easy to locate people who didn't believe this. It was way easier to find those ready to fight. *You know what they're like,* the comments said. *You know what their rules say about dogs. The angels do not enter a house in which there is a dog. Whoever keeps a dog will have his reward deducted.* His recent jihad post had added to the fuss and in the morning an animal rights group appeared on site.

The two protesting parties bickered until an anti-Islamophobia group joined the scene. They lacked the fierce bite of the others but provided a needed antidote to the rage. It was made up of a university crowd and older whites getting their steps in. A brown doofus in a thobe and fistful of beard held a sign that read, IF YOU'RE NOT SCARED, HUG ME. His head swivelled to follow two white women. My phone pinged with a new email to the listserv cancelling the day's events. A fourth group, an anti-Sharia-law mob, were on their way.

Natalie unleashed her managerial skills in the kitchen, ordering our workers around to comfort the two cops attending to a slumped man shivering on a stool. He had a thick moustache that appeared stapled on and when he spoke his head rattled like a toy. He was familiar, like old photographs of my father. He stank of pheromones my body instantly knew as fear.

Natalie came to me. I behaved. I pushed down my giddiness. I'd never had to re-seduce someone. Her fingers glid across the stainless-steel countertop. I loved her. I needed her to say it, again. I'd gone to the emergency room for stiches where Samir had cut me and told her that I had fallen. Her head cocked to the side, she chose to believe me.

"That's Imran," she said. "He's the other patient." She ordered a pot of tea, snacks for the cops with bottles of water. Abdul continued speaking Imran's story to the cops. Imran had been in Toronto one month after being snapped up at the Pakistan-Afghanistan border and held in Cuba for sixteen years. He had originally been resettled to Yemen, where he knew no one, as he was Pakistani. Through Abdul's intervention, he managed to be brought to Canada. His actual crime: selling burned Bollywood DVDs at a soccer match. Later, during a snatch of conversation, he confided in me that he had probably been sold for bounty to the Americans by a jealous husband.

Natalie and Abdul hadn't expected me so early, but quickly the Imran controversy — he was responsible for the brow slash on the fanny pack protestor — and the attending cops took over their attention. Abdul spoke to the police, the black line of his gums obvious; Natalie kept distance from me. For the first time, I noticed Abdul's angular, aquiline nose, and the polite, condescending way he spoke to authorities.

Like Mo', Imran had been inside since arriving, running through medical and security checks. Unlike Mo', he was eager for the world. Abdul had given him a small assignment: go outside and get coffees — two black, one latte, one capp. He was almost home when the protestor snuck behind and hollered into his ear. Imran dropped the coffees and swung. No big deal, really.

Abdul tried to explain trauma to the two officers, who seemed, understanding the complicated nature of the events, to regret responding to the call. When Imran tried to speak, Abdul interrupted with a puke of medical and Islamic jargon meant to confuse. The cops stood with their hands in vests, nodded with affirmative noises. The scuffle had ripped Imran's shirt open. The crowd had collapsed on him as the cops arrived, called earlier by a neighbour.

Natalie rejected a plate of lentils brought for the cops and told the worker to get sandwiches. "It's not good," Natalie said to me. "We've been getting too many media requests since the first protest … this is next level. Too much attention."

"It's all fine," I said. "We have some positive stuff scheduled."

"I'm getting government emails. They want to know what's up."

I tried comfort. We waited to find out which protest group the wounded belonged to. Fingers crossed for the anti-Islamophobia group but the woman's cargo-shorts-and-fanny-pack combo gave a distinct animal rights vibe.

Imran reached for tea and through the tear in his shirt I could see fresh scratches across his chest crisscrossed over old scars. He stood up. What I thought was him hunching in fear was his natural posture. A permanent happening to his back. There were red lashes on his stomach and the cops were inquiring about that now. Abdul turned his head and clucked. "He's been in Canada's gracious custody only for a month. These are from Guantanamo Bay."

"They're still doing that stuff over there?" a cop asked.

"You'll have to ask the Americans."

The officers tried to figure out if this was an immigration issue. When Imran jabbered in a language I'd never heard, the cops wrapped up the proceedings.

"We'll have more questions," a cop said. "Stay here."

I shuddered when the police left, finally fearful. I wished for the warmth of the fire that had burned my clothes. I had the tools to handle this problem. I was lucky in that. To push down an image until it disappeared into the confusing mass of memory's museum.

The last gasps of Samir, the red flesh of his wound opening and closing like a mouth.

I wasn't stupid; I couldn't confess, no matter how urgent the need was to discharge the burden. How simple to invite the relief that expression brings. I couldn't; it had to be my secret, molten and fused to me. I had to accept what I'd done in silence.

I had to talk to Abdul. That was all I felt. Through him I could create the one thing that was rare to me, rarer now, than death: hope. The ability to surmount yourself. To keep going.

•

I found him on the roof watching the sway of protestors below. A twirl of cigarette smoke rose above his shoulder. Not yet noticing me, he tossed his butt over the ridge and startled when he turned. His lips curled back, revealing sharp incisors and receding gums; but the flash of red and white disappeared into his customary smile.

"Brother," he said and motioned toward lawn chairs. The hidden rooftop garden had been done pro bono by a local to Abdul's specific instructions. It mimicked the Lodhi Garden in Delhi, with plants and shrubs that would withstand winter.

His black track suit crinkled when his arm rose to his mouth. The same track suit he'd worn when he stood outside my apartment and beckoned me into the night.

I had considered his mysterious visit a gift from Allah and a welcome distraction into my life: violence to act upon instead of thinking about Natalie. It was a message from above, like

Bagheera biting off Marwan's hand. Where Marwan had contemplated the deeper meaning, I had not.

Another coolie came out to deliver two cups of bitter tea. A mint leaf floated to the surface. I took a sip and Abdul sat, clearing his throat.

"You've heard about Mo'?" he asked.

"I was with him when he jumped."

"He's fine."

"He jumped in the lake!"

"He's at my home," Abdul said. "Resting. I was wrong about the situation. I shouldn't have let Samir take him."

"Can I see him?"

"He's recuperating," Abdul said. "I should apologize. About Marwan."

"He believes everything you say."

"Most people do. I shouldn't have let him believe about his hand, that it was a message from above."

"What doesn't have Allah's name written inside it?" I asked. "What doesn't have his hand guiding it?"

"I don't think like that," Abdul said. "Not so literally."

"So, Marwan losing his hand wasn't special."

"Not more than any other trauma," Abdul said. "I didn't want to take his zeal away from him … But I shouldn't have let him believe. What about your zeal? I tried to bring it out in many different ways. I tried so hard with you. Natalie told me you could be reached."

"Samir killed any zeal I have."

"Meaning?" His black track suit caught the sun in its material. The same track suit he wore when I stumbled upon him in the house with those two men. I always knew it was him. And I knew who those two men were: Imran and Mo'. I knew, finally, there was no point in ignoring everything I'd seen him do. We were the same. I'd killed a man, just as he had.

"Samir's been stealing from us," I said. "From the bank account. He's been using the donations to pay himself, pretending to be contractors. He's done it all under my name, so it looks like I've been paying myself."

"Should we call the police?"

"I spoke with him."

"Meaning?"

"We shouldn't involve the police," I said. "You didn't notice that he'd been taking money?"

"I don't look at the bank accounts," Abdul said. "Natalie handles that. She takes care of the money."

"Do you believe in God?" I asked.

Abdul laughed. He got off his chair and walked back to the edge of the roof to look down at the protestors below. He didn't want to answer. I needed him to answer. He spat off the roof, took a sip of his tea, and lit another cigarette.

"What a question!" he said.

"Do you?" I asked.

"In what way?"

"I don't know. God, Allah."

"It bothers you to say Allah."

"It doesn't," I said.

"You're not this typical, confused Muslim — I know. I'm not trying to insult you. Don't be upset at what I'm trying to say. All the same, you don't hold yourself as one. You don't look at yourself as one coherent whole. Is that not a problem? You think you're split into before and after. How much do you keep secret from yourself? Muslims have learned to develop the habit of keeping secrets. A Muslim should learn not to say more than what needs to be said. A lot of our work is clandestine by nature. Allah moves in shadows. A lot of harm has been inflicted by talking. Have you ever hurt anyone? Does it make you believe or not believe?" he asked. "When I shot the soldier I believed in Allah more than ever."

"I believe if I can see the hand that shapes."

"And are you supposed to see the hand that shapes?" Abdul asked.

"With Marwan I thought losing his hand would hurt him. But nothing hurts him," I said. "He acted like he got a nick while shaving. I really felt, maybe, for the first time, maybe, that there was guidance. Allah would not let him be hurt. He lost his hand! And he didn't crumple into nothing. That must be Allah."

"We really want Allah to be logical," Abdul said. "We want him to be reasoned. Scientific. For proofs. When your father saved you from drowning — was that logic?"

"Natalie told you about that," I said. It frightened me that he knew that story.

"Natalie loves to talk about you," he said and moved toward me. We sat side by side.

"He's my father. He had to save me."

"What's the memory? You were in a pool, visiting Delhi, a little boy, and you went down the slide too fast and choked on water. You were drowning. How hot it must have been that day. I can hear you sputtering. I can feel the pain in your chest. And he pulled your little body out. That was it. A father's swoop. And now what? You feel in debt to your father for his rescue?"

"No," I said. "I don't think so. He did what he had to do when he pulled me out."

"Did he?" Abdul asked.

"He's my father!"

"What if he didn't? That is harder to consider. He could have been inside. He could have been having a drink. He could have watched your little limbs and seen his escape from that life." Abdul laughed. He put his hand on my knee. His breath smelled of tea. "Natalie saved you," he said.

"That's love," I said. "What I have for her is love."

"The same love you have for your father?"

"My father does what he has to. It's not love. It's duty. A requirement."

"The minimum was saving your life. That's quite the minimum. You don't feel bound to him?"

"I have to be."

"Why?"

"He's my father! He came here, they came here, they worked, they left India, they did this for me. You've seen Marwan," I said. "He worships his father."

"Marwan loves his father."

"Good for him."

"You've kept that resentment well under wraps."

"I don't resent Marwan," I said. Abdul lit one cigarette with another. I wanted to escape this conversation but knew I had to see this to its end. "I don't resent him," I said. "It's hard. It's difficult. I love him. You're wrong. It's not resentment. I don't want to take it away. What can I do about jealousy?"

"And you're upset with Natalie, too, about leaving her parents?"

"Do you believe in God?" I asked again.

"*Milestones* was written in prison. ISIS is from prison too. Does that mean prison is where God is? What do you think came from Guantanamo Bay?"

"A lot of nothing," I said.

"Is God in prison?" Abdul asked.

"What did I say? His name is written on everything."

"Even Shaytan, then? I killed, you know, Allah was written in that act of mine," Abdul said.

"You had a reason. It was war."

"That's our language," Abdul said. "Isn't it still wrong? I acted from fear and abandoned Allah. I killed someone. I shot him. I never saw him; I shot him. They matched the bullets to a gun they found near me. How often do you imagine killing?" Abdul stood again and loomed over me. The sun seemed to hide behind him.

"I don't believe you didn't know about the money," I said.

"You're mistrustful in general. I'm not offended. Natalie loves to tell me how alike we are. Our arms, our biceps, our shoulders, our chest. She says that we were built from the same mould."

"We all come from Adam."

"That's a good one."

"Natalie loves to say you're doing good. Where's Mo'?" I asked. "And Imran?"

"You don't think that's doing good? Taking those terrorists in, those discarded, teaching them, showing them how to live again. Do you know what happens to most people who leave prison? You read about it, did you? Guantanamo Bay — imagine that. In Pakistan, Afghanistan, Morocco, Yemen; you think those released there all have Instagram pages? Even getting to leave a place like Guantanamo comes with its own burden. Its own weight. To be aware of life so fully. That's what happens when you're inside. All you can think about is what's outside. And then when they throw you back out ..."

"What are you doing to Mo' and Imran? In those rooms. In the house."

"I'm doing what's already been done. You think they know how to move among us?"

"You're hurting them."

"I am?"

"You're torturing them."

"Do they seem fearful? They've chosen to live at the Resettlement Centre, have they not? They've chosen to live with me and my methods. Do you know what it means to put a man in prison and then take him back out? What does that road look like? Do you know? No one has ever asked me if I miss it. It's inconceivable, isn't it? That's what truly makes me a monster. To bristle at my freedom."

"I'm sorry," I said.

"Do you care about Mohammad and Imran?" Abdul asked.

"Of course."

"Did you when you saw them in that room? Before you knew their names?"

"I was terrified when Mo' jumped."

"And when you saw him in the room with me?"

"That had nothing to do with me."

"You saw them being tortured."

"It could have been anything."

"You knew exactly what you saw," Abdul said.

"I needed to find Natalie."

"Because of Natalie you didn't care about those two men in that room."

"No. I'm sorry."

"How many people do you think have said sorry to me? It's fine. I'm doing well. Don't get that confused. That lust had to be directed. That ambition. It's difficult to direct ambition. What's yours for — money?"

"Whose isn't?"

"You're pretending," Abdul said. I stood up. Abdul startled. Was he afraid of me, too? We were the same height, the same weight, our frame the same. That first night I really met him, outside my apartment when Natalie left me. He called me toward him. He whupped my ass in the dark. I had wanted to be him more than anything else. Even as I learned what he was, I wanted to get closer and closer.

"Money is what you need," I said. "Why did your father come here? My father? For a 'better life.' What does that mean? Money, money, money."

"Would you kill for money?" Abdul asked.

"What did you kill for?"

"Fear. Lust. For Afri. I forgot Allah," Abdul said.

"You have ten million dollars. Did he remember you?"

"You offer money to the world and what else. Violence?"

"Yes," I said.

"Did you ever hit Natalie?"

"No."

"But you wanted to," Abdul said.

"I never thought of hitting her."

"You were worried about it. Worried about what would happen if you kept drinking. Worried about what would come out of you."

"It's not the same," I said. "I'd never hurt her."

"Isn't that why you stopped drinking?"

"I stopped 'cause I'm a good Muslim."

"We beat our wives," Abdul said. "We've always beaten our wives. All our men beat our wives, our children. That's what they say. What about —"

"Don't bring my mother up."

"I won't."

"You don't get it," I said. "Your father didn't beat you."

"What happened to a few spanks? How often did he hit you?"

"It doesn't matter," I said.

"I'm listening."

"He hates himself and so he had to hate me. I don't know what's wrong with him. He has no connection to the world. I don't know why he drinks. He's never shown me a single photograph of his family. Of my family! Not just his. There's no photographs of me as a kid. Or home videos. Every time I think of him I'm full of hate. He hates me and I hate him. So who cares? What good does it do? It's dragging me down to death. It's death. That's what it is."

"You said you love your father."

"That's not in the equation," I said. "That's not a factor. I love him. I can't do anything about that."

"You keep going back to him. Seeing him, visiting, bringing plant food. You give him hope. Does he love you?" Abdul asked.

I wanted to throw myself off the roof. I was trembling. Abdul took a sip of his tea. We did not speak for a minute. I put my hand into a bush in the garden and crushed leaves. He chewed the mint leaf from the tea. He continued, "How we waited for a woman in Guantanamo. All the men shackled waiting for a woman. The boy who could recite the soccer games from memory. He was beaten almost daily at one point. Can I show you how they took him out of his cell?" Abdul pulled me out of my chair. He put his hands on my waist and turned me around so he was behind me. He slipped his forearm across my throat and his other arm clinched my head. He pulled his forearm tight against my Adam's apple. He pulled tighter. "They took him out every day like this. He wanted a woman very badly. The cages were out in the open air. We could see each other. He wouldn't stop masturbating. Every morning, lunch and dinner he would masturbate. In open air, caged, starving, cold, this boy lived for masturbation. The guards laughed at him first, then pitied him, then were scared of him. He tried to hide it, but eventually when he went to the corner hunched over we knew what it was for. No matter how hard he tried, when he finished, he always ejaculated with a grunt." Abdul tightened his grip across my throat so the air was cut off and then he let go. I gasped. "A little taste of mercy," he said. "That's how they pulled him out of his cell every morning."

I moved away from him toward the edge of the roof. I waited for my breath to return. "Mercy?" I asked. "That's what you do to Mo' and Imran?" This stopped Abdul. His cigarette pinched between his fingers.

"Tell me, what was I doing to them?"

"What happened to them in Guantanamo Bay."

"How do you know what happened in Guantanamo Bay?"

"Everyone knows. I saw it on the news."

"Do you think Mohammad and Imran can go a day without wanting their old pain?"

"You can't believe that."

"You think they're in those rooms against their will?"

"They must be," I said.

"Why didn't you call the police?"

"What was I supposed to say to them?"

"Exactly what you saw."

"Why did you attack me?" I asked.

"Natalie asked me to."

"No, she didn't."

"She wanted to start a new life. She knew you wouldn't leave us alone."

"Don't lie," I said. "Let me ask you: did you do it? In Afghanistan — shoot the soldier on purpose?"

"I did what a fourteen-year-old boy, scared Allah had abandoned him, thought was right."

"Do you feel guilty about leaving Afri behind?"

"I had no choice. I was taken by soldiers."

"You could go back," I said. "You could have a son."

"I hope I have a son. Everything I did: the men in those rooms, dangling from chains, you ignored. For Natalie? What if she doesn't want you?"

"I can't think that far," I said.

"Remember: they have the watches, but we set the time," Abdul said and extinguished his smoke into a metal bucket of sand next to his lawn chair. "I love that home," he said. "Where I have my sessions with Mohammad and Imran. The first piece of property I ever bought. I could never sell it. I can't kick the tenants, here, in this building below us, out either."

"The building is yours."

"That's not the reality I want to make. They'll come around. This building is the prize. I can wait." Seagulls cried above circling for scraps. Abdul motioned to a small cooler next to his lawn chair. Whatever he seemed to say, I would do. I would never understand my compliance, except to say that I deserved whatever happened. I lifted the lid and opened a bottle of San Pellegrino for us.

"Let me come to Bombay with you," I said.

"No. You're important here."

"I can help. I speak a little of the language."

"We've arranged a translator."

"Let me come."

"It's not wise. You should stay here. You'll be good with the police. They'll be by tomorrow for more questions. We're leaving tonight." He patted his pocket for a cigarette and I took the opportunity to step close to him.

"I have a problem with money," he said.

"Samir has been stealing some. At least half."

"This is why you should stay here. Deal with Samir and the money. I can't decide if he's not what I thought he was, or if he's completely what I thought he was. Do you understand?"

"Knowing what I know and knowing what I don't want to know."

"Exactly," Abdul said. "Can you imagine my father now? I own two pieces of real estate downtown. Pieces of land. I wish we could do what the embassies do: my land, my rules."

"Ownership," I said.

"It was money," Abdul said. "Bringing me to Ahmed. That's all I saw. I got greedy."

"Natalie was right: we're alike."

"It made me act in ways I wouldn't."

"The posts: last night, you posted a video …"

"That seems to have upset a few people."

"Did you mean it?" I asked.

"We have to take our language back. Jihad isn't what they think it is."

"Was it smart? You know how people are going to react. They don't like that kind of talk."

"I'm no longer a good boy in this country. I'm scaring them."

"It wasn't smart," I said.

"Do you think Samir had a good heart?" Abdul asked.

"I think he did what he needed to do."

"What will you do to whomever took the rest of the money?"

"It depends who took it," I said. "I don't justify what I do. I don't need justice."

"Natalie told me what you do for your father and your mother. You stay in their lives."

"That's bare minimum," I said. "I haven't helped them."

"Bare minimum is doing nothing," Abdul said. "They see your clothes. Your smile. They know you're okay."

"Am I okay?"

"Mercy. Mercy, mercy, mercy. Every few pages in the Qur'an, Allah is merciful. What does that tell us? If Allah is merciful, what should you be? You should be rigorous. You should be hard-working. You should have high expectations. But what if you fail? You hold yourself accountable," Abdul said. "You have to earn mercy. You're the only one who can. But does that mean pain? Does that mean this darkness of night? When does accountability shift to indulgence? Consider it. Consider mercy. Consider the accountability of mercy." He stubbed another cigarette and paced. He needed to keep moving, otherwise his joints got rigid.

"Imran is learning mercy," he continued. "That's his first lesson. It's a hard lesson … hard methods teach it. They paid twenty-five thousand dollars for him. His bounty. If they kill your son, they pay one hundred dollars. But you can't keep that anger if you want to live here, within, to reap the West. Is that vanity? I want you to consider that there is vanity in you. I can see that you know it. I want you to think about other things that may rest in you that you ignore. Or maybe you don't want to see. No man is born with vanity. Let's not even say evil. No man is born bad. They are bent that way. Shaped. Knocked into their role. We're not brittle. Everything we know, man is not brittle. He can be moulded. Remoulded. You have a potential beyond vanity."

All his intensity focused on me. People paid money for these sessions. He sat with his eyes closed, cigarette on his lip, like he knew. The confession gathered momentum in my brain. I needed to hit myself. Stop. Stop. I wanted the bare steel blade, above my rib cage, underneath my heart, sliding in silently. The ring of blood around its silver hilt. Stop. I needed it to stop.

"You want me to give myself mercy?" I asked.

"I want you to give yourself forgiveness, yes. If I can ..."

"What you did was different."

"I'm telling you it was not. I killed a man. How do I repay that? I know the exact address his parents live at. Should I send them a gift? What did you do to Samir?"

"Nothing," I said.

"You took care of it. You protected yourself."

"I did what I had to."

"What did you do? Tell me what happened when you discovered he'd taken your money."

"I did what I was always going to."

"Do you think his family will miss him?"

"I can't give myself that mercy."

"Come to the home tonight. You remember where it is. What I do there. I can show you mercy."

•

I left Abdul promising to come back in the evening. As I drove down the highway toward Marwan's house, Natalie called.

"Can you come by the building tonight?" she asked. "We're going to talk to the couple upstairs."

"I have to see Abdul later," I said. "I can come before. You okay? You seemed shook this morning."

"Just the Mo' stuff. But I saw him," Natalie said. "He's fine."

"Did you talk to him?

"No."

"What happened with the money?"

"What? His? He has none."

"No, in the accounts," I said.

"What do you mean?"

"The money. The donations."

"Where's Samir?"

"Don't worry about Samir," I said.

"I don't know what money —"

"Almost half a million is missing."

"What? How?"

"Don't lie to me, Natalie."

"Hamid, I don't know. Where's Samir? Is he coming by?"

"I asked Abdul if I could come to India."

"… What did he say … ?"

"No."

"That's probably for the best," Natalie said.

"What do you want?"

"It doesn't matter."

"Of course it does."

"I want a future," she said. "I want things to be right."

"And?"

"And that's step by step."

"What's the first step?"

"India is like a work thing," Natalie said. "I love you."

"That's a time for you to say it."

"I'm sorry. I told you to stay away. I'm sorry."

"Why are you going?" I said.

"For work. You know this."

"Don't lie to me. Where's the money?"

"Hamid. I don't want you to get hurt or get in trouble. I told you not to get involved."

"Where is the money?"

"Come by the centre, okay? Let's talk to the couple. We can go over the accounts. I love you."

27.

I arrived in North York to find Marwan's washed, waxed, detailed, loved Corolla sparkling in his driveway like no Corolla ever should, parked behind the rust-rimmed maroon Plymouth minivan his father had been driving for two decades. The Corolla cleaned out. The regular plastic bag full of protein bar wrappers, smoothie boxes, and garbage from the various chemicals Marwan needed for his exercise were missing. A new deodorizer hung. Seats vacuumed. Marwan got his habits from his father and the Plymouth was full of its usual discontent: maps, documents, empty Timmies wrappers, junk that told family history.

More changes: the light bulb over the door to his hovel gone from a glaring white to an elegant yolk that spilled onto the new painted door, new brass knocker, new welcome mat. This productivity was not unusual. In high school he crushed on a girl on the soccer team and in a few days was dressed head to toe in Umbra gear and blathering about Messi, as well as forcing himself onto the boy's team. She, too, had a blond ponytail.

It was late afternoon, about thirteen hours since Britta had given him her number.

I went down the stairs to his basement unit. The wound on my head throbbed as the numbness from shock, pills, and the cream smeared over the cut wore off. Soreness spread through my body from my shoulders and back, down to my thighs and calves. It had taken all my strength to hold Samir down.

I did my one-two knock and opened with my key. The redecoration continued. Milk crates gone, the futon, previously permanently a bed, back as a couch, and arranged neatly with new sofa pillows and a throw. A white fake-fur rug brought the room together. The minuscule red dot of a burning incense stick. The TV was off the floor and on a stand. A bed frame! Garbage and recycling bins empty, a new toaster and coffee maker. He'd managed to eliminate the wet gloom that stalked basement apartments. The key piece: on the far wall, across from the window, was a light patch of paint; paint that hadn't seen the sun from where Britta's bodybuilding calendar had been taken down. He came out of the bathroom cologned, wearing dark green chinos and a maroon button-down with a tacky gold watch. His beard shortened and his fade returned.

"You did this since last night?" I asked.

"Just the door," Marwan said.

"You lie."

"Just the door. I'm not doing this for a girl."

My phone buzzed. My father. I couldn't tell Marwan what I had done to Samir this morning. I couldn't get a grip on the images. It was a bright light in my mind blinding me from thinking.

"You good?" Marwan asked. "Last night finish okay? They found Mo', I heard."

"It was fine," I said.

"How's Natalie?"

"It was nice."

"You two?"

"We had a thing," I said. "A moment."

"That's good."

"How about you?"

I pointed to a KitchenAid mixer on the countertop. We did not sell it. Self-conscious, Marwan patted down his shirt and pants.

"Don't judge," Marwan said.

"Me? Me? What am I gonna judge?"

"Me and Britta had lunch."

"Today? Already? She didn't freak out?"

"Nah," Marwan said. "I said what I said."

"What you say?"

"I said what I said. Don't worry about it. I didn't lie. I was honest."

"And what she say?" I asked.

"She thought I was charming."

"You are charming," I said. "You look fresh."

"We're dating. That's it. She gets it."

"You're dating? It's been half a day."

"She gets it."

"Gets what?"

"We aren't going to sleep together," Marwan said.

"Wow."

"It's a different vibe. Serious."

"That's all the redecorating?"

"Nah. My mom came downstairs for the first time in a year and flipped. Me and my dad went to Home Depot and did this in two days. She was mad-mad."

He passed me a can of club soda and sat on a new high stool. He wanted to know about Natalie. What could I tell him? I was ready to do whatever to bring her closer to me. I admitted her enigmatic pull: that it was a mystery I had allowed to capture me. Marwan knew this. He'd been trapped in Britta's orbit for two years.

"Me and Natalie is me and Natalie," I said. "You know how it is. What you want me to say? It's the same thing as you and Britta."

"Britta, all that — it's the promise. It's her promise. I don't know what happened between us that did me in so hard. But I know a part of that was the potential of us. Why she unlocks it, I don't know. You and Natalie? I mean, y'all been through a lot. This revert stuff?"

"You don't think it's real?"

"I've been watching her, it's real. That's the weirder thing. You have love for each other but the actual parts, the things you have to do to be together … Can you sit on a couch with her without losing your shit?"

"We had that."

"You had that a year and a half ago," Marwan said.

"Whatever, man. You're talking big because it's working out right now. All your marriages are off?"

"I told my parents. They wanna meet her. We're meeting next week."

"Britta is meeting your parents next week?"

"I told you it's for real," Marwan said. "We sat down and talked about what we wanted. Like, I spoke to her, I said to her, I want it, I want the relationship. That's it."

How could I explain Natalie to him? I did not want to be free. I was scared of freedom. I don't know if that was love.

"Did you see Abdul on TV today?" Marwan asked me. I hadn't. The interview yesterday was scheduled to air this afternoon. I'd pushed for it with a news channel so he could talk about his before-Guantanamo life. Marwan brought up the video. Abdul led a female reporter down a leafed street with children riding on tricycles and a father washing his car. Abdul stuck out with kohl eyes and a black, ankle-length thobe that billowed on his body. Abdul at a clearing in the park that broke into a path that led to his old high school.

"This is a beautiful place," Abdul said. "The grass holds magnificent green. I call it a Canadian green; it has a luminosity caused from snow falling. Green is an Islamic colour. The Taliban would have loved this area. It's flat, see, and the clearing has enough space to have an audience. They would have stoned a woman here: a cheater, fornicator, extramarital relations before marriage. Can you imagine, in Canada? Maybe the girls I went to school with and their short skirts. There is an epidemic in this country of licentious behaviour that should not be tolerated. You are willfully allowing them to stray. Technology does not mean morals." The host, befuddled, fumbled through questions before cutting to a priest discussing Abdul and his ideas.

"Did you tell him to say that?" Marwan asked.

"No," I said. "Let me hear it again." We listened. I brought up his Instagram page. His entire profile had been wiped except for the news clip.

"Maybe he meant … empowering girls," Marwan said. "You know. Respecting themselves."

"Bro, no one who brings up short skirts means good."

I texted Natalie, we should probably talk about Abdul. The scrubbed IG page threw me off. Even the avatar was replaced into a sterner photograph of his face. My phone buzzed. My father. Natalie texted back saying we could talk about it tonight.

•

When I left the basement my anxiety settled. Marwan's warmth brought me back to the real world and I didn't mind going to my father's. There was, and always would be, a home with Marwan for me.

This is silly, but I remember the first time I slept over at his house. We were fifteen years old and in the morning over breakfast his father asked me if I wanted scrambled or fried eggs. I couldn't answer the question. It was the way he said it: the curiosity in his voice, the extension of himself — he would make me the breakfast I wanted for no other reason than it was what I wanted. No one had asked me a question like that before.

No matter what happened, the space Marwan created in his home for me would always be there. No matter what happened, Marwan's love was the bedrock of my life, a foundation I could step toward and be confident of my landing.

Sliding my key into the Integra's ignition my eye caught two crows on his front lawn playing with a piece of reflective plastic. It was a game of keep away, one crow playfully pecking at the other, and then the other returning the favour.

I pulled away smiling.

I didn't know it would be the last time I saw Marwan.

•

I'd ignored my father since peeking into the storage locker. Busy, sick, any excuse worked, stand-ins for what I really wanted to say. I'd texted him my assessment — worth jack shit but you could wring a hundred bucks out of it — which he did not agree with but also refused to visit the locker himself. I didn't bother asking my mother what she thought.

As I drove toward him, I waited to relish the familiar anxiety that appeared near him. It did not come. The buildup of venom and fear that usually accompanied my visits was not there.

I stopped for more plant food and it was 5:30 p.m. when I pulled into visitors parking. Very close to drinking time. I shared the elevator with a Bengali family. The son played with a red toy car, driving it up and down the wall growling engine noises. He drove the toy up my thigh, then down, the mother watching him quiet.

The two recliners were skewed away from their usual position. A half-full ashtray lay on the ground. He never smoked inside. The kitchen was tidy, but the sink full of plates and plastic trays. When he said salaam, I knew he was drunk. Wet eyes and sagged mouth. He took the blue packets of food.

"You don't think the locker is worth anything?" he asked.

"I don't."

"It doesn't matter."

"She's been there for years," I said.

"She'll come back. We're married."

"She doesn't want to be."

"What do you want? Why are you sticking your nose into it? Just do what I say."

I'd never spoken to my father about the New Year's my mother came over to my apartment bruised. My anxiety about the evening had been replaced by a coolness. I wanted to know. I was desperate to see what it revealed about me.

"Why'd you hit her?" I asked.

"Hit who?"

"Her."

"No one knows what happened that night," he said.

"She came to my door."

"It doesn't matter. It's between us."

"She came to my door," I said.

"It doesn't matter."

"Why did you do it?"

"No one knows," he said. "It was years ago. Years ago. She has a life here."

"Okay."

"Okay, okay. Okay, okay. That's all you say."

"What is there to say?"

"She has a life here," he said.

"Why did you hit her?"

"I didn't hit anybody."

He sank into his recliner. I touched the wall to ground myself. The TV on mute: Prince Harry as a child. Where did my father go in his lowest moments? Did images of death and disturbance flick into his mind like they did for me? Or did I get it from my mother? Or was it all me: my actions all mine, the root cause of me, me.

"Why'd you hit me?" I said.

"I didn't hit you."

"Uh."

"I never hit you," he said. "You watch too much TV."

"Are you serious?"

"When did I hit you?"

"You want a list?"

He stared at the TV but was not watching. His body and mind in different places. I had no memories in this apartment. It was his. I'd never lived here. I stood behind him, accounting our differences. I was bigger, stronger, I probably made more money than him … Pathetic, even now, all I want is to not make him angry.

On the seat, he was alone. In the apartment, he was alone. It was not my sadness. I had no debt. His head bobbled to his internal monologue.

He had repeated a few stories all his life: his father, an orphan from Afghanistan stumbling into wealth and falling out of it by the time he was born. Family lore was that Grandfather was a gangster in Bombay and had to retreat to the countryside after being shot in the gut.

There was the India Emergency in the '70s when the government abandoned law. Buying a single cigarette from a vendor, struggling with the lighter that hung from string. Down the street, his best friend coming to visit him on a Royal Enfield motorcycle, stopped by a policeman. My father always jealous of that motorcycle. They were chatting, who knows what. The wrong thing said. A gun, its bullet, his friend's head burst on the side of the road, falling off his bike, the police taking it, leaving the body, the blood-brain mix on the dust dirt road. He went home. What could he do? There he discovered his father had been taken into police custody: they were Muslims, remember. Always we were Muslims in that country, he told me. How do you live in a world that makes decisions for you?

I wanted to understand all the different ways the world moved to make him what he was. I was stuck. I couldn't blame him. I couldn't forgive him. What was left? I was his son; not him. I was his son; not him. I tried the words out in my head — not the first time. I was his son; not him. I could move through the world separately from him.

I was his son; not him. I'd avoided the future I was most afraid of. I'd become my own man. I'd become worse than him by committing an atrocity he hadn't come close to. All the bruises he gave me disappeared eventually. Even the pain in my body, from the screeching wound on my forehead, to the stiffness in my lower back, the pain I'd created hurting Samir was worse than anything he'd ever done to me. If I was worse than my father, what was I? I was his son; not him.

He was about to speak. From behind, I put my hand on his shoulder. The first time I'd touched him in years. He dug into his pocket.

"Take this," he said.

"I don't need twenty bucks."

"Take the money. Who doesn't need twenty bucks?"

"I don't want this," I said.

"Don't say no to your father."

I pocketed the bill and left him with the couch, his TV, the withering plants.

•

I drove downtown to meet Natalie, except she texted me she wouldn't be there. We would talk later. She texted apologies and asked me to continue the task. The tenants upstairs were not leaving and not making plans to leave. This meant renovation work had to halt and a donation earmarked specifically for renovations by a Muslim cement company would not be injected into our bank account. It had become urgent: visible renovations were the biggest sign of progress when prospective donors toured the facilities. Abdul would not kick the couple out. Natalie couldn't kick them out. Natalie could get me to kick them out. This was the kind of job Samir would have bumbled his way through in the past and I was glad to take it. I was moving automatic, still pretending the day's transformations were not permanent. I believed there was a way back to Natalie and my money.

Mr. Ahmadi, my tax victim from two years ago, came to my thoughts. True to my word, I hadn't hit him up again. His family didn't cause further fuss. Light violence had been the answer there; the shattered lamp had made the decision for them. I told Natalie about it one night, not knowing why I was confessing or what was wrong about what I had done to him. It wasn't the fear in Mr. Ahmadi's face I remembered, but the way his wife processed what was happening and lost faith in her husband. Her face contorted, became rigid. People like this couple, like Mr. Ahmadi, welcomed trouble. We gave them warnings. That was the way things were balanced. It was mercy.

My own mercy would be soon. I needed to balance what I'd done to Samir.

It was like entering into a new world when my elevator opened. The top floor concrete walls and piping. The dings and hisses of the building were bare naked. City noises. Sweet and dusty smell of forgotten candy. I put my ear against the door and heard a radio or a fan, steady mechanics. What was a friendly knock? Rap, rap-rap rap, rap-rap.

A little Chinese opened the door. Short hair and thick glasses. She sized me up and left me standing there. It was a jungle inside: low, luscious plants hung from the ceiling, and three heavy fans cycled humid air. A grab bag of plants wherever my eyes fell. My mother would love it here. A man in a fishing vest sat on an orange couch facing a cutting-edge TV. It was the single new appliance I spotted and out of place in the unit. Ceiling-to-floor windows covered a wall, and in the very corner, a space devoted to canvases. The man rummaged through a stack of newspapers. Canvases piled up, dozens, maybe hundreds, all small or mid-sized, and an easel positioned for maximum sun.

The man took off his glasses for a look and mutter and went back to his papers. The woman pulled out a pizza slice from the microwave. I wandered to the paintings: they were famous, I don't know what, landscapes and lilies, orange sun, pastel waters, green grass I wanted to grab. I picked one up, freshly done, left standing to dry, and moved it under light. A man rowing in the middle, with blue-purple light all around him, so the water and sky came together, the bright orange sunlight the vivid moment. I could see the objects in the picture relied on their distance from the man in the boat for it to come together.

"You sell these?" I asked.

"What do you think?" the woman said and shoved pizza into her mouth.

"How much?"

"That? One hundred," she said.

"They go for that much?"

"More, even!"

The man interrupted. "We can't crack the real market," he said. "The real fake market. We try and try."

"What real fake market?" I asked.

"All those paintings you hear about being sold? Half are fake." The man pulled out a folder stuffed full of crisp printed pages. It was the same certificate of authenticity, multiplied in dozens. "I don't think it's our fault," he said. "Look how good that one is. It's the dealers. It should be easy."

This audacity going on upstairs. I was impressed.

"What do you want here?" the woman asked.

"You gotta move out," I said.

"We spoke to Mister Abdul," she said. "We aren't moving."

"I thought it was kids living here?"

"Our son died," she said.

"I'm sorry."

"None of your business."

"Right."

"We're not moving," she said.

"We can offer more money."

"Beat it."

"How much money you want?" I asked.

Natalie had set the ceiling for my offer at seven thousand for "moving expenses."

"Wait for us to die," she said.

Their wrinkled skin like crumpled paper bags. The woman walked with a hitch, even as she moved steadily across the room, and spoke in a firm voice. They took turns speaking, each one aware of their joint position. She invited me to sit and when I lowered into the chair my back locked up, my forehead cut pulsed. She eyed the wound but did not comment on it. My hands hurt. I could no longer make a fist.

"We can do three thousand," I said. "Cash."

"Do we need money?" she asked.

I couldn't tell. The place was rundown, but hearing their son died clicked the dishevelment into place. There were memories. Stools not moved in years, a stereo covered entirely in dust.

"We're old!" she said. "We'll die soon."

"How old are you?"

"It's a joke."

I needed to get confirmation out of them. My failures for Abdul were adding up. Natalie asked me to secure an agreement that they would move out so that a contract could be signed for renovations and cash influx. What was I supposed to do with people like this? I'd move into a dumpster for 7K. They were monied. I noticed a black Chanel bag near the entranceway.

"He's going crazy downstairs anyway," the man said.

"What you mean?" I asked.

He picked up the remote and navigated to the YouTube app on the TV, brought up Abdul.

"There is too much haram things going on in our world. And because of our culture, our mind-your-business West, we mind neighbours, we say nothing offensive, we don't want to hurt people, we do nothing. But this idea of neighbourliness is wrong. Who else is going to do it? If you see a woman doing something out in public that is not approved, say something. If you see a man failing his obligation to his family, say something."

I brushed the video aside.

"I understand he's strange to you guys."

"You guys?" the man said. He turned the pages of his newspaper. The man was comfortable and at ease, which bothered me. He wasn't taking in my physical presence at all. He didn't care about me. He wasn't scared.

"You guys — Chinese people, old people," I said.

"We're from Hong Kong," she said.

"That's different?"

"We're not provincial like you people."

"Yo, easy. I was born in Bombay."

"Really? Same-same," she said. "Cosmopolitan."

"See, relax."

"No, not really. Don't be silly. Indians." She did a little bobble of her head to mock the Indian gesture, then put a biscuit in my palm. What was I supposed to do? What did Natalie expect me to do? What did Abdul? The couple responded to me like a fart in the wind, soon to be gone. They changed channels to a news station. "English Breakfast or Earl Grey?" She waved the kettle in her hand.

"Is that a good kettle?" I asked. "I can get you a deal on kettles."

"We're good for kettles." She plopped a tea bag into the cup, hot water, milk. I sat on the chair.

"You don't want to leave?" I asked.

"Why should we?"

"Downstairs — it's a good cause."

"We're a good cause," she said.

Was I supposed to hit them? Their nonchalance caused panic in me. Should I break the TV, be rude, be violent? Was that what Natalie and Abdul understood me to do? Was that the invisible assignment?

The loft had relics of their son's past. Photographs of him next to dust bunnies next to a white electric guitar.

"How did your son die?"

They looked forward to the TV. I was sorry for my rudeness, but I needed to know. The father twisted in his seat and pointed to the corner where the easel sat, where the sun burned strongest.

"He hung himself," he said. "They didn't find him for one week. We sent him here for school and he … had no one close to him who would check in."

"God," she said. "God is good. Put your faith in that. I like Mister Abdul for that. God plans."

Their faces changed separately; he did not agree. Did it matter? What I'd sensed as a warmth between them was now ice. It didn't matter. They were here together. He squeezed her thigh and she brushed his hand off. I wanted to ask them if they were happy but knew they would scoff. They wouldn't move out. The money would not have any influence. A beating wouldn't, no violence would. They'd gone to the far edge of horror and what they brought back made the real world irrelevant.

I thanked them for their time and left.

28.

Text from Abdul:

Please meet me at the house. I'm ready.

I hobbled to my car and had the same out-of-body experience I'd had when my mother knocked on my door with swollen black eyes to tell the story of my father. I hovered over myself, understanding there had been a change in my life. I was on a new path.

The house seemed taller than before. Farther back and worn down. In memory it was pristine and modern. I could see the shabby work now, the water damage in the bricks, a broken window frame, a brown patch of grass.

I was scared walking through the front door. Would anyone greet me with fists at the top of the stairs? The same bleach smell as before. Magazines in the living room replenished. I heard thumping again, a light wallop, a punch or love smack. In the kitchen I poured myself water, impressed by the weight of the glass. There was a Le Creuset pot on the stovetop, WÜSTHOF blades in the drawer.

Put the final moments of this life off.

Abdul from upstairs.

"Come up."

An order. My body knew the pain from his blows. He shouted again. Shaking, I took the stairs slow. I relinquished myself. I was always on my path.

Three of the doors were closed. One led to his office. Light fell onto the green carpet. His demand came from there.

I pushed the door open. I recognized dark oak bookshelves from his videos. A bare desk. A Corb LC3 armchair, the famous one that cost at least five thousand dollars. Two plain chairs in the corner next to a jug of water on a small table with a box of tissues. A therapist's office. Abdul sat in the Corbusier in his familiar black track suit. What had he said before? It's finished. Do you understand? It's finished.

Thick blackout blinds covered the windows. Three lamps cast hard shadows across the room. It smelled like sandalwood. A rug on the floor stretched across. Birds embroidered on it. Three lemon slices floated in the water, their white skin loose.

"I knew you were special when Natalie talked about you. And then there was the fighting. You could fight. And you wouldn't stay away. You remind me of my brother. Or a dog."

"Where's Natalie?"

"She's packing. We're leaving. We're going to Mumbai in a few hours. First stop."

"She's with you?"

"Maybe not the way you think, but yes. You're confusing a lot of events. You missed so much."

"The money?"

"Surprisingly, the bank unfroze the two hundred thousand," Abdul said. "The money went through to my bank account this evening. It took another urgent call from me. That's the last of my luck. The whole thing was my fault — Samir told you? Samir was right. I should have gone to him first. His outward appearance and behaviour betrayed a core stillness. He was very organized. Samir explained it to me. FINTRAC. Money laundering, a big no-no. The fifteen thousand we — I — took set off all sorts of alarm bells and phone calls. Samir found out immediately. It became a competition. Who can take the most money from Hamid and run." Abdul stood and gestured to the hallway. "Let's go to the other room."

I was tired. My heart gone. I wanted what was next; I needed it. I wanted it over. Natalie was leaving …

Abdul stepped past me. I followed. A room with a door open. Blank white walls ready for me.

Another room with the door closed.

Abdul knocked twice and opened.

Mo' in the centre of the room. He had a chain wrapped around his torso and fixed through the grate affixed to the ceiling. His skin was red from where he'd been hit recently.

"Abdul told me you were coming," Mo' said.

"Shit! Are you — are you okay?" I asked. "Do you need help?"

Abdul stood at the doorway.

"No. No, I'm fine," Mo' said.

"You're bleeding."

"I'm fine. Don't touch me. Why did you come here?" he asked.

"You're —"

"What? Please, what am I? Abdul does what we ask him to." Mo' stood straight in the chains. He looked past me to Abdul. "We come into this room the same reason you have," he said. A line of blood from his temple drew down to his mouth. "Please, it's okay. Go to Abdul. He will show you."

I stepped out of the room into the hallway. From behind Abdul blasted me with a cattle prod. Electricity zapped through to my body. I dropped in a heap.

Abdul pulled me by my legs through the hall and into the room.

"I told you," he said. He kicked me in the ribs three times. Sharp pointed pain that went away as fast as it came. A steel chair in the middle of the room. Grabbing under my armpits he shoved me into the chair. I'd seen the room before. A stereo screwed into the wall. I wiggled my fingers. I was losing feeling. Sweet sweat stink. Mine or his? He drove the prod into my rib again. Blue clicks of electric. White light. I was zip-tied to the metal frame. Electricity in my fillings. He rummaged through a cardboard box and yanked a coarse hood made from a potato sack down my face and blood from my wound gushed into the material. "Natalie has been really good at helping," Abdul said. "She's patient. When I went into Guantanamo, someone giving me ten dollars would have been a fortune. I was a kid, my mind only on how many chocolate bars and Cokes could I buy. Then, the settlement! An adult, now. I paid my lawyers of course. That building I bought is so small and decrepit. Zoned badly. All these things I learned after. Even then it was a deal. It took most of my money. I had to bring other people in. Developers. But it would make it okay, it would give me permission to be here, in the West."

Abdul scratched my face pulling the hood. My skin under his nails. My blood on my tongue. I heard water then I was in the sea, in its guts, water in my nose down my throat, I couldn't breathe. He stopped. "This is part of what they taught us," Abdul said and paused so I could breathe; grabbed my hair through the cloth and pulled my head back and the water gushed onto my face again. Cool, refreshing, it washed away blood but the cloth drenched, I gagged, I sucked in water and choked. I thrashed in full panic, cutting against the ties and Abdul let go of my hair allowing me to crash to the ground with the chair. He let me squirm then pulled the mask off my face so I could breathe once more. When I had regained control he pulled me up. I was his. The water into my nose, in my mouth; I gagged, coughed, I tried to scream but took in more water. My nose burned. He stopped again, taking off the cloth, allowing the water to stop, for me to cough up water and puke. My vomit clear with strands of green. That sharp-cheese stink. Shivering. The mask on.

"Is it all right if I tell you this?" he asked. "The doctors say it helps … When I came out … the government was eager to do good … but what was that to me? All the Muslims, from all the mosques we went in and out of … many wanted to help now that I was free. Each night I was in Guantanamo, I thought, I don't deserve this. Each night. Until, one night, years into it, I thought, so simply, what if I do? You are where you are meant to be. You, here, now; so what was I being punished for? Why couldn't I even know what it was?" He pulled a thick metal chain from the box, looped the chain through my tied hands and threw it up so it went through a grid in the grill above me; holding the chain he leaned back with his body weight and cranked me upward, my arms howling as they pulled behind me, tearing my shoulders, and I fainted for a few seconds and he loosened his grip so I could support myself standing and then slammed me into the wall. Pain through my ribs out to my limbs. "I didn't deserve bad," Abdul said. "But I didn't deserve good either. No one prepared me for a cage. You know: 'And the heaven he raised and imposed the balance.'"

I couldn't support myself. The chain tore at my flesh. Abdul pulled tighter. A scorching pain. I couldn't feel my body anymore.

I fell out of my body. I was terrified.

It was good. I was good.

"Please stop," I begged.

It was needed. A cleanse. Mercy. No control.

"Please help me," I begged; I needed Abdul's mercy.

"That you not transgress the balance," Abdul said. "And establish weight in justice and do not make deficient the balance." With one hand he tore my shirt off my body. I was wet with sweat and blood and bile. "Natalie told me you used to wet the bed as a child," Abdul continued. He rolled the shirt into a ball and inhaled my smell. He kneaded his fist on my torso, my stomach, searching; the strong latex smell of gloves like sniffing salts. "Here it is," he said. "Your bladder. Same as my bladder."

The electric prod into my torso. I winced. It didn't come. I opened my eyes. He was staring at me but in a different place, city, country, world, universe. Abdul pushed the button and electricity shattered me as I tried to curve into myself for protection. The chain he'd hooked through me stopped me from falling.

I pissed myself. I needed to run for clean air — I needed clean, bracing air.

"My lawyer recommended a therapist," Abdul said. "I put it off. I had to buy the building. That was my therapy. I had vague plans for it. A kind of community centre. I was honest; optimistic, truly. My father. Remember what I told you about my father. Why not pick up his plans?"

I hung while Abdul went through his tools. I gagged; I gagged again, choking. He pulled my hood off stuck his gloved hand into my mouth and bent me over so I could vomit. I heard him go down the stairs. Quiet. Then up the stairs. He tilted my head so I could drink water. He left again I don't know how long after came back. He unzipped his jacket, revealing a torso criss-crossed with scars, almost as if he was built layer by layer of cuts. There was a sling wrapped tightly around his shoulder through to his torso and he unclipped it: his shoulder sank, shifted to its new natural position. His relaxed body drooped. Hip and leg beaten into new positions so he couldn't stand evenly without effort. His back curved like the tail of a comma. Old and new marks on his body. Fresh scar tissue over hard ridges of skin.

"Finally, out of prison for a year, then two years, I couldn't sleep," Abdul said. "My lawyer kept telling me I needed to get help. I needed work. Not sleeping was too much for me to handle. I wanted to try therapy. There were so many people in my ear begging me to be okay. Even in Guantanamo I slept.

"We met at her office. The therapist wanted to try a new technique. To reintroduce me to my captors in a safe environment. They put me in a room, a small room, with strong white lights, a metal chair, a table. That's what they thought happened to me! The therapist came in, talking to me, asking me questions. The room was supposed to be mimicking my ordeal. The room was designed to look like the Guantanamo

Bay interrogation rooms. It was here, she said, safely, we can reintroduce you to your trauma! With civility and gentleness, we would walk through what had happened to me and rewrite my memories. They knew so much of what happened to me without me ever having to tell them. They read all the reports and documents and books and watched the movies. They had recreated the room perfectly. They wanted me to put on the famous orange jumpsuit — if I felt comfortable, they always insisted — and sit in the chair. She would be the interrogator. I would be the victim again."

Abdul opened the cubby door to the left that had held Imran in the past. I was high on my pain; I could not talk, I wanted to beg. He pulled out a wooden box from the room and compared it to my frame.

"One of the few things you don't hear about: for months you don't see yourself in a mirror. Six months will go by and you'll catch a glimpse of yourself in a steel reflection; every feature grown in a distant way. And being a teenager. I don't recognize this body. None of us do."

How awkward his movements now that no one was watching. His body different slashes, short, deep and not, some like they'd tried carving meaningful shapes into him. From his wrist to bicep was a journey of cigarette burns. His skin in places coloured blue and red. Alien skin.

"Your father stopped hitting you at thirteen?" Abdul asked. "My father never hit me. It's like we had a hand-off. The room … the therapist my lawyer recommended thought the room would mimic my time. That it would allow me to reorganize and understand my memories. To write my own narrative. I was flabbergasted. They had documents. They had news reports. They knew what had happened. And they thought this therapy room would bring justice to me … The strangest thing, the truly strange thing, was the idea I'd move on. The expectation I'd heal. You thought that too. But they weren't wrong. Not totally. I found peace in this house. Peace in this room: bringing Imran and Mohammad here. You heard Mohammad just now. Imran is the same. They're greedy for it. They miss Guantanamo. It's all we know. Those years in prison erased everything we had before. We are forever in those cages. They came to me and asked for it. And my lawyer, my therapist: they were right. That cage was where I belonged. But I no longer wanted to be the captive. They could never understand that. I wanted to be back in the cage. But not to be the prisoner. Who would that help? I would re-enter the prison for my brothers, but now I would be the victor."

He disappeared from the room. I heard his voice far away like an echo. I passed out. He slid a broomstick behind my arms so I was standing like Mo' in the other room. He ran his finger down my torso to my crotch and back up. He squeezed my testicles so hard my eyes opened.

"What did I tell you?" Abdul asked. "I asked you to leave Natalie alone. I asked you to leave it all alone twice. I came to your home and relayed the message with kindness. I asked you to listen. But you are like Imran and Mohammad: you asked me for this." His shoulder drove into my chest and I crashed into the wall. It smelled like rotten eggs. An abandoned toilet. He'd torn open a wound on his body. Burst flesh. A pomegranate. "What's the story that Natalie likes to tell?" Abdul asked. "You're a little boy coming down a waterslide too fast and your father saves you from drowning? She thinks that's the key. Did she ever tell you that? She thinks that's the one memory that keeps you like this." He pulled the coarse hood over my head once more. I braced.

Cold water rushed over my face. My nose burned. Water in my lungs. I couldn't breathe. He stopped.

I begged him to let me free. He punched me in my stomach.

I took deep breaths.

He waited for my breathing to slow and then water rushed over my face again. In my lungs. I tried to break free and the ties cut into my wrists. I choked; gagged.

I died in that chair. I must have. I could not speak. He stopped.

I heard a lighter spin. Oh god I was tired. I couldn't stop him. I prayed. The steel spun once more searching for flame. I tensed and tried to rise to my feet. I smelled a lit cigarette and relief rushed into me. I fell back to my knees. Dizzy relief.

"It's not impossible that I'm that other person you've seen … that other Abdul. It's not. I like to think to myself that it's me, the other me, the me with none of my past. I like to think I can be both." He exhaled. "I'm going to try to find out again. These things happen, opportunity comes."

He blew smoke in my face, making me spin, and put his cigarette out on my bicep. I begged him to stop, the words spilling out of my mouth.

29.

Light cut through my eyelids. I'd puked and shat myself. I'd passed out next to the metal chair on the ground. He'd removed the ties and chain. I had to get out of the room. Was Abdul in the other room? There was a bitter metal taste on my tongue. I'd bit my tongue off — I reached into my mouth and grabbed for it — it was there, I hadn't bitten it off. I searched the room for a weapon and took the broomstick.

On his desk, water and a small orange bottle with a label that said ABDUL MOHAMMAD, PERCOCET. Two pills.

I leaned against the chair and popped the pills with water. I sat back down in my mess until I realized what I was doing.

I patted my pockets. My phone, wallet, car keys. I went to the office and in the drawers I found a charger and a pair of plain black pants and white collared shirt. While I waited for my phone to charge, I fell asleep.

I blinked. I couldn't see straight. The percs moved through me. I stepped into the shower. I didn't want to put on Abdul's clothes but had no choice.

I remembered: Mo'!

I ran to the room. Not there. I checked the other rooms. Gone.

What had Abdul done to me?

He'd drowned me. I'd known that before, in the story Natalie told him.

I went down the slide too fast and was stunned how I broke through the water, the water in my mouth and nose, in my lungs.

My father saved my life.

Four

30.

In Bombay, I gave my cousin Dabir four hundred dollars to borrow his Hero Honda for the week and never ask me a question again. The motorbike was a beauty. A slim machine with a black-and-purple fuel tank, new fake-leather seat, and, a rarity, working lights, front and back. It had a single surviving side mirror. Built for Bombay traffic. Sorry — Mumbai.

I don't like this name change. I never got into the shift. Movies, newspapers, and TV referred to the city as Mumbai, after politics changed the name up to rile the locals in the '90s, yet almost every person I spoke to, back home and here, called it Bombay. I'd been born in Bombay. Calling it Mumbai erased my history.

But wasn't that what I came in search of — my own eradication. The traveller's cliché. Here, I'm cut off from my personal past, my wandering Western years; I'm anonymous in this megalopolis and it's that distance that allows me to thrive and look back cleanly at those last days. Memory has become a hard surface. I know no one in this city. I'm not part of it.

Twenty-four hours after my meeting with Abdul, I burped out of Mumbai International airport into the bulging threat of monsoon.

My black-and-yellow took me to Fort where I'd booked a hotel room on my layover in Paris. I'd packed few clothes, the fifteen thousand USD I'd hidden in my apartment and the world's biggest bottle of painkillers, which was mostly useless against the noise in this dust bowl, but it helped quiet the slash on my forehead. The scar is Samir's last mark on the world. A reminder of what I'd fled.

I'd been moving for days powered by shame. I needed Natalie, still.

I slept for two days after I landed.

I arranged a new SIM, texted Dabir, cut the line at Victoria Terminus train station, and inserted myself into a muggy cart full of Indians. This was the first time I'd come to the country on business and not to ogle sights and sounds. I was determined to get my money. Lying in my hotel, the TV whirring in the background, staring at the red paan stains on the walls, I was convinced the chase for Natalie was still the most important.

I shoved in between bodies on the train cart. I had local lessons to learn. When to travel on the train, which direction was a no-no during rush hour. I almost fell out trying to navigate the tightly packed cart. I limped but my swelling went down. The bruises across my torso lighter. No longer purple coming close to black. It would take me weeks to shower; rushing water scared me. As time took my rage, fear pushed forward — those first days Abdul was in every loud noise, on every anonymous face.

I knew Bollywood, Hindutva, food, but nothing about the granular details of social life in the country. So, I played pretend. No, being crushed by a platoon of men coughing into my face during train trips did not bother me. The heat? No, it was fine, thank you, it didn't feel like my crotch was held captive in a Turkish bath. The mosquitoes? Please, I have too much blood — take some. No wonder the Arab thought venturing into Canada would be easy. This city was like a tar pit in hell compared to the oasis of the West.

I could be a local. I was born here; I was six when we moved into the West's tundra blast. Visiting, I'd never ventured out of the reach of a practised Bombayite, always taking in the city with my cousins, tagging along as an illiterate, unable to read signage but able to speak with the skills of a slow child. It was incredible to be in a city and realize I could not impact it at all.

We were on a dirt strip behind Dabir's apartment complex near JJ Road where he lived with his mother, who was my mother's sister. And my mother.

Dabir instructed me in an Indian accent singed with American, a stain on his voice from ten years of call-centre work. He asked if I approved of his work name, Dale, and didn't believe me when I said I'd never actually heard that name spoken out loud.

It was like wearing a wetsuit, being outside. I couldn't confess the effects of the weather to Dabir. Locals pounced on weakness from Westerners. My Hindi was bad enough. Whenever someone spoke a basic sentence to me, he would turn to make sure I understood the man said be careful with the hot samosas or whatever. It was cute when it didn't make me feel dumb.

Sticking my fingers into my nose there was black snot already. A thousand nose hairs grew to combat the startling range of pollutants trying to kill me. I loved it.

All looked like me: dumbfounded faces doing their daily thing. I slipped under the skin of this medieval city.

I saw a horse trotting alongside cars earlier. Who had the right of way? I tested the Hero Honda up and down the strip while Dabir shouted a list of video-game systems at me, stunned each time I said I did not own it. For a full fuel tank, I promised him a PS4. He bargained for an iPhone.

Dabir was a skinny boy with a drooping face and a hooked nose that hung over his mouth like a last-minute addition. With a turn of his head he reminded me that my mother lived in the building. I'd reached out to him because I needed his bike and I'd asked him not to tell anyone I was in the city. He agreed but was nervous. He viewed withholding as a lie. He worked his hand through his oiled hair, then fiddled with the handlebars as he told me how much they'd enjoyed having my mother there. There was strain in his voice.

My mother in the building. I'd not planned on visiting her but Dabir begged me. I owed him that much. The repercussions if they found out I was in town would be huge for him. It was the kind of deception that would shroud his entire life, brought up at inopportune moments to humiliate.

They lived in a five-story building with a synagogue on the topmost floor. Because it was on a main street, near a major bridge, there was always a hustle in and around it. The exterior had been painted blue many years ago but all that remained were spots of the colour over cement. Entering the lobby into the coolness of its dark corners gave a needed break from the heat and noise. Each floor had simple grey walls and the colour came from the doors, either brown or painted red or orange. Because it was so bare it didn't have the falling-apart appearance of so many weather-beaten buildings in the city, but it hadn't been designed either, not like the art-deco residences across Bombay. It simply existed, like an old tree might.

The hundred-year-old watchman snoozed on his cot. The familiar stairs and even the smell of goat shit went back through my catalogue of memories and found a nostalgic connection. A fake flutter of comfort and home. Most of my thorny memories existed after India and before I started drinking, a window where my parents were made up entirely of disappointment. Were they not who they wanted to be? Did they fall short of their own expectations, never mind mine?

This apartment had been in my mother's family for decades and we'd visited often when we lived in the city. I used to knock cricket balls out from the window with cousins. I wouldn't have been able to name them now. When I remembered my childhood, this apartment building was prominent and it was odd approaching it as an adult, like I was cutting myself into a film I'd watched long ago.

A servant in a pink outfit squatted over a wash bin in the hallway. Did I know her? She paid no attention to me as I surveyed the different doors and tried to see if they matched my memories. She dipped a plate into water, wiped, and put it on a rack. I recognized her face; the oval shape or the bunch of her brows. Or was it the plait in her hair? Would I have ever been taught her name? Probably, yes — but maybe not. I would know the domestics in our family unit but perhaps not my auntie's. I never had a handle on the relationship between the workers and their employers and I found the idea of servants too many things at once: disturbing, powerful, easy, horrifying, amazing. On later visits back, my father would monitor one hanging laundry and tell me with sadness: she cost fifty dollars a month, max. They live over there. And he would nod with his head to a row of huts behind the building.

The door was open. A TV on a news channel: Hindi phrases flecked with English as they discussed the latest Tata scandal. I stepped into the living room and found my mother and auntie drinking tea and staring into their phones.

My appearance knocked them into craziness. Auntie scrambled for biscuits and tea, shouting at her servant and made sleeping arrangements for me and asked me four times if I wanted McDonald's, she would send Dabir, he'd be so happy to see me.

My mother silent. I'd not prepared for the questions visiting relatives receive and told lies: the gash, the bruise, the odd limp all caused by — my brain stung by jet lag — falling off a horse. I made up a friend who took me horse riding, then a friend who owned a horse farm, then a last-minute consulting job for a car manufacturer wanting to open a call centre in India. Then I had to resist the onslaught of people she knew who worked at call centres. Yes I brought gifts, I forgot them in the hotel, yes the company is paying for the trip, and finally, yes, I was examining prospects of two doctors, one engineer, and one lawyer, all driven delirious by their desire to marry me. She suggested two ambitious and Westernized daughters she knew. What would my ad be like in the matrimonial pages?

FUCK UP AVAIL, SAYS HE'S 5'10", DARK-SKINNED, NO JOB, NO REAL PROSPECTS, ODD FAMILY DYNAMICS, PROLONGUED PSYCHOLOGICAL PROBLEMS, A TOTAL WASTE OF HIS PARENTS' JOURNEY WESTWARD, LOOKING FOR A WIFE TO

BLAME; CASTE NO BAR, ABRAHAMIC RELIGION PREFERRED, ILLITERATE INDIAN; MUST SPEAK ENGLISH

Fibbing made Auntie happy. Satisfied I was not a loveless loser without a job, she retreated to the kitchen to harass her servants while they prepared lunch.

Me and her alone. I'd grown up calling her "Mummi" but stopped because it was childish. I didn't replace it. No name for her now. When was the last time we'd been alone in a room together? I touched her on the shoulder. I said hello once more. She wore a cream shalwar kameez I recognized as her home wear. Hair cut short and gone white. Wrinkles alongside new freckles and dark spots. She'd lost weight. Distance and time meant she was old now. She refilled her tea and a grimace broke on her face.

"It's not what you think here," she said.

"Are you working?" I asked.

"It's not been easy. You can't trust the doctor will come. Just last week, a neighbour called the ambulance and it never arrived. He died. Heart attack. How long are you staying?"

"Depends on work. A week or two. Longer, maybe. The apartment looks nice."

"Do you want to be living with your sister at sixty?"

I expected serenity; a woman happy to be home. Her emails to me were fact lists about her life. A job, old friends, colleagues. They never carried emotion. She was surprised those decades in the West had shaped her. She thought she'd be too old to change. Coming back, India was different. Her relatives weren't as happy to see her as she'd wanted. She'd forgotten they took bribes here for every small thing. There were no ethics attached to it, it was just custom. She laughed:

it made her miss being put on hold by civil servants. She had lost her job a year before. My father sent money each month. That I didn't know.

"Did you see the storage?" she asked. "Everything is there?"

"Of course."

"Good. I'm coming back next month."

"Where — hunh? Coming back where?"

"I'm going to live with your father," she said.

"What? Why — what did — after what —"

"What he did is what he did."

"How can you go back to that?"

"He's different. He's calmer. Old age."

"You don't remember what it was like."

"I remember," she said.

"You don't remember what he did to me."

"What did he do?"

"He used to beat the shit out of me!"

"I didn't know that."

"You knew."

"If I'd known I would have said something," she said.

"You knew."

"I didn't."

"I don't think going back is a good idea," I said.

"And what is a good idea for me?" she asked. "I can't work here. I can't live with my sister forever. Where would I go? Should I live alone?"

"No, I don't know … you have … you can work for a few more years …"

"And then what? I'm sorry, I shouldn't have brought it to you in the first place. It was wrong of me to put our marriage problems on you."

"You came to my house after he hit you. That's not a marriage problem."

"He wasn't himself. I've talked to him," she said.

"I don't think you should do this."

"I understand."

"I want you to be safe."

"I am safe."

"Here you are."

There had to be solutions. There were a million roads for her to take. A thousand different approaches. Not this road back. Five years should have snapped her free of the old life. I couldn't do anything. I couldn't think like that. Had she weighed her options? This was the best thing?

"It's not what you think here," she said.

"It's better than being with him."

"You don't know what you're even saying. You can't understand."

"It doesn't mean anything that he beat the shit out of me?"

"I didn't know that …"

"It doesn't mean anything that he beat the shit out of you?"

"That night — what happened that night. No one knows. It was … no one knows. You can't forget the good and remember only the bad."

"You haven't tried here."

"Don't be silly," she said.

I was wrong. She had tried: at fifty-five she uprooted to live as a single woman in India. Of course that didn't take. How much longer could she keep going? How long until she convinced herself that what was before was easier? She loved, continued to love, always loved, my father, even if I couldn't believe it, even if I couldn't say it.

"I don't want you to go home — there."

"You can't … this doesn't have to do with you."

I could send her money. India is cheaper than Canada. I could. I had to stay here for a while, we could share an apartment. How could she not get a job? She hadn't been trying hard enough. I could help her. She was sad, depressed. I could help her with that. The government here hated Muslims — who gives a shit? That was the same all over. What if she went back? That would be harder … she had some friends from her old job … I could contact them, rent her a room. They loved her at the job … she could get it back … the cold … she hated the cold. Her family was here … maybe Marwan would move out of the basement soon to live with Britta … I could move her in there … pay some of her rent …

A new thought, banal but precise in its simplicity, came to me. What if I'd deleted five or ten memories? My entire personality would shift from that small shuffle of remembrance. I'd be kinder and malleable, built to approach the world with curiosity and not rage. My mother did it in front of me. She had said he'd hit her before, a handful of times over their marriage. Those memories receded when she had to make choices.

"I know you don't understand," she said.

"What's to understand?"

"He's not what you think."

"What is he?"

"He's complicated," she said.

"What does that mean?"

"What do you want me to say? You're interrogating your mother like this? What are my choices?"

"Stay here."

"And do what? I can't find work. I'm an old woman in India — what do you want me to do?"

"Don't say that."

"Tell me, then. Will you send me money each month until I die?"

"Instead of him sending you money? Yes."

"He's my husband," she said.

"I'm your son!"

"And this shouldn't be your concern."

"I want you to make sense."

"You're not listening," she said.

"I don't want to listen to this."

She put her hand on my leg and patted my face. She went to the kitchen to help.

31.

"You look like shit."

Ahmed was not wrong. I'd never been knocked around this much in such a short period of time.

I held my side in pain when I got off my motorbike at his villa, about an hour away from my hotel, near Sanjay Gandhi forest, where they said tigers roamed. The pain poked me out of my gloom.

I was angry at Ahmed's. I wasn't sure about any of my memories anymore, or the way I'd accepted them — why could I not forgive the way my mother did?

Ahmed would know all. Or his dad would. I had texted him through Samir's phone and the reply came to me on my own, which didn't completely surprise me. I didn't know anything about the world.

"You need to know where Abdul is?" he asked. "And your girl, Natalie?"

He lived in a walled compound. The entrance was manned by two surly smoking guards, one who stood back while the other waved me in after a few questions. I walked my motorbike to the circular drive, over two dead patches of grass, and parked it in front of a bungalow blasted by years of dirt and dust. There were two more guards at the door watching cricket.

Inside, ceiling fans whirred and a small man took me through the open area in the centre of the complex, past one lady flipping rotis over flame, and another who hung laundry.

Ahmed's father and elder brother lived in Dubai. They had built their empire through smuggling and other assorted crimes; their names weren't famous but they were associated with Dawood Ibrahim, international gangster, and Ahmed's family's power came from their proximity to this Don.

They'd cemented their relationship by taking part in the '93 Bombay Blasts — bombings, said by some to be organized by Ibrahim in response to the riots across the city that took thousands of Muslim lives. This moment of history fused the families forever and Ahmed's long leash was the result of his father's work.

My last memories of Bombay had been these riots, huddled close with my family in my auntie's building, not allowed to leave. I may have invented the memory: close together, observing through a window at a street lined with police. My parents never spoke about the riots or the bombings. We'd left after the riots and before the blasts but I didn't realize that for a long time.

Two wooden doors led to a room tiled aquamarine. The Arab — Ahmed — sat on a black leather chair in front of bookshelves that held cricket, badminton, and field hockey trophies. The door closed behind me and we were in a glimmering submarine.

"What happened with Samir?" he asked. I was honest. What else could I be? I didn't know when I could go back home so I told him all. He listened cautious, nodding along as if I was confirming details. He turned his computer monitor so it faced me. "Watch," he said.

Black-and-white footage of the night. A security camera pointed to Bagheera's room after I'd left Samir there, bleeding. She approached him with curiosity. What did he always say about her? His first pet. She moved closer to Samir. Her jaw opened. She lowered her mouth. I recoiled and pushed the screen back to him. Ahmed laughed. Tension released. There would be no one to call the police about Samir. Forgotten, a loose end permanently flailing in the wind. Ahmed's people had taken care to make sure nothing reached back.

"My father loves Abdul," Ahmed said. "He thinks he's principled. He's helping him — he's got him documents, passport, all that. Abdul is going to Kandahar soon. First, by boat to Pakistan, taking off from our little bay down here. I don't know what the details are with her. I don't know if she's going. You want to know where they're staying?" He lit a cigarette and acted like he was thinking. They'd known Samir was a delinquent and had learned about his graft before I had and had been putting together a plan before I acted on my own. Now, Samir's family here would be given money and told not to worry about him. What was left of him after Bagheera dined would be buried in Ahmed's own backyard by a cousin. "I'm back here now," Ahmed said. "Permanently. My father ..." He paced behind the desk, oblivious to me as he tried to work out what to say about his father without revealing too much. He hadn't come here for a wedding. That was cover so Samir wouldn't get suspicious. He'd been pulled back to Mumbai by his father, declared an overseas screw-up as they opted out of expanding their North American footprint. Punjabis had a firm grip from Vancouver to Toronto and Hell's Angels in Quebec. ArabTarzan had caught too much heat from his association with Abdul and his new, stern videos. He abandoned it easily. The house would be packed, sold. The animals given away. "You want their address?" he asked. "Help me out. We can use your skills."

There had been new news: Ahmed's oldest brother had been knocked unconscious in a motorcycle accident and the second oldest wouldn't leave the comfort of Dubai for India. It wasn't sure if the oldest would ever wake up. Their hold on Mumbai would be tenuous without family in the city conducting the nuts-and-bolts work. My opportunity came in the briefest gap this created.

That was how I created my future. That was how, finally, I took over Samir's spot.

•

We drove to a four-story building held together with bamboo poles and concrete slabs. Ahmed said I could spare a few days — he could delay Abdul from leaving the city — if I went upstairs and gave pointers. Without his permission, I promised Dabir as collateral, knowing he would excel. He needed the work. His English was going to waste.

It was three small rooms with water stains on the walls, fans blowing erratically, and a pack of Indians huddled over desktops and phones. Four men at each workstation, each with their own specialized job: one held the thick stack of papers with contact information, one on the phone connected to two headsets, one typed, and one manned the mouse. It was a moron operation handed to Ahmed's father in repayment for a debt and now Ahmed's to fix up.

They were expecting me. A man in an oversized shirt brought me chai. They were connected to Toronto with a family that finished the job — they were being stupid, confusing, trying to run a service scam; A/C replacement, furnace updating, duct cleaning, services that could be drawn out for multiple payments. But it was too difficult. Risk too high. I had to be blunt. They weren't good enough.

The entire floor housed several phone cheat companies and I knocked on a few doors until I met someone who promised me the list I wanted: a Canadian scroll of names with SIN numbers. On the first round, skip the white names — Douglas, Ellis, Williams — go for the Indians. If they sound old, hang on to the phone call as long as possible.

Explaining it, I regretted not trying a SIN scam myself. Recalling accurate information, a full name, address, and especially the SIN number, can terrify many into compliance. I came up with a list of allegations we could accuse them of — failure to pay, administrative fee change — and then demand it be paid out on prepaid credit cards. That was the tricky part. It was stupid, but only the stupid would fall for it.

This is blunt-force trauma: expect to go days without success, but latch on to the right person with the right combination of words and a month's rent is to be made. Write down each name and amount scammed for. This would become a second line of income for Ahmed — we could sell this list to other workers as proven marks. They were eager students.

Ahmed complained about their English. It was generally fine, if stilted, jagged, awkward, and studded with outdated

British phrases. The hardest habit to break was getting them to stop saying "Madam" instead of "Miss"; it was the biggest giveaway of foreignness. While I waited for the first list, I tried to inspire looseness in their English. They asked about *Goodfellas*, *The Wolf of Wall Street*. I rolled my eyes to the back of my head. They were more than happy to watch *Friends* and Jennifer Aniston.

Dabir took it all in. He was a good kid. I had cash for days so I promised to keep him afloat until the operation took off if he promised to manage the situation. Ahmed came by that evening, after a day of lessons and TV, and was delighted at the simple direction I'd given them.

•

I followed Ahmed into his black Škodas and flipped the Hero's keys to one of his men. He wanted to take me to his favourite restaurant. In traffic for forty minutes while he stared at his phone, separated from the madness outside. We turned a corner and drove by a mash of people: peanut sellers peddling the roasted nut in coned newspaper, clothes hawkers hollering at passersby, skin-and-bone men hobbling down a lane that broke from the sidewalk and pushed to the sea, over sand, and toward a white mosque in the distance. Ahmed asked the driver to slow down. The lane lined with food and flower sellers, beggars, and a crowd moved in and out of the building.

"You know about this place?" Ahmed asked. "For Saint Pir Haji Ali Shah Bukhari."

"The mosque?"

"My dad loves it. I think he'd really lose his shit if anything happened to it."

"Is it sinking?"

"The tide comes up and takes away the laneway, but no, not really, I don't think. The mosque is for this saint. My dad says the story is he went to Mecca for Haj, died, and his casket floated back. I don't really get it — isn't Mecca the place? But it's important. Four, five hundred years ago. Back when they believed in magic."

"You know how Indians are." I don't know what I meant but Ahmed nodded.

"Why are you back here?" Ahmed asked. "No one is going to find out about Samir. You worried about the bank?"

"I guess."

"It'll get sorted. No one important was embarrassed. No one cares about a couple hundred thousand."

"For you, maybe. I don't have a lawyer."

"What's your plan with Abdul? Or is it Natalie?" he asked, then put his hand up to stop me from speaking. "Don't tell me, actually. I don't want to get involved. Why even worry about her? I know what they did."

"What they do?" I asked.

"They took the money. I know it wasn't just Samir."

"You know Abdul took money?"

"What can you do? My dad likes Abdul. He likes that there's someone out there saying this kind of stuff with such a big audience. The last two weeks Abdul has been on Instagram going crazy fundamentalist. I sent the links to my dad: he loves that shit. He was probably preparing to go back to Afghanistan. They don't go for that liberal Muslim nonsense."

"Don't you have to do something about Abdul taking the money?"

"Why?"

"How's it gonna look?"

"Who knows?" Ahmed said. "He wants to go back to Kandahar to get blown up? Who cares? If he actually does something there, makes a name for himself, my dad can say he funded him. What happens if we do something to him? It's just a sad thing to a sad dude. And the girl?"

"Bro, come on —"

"It is what it is," Ahmed said.

"I could go to jail."

"You're not. You're here. Why'd Natalie take the money? She's not going to Kandahar?"

"I don't know ..."

"See," Ahmed said. "You don't know. I don't know. How much did they take? Maybe five hundred thousand — I mean, it's not even really mine, right, donations we hadn't even fully counted yet. And whatever, the future — all the big dreams we all had. Whatever. We sell the house. We expect it to go way over asking. It'll go for more, way more. We sell a bunch of the other shit. Three cousins are staying there, they got PR. They like it there, they can have their families and everything. I minus the five hundred thousand from that, I'm still fine. So why get worked up? Stay here, make money with me. You helped me out with the cat, the store, the donations. Now the call centre. We already work together." He nodded and went back to his phone. I watched the mosque disappear as we drove away, the mass of people throwing shadows against its surface. They were pilgrimages, sellers, street children, and businessmen, wave after wave of the city's people, crashing into each other. The tide threatened to take it all away.

His driver jerked to a stop and we entered a white-cloth restaurant where waiters stood taut and formal in colonial-style costumes. The restaurant crammed but space made for us in a corner and we were left undisturbed for the last time that evening. After a meal of biryani and daal, we bounced to a bar with twenty-dollar cocktails and Eastern European women sitting in a row on stools. His friends joined us and men lined up for favours and short meetings. They were discussing new business. Ahmed asked me my opinion: I vetoed roulette and suggested card games instead. Then a car ride to a club with two-hundred-dollar bottles of vodka, a near constant stream of men asking for favours. Skinny, light-skinned women in short dresses joined our tables and rotated out throughout the evening. Ahmed wanted me to choose one but could see I was limping around and gave up with a laugh.

I'd written him off as a strange, odd son, the last-in-line-for-the-throne rich kid who fled to hide himself in Western comforts. The stories of his appetites were enormous and pathetic in their predictability: prostitutes, rub and tugs, parties that stretched from afternoon to the next day's dawn; people enchanted by his Instagram follower count and social might; his unending bank account.

He was different here, even in the nightclub. He was relaxed. I didn't realize he hadn't been relaxed in the West until I saw him speaking easily with whomever approached our table. I'd thought ArabTarzan was a stupid side gig, but it was his creativity creating an outlet for the striving ambition he had to suppress as third-in-line. Now that his brothers were out of the way, he assumed a role he'd observed his whole life, never expecting to take it on, and to everyone's surprise, his observations easily turned into action. His ideas for business and money were sharp, specifically located on the kind of clientele we'd be receiving. He knew how to juggle different parts of an organization and pull them together into a whole. The self I saw in the West was different. A child biding time until he was allowed back. It was true, for people like him, and I was learning, for people like me — we would rise to what was expected.

We spoke constantly that night. The first of many face to face, our hot drunk breath in each other's ears. The night ended with the liquor doing its work. We stumbled from the club onto the street as a pack but we peeled off ahead of the others. In Bombay, Ahmed wore Western clothes: cream-coloured blazers and dark slacks, aviators that reflected his surroundings back out. His friends yelled at each other about Koli and cricket and the yellow flush of streetlights held us as we walked away, our eyes open to the sky and the possibilities of our new business.

The next morning I had a text with Abdul's hotel address and itinerary and a lingering pulse from last night telling me that maybe I'd found the place I needed.

32.

I guide the backroom mongrels for Ahmed now. We have poker and blackjack mainly and I'm given four or five important clients to monitor and entertain. The blank-faced lessons of Abdul come in handy then, as does the talon sharpness of Samir.

The vastness of this city compresses me into coherence. There is simply too much going on for me not to operate as one solid blade, to be a person in sync with himself. Everything superfluous has been thrown out. There is nothing left inside me to surmount.

In the background, guiding Europeans from brothels to hotel bars, sewing myself close to wealth and notoriety, I've become singular with power. It's not much — I'm a noiseless gear in the machine — but it's enough.

Samir bled on that ground, the wet tapestry of his skin loosened from his skull, a whistling from the gap between bone and flesh; Bagheera's nose twitched and the wave of instinct took over her body. For her, it was preordained: weakened flesh meant prey. It didn't matter how much she'd meant to Samir. The thread that wove through her life was violence and death and there wasn't an argument otherwise. Was it the same for me?

I slipped on a toque the other day — I was in Delhi for work, where it gets cold in the evenings, sharp without wind — and the coarse fabric sliding over my skin caused a shudder of fear. The potato sack over my face. Water in my throat; out my nose. In an auto near Gurgaon I clutched the cold metal railing between me and the driver, willing myself back to reality: for a minute, I was back in that abscess, sniffling my blood and phlegm, Abdul's blows thudding against me.

That night with Abdul frames my entire life. It was the true, fullest possibility of what we could do to each other and it marked me; as it should.

I've said I was born here in Bombay and I hold a child's memories of it, shapes and smells mostly, bad photocopies of memories. Almost no solid memories for me to anchor on — except one.

In the winter of '92, the day the Babri mosque was demolished, a few weeks before we left, my father walked me down the street toward the barber in the evening. I'd be the last haircut for the night.

What I wanted most in the world was to whistle. It was pure magic to me that the mouth could produce beautiful music and my father was the ultimate magician, capable of high notes and low slinking songs, tones that jumped and whispered with familiar TV jingles. He held my hand and shaped his lips into an O while instructing me. I blew out spit and air while he showed off his wide range. The frustration built. Why could I not produce even the smallest sound? I would have traded my life for the smallest sound.

His whistling was overtaken by shouting, swirling sirens, and a four-by-four with no roof driven down a street suddenly full of soldiers, with one shouting through a bullhorn. My father took me into his arms and 180'd back home. For the next two weeks we didn't leave the apartment. Each morning we looked out the stairwell window to the quiet street — the city, maybe, had never been so quiet — and reminded ourselves we could not leave. In other neighbourhoods there were riots and murders; bodies burning and families destroyed.

No one filled me in and after two weeks we moved to Canada as planned. I didn't remember the events for years, until watching a World War II movie in high school, my head hidden into my arms, napping, when on the TV at the front of the room, a small European town was evacuated with sirens.

Memories came back. Not one at a time: they were just there. I snapped up in my chair aware of an entire shelf of new remembrance.

At home my parents shrugged me off, my father with his Typical Indian Bullshit is what it is, my mother with "We'll talk about it later."

Mental math and an internet search took me to the Bombay riots, the Babri mosque, *Black Friday*. A mosque torn down nowhere near us made nine hundred Muslims in my city die. I read in detail about fires, riots, families destroyed. The same types of agitators wanted to change the name Bombay to Mumbai. Around the time the memories came back, the Gujarat riots had happened; Muslims lit on fire in trains. Those same people continued to design the country today. Hidden history.

For a month after the memory of the riots came back I would stalk the internet for video clues, testimony, evidence to flesh out the vivid but empty memory I had.

It wasn't until I moved back here that I remembered my memory's trick. After a few years, I'd thought the memories were a constant in my life, and I'd forgotten all about my rediscovery, the World War II movie, and my month spent on the internet searching for information to fill out the small parts I recalled.

What else will I forget?

What else can I forget?

33.

Abdul and Natalie were here. Yes, where we are now, the grand Oberoi. A full view of the Arabian sea. Dinner on white plates. A white sommelier on staff. A white European-trained Indian chef, reinterpreting Indian food for Indians who don't want to be Indian. Fake floral smells, manicured attendants, yes sir, no madam, and a thousand miles away from the street. It's an honest relationship with money. No one here hides it. There is only flaunting. Which is what you're supposed to do with it. If the Taj Mahal and elephants were our previous clichés, today's equivalent is just outside: a candy-green Lamborghini snug to the ground, the Indian CEO of a tech company; three generations of beggars — the eldest, the father, asking for a rupee or two, a concave depression where his nose should be. Behind him are slums, slum tours; behind that, luxury apartments, a different planet. The sea takes us to the rest of the world.

For four days after Ahmed sent me Abdul's itinerary I parked outside the hotel under shade next to a spread of autos, taxis, and painfully white Škodas waiting to pick up their passengers at the hotel. A paan seller on my right, globs of red spit smattered on his stand, and a cloud of beedi smokers.

I arrived to my spot early each morning and took my fried-egg breakfast from a man on the street. Grease-laden pakoras fallen from heaven roared in my gut. I found shade under a tree with leaves like blankets.

I must have missed them on the first two days — I had to piss, get water, eat different food — but on the third I saw them come out. A white car pulled up to the entrance and the driver hopped out like a schoolchild eager to please teacher. Abdul and Natalie were like cosplayers in their shalwar kameez. They allowed the boy to open and close the door and nothing about them told of the disaster they'd left behind.

Ahmed sent their itinerary while I slept. They were here for at least a week, obnoxiously attending an academic conference on Islam. The rest of the ambitious plans to Delhi, Malaysia, Korea, and all, had been trashed.

In the mornings they went into a local Café Coffee Day and then each afternoon disappeared into a crumbling office building, coming out after two hours. They would eat a meal and then repeat the process. In the evenings, they went for dinner, drinks, or a movie. Back into the hotel by 6:00 p.m.

On the fifth day, as I finished my breakfast, I noticed the Indians that normally chattered around me had gone into hiding. A driver told me I should be mindful of the weather. As he finished his sentence the monsoon broke, like a switch flicked.

One blink, water to my ankles. Two blink, water to my knees. I waited pathetic under the tree, watching as Abdul came down to shoo the Škoda away.

Not wanting to test the roads, and finding plausible cover under the canopy I was now hiding under, I waited for an hour until an SUV pulled up and Abdul and Natalie ran from the lobby to the car while their driver soaked up the rain as he held the door open. I ran to my bike and followed until the gushing water overwhelmed my poor driving skills. My bike fell to the side and pinned me down. A group of randoms saw me struggle and helped me escape but the SUV was gone.

I retreated exhausted and forced into submission. Hiding in my room, clicking channels, realizing the furniture had been arranged to hide various stains.

By night the rain stopped and the streets were as before. I puttered my bike to a gully a little distance from the hotel and ordered a paneer dish on an app. The driver's scooter cautiously entered the alley I was hiding in. He was dressed as I wanted, in a branded red hat and T-shirt bearing the Zomato insignia and holding a plastic bag of food.

We negotiated: I offered him ten, then twenty — we're talking USD — and he gave up the shirt, hat, and food for thirty. I couldn't stand his frail rib cage and so with some reluctance I handed over my four-hundred-dollar Acne T-shirt, making him pinch the cotton to understand the quality. He did not. I sent him away with an extra ten bucks.

The rest was easy. I wasn't sure how far they would let me through but a stiff-chest confident walk got me past security alongside mentioning that the customer insisted on being handed the food directly. I had the room number already.

There was no camera in the hallway. A Do Not Disturb sign hung on their doorknob.

I knocked twice, waited, knocked twice, waited, then four times in a row till I heard a shout, "Coming!"

The knob turned.

Natalie opened.

Her brain stalled at my outfit and presence in India. I peered into the room. No one else. She invited me in. I put the paneer on a side table. Her hair in a bun.

"Where's the hijab?" I asked.

"It's too conspicuous here."

"It's real subtle in Toronto."

There was a bottle of gin on the table with a heavy glass. Ice cubes melting. The TV on low. The room stunned me: it was unlike anything I'd seen in India. Wood floors, high ceilings, and modern furnishings; hotel art on most walls and short lamps scattered across the room. A claw-foot tub in the bathroom was separated from the sleeping area by a glass wall that automatically fogged. A view of the sea. I was foolish in my clothing. She wore white pyjamas and a hotel robe, her hair pinned back.

"Food?" I asked.

"I'm sorry," she said.

"You hungry?"

She burst into tears. I let her into my arms. She pulled me to the bed so we could sit.

"Where is he?" I asked.

"He's gone."

"Back to Toronto?"

"Kandahar, to Afghanistan," she said.

"He really go full Taliban?"

"He went back for Afri. He's not … he's not … he looks good, he talks good. But he's not well. He went back for Afri, for his son, or daughter."

"They're there?"

"He wants to find them if they are," she said.

Natalie sat cross-legged on the bed and I put my head in her lap.

"Samir noticed we were skimming money."

"Because he was stealing too," I said.

"And Samir threatened Abdul. Samir was going to do something — who knows what. Tell Ahmed. Tell the cops. It wasn't my idea. So we decided to take all the money. It's going to last him ages in Afghanistan."

"You stole from me," I said.

"I told you to leave it," she said. "I told you to leave it alone … Abdul didn't understand things, like, daily, real things. You know his cell phone had no SIM card in it? He was too scared to have a phone on him. He used it to take videos. He wanted to do good. He did, so badly, in the beginning. But it just left him. He just thought he would never make it work. Like that, it changed. He wanted the Resettlement Centre to work. He did. But he couldn't keep it up. He just deteriorated. The closer he got to Mo' and Imran, the worse off he became. All his money went away. He didn't understand what to do with ten million. Lawyer fees, the house, the centre, it felt like it vanished. He didn't know what money was, not really."

"And you?"

"I'm sorry," she said.

"Was that the plan from the beginning, to use me?"

"I told you to leave it alone. To not get involved."

"Was the plan always to use me?"

"It started coming together. Abdul saw the benefit of Ahmed. And then you were there, able to pull things together. Ahmed meant access to all this money."

"You didn't tell him to stop?"

"We told you to leave it," she said.

"What do you want with the money?"

"It's for my parents."

"You don't even like your parents."

"I didn't know it would be like this. We wanted Ahmed's money, we didn't know Samir would pull you in so deep."

"What's we? Where is he? He's gone. What did you need all that money for?"

"Why not?" she said. "What do you need all your money for?"

"He just wanted a buck? The Resettlement Centre, it was all nothing?"

"I don't know what people expected from him … Those Instagram videos where he looked so pulled together. Did you think that was what he was really like?"

"I spent time with him. He was fine."

"What time?" she said. "A few meetings? A few lectures? When he was alone, in private with me, he crumpled. There was nothing left inside him."

"No one asked him to start that Instagram page," I said. "He went on social media himself."

"Everyone asked him to be okay. Everyone needed him to be fine. They gave him the ten million and said — this is it. Be healed. No one told him how to come back from that decade."

"He helped people," I said. "He did. He helped me. His last night in Toronto … he helped me."

"What did he do?" she asked.

"I promise. He helped me."

Natalie looked away. Did she know what Abdul did in those rooms? I wouldn't ask. I wouldn't tell her.

"What happened with you and him?"

"Really?"

"Really," I said.

"That's what you want to know," she said. "After all this. You flew to Mumbai to ask if I slept with him."

"Kinda, yeah."

"No," she said.

"Don't lie."

"Hamid, stop."

"Don't lie. Did you?"

"No," she said.

"I don't think I thought you were going to say that."

Her fingers on my temples. I closed my eyes when I asked questions.

"Do you love him?"

"We are friends."

"All this Muslim shit?"

"It's not fake," she said.

"Yeah, right."

"It's not."

"You were friends. He was your imam. For real?"

"Can you not be a dickhead?"

"Yes."

"It was … he needed …"

"Kindness."

"Yes," she said.

"But what about you?" I asked.

"I heard what my mother had always talked about. A voice that was outside of me and from me at the same time. I was there for how long? Two months? It was quiet. It was peace. It was rhythm. It was organized. My life was never organized before. Not like that. Not inside, not in me, not like that."

Her fingers on my temple.

"How much money you got?" I asked.

"Don't ask me," she said.

"How much?"

"One hundred fifty thousand."

"Damn. What you doing with it?"

"Giving it to my parents," she said.

"Yeah, right."

"I am."

"Don't say that to me. What are you doing with it?"

"I am," she said. "I'm going there now."

"Vancouver?"

"Near Manila. I can buy them a house."

"I don't like that."

"Because I'm doing something for my parents?"

"Are you going to buy yourself something nice?"

"Yes," she said. "A house. For my parents."

"You going to be that girl?" I asked.

"It's important."

"For who?"

"For me," Natalie said. "To do one thing for them."

"Are you going to live in Manila?"

"I'm going to do this. That's it. This one thing. And then it's done. I don't have to worry about them anymore. I don't have to think about them ever again if I don't want to. I have to do this one thing. I can't stop thinking about them. I tried to stop. That's why I moved to Toronto from Vancouver. But it wouldn't go away. I always thought about them. I would wake up in the middle of the night and think about them in their horrible basement. Why don't they have any money? I could never understand it. They worked for so long for so hard. But I hated it. They weren't even that bad. They were just never around. It was so mild. They never hit me. They never yelled at me. They didn't know anything. They were never there. And because of that absence, I felt so much … what was it? Anger? I resisted them. I resented them. And I resented that I did. I resented any feeling I had toward them. I resented any feeling that I had. But this is it. This house. It's not for them, don't say that. Nothing is for them. The house will stand forever. But it's for me. It's mine."

"Wow," I said. "I bought them a house. And I never even got to meet them."

"Shut up. Do you get what I mean?"

"What's to get? You think you'll forget? You never will."

"I want to think about them in a different way. I want to have done a thing for them. For there to be a concrete reminder."

"So why are you here?" I asked.

"Ahmed's connections. Abdul needed documents — forgeries."

"But why are you here?"

"I told you — he can't … daily stuff. He can't anymore. You know what he's like. He has medicine he has to take."

I was sorry for him. I understood he needed more from life than he'd ever be able to get. Moments of kindness would be his respite. Her kindness. In that moment my love for her flared once more.

"What's going to happen in Afghanistan?"

"He has family."

"And you?"

"Are you going to ask about my drinking?" she asked.

The following evenings in that hotel room stand out like a jewel in my life, a moment in my past that I see from different angles to perceive different depths. I was humbled by the generosity of her spirit, and how, over our relationship, she'd lent me that spirit to support myself. Her kindness, extended to Abdul as an absolute, allowed him to change his life. What had we talked about on the roof? Remoulding yourself through mercy. The same furious energy that drove her to drink was responsible for her kindness and how she was able to extend herself into the world without judgment.

For so long I had focused on the drink and lost sight of the marvel in front of me, the woman who could change lives, administer organizations, use me like a cheap pawn for money, but was herself stuck in the mud, unable to move in any direction.

What they preach at Al-Anon is that booze is a disease, a symptom of a malaise that infects the soul. Did I believe that? I was scared of her and to ask myself what motivated her. I was content for it to be booze.

I was flooded with gratitude. At the same time, recognizing her separately from me, the heat of our love cooled, and after momentarily seeing her firm, she became abstract once more, like she had been at the height of our relationship. Mystery came between us again but now with none of the curiosity needed to pursue her. In front of me she became a memory. It was over and I felt great joy for having known her. There was no anger. The money didn't matter. The drink didn't matter. I had been to the edge of myself.

She was brave or a coward or both; she was neither and made choices she needed to.

I didn't want to see her stuck anymore. She had worked to give Abdul and her parents new lives.

"I don't know how you drink that shit but you can drink as much as you want."

"You don't care anymore?" she asked.

"You're rotten with it."

"Why are you here?"

"I thought I was going to kick the shit out of everyone," I said.

"And now?"

"Now? Now, I just kinda wanna be with you."

She smirked. It was over. I pulled her to me. We'd spent two years with each other. I missed her. I loved her; that would never change, but she wasn't my life. I surprised myself. I wasn't angry. Her hustle was clean. I didn't know what was true and what not, but I didn't care, and it didn't matter.

34.

We spent a week in the city, drifting down its streets on my motorbike, her arms fierce around me. A chatter of black crows followed us for a day before spiralling upward and away.

I showed Natalie where I was born, my first school, all the monuments of my early childhood. We drank on Chowpatty beach and played tourist, searching out the best bhel puri vendor. I took her to a club and we danced drunk and eager like we'd just met.

Each night we came home to the other.

On the seventh morning I woke to an empty hotel room.

No note, nothing, no need.

She knew she'd be with me, forever.

35.

Samir was never in the news and no one who may have cared, cared. Abdul made the news, yeah, and so did I but I'm on top of it. Money takes care. I'm not worried.

Samir had been good for a while and then he wasn't. It'll happen to all of us — we wait for our turn. In that mercy I found a path forward.

Samir lurks behind every action of mine. Every word has the echo of Samir. Every meal I eat I share with him, every drive down the balmy coast.

Ahmed still wants to bring in roulette, but I don't know, I told him to chill. I do other stuff too. International clients; that's my specialty. Indians are good at luxury, I'm not gonna lie, but all that head-bobbing only goes so far.

I'm the middle man — the twenty-first century's perfect job.

We do more, sure. There's a lot I can offer. What do you want? Money comes, money goes.

Samir's cash? I'd been moving it for years from our wire transfer set-up in the store. Right after Natalie left, I had Marwan text me all Samir's account numbers and info. It wasn't just the dough Samir skimmed from us — that boy liked to save. He sent it to a bank in India, that was convenient. I had Samir's phone and its dumb password; it took a super-intelligent street kid ten minutes to get into his bank accounts.

I had to take Samir's phone back to answer the security question. The kid couldn't answer it for me.

What was the name of your first pet?

ABOUT THE AUTHOR

Photo by Calvin Thomas

ADNAN KHAN is a screenwriter, novelist, and journalist. He has won a National Magazine Award and the RBC Taylor Emerging Writer Prize, and his debut novel, *There Has to Be a Knife*, was named a best Canadian novel of 2019 by the CBC. His debut feature film, *Shook*, made its premier at the 2024 Toronto International Film Festival.

The author would like to acknowledge the support of the Canada Council for the Arts, the Ontario Arts Council & Government of Ontario, and the Silk Road Institute.